VOICE:

NIGHT

s. He walks slowly,
turns. APPROACHING
reminiscent, lifted,
ice speaking on the
CLOSE SHOT, CAMERA
DS as Fonda stops,

VOICE:

we want slavery;
the earth, where
rest of the way

ands, waiting for it to go on,
is, looks about to see that all

NDA

MUSIC THEME from CANTATA has entered.
his feet moving unconsciously
gain, as the SOUND of FREEDOM TRAIN
IC as the SOUND of FREEDOM TRAIN
ightly stronger.

GRANDFATHER'S VOICE:

ER)
was here, right here that
ghteen-sixty-five, right here
same platform with all the other
at had come in from the farms
towns, that had been coming in
ning in, in wagons and buggies and
eback and some a-walking in the
and the mud, a-coming in and a-coming
er since that shot had sounded a
sand miles away in Washington.
ding here waiting outside the
egraph office, and the old Jake
zel come out ... and the old Jake

again, listening, CAMERA STOPPING with him.

(CONTINUED)

Faulkner

A Comprehensive Guide
to the Brodsky Collection

Volume IV: Battle Cry
A Screenplay by William Faulkner

Faulkner

A Comprehensive Guide
to the Brodsky Collection

Volume IV: Battle Cry
A Screenplay by William Faulkner

Edited by
Louis Daniel Brodsky
and
Robert W. Hamblin

UNIVERSITY PRESS OF MISSISSIPPI
Jackson

Center for the Study of Southern Culture Series

Manufactured in the United States of America

Library of Congress Cataloging-in-Publication Data

Faulkner, William, 1897–1962.
 Battle cry.

 (Faulkner, a comprehensive guide to the Brodsky
Collection ; v. 4)
 1. World War, 1939–1945—Drama. 2. Faulkner,
William, 1897–1962—Moving-picture plays. I. Brodsky,
Louis Daniel. II. Hamblin, Robert W. III. Title.
IV. Series.
Z8288.F38 1982 [PN1997.3] 791.43'72 85-10049
ISBN 0-87805-253-4

CONTENTS

LIST OF ILLUSTRATIONS

ACKNOWLEDGMENTS

THE EDITORS are extremely grateful to Warner Bros., Inc., for permission to publish the two versions of "Battle Cry" contained in this volume. We are especially appreciative of the efforts of Marshal M. Silverman, Warner Bros. executive in charge of legal affairs for theatrical feature film production. He not only coordinated the legal arrangements but also proffered his personal support and friendship.

Like its predecessor, *The De Gaulle Story,* this book would not have been possible without the cooperation and assistance of two particular individuals. Warren R. Howell, the late, distinguished San Francisco bookdealer, arranged for a group of Warner Bros. scripts to be placed in the Brodsky Collection and also handled the preliminary negotiations regarding publication. A. I. "Buzz" Bezzerides, a close friend and colleague of Faulkner during the 1940s, kindly allowed the "Battle Cry" materials in his possession to be deposited in the Brodsky Collection. Our indebtedness, as well as gratitude, to both of these gentlemen is immense.

Meta Wilde and Orin Borsten not only contributed the essay that graces the early pages of this book but also answered numerous inquiries about Faulkner and Hollywood. Glenn Horowitz, New York bookseller, has offered professional advice and friendly encouragement over a long period of time. Paul Lueders continues to produce outstanding photographs for use as illustrations in the Brodsky series. To these persons, too, the editors express heartfelt thanks.

As the introduction to this volume makes clear, the editors were privileged to have access to the materials in the Howard Hawks Collection at Brigham Young University. We wish to thank James V. D'Arc, curator of the Arts and Communications Archives at Brigham Young University, for supplying photocopies of pertinent documents from the Hawks Collection. We also thank Leith Adams, archivist of the Warner Bros. materials at the University of Southern California, and Cathy Henderson, curator of manuscripts at the Humanities Research Center at the University of Texas at Austin, for graciously providing information and documents.

We continue to be indebted to the following individuals who share in the partnership that is making possible this series based on the Brodsky Collection: William Ferris and Ann J. Abadie, of the University of Mississippi's Center for the Study of Southern Culture; Barney McKee, JoAnne Prichard, Seetha Srinivasan, and Hunter Cole, of the University Press of Mississippi; and Bill W. Stacy, Leslie H. Cochran, Fred B. Goodwin, Henry Sessoms, and James K. Zink, of Southeast Missouri State University.

For numerous acts of general assistance and kindness we wish to thank Dolores Cleve, William Lane, Kay McBride, Maribeth Needels, June Nivens, Bruce Parrish, Ralph Sipper, Pat Williams, and Harriet Yeargain.

The editors also wish to acknowledge the financial support and personal encouragement generously provided by Saul and Charlotte Brodsky; Biltwell Company, Inc., of St. Louis, especially its Chief Executive Officer, Edwin J. Baum; and the Grants and Research Funding Committee of Southeast Missouri State University.

Finally, we are very, very grateful to our immediate families—Jan, Trilogy, and Troika Brodsky and Kaye, Laurie, and Stephen Hamblin—for their love and support during our work on this project.

FAULKNER: HOLLYWOOD: 1943

In that rainless summer of 1943, William Faulkner worked conscientiously on his screen treatment of "Battle Cry." On his way to June Lake for story conferences with director Howard Hawks, he commented on the sedge and grasses leeched of green by a merciless sun. On all sides the hills were the color of dirty lion fur. Almost everything at that time of his life—Southern California's tawny landscape beyond the well-tended lawns of its cities and towns, a horse in playful gallop, a weathered barn, cotton fields no more than two hours away from Los Angeles—gave him a sense of unbearable displacement and awoke in him yearnings for Oxford.

Although in his letters to Oxford Faulkner expressed discontent, ill-being and longings for home, he had no genuine wish to leave Hollywood. He desperately needed the shameful $350 per week paid him by Warner Bros.—the greatest bargain a studio ever struck with a ranking novelist. Assigned by Hawks to write the script of "Battle Cry," Faulkner threw himself into its completion with energies at a high crest and found, for perhaps the first time, a degree of creative satisfaction in this form of writing.

"Battle Cry" was no ordinary project. Designed as a celebration of the human spirit under threat of extinction, it was a conduit for his reverence for the embattled and suffering peoples of the war. Morever, the shape and breadth of the screen treatment and the projected screenplay that was to follow occupied his thoughts, bubbled in his mind, more than any other film project on which he had worked. It was something new in form, cycloramic, with jumps in time and place, and with the camera utilized beyond any previous attempt.

In screenwriting there was never the fervor that went into his books. His novels and short stories seemed to emanate from the deepest part of his creative furnace. Evenings at the old Knickerbocker Hotel in the mid-1930s, I had listened as Faulkner reread a few pages of *Absalom, Absalom!*, completed days before; instantly, mystically, he was drawn into the metrical patterns, the Faulknerian flow, as ordered and as passionate as music. Screenwriting, on the other hand, was a business of bits and pieces, scene after scene—mechanical, fragmentary, detached—by the very nature of its structure. Faulkner required the hurtling force of life without impediment to experience his own work to the fullest. But in 1943, before movies were conceded to be the director's medium, writers were asked to indicate camera positions (close, medium and long shots), point of view, over-the-shoulder shots, dissolves, fade-ins, fade-outs. For Faulkner they were so many stride-breaking interruptions.

Screenwriting was not his forte, but from his introduction to Hollywood in the early 1930s he was reasonably good at it and by 1942, when he came back to Hollywood, he was a pro—the equal of lesser scribes earning five or more times his stipend. His dialogue was not fashionably terse, but it was colorful, alive and could be spoken without difficulty by actors worth their salt. Above all, he was a fine play doctor, a fixer. Saddled with a writer lacking invention, Howard Hawks would summon Faulkner for a swift solution to a bogged-down script. Faulkner worked with character; out of the dynamics of character came the confrontations, the conflicts, the ironies, the joys, and the torments that propelled his books and screenplays.

While Faulkner was preoccupied with "Battle Cry," I was holding script on the musical numbers of the film version of *This is the Army* at Fort McArthur and, later, for additional photography, at the Warner Ranch. What had started as a successful Broadway revue with enlisted men was now one more in Lt. Col. Jack L. Warner's succession of motion pictures concerned with World War II—films urged on Hollywood by the War Department to build morale. Theater marquees across the country blazed such titles as *Destination Tokyo, Action in the North Atlantic, Air Force, Dive Bomber, Background to Danger, Desperate Journey, Edge of Darkness, Underground, Across the Pacific,* the British-made *Flying Fortress,* and *Casablanca.* Even that old, weary dray horse of a musical, *The Desert Song,* was given a war theme.

William Faulkner was better equipped than most writers at Warner Bros. to work on war films, especially those requiring knowledge of aerial combat. I remember that he was in a state of contained excitement over "Battle Cry." As he puffed contentedly on his pipe, his eyes shone with the clarity that comes with good prospects. His step was jaunty. He was not drinking to excess. Never one to talk shop (his work was as private as his persona), he did tell me that his screen treatment, with pages and pages of dialogue, was coming along with only minor hitches. He mentioned the character of Mama Mosquito in the Chinese section. Who should play her role? he asked me. He spoke of Luise Rainer, whom he had seen years before in *The Good Earth,* and who, after being blackballed by Louis B. Mayer, had now been cast in *Hostages* at Columbia. Nazimova? Gale Sondergaard, who had played an oriental in *The Letter* with Bette Davis? At that time, I believe, Faulkner was the solo writer. He had learned to limit his output of pages in accordance with the expectations of producers and directors, lest their suspicions be aroused. For Howard Hawks, however, he turned in great chunks of material. The pages seemed to write themselves. Hawks was in control, brooking no interference from studio heads. With *Dive Bomber* and *Corvette-225*, the latter produced for Universal, Hawks negotiated from their own acknowledgment of his standing as one of Hollywood's most successful directors. Hawks assured him, Faulkner said, that "Battle Cry" would bring him his first screen credit since *Today We Live, The Road to Glory*, and *Slave Ship*. It would also force Warner to tear up the present contract and restore his four-figure salary.

The confidence, the sense of a corner to be turned, continued for weeks. The move from the noisy writers' building, where garrulous colleagues interrupted his work and secretaries gossiped, to Hawks's own private quarters on the lot buoyed him up further. One evening, as we dined together, he could not withhold from me the possibility of a permanent berth with Hawks, a move that would spell an end to his financial woes. More than that, he could not say, but I read in his inward smile an expectation for the two of us. Of course, that could never be, as much as we wanted it. Then came the great letdown. Either Hawks clashed with Jack L. Warner, as it is commonly believed, or "Battle Cry" was canceled because of story elements within it (i.e., the over-sympathetic Russian section) or the staggering cost to the studio of such an epic motion picture.

Faulkner was crushed. He began to drink heavily, and once again, he brooded over being turned down for a military commission because of his age and lack of higher education. Women were flying planes, he knew; perhaps he still had a chance. This was not to be, not any of it—"Battle Cry," active war service, a salary hike of any consequence, an overdue screen credit. Soon he was back at the writers' building, steeled to disappointment, collecting his pittance each week, earning the damned money many times over. But Hollywood was still better for him than Oxford. In Hollywood there was love. And Hollywood was alive with the pulsations of war, and something in him needed to be in the dead center of it.

World War II was graphically indicated in Los Angeles as it never could have been in Oxford. Servicemen, WAVES, uniformed nurses, and British, Canadian and Free French soldiers and sailors enlivened the passing parade downtown and on Hollywood and Sunset Boulevards. Endless convoys with lights glowing in the daylight passed along main arteries between military installations, and in transit between San Diego and San Francisco, then onward to Portland and Tacoma and Seattle. Newspaper headlines screamed of death and disaster. Faulkner, hunched forward in his chair, listened intently to the terse broadcasts about war by Edward R. Murrow and William L. Shirer. He would pause in his writing to turn on the radio at the Highland (Avenue) Hotel to hear Lowell Thomas, Gabriel Heatter, and Raymond Gram Swing. (A fire charred the interior of the hotel a few years ago, requiring extensive repair; Faulkner's top floor "penthouse" and deck escaped damage.)

The tensions and turbulence of wartime Los Angeles stretched Faulkner like a fine wire. Even at the studio, his need to share, feel, and experience was satisfied. More war films were added to the production slate. Censorship was a fact of studio life. Security was never to be as tight. Only those who could prove American citizenship could enter the gates each day. (The Manns and Feuchtwangers, had they chosen to write for the screen, would have required special dispensation.) Day and night, production was interrupted by bombers roaring over Burbank; planes were being tested, pilots trained. Because of the blackout, great blankets and tarpaulins covered the sets when we filmed on sound stages at night to prevent the smallest splinter of light from showing. There was a climate of nasty suspicion engendered by the Jack Tenney Assembly Committee investigating, even then, Un-American activities; some actors had already appeared before the committee. Employees complained that their desks were rifled by studio snoops overnight and sometimes during lunch hour. New faces appeared on the lot, whom some believed were FBI stalwarts posing as hired help. Posters commanded studio personnel to zip their lips, join Civilian Defense, contribute to British War Relief, Greek War Relief, every kind of war relief, and give blood, blood, blood. Rumors fanned over the lot that some employees of German ancestry were sending money back to Hitler. We were fingerprinted and were made to carry identification cards. Employees who spoke with the faintest of accents were looked on with grave suspicion. There was talk of a fifth column.

The armed services stripped Warner Bros. of key people without any regard for what it would do to production. Month after month, actors, mailroom youths, messengers, sound specialists, boom operators, cinematographers, camera operators, best boys, assistant directors, art directors, backlot laborers, and production managers, among others, vanished from those environs. Shipyards commandeered gaffers, electricians, carpenters; defense plants took welders and pipefiters. By the end of 1943, Warner Bros. had lost more than a thousand employees to the war effort.

The largely unapproachable William Faulkner made close friends in spite of his insularity: Thomas Job, A. I. Bezzerides, Stephen Longstreet, Marc Connelly, Jo Pagano and, through our relationship, my own friend John Crown, a brilliant pianist. Perhaps Crown familiarized Faulkner, who couldn't be dragged to a symphonic concert, with Dimitri Shostakovich's Seventh Symphony and the Iron Rats movement that figures so movingly in the Russian sequences of "Battle Cry." In addition to these new friends, Faulkner had another group of drinking buddies.

Although he expressed no great affinity with other writers toiling in Hollywood, he nevertheless derived a quiet pleasure when he found himself in their midst. At Warner Bros. and on other lots, or to be encountered at Musso and Frank's back bar on Saturday afternoons after studio quitting time, were Frederick Faust (also known as Max Brand, he would meet his death the following year as foreign correspondent for *Harper's*), Alvah Bessie, Dalton Trumbo, Lillian Hellman, Dwight Taylor, Keith Winter, Dawn Powell, James M. Cain, Raymond Chandler, Dashiell Hammett, Elliot Paul, John Fante, Tess Slesinger, Carl Sandburg, Horace McCoy, Clifford Odets, W. R. Burnett, Louis Bromfield, and John Steinbeck. Of the latter two Faulkner asked incredulously, "You mean they need the money?" At our table he spoke only to me, occasionally lifting his glass politely in recognition of a passing writer's nod, but he would not have wanted to miss a pleasant Saturday afternoon among his peers in 1943—breathing the same smoke-laden air, hearing snatches of their conversations, often diatribes against studio heads, producers and directors. It was in some odd way a rite of tribal identification. In turn some of the others, aware of him as the author then of *The Sound and the Fury, Light in August, As I Lay Dying, Absalom, Absalom!* (which he was writing when we first came to love each other), *The Wild Palms,* and *The Hamlet,* cast glances that ranged from awestricken to curious. If they had not read his books or his short stories in *The Saturday Evening Post* and *Harper's,* they knew of his growing reputation through the *New York Times Book Review.*

Faulkner, in spite of all that's been written to the contrary, was no more miserable than any other writer imported that year by Hollywood from New York City or Westport or any other place. Nor was he lonely—that least of all. If his letters indicate the opposite, one should remember that Hollywood—that amorphous piece of real estate within Los Angeles proper—has never been a place to love, with its

contents of pure sleaze and architectural splendor. The movie industry offers little to inspire love, especially to writers who continue to
this day to be thwarted by continued requests for rewrites, interference from actors, trivialization by story editors of scripts too literate,
or too different, and finally, by the consignment of screenplays to
shelves that hold thousands of others that never reached production
stages. The publishing world and the legitimate theater are better by
far for the writers.

In 1943, Faulkner needed, wanted, chose to be in Hollywood. This
was the romantic dream that only he, of the two of us, held to the
promise of higher earnings, a screen credit at long last, perhaps a
communication from the War Department: "We have reconsidered
your request. . . ."

What he drew from Hollywood from 1942 through 1945—the love,
the financial security, the unexpected friendships, the terrible frustra-
tions, the bitterness—would fuel the great work yet to come upon his
return to Oxford and Rowan Oak.

Meta Carpenter Wilde and Orin Borsten

INTRODUCTION

I

BY THE END of 1941 William Faulkner was financially and spiritually bankrupt as a result of his failure to make fiction writing support and satisfy him in a climate of well-being. During late November and into December, from his home base in Oxford, he attempted unsuccessfully to gain employment with Warner Bros. Pictures by producing, at the studio's request, an original story line for a previously rejected screenplay entitled "The Damned Don't Cry." Additionally, during the next several weeks he wrote, as he later recorded, "5 20–25 page story lines for various studios or individuals, none of which came to anything."[1] In February 1942 he resumed his efforts to produce short stories for magazines, but with equally negative results. In late June he confessed in a letter to Bennett Cerf, "I have 60¢ in my pocket, and that is literally all. I finished a story and sent it in yesterday, but with no real hope it will sell. My local creditors bother me, but so far none has taken an action because I began last year to give them notes for debts. But the notes will come due soon and should I be sued, my whole house here will collapse: farm, property, everything."[2] A few days later, even more desperate to secure work, Faulkner outlined for Harold Ober the generous remuneration he had received in Hollywood in the 1930s but added: "I believe the agents who have tried to sell me have talked about $1000 per week. I don't think I am or have been or will ever be worth that to the movies. It just took them five years to find it out. I will take anything above $100.00. I must have something somewhere, quick."[3]

Finally, with the dubious and ultimately detrimental assistance of William Herndon, a West Coast agent, Faulkner managed to secure a contract with Warner Bros., but only by committing himself to a complicated series of options that he would eventually view as servitude.

1. *Selected Letters of William Faulkner*, ed. Joseph Blotner (New York: Random House, 1977), p. 159.
2. *Selected Letters of William Faulkner*, pp. 154–155.
3. *Selected Letters of William Faulkner*, p. 155.

But that harsh judgment would come later; for the present he had
employment and the promise of a steady income: thus he excitedly
prepared to make the first visit in what would become an off-and-on
four-year sojourn in Hollywood as a wartime screenwriter. Before he
left Oxford, in a letter regarding his initial assignment, a proposed
movie about France's emerging military hero, Charles De Gaulle,
Faulkner expressed his renewed optimism to James Geller, head of
the Warner Bros. Story Department. "Your letter of July 15 at hand. I
also have Mr Buckner's letter describing the job he has in mind. It is a
good idea and I will be proud to work with it and I hope and trust I
can do it justice."[4]

Officially, Faulkner went on the Warner Bros. payroll on July 27,
1942, at a salary of $300.00 a week. In the beginning, and for quite a
while, Faulkner actually believed that the work he was performing
would deliver him from his financial and emotional abyss. Not only
did he once again have a regular income, but he was also engaged in
purposive action that was helpful, even necessary, to winning the war.
Though he had failed three months previously in his efforts to enlist
as a navy pilot, he had found a means of contributing to the war effort
after all—and actively, not as a civilian commander of air raid observation posts or even as a uniformed officer sitting at a desk in Washington. Indeed, bolstered by the patriotic fervor that engulfed the
film industry during the war years, Faulkner logically perceived an
element of the heroic in his Hollywood "service" status. And for much
of 1942, until the end of November at least, deducing from the mas-
sive, exuberant outpouring of material that became "The De Gaulle
Story,"[5] Faulkner actually derived gratification as well as recompense
from his work as a scriptwriter.

However, by December 1942 Faulkner had become frustrated with
the lack of success on his first major writing assignment. Despite the
enormous amount of time and energy invested in "The De Gaulle
Story," circumstances beyond Faulkner's control had led to the shelv-
ing of that project. Moreover, Faulkner was homesick; and, worse, he
was rapidly becoming convinced that his arrangement with Warner
Bros. was catastrophic: his pay was paltry, not generous as he had
originally perceived it to be. All such factors—his low pay, his loneli-
ness, his unfortunate contract that assigned the studio the right to

---

4. *Selected Letters of William Faulkner,* p. 157.
5. For a detailed record of Faulkner's work on this project see Louis Daniel
Brodsky and Robert W. Hamblin, eds., *Faulkner: A Comprehensive Guide to the
Brodsky Collection, Volume III: The De Gaulle Story* (Jackson: University Press of
Mississippi, 1984).

seven annual renewals, and the deep-felt suspicion that his "war work" was not as essential as he had thought and hoped—contributed to his growing cynical conviction that he had been misguided, even duped.

Faulkner reflected his current pessimism in a letter[6] to his stepson Malcolm Franklin just prior to leaving Hollywood for a brief Christmas visit to Oxford. In an uncharacteristically garrulous letter that foreshadowed much that was to follow in his life and work, Faulkner listed his principal concerns. One was his acerbic belief that only soldiers and those working directly on the construction of war materiel were essential to the war effort. In the group of persons engaged in work superfluous "to winning a war or anything else," Faulkner included "real estate agents and lawyers and merchants and all the other parasites who exist only because of motion picture salaries." Apparently Faulkner was already sensing himself a party to this specious breed, and his self-consciousness was exasperating. How much luckier, Faulkner believed, were those who had an active role in the conflict. Thus Faulkner implored his stepson to enlist. Ultimately, going off to fight was a question of manhood. "It is the biggest thing that will happen in your lifetime. All your contemporaries will be in it before it is over, and if you are not one of them, you will always regret it." Faulkner went on to reassert his own preference for actual, physical involvement: ". . . it's a strange thing how a man, no matter how intelligent, will cling to the public proof of his masculinity: his courage and endurance, his willingness to sacrifice himself for the land which shaped his ancestors. I dont want to go either. No sane man likes war. But when I can, I am going too, maybe only to prove to myself that I can do (within my physical limitations of age, of course) as much as anyone else can to make secure the manner of living I prefer and that suits my kin and kind."

However, as his parenthetical remark implies, and the remainder of the letter makes clear, Faulkner's desire for an active combat role was mere dreaming, a wish-fulfillment resulting, perhaps, from his failure to become a pilot in not one but two world wars. In continuing the letter to Franklin, Faulkner acknowledged that he must now find his purpose in another direction. Wars must be fought by young men, but "then," Faulkner added, "perhaps the time of the older men will come, the ones like me who are articulate in the national voice, who are too old to be soldiers, but are old enough and have been vocal long enough to be *listened to* . . ." [emphasis added]. Here one finds not merely the rationale for writing patriotic movie scripts but a *raison*

6. *Selected Letters of William Faulkner,* pp. 165–166.

d'être for the remainder of Faulkner's literary career. If he wanted to prove his manhood, his soldiering henceforth would have to be "vocal"; moreover, if he were going to be "listened to," he would have to "articulate in the national voice."

After his brief respite home for Christmas in Oxford, Faulkner returned to Hollywood in January 1943 and resumed where he had left off: trying to write a war-effort screenplay. This one was entitled "The Life and Death of a Bomber." The previous November 14 Faulkner and Joe Berry, of the Warner Bros. Location Department, had toured the Consolidated Aircraft factory in San Diego to gather information for a proposed script about the civilians involved in building American bombers. According to Faulkner's notes from the tour, the movie was supposed to provide favorable publicity for Consolidated in the way *Wings for the Eagle* (Warner Bros.; 1942) had done for Lockheed. On January 21, 1943, Faulkner submitted a twenty-page "Outline for Original Screenplay," the theme of which is the need for national unity in support of America's servicemen. In showing how a labor dispute and a love triangle interfere with work at the factory and cause a defective bomber to be sent overseas, Faulkner dramatized the tragic consequences of placing selfish motives ahead of national security interests. However, like "The De Gaulle Story" before it, and far more quickly, "The Life and Death of a Bomber" was canceled.

For the next two months Faulkner worked on a succession of unfulfilling projects,[7] none directly related to the war. Possibly as a result of this last fact, Faulkner found himself living "a damned dull life" and vowing, again, "to soldier, if possible."[8] Then occurred, suddenly, a development that once more stirred Faulkner's enthusiasm and pride. Howard Hawks wanted him as scriptwriter for his next war movie. Faulkner would be given another major opportunity to prove himself useful both to Warner Bros. and the nation. A month later Faulkner described the project in a letter to his daughter Jill: "I am writing a big picture now, for Mr Howard Hawks, an old friend, a director. It is to be a big one. It will last about 3 hours, and the studio has allowed Mr Hawks 3 and ½ million dollars to make it, with 3 or 4 directors and about all the big stars. It will probably be named 'Battle Cry'."[9]

7. Faulkner spent brief periods of time, respectively, on *Northern Pursuit* (for which he received no screen credit) and two unfinished scripts, "Deep Valley" and "Country Lawyer." See Joseph Blotner, *Faulkner: A Biography*, rev. ed. (New York: Random House, 1984), pp. 448–449.
8. *Selected Letters of William Faulkner*, pp. 169, 167.
9. *Selected Letters of William Faulkner*, pp. 173–174.

II

Intended as "a United [i.e., Allied] Nations picture told from the American viewpoint,"[10] "Battle Cry" was conceived as an epic film with separate chapters depicting American, British, French, Russian, Chinese, and Greek resistance to the Axis powers on various fronts. The idea for the movie seems to have originated with Howard Hawks and his agent, Charles Feldman, whose company, Charles K. Feldman Common Man Production, owned the movie rights to the four properties that provided the original basis for the film.[11] These properties included "Abe Lincoln Comes Home," a musical cantata with music by Earl Robinson and libretto by Millard Lampell; "Diary of a Red Army Woman," a story development prepared by Violet Atkins and William Bacher from their Treasury Star Parade[12] radio script of the same title; "Ma-Ma Mosquito," a news feature by Dean S. Jennings treating the military career of Madame Chao Yu-tang, the sixty-five-year-old Chinese patriot who commanded an army of 30,000 guerrilla fighters against the Japanese;[13] and "American Sequence," two respective story ideas by Howard Hawks about American soldiers in North Africa and an American war correspondent in Malta. As the project proceeded, other source material was added to these four original properties. Altogether, as many as eight additional short stories, five of which had been previously published, were used, though some of these were later discarded.

10. This description of the film is taken from a memo by Earl Robinson to Howard Hawks, dated July 15, 1943. Robinson's memo (summarized below), along with other materials identified in this introduction by the initials BYU, is contained in the Howard Hawks Collection housed in the Harold B. Lee Library at Brigham Young University. The editors are extremely grateful to James V. D'Arc, curator of the Arts and Communications Archives at Brigham Young University, for providing photocopies of the "Battle Cry" materials in the Hawks Collection.

11. These properties are listed in a Warner Bros. Inter-Office Communication from R. J. Obringer to Steve Trilling, dated April 10, 1943, and a related letter from Charles K. Feldman to Obringer, dated April 23, 1943, both of which are included in the Warner Bros. archives at the University of Southern California (USC). The editors express appreciation to Leith Adams, archivist, for providing access to pertinent materials in this collection.

12. "The Treasury Star Parade" was a series of radio dramas sponsored by the United States Treasury and designed to promote the sale of War Bonds. Coordinator of the program was William A. Bacher, who also edited twenty-seven of the broadcasts for publication as *The Treasury Star Parade* (New York: Farrar and Rinehart, 1942).

13. Dean S. Jennings, "Ma-Ma Mosquito," *Collier's,* 105 (April 13, 1940), 17ff.; condensed as "Mother of the Guerrillas," *Reader's Digest,* 37 (October 1940), 117–118.

Actively collaborating with Faulkner in fusing these diverse materials into a workable script were Hawks, Bacher, and, to a lesser extent, Steve Fisher, a twenty-six-year-old scriptwriter who was assigned to the team two months into the project. Hawks, the director, supervised the story conferences and supplied the title as well as the American story line. Bacher, who served as Hawks's principal assistant on the project, wrote brief passages of continuity, edited Faulkner's arrangement of scenes, and, together with Violet Atkins, co-authored the initial scripts for the Russian and Chinese segments. Fisher revised four sections of the screenplay, including three of Faulkner's segments, although none of Fisher's material was ultimately retained in the most advanced version of the screenplay, the "Second Temporary Draft" (Part II of the present volume). Three other individuals—Atkins, Robinson, and John Rhodes Sturdy—became marginally involved in the project, though none of these apparently had much, if any, direct contact with Faulkner. It was Faulkner, however, who was given the principal responsibility of pulling the separate strands of the story into a unified script; and the title page of the Second Temporary Draft rightfully acknowledges the work as a "Screenplay by William Faulkner." Precisely because it is a composite and derivative work, "Battle Cry" stands as an important document in Faulkner's Hollywood canon, providing as it does a significant perspective on his work as adaptor and collaborator.

Faulkner started work on "Battle Cry" on April 7, 1943 (XXI).[14] In the early stages of composition he benefitted from story conferences with Hawks (and probably Bacher) held at June Lake, California. By April 21 Faulkner had completed a temporary treatment, with some dialogue, of 143 pages (II). This version, subsequently revised and expanded, opens in early 1942 at a railway station in Springfield, Illinois, where Fonda,[15] a young recruit, prepares to depart with other draftees for the war. Seeing a reluctant Fonda off is his grandfather, who challenges his grandson to emulate the example of an earlier Springfield citizen, Abraham Lincoln, in waging war against tyranny. In words that echo the sentiment of Faulkner's advice to his stepson in the letter cited previously, the grandfather exhorts: "Go on, now. When the shoving comes, let the rest of them be late to it, but

14. The Roman numerals in parenthesis throughout the text refer to the Brodsky materials listed in the bibliography printed at the end of this introduction.

15. This character is named "Flynn" in certain scenes, but he is described as "the Fonda type" and he is called "Fonda" more often than "Flynn." Faulkner's reference, of course, is to Henry Fonda, popular American star of stage and screen.

not my blood and kin! Go on." Throughout this scene Faulkner identifies the train carrying Fonda to military service with the Freedom Train that brought Lincoln's body home to Springfield following the assassination. The music of the Lincoln cantata provides an appropriate background.

Faulkner now flashes forward to the North African desert, where Fonda is a member of a platoon engaged in a special mission to hold a strategic well against an impending German attack. The commanding officer (named Whitesides in later versions) has been mortally wounded, and command of the unit's seventeen survivors has passed to a slow-witted, middle-aged sergeant named Reagan.[16] In the company of these American soldiers are an English corporal, Albert Loughton (who has with him two prisoners—a German and an Italian), and two stranded soldiers from another American unit—America, a black youth who is paralyzed with a bullet in his spine, and his white companion, Akers, a Southerner. Led by the courageous but indecisive Reagan, this motley crew of soldiers, cut off from the main army, must decide whether to retreat or dig in to face the approaching German forces.

At this point Faulkner cuts away from the battlefield setting to introduce the first of three extended segments of the Lincoln cantata.[17] Based upon an American Negro folk legend which holds that Lincoln still lives to carry on his fight for freedom, the cantata conveys the theme that will unify the various international episodes of the film: "Freedom's a thing that has no ending, / It needs to be cared for, it needs defending; / A great long job for many hands, / Carrying freedom across the land." The separate episodes in the script are intended to demonstrate that Lincoln's dream of freedom must be extended to all nations. It is this realization that will ultimately supply the answer to Fonda's question about why he and his fellow soldiers are fighting on foreign soil.

The American sequence and the Lincoln cantata become the warp of the text onto which are threaded the successive episodes that show the worldwide challenge facing the Allies. As noted previously, most of these international incidents were adapted from works by other authors. For his version of the British sequence, subsequently re-

16. Other than the similarity of name, there is no evidence that Faulkner associated this role with Ronald Reagan, the Hollywood actor who would later become President of the United States.

17. Faulkner worked from a handwritten manuscript of this work (BYU), which was later published as *A Cantata: The Lonesome Train* (New York: Sun Music Company, 1945).

placed by other material, Faulkner blended five separate story strands. The first, possibly by Faulkner but just as likely adapted from an unidentified source, describes the actions of a young RAF pilot, Ackroyd, who helps to design a platform deck that will enable his fighter plane to return to freighter ships at sea.[18] The second narrative, also of uncertain origin, describes the heroic death of John Loughton, Albert's older brother, in the sabotage of a German warship. A third segment, the account of a developing love affair between Margaret Loughton and an American correspondent (a "John Garfield type," Faulkner notes), seems to be the Howard Hawks story, "Malta," mentioned in Warner Bros. file memos (BYU;USC) relating to "Battle Cry." The other two pieces of the British sequence are adaptations of two published stories by Guy Gilpatric and I. A. R. Wylie, respectively.[19] The Gilpatric narrative, "A Bomber Goes Back Home," describes the use of a captured German plane in a kamikaze mission by six Britishers, four of whom are Jewish, against the Berlin chancellery. The Wylie story, "A-Hunting We Will Go," recounts, in a seriocomic vein, how several Englishwomen, who steadfastly maintain their club's foxhunting tradition while their husbands and sons are away at war, discover and capture some German commandos who have parachuted into the English countryside. In reworking these published stories for the purposes of the script, Faulkner retained the plot lines but altered the characters' names and added or deleted personages at will. More significantly, he sought to link these and the other British episodes through the insertion of Fonda, who, as an

18. The Ackroyd story, although a minor incident in the plot, may have held a special poignancy for Faulkner. Setting the scene in which the young Britisher, a convoy pilot for a group of freighter ships, must choose among trying to reach land, parachuting into the ocean, or crash landing onto the ship's deck, Faulkner notes: "He is against going up, he doesn't want to, *no sane man would want to.* But it must be done, someone must fly the damned kite and *the government sent him to do it, is paying him to do it,* etc." [emphases added] Perhaps it is not entirely coincidental that Faulkner in this passage repeats the phraseology he had used in recent letters to his stepson and nephew, both servicemen. "No sane man likes war," Faulkner had written to Malcolm Franklin in the letter previously cited; and he counseled Jimmy Faulkner on April 3, 1943 (*Selected Letters,* p. 170), to be faithful to his responsibility, in part "to pay back to the Govt. the cost of training you." At the time the nephew was training to be a cruiser pilot, much like Ackroyd, in the American naval forces.

19. Guy Gilpatric, "A Bomber Goes Back Home," *Collier's,* 106 (February 8, 1941), 11ff., and I. A. R. Wylie, "A-Hunting We Will Go," *Saturday Evening Post,* 213 (July 27, 1940), 12ff.

acquaintance of Albert Loughton, either participates in or hears about the various adventures.

Three other published short stories were similarly incorporated into this early version of "Battle Cry." Budd Schulberg's "The Bell of Tarchova" dramatizes how a small Czechoslovakian village, particularly one muscular young man named Stefan, thwarts the efforts of German soldiers to confiscate the village bell and melt it down for use as a cannon.[20] In Faulkner's slightly altered version the setting is a Serbian village, the hero is a Greek named Demetrios (this change enabled Faulkner to link the incident with the Greek episode to follow), and the story is recounted by the Italian prisoner to illustrate the fierce resistance of the Europeans conquered by Hitler's armies. Georges Carousso's "The Weapon" describes how a Greek patriot, known to his enemies and the general public only as "the man with the cough," uses a secret radio to encourage Athenians to defy the occupation army by hanging small Greek flags from the Acropolis.[21] In this instance Faulkner's revisions went considerably beyond changes of name and location. He borrowed Carousso's characterization of the Greek spirit of resistance, the portrayal of the German commander as an insatiable glutton, and the humorous episode in which young boys play tricks on two Italian soldiers; but the principal element in Faulkner's version, the repeated blackballing of the German officer, does not appear in the original story. The third narrative, C. S. Forester's "The Dumb Dutchman," recounts the adventures of a Dutch tugboat captain, Jan Schuylenboeck, who, while ostensibly in the employ of the Nazis, directs a chain of barges loaded with German troops into an English ambush.[22] Forester's story, unlike the others, was not given independent treatment in the script but was utilized as the climax of Faulkner's otherwise original French sequence.

For this French episode Faulkner recreated the milieu he had treated the previous year in "The De Gaulle Story." The principal characters are Albert Loughton, the British corporal, and Clemente Desmoulins, a young Frenchwoman who was formerly a prostitute. These two meet and become lovers in Paris in 1938, but their marriage plans are interrupted first by Albert's discovery of Clemente's

20. Budd Schulberg, "The Bell of Tarchova," *Saturday Evening Post,* 215 (October 24, 1942), 12ff.

21. Georges Carousso, "The Weapon," *Saturday Evening Post,* 215 (April 24, 1943), 23ff.

22. C. S. Forester, "The Dumb Dutchman," *Saturday Evening Post,* 215 (July 11, 1942), 16ff.

past and again, following a reconciliation, by Albert's enlistment in the British army at the outbreak of the war. When the Germans invade France, Albert escapes with the remnants of the French and British armies at Dunkirk; but Clemente is trapped in Paris, where she is raped and forced to become the mistress of a German officer. Later, having been abandoned by the officer, she manages to survive only by resuming a life of prostitution. Faulkner makes it clear that Clemente's situation is allegorical: "She is now a symbol of France itself: conquered, debased, prone and dazed and for a time apathetic beneath the conqueror's heel." Finally, in desperation, Clemente turns to Henri Ballin, a former acquaintance who has become, without Clemente's knowledge, an Underground agent for General De Gaulle. Fearful that involvement with Clemente might jeopardize his secret mission, Ballin at first seeks to ignore the woman; but when he learns that the Gestapo is attempting to coerce Clemente into locating and betraying him, Ballin arranges for the Underground to kidnap her and keep her in hiding. Now privy to the Underground's activities, Clemente learns that Ballin and his fellow conspirators are plotting to sabotage a planned German invasion of England. The strategy calls for one member of the Underground, a Dutch tugboat captain who has the trust of the Nazis, to lead a convoy of German barges into the line of British fire. Seeing an opportunity to escape to England and perhaps be reunited with Albert, Clemente secures Ballin's permission to accompany the tugboat crew on the mission. At the last moment, however, Clemente forgoes her chance for freedom and happiness, choosing instead to remain behind and seduce a German officer to prevent his giving the order that might halt the debarkation of the doomed German troops. The climax of the French sequence essentially follows Forester's story, except that Faulkner has his captain and crew sacrifice their lives by disdaining to cut loose from the barges and sending a continuous radio signal that enables the British to guide their torpedos unerringly to the targets.

III

Two other international episodes, Violet Atkins and William Bacher's adaptations of the Russian and Chinese stories, remained unfinished at the time of the April 21 treatment, but Faulkner noted their intended placement and included brief synopses of their contents. On page 18, following a segment of the Lincoln cantata, Faulkner shifts the scene to a Soviet airfield in 1937–38 and notes: "We play the Russian story, of the woman aviator, Stalingrad siege, the fetching in of musician soldiers from the front line as far away as Moscow and

Leningrad, to play the symphony, on to the end of the Russian story."
Faulkner had obviously read or heard described "Diary of a Red
Army Woman," which blends the fictional love story of Tania and
Semyon Doronin, two Russian flyers, with a dramatization of the his-
toric premier performance of Dmitri Shostakovich's Seventh Symphony, part of which was written in Leningrad during the German
siege of that city in 1941. The Chinese sequence was likewise handled
in summary fashion. On page 22, following the burial of the American officer in the African desert, Faulkner shifts to another burial site,
this one in China, where the grandson of Mama Mosquito is being
interred following a Japanese air raid. Faulkner notes: "We tell the
Mama Mosquito story: the moving by hand of an entire munitions
factory, piecemeal back into the hills where the Japs can't bomb it, on
to where General Chiang decorates her." Faulkner may or may not
have read Jennings' account of Mama Mosquito's exploits: the moving of the factory is not mentioned in the feature article but probably
derived from the story conferences with Hawks and others.

Faulkner's arrangement of the separate episodes in his initial treatment of "Battle Cry" calls to mind the complicated plot intersections
in such novels as *The Sound and the Fury, Light in August, The Wild Palms*,
and *A Fable*. Indeed, of all the movies with which he was associated,
"Battle Cry" seems the most compatible with Faulkner's concept of
novelistic form. The following outline of the major divisions of the
April 21 treatment suggests something of the complexity of Faulkner's structure.

I	Part 1 of American sequence (Springfield)
II	Part 2 of American sequence (North Africa)
III	Part 1 of Lincoln cantata
IV	Russian sequence
V	Part 3 of American sequence
VI	Chinese sequence
VII	Part 4 of American sequence
VIII	Part 2 of Lincoln cantata
IX	Part 5 of American sequence
X	English sequence
XI	Part 6 of American sequence
XII	Serbian sequence
XIII	Greek sequence
XIV	Part 7 of American sequence
XV	French sequence
XVI	Part 8 of American sequence
XVII	Part 3 of Lincoln cantata

As noted previously, each of these segments contributes to the overall conviction that nothing less than a global commitment will be required to defeat the Axis powers. However, since the film was to be directed to an American audience, the American sequence predictably received the greatest emphasis. This section of the plot features the conversion of the Italian prisoner to the American cause (as demonstrated by his shooting of the German prisoner) and an exercise in democracy in Reagan's decision to allow his troops to vote on whether to defend the well or retreat. They vote unanimously to hold their ground, and the sequence concludes with the Americans bravely fighting to the death as they are overrun by superior German forces.

What readers of Faulkner's novels and stories are likely to find most engaging about the American sequence, however, is not the battlefield action but the treatment of the American civil rights issue embedded in the text. Significantly, Faulkner could not write about the quest for freedom around the globe without addressing the shortcomings of his own society in relation to this ideal. Perhaps it was the linkage of World War II with Lincoln and the Emancipation Proclamation that made it impossible for Faulkner to ignore the discrimination against blacks in the United States, especially the South. In any event, the insertion of a Southern black named America, who has been wounded and now suffers paralysis, seems an obvious, if vaguely realized, allegory on American race relations in the 1940s, as does the characterization of the ambivalent Southerner, Akers, who is capable of an impressive sensitivity toward his wounded comrade but nevertheless embodies a strong regional and even racial bias.

It is Battson who raises the specter of the Negro problem when, upon hearing the Italian prisoner characterize America as a place "where all men have a vote in what all are or are not to do," Battson interjects: "All of them except America's folks. There are parts of it where America's folks don't have any say. Ask Akers." However, it is not Akers but the Italian who rallies to the South's defense. The South will change, he insists, "just as soon as the people outside that part of the country, whose concern it is not, stop trying to force them to give America's people a vote." When Battson, playing the devil's advocate, rationalizes, "They are free to leave, whenever they don't like it," the Italian responds:

> If the rest of the United States' house were as clean as it should be, as it had given its promise to be on that first day of January, 1863, making them as welcome into it as that old promise implied, I think the Jim Crow people would need much more than just a vote to bribe America's people to remain in the Jim Crow land at all. But

perhaps not. Perhaps it is not that simple, not that easy to turn your back on the land, the earth, where you were born and where the only work you know is and where your mother and father and sisters and brothers and children, too, are buried—even if it is only a tenement in Harlem or Chicago or Detroit or a farm in Jim Crow land—

There is something patently ludicrous about an Italian prisoner lecturing American soldiers in the North African desert regarding discrimination against blacks in the United States; and Faulkner was undoubtedly wise to delete the Italian's remarks in the revision of the script. But it is interesting, and helpful, to know that Faulkner was already, in 1943 (five years before the formation of the Dixiecratic States' Rights Party), thinking about the themes and issues that would eventually find expression through the voice of Gavin Stevens in *Intruder in the Dust.*

IV

By June 2 Faulkner had assembled and submitted to the Story Department an expanded script (Part I of this present volume), numbering 232 pages in its retyped format (V, VI), that incorporated a fifty-page "Diary of a Red Army Woman" section and a forty-three-page "Mama Mosquito." segment into the earlier treatment. As noted previously, these Russian and Chinese sequences were prepared by Atkins and Bacher, though there is some evidence that they were working under the close direction of Hawks. For example, a two-page set of notes entitled "Suggestions on Russian Story" and initialed by Hawks (BYU) recommends having Tania and Semyon meet after the parachute jump, presenting their love story as "a rather violent affair," using loudspeakers on the streets for public announcements, and placing Tania and Semyon at the premiere of the Shostakovich symphony. Atkins and Bacher almost certainly drew upon these notes, since their version of the Russian story incorporates all of the above suggestions. Moreover, the June 15 and June 18 memos by Bacher, discussed in detail below, allude to specific elements in the Chinese story that had been inserted at the request of Hawks.

The rest of the content of this June 2 treatment remained unchanged from the April 21 version, but there was one notable alteration in structure. The "Mama Mosquito" section was moved from its originally designated position on page 22 to occupy pages 157–199 in the second version. This shift resulted in the division of the French sequence into two roughly-equal halves that now appeared, respectively, before and after the Chinese story. This curious arrangement created a flashback that interrupted another flashback—a complicated design that will hardly surprise any reader of Faulkner's novels but one that understandably was not allowed to stand in subsequent versions of the screenplay.

Although he seems to have had no hand in developing or writing the June 2 script, Steve Fisher had become a member of the scriptwriting team on May 31 (XXI). Fisher's first contribution to the project was to put the Russian sequence into screenplay form, a task he completed on June 16. Actually, Fisher's script (VII) represents little advancement over the one submitted by Atkins and Bacher. Except for the addition of camera angles for the various scenes, Fisher made few substantive changes in the previous text. Although he doctored a scene here and there, as in adding a view of Semyon's parachute floating to earth and in having Tania's rape take place off-camera, for the most part Fisher limited himself to filling out sentence fragments and making slight alterations in dialogue.

Two sets of notes dictated on June 15 and 18 by Bacher for the attention of Hawks (BYU) indicate the status of the project at this point, as well as something of the nature of the collaboration. In the first of these memos Bacher generally approved Faulkner's June 2 composite script, but he felt that particular episodes should be deleted and the tie-ins for the separate sections improved. Bacher suggested eliminating the complicated British sequence, including the investiture at Buckingham Palace and the stories of Ackroyd, John Loughton, Margaret Loughton, the suicide mission, and the hunt. In place of these unrelated episodes, Bacher preferred using a script by John Rhodes Sturdy of Sturdy's own unpublished short story, "Maitland's Reply," the account of a fourth Maitland son who follows his three deceased brothers into service with the Royal Air Force.[23] Bacher also advised Hawks to drop the Schulberg story about the villagers and the bell, to cut down on the lengthy speeches by the Italian prisoner, and to delete Faulkner's allusion to Lidice, the

---

23. The twenty-six-page script of this story (IX) carries the typescript date "5/17/43" and the notation "Original / by John Rhodes Sturdy." The story version was subsequently published as "Maitland's Reply," *Scholastic*, 45 (November 13, 1944), 21ff.

Sturdy, formerly a newspaperman in Chicago and Montreal, was at this time a lieutenant in the Royal Canadian Navy on assignment in Hollywood as the technical advisor for *Corvette K-225*, a Howard Hawks-produced film about a warship constructed in a Canadian shipyard. The movie, directed by Richard Rosson and for which Sturdy wrote both the original story and the screenplay, was released on October 19, 1943.

Czechoslovakian town that was leveled by Hitler's troops in retaliation for an attack upon a German general. "Also," Bacher added, "cut out the Jim Crow stuff."

A considerable portion of Bacher's June 15 memo relates to the Russian, Chinese, and French segments. Regarding the first, Bacher noted: "All of the 'Red Army Woman' incident is ready for the screen dialogue, but we need a better transition device from Fonda and the Freedom Train theme to the Russian story." Although he was undoubtedly aware of the fact, Bacher made no mention of Fisher's recent assignment to the Russian sequence. Continuing, Bacher insisted that the "Mama Mosquito" story, pages 157 to 199 in the June 2 script, should be moved back to the position designated for it in the April 21 treatment. Bacher also pointed out that "Bill Faulkner is inserting more of the character of the old woman at the beginning" and that the climax of the Chinese sequence employs "the action desired by Mr. Hawks—immediate and catastrophic." Bacher further noted, "The story of the French girl is excellent"; but he questioned whether an American audience would accept Clemente's role as a prostitute. Nevertheless, while he advised that Clemente's "crime" be made "less heinous," possibly "just one act of indiscretion, forced by necessity," Bacher conceded that "I don't think there is anything the girl could have done, even stealing or killing, that will make our story quite as powerful as the Faulkner device, so if Bill Faulkner can soften that just a little . . . , I think our story will be all right." Bacher also recommended that Clemente's trip to England to visit Albert's parents be deleted. On balance, though, Bacher liked the French segment: "It still [needs] a lot of work on the dialogue, but I think that can be done in screen form from now on in."

Upon receiving this June 15 memo, Hawks went through his reading copy of the script (VII) and penciled marginal notations recording some of Bacher's suggestions. Apparently, as he transferred this information to his copy of the script, Hawks lined out the corresponding sections of Bacher's memo. This procedure accounts for the markings in the memo that at first glance appear to be Bacher's own cancellations. Close examination of Hawks's marginal entries reveals that he accepted most of the revisions recommended by Bacher.

By June 18, when Bacher dictated another set of observations for Hawks, several of the proposed changes had already been incorporated into the script. Principal among these were the substitution of Sturdy's story for the previous British sequence and the insertion of new transitional material between the successive episodes. The new ties included Battson's background story of the diary as a lead-in for the Russian sequence and the exchange of dialogue between Fonda and Loughton that introduces the British section. Bacher wrote some of this new material. Regarding the adaptation of "Maitland's Reply," Bacher noted: "In the beginning of the story, I have made the voice that speaks of the battle cry of the English Loughton's, and have done the same at the end of the episode." Bacher indicated that he had followed Hawks's advice in revising the Freedom Train motif. "I have put in the beat of the Freedom Train, as you suggested, at the beginning and ending of each of these separate sequences, and you will find that they are integrated so that instead of 5 or 6 separate stories, we really have one." Bacher added that he had shortened the final scene of the script by moving the last section of the Lincoln cantata, leaving only, as a finale, "a single chorus of the Freedom Train and the passing of the cars until we come to the last one, 'Berlin, Tokyo, or Bust'."

Faulkner drew special praise from Bacher on two counts. With regard to Faulkner's revision of the Chinese story (a revision, as it turned out, that went considerably beyond the reworking of the opening that Bacher mentioned in his previous memo),[24] Bacher remarked: "Faulkner has done an excellent job on the screenplay for 'Mama Mosquito'. He has saved all the best elements and, at your suggestion I understand, has contributed a very vital piece of business in the foot bowl." Of the French segment, still in summary form at this stage, Bacher stated: "The French story, along with its underground sequences, is ready for screen play, and I think you suggested that since Bill Faulkner had already done so much work on it, he would, perhaps, be best suited to put it in its final form." Then, in a remark that may surprise those critics who hold that Faulkner was temperamentally and technically unsuited for scriptwriting, Bacher added, "I think he's a swell craftsman, Mr. Hawks, and he'll come through with a great job on it." Bacher was still concerned, however, about the Jim Crow language that surfaced from time to time in Faulkner's script. "We must watch the use of the word 'niggers'," he warned.

Another of Bacher's concerns was the form of the "Red Army Woman" material "as adapted for screen play." The initial "rape se-

---

24. In one of Faulkner's most fascinating additions Wei Lin says to Lu Ping, "Thy name is like a little temple bell that the wind trembles." Faulkner had twice previously associated a lover's name with a bell (in a fragment draft of a letter to Helen Baird in 1926 and in *Mosquitoes* [New York: Boni and Liveright, 1927], pp. 268–269); and he would do so again in a letter to Joan Williams in 1952. See Carvel Collins, "Biographical Background for Faulkner's *Helen*," in William Faulkner, *Helen: A Courtship and Mississippi Poems* (New Orleans and Oxford: Tulane University and Yoknapatawpha Press, 1981), p. 33.

quence," which had been suggested by Hawks, "seems right in concept," according to Bacher, "but I don't think it has worked out so well
in the writing." In addition, Bacher thought that Nina and Fedya
were given too much attention in the plot, and he objected to the
scene in which Tania and Semyon maneuver their planes to "play like
birds in the air."[25]

One statement in Bacher's June 18 memo explains an anomaly that
would be carried forward into subsequent versions of the script. In
noting that the scenes had been numbered for continuity (a fact that
indicates that the screenplay, at least in Bacher's judgment, was nearing completion), Bacher explained that the Greek story had not been
separated from the main text as the other international episodes had
been. Rather, Bacher explained, "we numbered it in with our regular
continuity, because it was so short and seemed to fit so well into the
spirit of their [the American soldiers'] conversation." This inconsist-
ency of enumeration would be continued, eventually being copied
into the Second Temporary Draft.

Bacher appended to the June 18 memo a definition of the title
phrase, "Battle Cry," for Hawks's consideration as a possible foreword
to the film. The brief statement (BYU), surprisingly Faulknerian in
tone and substance, opens with the assertion that " 'Battle Cry' is the
sound that wells up out of the human spirit when you attempt to take
away from man all those things with which he has lived—the things he
holds most dear and that have made his life worth having." Bacher
identified these values as "the dignity of his home, the integrity of his
land, the honor of his women, and the happiness of his children."
When such things are in danger, Bacher concluded, free men will
always respond with "a defiance, an affirmation and a challenge
against which lust and ruthlessness shall not stand, and before which
tyrant and oppressor, each in his ephemeral and bloody turn, shall
vanish from the earth." Beneath this statement Bacher added an
"apologia": "Maybe this is a little flowery, Howard, but I think it has

---

25. This last point makes it clear that Bacher is here addressing the original
Russian story, not Fisher's rewrite, since the incident in question is unique to
the earlier version. Apparently Bacher had not yet seen the Fisher revision
dated two days previously. But Bacher must have already discussed his reservations with Fisher: the Fisher rewrite incorporates the alterations Bacher
advised in this memo to Hawks.

Bacher's objections to the Russian story raise questions about the extent of
his involvement in the authorship of the piece. Perhaps Violet Atkins had
done most of the work on the story treatment developed from the radio
script; or perhaps Bacher was now having second thoughts about his own
work.

the dignity which your play may require." Hawks agreed, and the lines appear as the opening lines of the Second Temporary Draft (XVII) of the screenplay.

V

In the days and weeks that followed, Hawks and his writers continued to juggle and revise the script as they searched for the best configuration of incident and theme. A copy (IX) submitted to the Story Department on June 21 and identified in the Warner Bros. files as a "Complete Temp. Script" and on the title page as a "First Temp. Draft" substitutes Fisher's Russian narrative for that of Atkins and Bacher. On June 24 (XXI) both Faulkner and Fisher turned in scripted versions of the French story (X, XI). Although Bacher had indicated in his June 18 memo that Faulkner would be the choice to put the French material into screenplay form, the decision had been made to let each writer independently try his hand at the task. Fisher worked from Faulkner's treatment, inserting additional dialogue and occasionally providing specific narrative detail in lieu of Faulkner's general summary. Fisher changed the name of Henri Ballin to Jacques Duval and, in keeping with Bacher's previous suggestions, toned down the references to Clemente's past (in Fisher's version Clemente is mistakenly arrested as a prostitute during a police raid on a restaurant of questionable repute) and deleted Clemente's visit to England. Further compression was achieved by ignoring the background of the Dutch captain and by using numerous voice-overs to summarize some of the action. For the most part, however, Fisher remained faithful to Faulkner's account and even occasionally lifted whole passages of description and dialogue directly from Faulkner's pages. Faulkner's screenplay version of the French material provides an interesting contrast to Fisher's rendition. Faulkner, too, followed Bacher's counsel in eliminating Clemente's trip to visit Albert's parents, and he also tightened the overall plot in the retelling. But, unlike Fisher, Faulkner devoted considerable attention to Clemente's former prostitution and her present illicit affair with Albert. Faulkner obviously felt no compulsion to downplay the scandalous details of his story as a concession to a squeamish American film audience.

Faulkner next turned his attention to putting the American sequence into screenplay form, and he submitted his new version (XIV) to the Stenographic Department on July 5. Retaining the basic plot from the original treatment that had been incorporated into the First Temporary Draft, Faulkner here blocked the material into individual scenes (though unnumbered), reworded the narrative in places, and inserted considerable dialogue. The principal alterations were the expanded role assigned to Battson, the addition of the speeches in which the German prisoner analyzes the American temperament, and the deletion of the Italian's civil rights preachments. This July 5 version also includes, for the first time, the four scenes involving Paul Robeson, the legendary black actor, and incorporates the foreword and the Russian prologue provided by Bacher. Faulkner also supplied, on a separate sheet following the title page, a *dramatis personae* listing the names and the ages of the characters appearing in the desert episode. This list, which includes a Sioux Indian, a Negro, a Mexican, a Chinese, a Jew, an Irishman, a Pole, and a Swede, seems consciously designed to capture the "melting pot" quality of American society and thus, by extension, to relate the American sequence to the various international episodes of the film. Although none of these international segments is included in this version of the "Second Temporary Draft," their intended placements are identified by specific notations or introductory tie-ins.

The speeches of Battson in this Second Temporary Draft call to mind Faulkner's expressed desire, as previously cited in the December 5, 1942 letter to Franklin, "to articulate in the national voice" and "to be listened to" by others. In an eloquent extended soliloquy tracing the history of the American nation, Battson contends that the United States was "conceived" in the "honeymoon" of 1776 as "a dream, a shape, a splendor in human dignity dreamed by men who were not politicians but poets," but the nation was not born until the "confinement" of 1861–65; "the suffering, the agony, the blood and grief and travail out of which rose a nation which can become in reality the shape of man's eternal hope and which, for that reason, must not and shall not perish from the earth." Battson is unquestionably Faulkner's mouthpiece in such passages; and, as though to underscore the point, Faulkner echoes another sentiment he had verbalized in the letter to his stepson. Like the Faulkner who cannot be a soldier, Battson is made a discoverer, a creator, of music, but not a performer. "I can't play any of it," Battson confesses. He continues: "It was the theory of music, making music for other people who can play to play it. . . . To put America into a piece of music as Wagner had put Germany and Tchaikovsky had put Russia. . . ." The implication is that Faulkner/Battson as writer/composer, not fighter/player, will seek, assimilate, and communicate through art the truths that others, artists of another sort, may read/hear and live by. The idea, of course, is a common one in Faulkner's work. It reaches backward not only to the recent letter to Franklin but to Bayard Sartoris' observation in *The Unvanquished* that "those who can, do, those who cannot and suffer enough because they can't, write about it"[26] and ultimately to the metaphorical dialectic on life and art in *The Marble Faun.* In the other direction, Battson and his sentiments anticipate the fictional Gavin Stevens of *Intruder in the Dust* and the real-life William Faulkner delivering pronouncements on segregation, nuclear war, privacy, literature, and other topics.

The speeches of the German prisoner also reverberate beyond the pages of "Battle Cry." In contrasting the American dream of individual liberty and equality with the German will to power, the captured officer enunciates a theme that will become a major concern in *A Fable,* already in gestation but not published until eleven years later. Indeed, in asking the American soldiers to imagine themselves atop the Rocky Mountains, "looking out upon America from the backbone, the roof-peak, of your hemisphere" and making judgments about America's potentialities, the German captain becomes a precursor of the old general in *A Fable,* offering the corporal various temptations from the hilltop above Paris. Like the general, the German believes that the value of humanity is to be found, not in "the moiling worthless mass of mankind,"[27] but in those few individuals, like Hitler, who dare to seize power on behalf of that select group "which has the strength to declare its own godhead, and so becomes godhead." Interestingly, the German officer is denied the ambiguity afforded his counterpart in *A Fable.* "Kill him!" an American soldier shouts. "They're monsters! There ain't any hope for them! . . . We got to kill them all to save ourselves!"

VI

On July 15 Earl Robinson wrote Hawks (BYU) at June Lake Lodge, conveying his impressions of "both scripts you gave me," presumably the first complete temporary draft and Faulkner's rewrite of the desert episode. Robinson felt that the screenplay held promise of "an honest-to-God great picture," with "scenes that will really be new and startling but at the same time simple and true and embodying real people and believable characters and situations." However, Robinson continued, the work was "spotty and confusing in places," and "the Lincoln integration still isn't solved completely." Robinson's major

26. William Faulkner, *The Unvanquished* (New York: Random House, 1938), p. 262.
27. Cf. the following passage from *A Fable* (New York: Random House, 1954, p. 30): "It is man who is our enemy: the vast seething moiling spiritless mass of him."

objection related to the tone and focus of the script. "The mood of so much of the picture," he complained, "is a sad one, one of brave people fighting against almost unconquerable odds, gallantry and courage in defeat, etc." Robinson believed that an American audience might find the mood too pessimistic, especially in view of the current Russian success on the Eastern front and "Eisenhower's terrifically organized and coordinated attacks" in Europe. Furthermore, the American involvement in the war should be given the predominant emphasis. In Robinson's view, the film should be "told from the American viewpoint, by Americans." For this reason greater care should be taken to integrate the Lincoln material, which would serve to dramatize the parallels between the Civil War and World War II. As Robinson stated the case, "The dirty dealings of the copperheads in Lincoln's time have been reflected all through this war—not only in the unprincipled attacks on [the] President and his policies for winning the war but of course more particularly in the various Fifth Columnists and the Quislings of the occupied countries."

Continuing, Robinson noted that "some of the qualities and character development in the rewrite by Faulkner are swell," but Battson's "search and discovery of the Lincoln legend is a little forced." Neither was Robinson impressed with the role assigned to Robeson, who seemed intended as "a kind of huge mystical concept." Perhaps Robeson should play the role of America as well as sing a part of the cantata. Robinson also pointed out that the scene in the Negro church imitated scenes in previous movies, notably *Green Pastures* and *Cabin in the Sky*. Shifting the locale to the seaside, where Negro fishermen could be shown loading their nets into boats, seemed preferable.

Though he generally approved of Faulkner's work, Robinson took harsh exception to two parenthetical remarks Faulkner had entered into the script. Regarding one quotation attributed to Lincoln by Robinson and Lampell, Faulkner had noted: "Can't vouch authenticity of this." Beneath the cantata passage that cited Lincoln's famous remark about "the common people," Faulkner had written: "If I remember correctly, Lincoln said, intent humorous, 'God surely must love the poor people; He made so many of them.' Am a little inclined to think the author stopped being a musician at this point in order to insert a little foreign matter." Robinson was not amused. He wrote Hawks, "I can't forbear remarking, before I finish, on one of your authors who not only doubted two of the direct Lincoln quotations we used near the end of the cantata but without bothering to look up to see whether they were right or not, inserted his insinuations as to their authenticity right into the script for everybody to read." Robinson assured Hawks that Lampell and he had checked and rechecked all of the quotations attributed to Lincoln. "If you want documentation," Robinson added, "we will give it to you."

VII

Even as Faulkner and Fisher continued to revise portions of the script, Hawks was proceeding to put the film into production. Records (BYU) show that screen tests for three individuals being considered for roles in the movie—Lauren Bacall, Leah Baird, and Earl Robinson—had been completed on April 26; and budget meetings had been held on July 7–8. Notes from these budget sessions, probably recorded by Margaret Cunningham, Hawks's personal secretary, reveal plans for filming the French, Chinese, Russian, and Freedom Train sequences. The last of these was to be under the direction of an assistant director, Jean Negulesco. As the notes indicate, cutting costs for the project was of paramount importance. Suggestions were made to borrow stock shots from such previous films as *The Good Earth*, *Sergeant York*, and *The Old Maid* and to procure an airplane from the United States Armed Forces. The military was also being approached regarding possible use of some recently-captured film footage showing Japanese troops in action in China. Perhaps the orchestra set required for the Russian story could be leased from Twentieth Century-Fox. The need for a Russian fairgrounds setting could be eliminated by having Semyon land his parachute in Tania's father's chicken yard.

By this time, Hawks's casting office had been instructed to send out calls to various agencies for actors and actresses. Some agencies had already contacted Hawks on behalf of their clients. Arthur MacArthur nominated Roscoe Karns, Robert Barratt, and others; Tom Conlon suggested Edward S. Brophy. Julian Olenick later wrote to recommend Hugh Southern for the role of Fonda's grandfather; and Bill Tinsman, who worked in the casting office, suggested Paul Fung, a Korean actor, for a role in the Chinese sequence.

The Location Department had been asked to secure a field of grain to be used in photographing scenes in both the Chinese and Russian sequences. A site was obtained on Moorpark Road in the San Fernando Valley, and on July 28 a production crew under the direction of Roy Davidson spent twelve hours shooting straight shots and keys of a burning wheatfield. The Daily Production and Progress Report filed on that date shows that four actors and thirty-six extras were involved in these scenes. The actors were identified as George Suzanne, Cab Severn, Alan Pomeroy, and Richard Talmadge. As matters subsequently developed, these were the only actors and scenes ever to be filmed for "Battle Cry."

During the latter part of July Faulkner and Fisher worked independently to revise, respectively, the Russian and Chinese segments of the script. Faulkner was at work on the Russian story at least by July 26, and he submitted his completed revision to the Story Department on August 3 (XV). This thirty-nine-page version represents essentially a compression of the earlier material. The compression is achieved partly through a greater reliance on Tania's voice-over as she records her narrative in her diary. But Faulkner also made some notable deletions, including the opening fairgrounds scene, the role of Fedya, the graphic on-camera view of the German invasion of the Russian village, and the meeting between Tania and Semyon just prior to his death. Only the Shostakovich element of the story remained virtually unchanged. Even as he condensed the story, however, Faulkner added certain specific details, such as the prank the wedding guests play on Tania and Semyon and, more significantly, the lines in which Semyon identifies Tania and himself, through their expected son, with "the long cavalcade of man's immortality, coming from where, he does not know, going where, he doesn't know either, except that he has a destiny, to have so endured." This latter detail represents a genuine improvement in the story, since it elevates the story of the two Russian lovers to a universal level. As Semyon expresses it, "So we are more than Russia. We are Man." And Tania responds, "Yes. We are Man."

Undoubtedly, Faulkner's revised version of the Russian story is more workable as a screenplay than the previous one, especially in view of the concern about the mounting expense of the total project;[28] but much of the narrative power of Atkins and Bacher's initial treatment has been sacrificed. Faulkner's willingness to make such concessions, however, says something about his development as a scenarist. A year earlier Robert Buckner, the producer of "The De Gaulle Story," had criticized Faulkner for his impracticality. Now Faulkner was demonstrating that, when the budget crunch demanded it, he could be as pragmatic as anyone else. Unfortunately, it would require more than the deletion of a few episodes to salvage "Battle Cry."

By July 31 Fisher had completed his revision of the Chinese se-

---

28. Faulkner commented on the financial crisis in his letter to his wife Estelle on August 1, 1943: "We had a meeting with the studio finance mgr. last week. Hawks asked what this picture will cost. The mgr. said $4,000,000.00. That is too much. So we must cut it down." *Selected Letters of William Faulkner,* p. 176.

quence (XVI). This new version, like Faulkner's reworked Russian segment, was apparently designed to cut costs of production by condensing the action and eliminating marginal scenes. The most significant alteration was the removal of the character Wei Lin from the story—and, with him, the love relationship with Lu Ping. The remainder of Fisher's plot—from the initial migration of the Chinese peasants, through the growing rebellion of the guerrilla army and the poisoning of the well, on to the decoration of Mama Mosquito by Chiang Kai-shek—represents essentially Fisher's editing, with very little rewriting, of the previous version by Faulkner.

On August 5, 1943, the Warner Bros. Stenographic Department distributed mimeographed copies of the complete "Second Temporary Draft" of "Battle Cry" (XVII). This version (printed as Part II of the present volume) represents a composite script fashioned from various segments of the previous material. The American sequence (including the Freedom Train scenes and the Greek story) is the revised text Faulkner submitted to the Stenographic Department on July 5. The Russian story is Faulkner's revised, condensed version, dated on the part-title page, "8/3/43."[29] The Chinese segment is Faulkner's revised version from the First Temporary Draft of June 21. The French story is Faulkner's text of June 24. The English sequence is the John Rhodes Sturdy narrative which, as noted earlier, was adapted by Sturdy himself.[30] It is significant that nothing in this August 5 copy of the screenplay is by Steve Fisher. Although Fisher had written four episodes totaling 140 pages, none of his material found its way into the final Second Temporary Draft. Thus, except for the Sturdy story and the foreword and other brief passages by Bacher, all of the final version of "Battle Cry" was written by Faulkner. Undoubtedly, had the movie been filmed, he would have been given undivided screen credit for the screenplay.

But the movie was never filmed. As the project dragged on and costs escalated, relations became more and more strained between

29. In the Brodsky copy, alone among the copies of this version that the editors have seen, the Russian story is not mimeographed but rather is a carbon typescript.

30. In the August 24, 1943 memo cited in note 32 below, Steve Fisher states that "Howard [Hawks] told me that we were going to do a new English sequence, and not use the one which is in the script at present." Hawks's dissatisfaction with the Sturdy narrative may explain why the copy of the Second Temporary Draft in the Faulkner collection at the University of Texas contains no English segment. The editors are grateful to Cathy Henderson, of the Humanities Research Center at the University of Texas at Austin, for providing a photocopy of the Texas copy of "Battle Cry."

Hawks and Warner Bros. Hawks's contract called for a twenty-week salary of $100,000 with a proratable figure of $3,000 for each extra week up to a maximum of an additional $50,000.[31] Now, with the initial time period drawing to a close and no production in sight, Warner Bros. officials were losing their patience. Hawks was living up to his reputation as a budget-buster who seldom delivered a film on schedule. Suddenly, starkly, the project was canceled. Faulkner's time on the film was credited until August 13, when, according to his off-payroll notice, his contract was "suspended for approximately 4 months." On August 16 Faulkner turned in to the Story Department a nine-page fragment of a further revision (XVIII) of the Chinese sequence (dated "8/4/43"), executed a contract assigning all rights to his "Battle Cry" materials to Warner Bros. (XX), and began preparations for his return to Mississippi.[32] He would be glad to get back home, but he must have been exceedingly disappointed that twice now in little over a year projects for which he had held such high hopes had come to nothing.

VIII

The shutdown of "Battle Cry," which during its four-month existence stimulated Faulkner to generate hundreds of typescript pages forming an early treatment, an expanded treatment, and two distinct drafts of the screenplay, must have come as a bleak and sickening revelation. Not a week before the cancellation of the project Faulkner still had considerable hope of success, as he revealed in a letter to his wife Estelle: "When I come home, I intend to have Hawks completely satisfied with this job, as well as the studio. If I can do that, I wont have to worry again about going broke temporarily. The main problem I have now is to get myself free from the seven-year contract for a pittance of a salary. . . . I have a promise from the studio that, when I have written a successful picture, they will destroy that contract. This is my chance."[33] In discussing his latest problems with the agent Wil-

31. This information is taken from the April 10, 1943 memo (USC) from R. J. Obringer to Steve Trilling cited in note 11 above.

32. The "Battle Cry" saga did not quite end with the departure of Hawks and Faulkner. Two memos (USC) dated August 24, 1943—one from Steve Fisher to James Geller and the other from an unidentified individual, probably Roy Obringer or Steve Trilling, to Jack Warner—suggest that the studio hoped to salvage the project, if possible. A one-page synopsis of the script prepared by Judith Meyers on December 13, 1943 (XXII), possibly for circulation among studio executives, further evidences a lingering interest in the film.

33. *Selected Letters of William Faulkner*, p. 177.

liam Herndon, Faulkner noted: "Naturally he doesn't want to let me go, *now that I have written a good picture . . .*" [emphasis added]. But now, the unhappy climax to his highly concentrated attempt to prove himself not merely a competent but an exemplary screenwriter could only reinforce his cynical judgments about Hollywood, and perhaps even break his spirit. Certainly, after the back-to-back failures of "The De Gaulle Story" and "Battle Cry," none of the film projects on which Faulkner worked in 1944 and 1945 would compel him to the same level of excitement or delude him with expectations of becoming what perhaps, after all, he was not essentially equipped for in temperament or sensibility: that is, a scriptwriter.

Yet, on returning home to Oxford in mid-August 1943, Faulkner did retain, along with some less visible alterations to his literary psyche, one immediately tangible legacy from his work on "Battle Cry": he had a check for $1,000, a loan from William Bacher, who, impressed with Faulkner's work on the aborted project, was confident that Faulkner could translate some legends about the Unknown Soldier of World War I into a saleable movie property. Once situated at Rowan Oak, Faulkner wrote to Robert Haas about the challenging new concept: "The argument is (in the fable) in the middle of that war, Christ (some movement in mankind which wished to stop war forever) reappeared and was crucified again. We are repeating, we are in the midst of war again. Suppose Christ gives us one more chance, will we crucify him again, perhaps for the last time." Then Faulkner added: "That's crudely put; I am not trying to preach at all. But that is the argument. . . ."[34] Faulkner failed to recognize that he *was* trying to persuade by preaching. Nor did he realize then that he had actually arrived at that juncture in his career where propagandizing, Hollywood's severest and most ineradicable legacy for Faulkner, had already begun to dominate his work. Ironically, Faulkner later expressed to Malcolm Cowley the belief that he could keep "Hollywood" and his other work separate, mutually exclusive: "I can work at Hollywood 6 months, stay home 6, am used to it now and have movie work locked off into another room."[35] Referring to the "Appendix" to *The Sound and the Fury* that he had written for Cowley's *The Portable Faulkner,* Faulkner similarly repeated, "I think this is all right, it took me about a week to get Hollywood out of my lungs, but I am still writing all right, I believe."[36] Indeed, the "Appendix" belongs with the finest prose Faulkner had ever written, but little did Faulkner realize

34. *Selected Letters of William Faulkner,* p. 180.
35. *Selected Letters of William Faulkner,* p. 186.
36. *Selected Letters of William Faulkner,* p. 205.

that he would ever afterward find it increasingly difficult, even impossible, to lock Hollywood away in "another room" or get it "out of [his] lungs." All too soon, propagandizing would become a way of life.

What Faulkner had mentioned privately to his stepson in his December 5, 1942, letter about men like himself "who are too old to be soldiers, but are old enough and have been vocal long enough to be *listened to*" [emphasis added] would be reiterated and proclaimed publicly in the Nobel Prize Acceptance Speech eight years later: "So this award is only mine in trust. It will not be difficult to find a dedication for the money part of it commensurate with the purpose and significance of its origin. But I would like to do the same with the acclaim too, by using this moment as a pinnacle from which I might be *listened to* . . ." [emphasis added].[37] Most shocking and stunning to those who had been familiar with Faulkner's fiction for more than a score of years was not the lofty, eloquent rhetoric of his moving speech, but Faulkner's unreserved faith in man's ability to endure and overcome oppression and tragedy because of the invincible, immortal qualities in the collective human spirit and will. Few Faulkner readers in 1950 could have known that what seemed a reversal of attitude was actually the residual product of his mature years in Hollywood. After all, neither "The De Gaulle Story" nor "Battle Cry," his two major works of affirmation from that period, had been produced. And those scripts that were known, such as *To Have and Have Not,* were so inextricably collaborative as to muffle and distort whatever positive voice Faulkner might have loaned to them.

Nonetheless, the hallmark—or stigma—was in place, even if the public remained at a loss for adequate explanations for Faulkner's apparent sea-change. Less than six months after the trip to Stockholm, on May 28, 1951, Faulkner again took to the podium. And again he preached his seemingly new gospel on mankind, this time to an audience gathered in the University High School auditorium in Oxford for the commencement exercises of the Class of '51, the valedictorian of which was his daughter Jill. This address, which has come to be known as Faulkner's "Never Be Afraid" speech,[38] was laced with two very remarkable echoes. One theme would imply a path directly back through the Nobel Prize speech to that December 5, 1942 letter to Malcolm Franklin, in which Faulkner posited "articulat[ing] in the national voice" and "be[ing] listened to" as a legitimate alternative to youthful fighting in the field. In his com-

37. *Essays, Speeches & Public Letters by William Faulkner,* ed. James B. Meriwether (New York: Random House, 1965), p. 119.

38. See *Essays, Speeches & Public Letters by William Faulkner,* pp. 122–124.

mencement address Faulkner spent the initial two of the five paragraphs distinguishing between youth and age, highlighting with the French proverb, "If youth knew; if age could," the obvious paradoxes inherent in the two conditions. Then he proceeded to offer some relevant observations that he hoped would be listened to, and acted upon, by those in attendance still young enough to shape the future: "So you young men and women in this room tonight, and in thousands of other rooms like this one about the earth today, have the power to change the world, rid it forever of war and injustice and suffering, provided you know how, know what to do." The fearlessness that Faulkner went on to advocate was a quality he knew well. He had expressed it most recently through Chick Mallison and Miss Habersham in *Intruder in the Dust,* but he had also learned it, in part, from the characters of "The De Gaulle Story" and "Battle Cry": Georges, Catherine, Coupe-tête, the priest, Kereon, and De Gaulle; Fonda, Battson, America, Akers, Reagan, Ackroyd, Tania, Mama Mosquito, and Clemente. One part of Faulkner's commencement address links directly to a passage in "Battle Cry." Faulkner told his listeners, "What threatens us today is fear. Not the atom bomb, nor even fear of it, because if the bomb fell on Oxford tonight, all it could do would be to kill us, which is nothing, since in doing that, it will have robbed itself of its only power over us: which is fear of it, the being afraid of it." In "Battle Cry" the Italian prisoner relates the story of a fat German general humiliated by his captives, despite his tyrannical domination over them. At the end of the story Battson says, "Well? Is that all?" The Italian replies, "It will never be all, as long as they can laugh. How can you conquer people who can still laugh at you?" "You can starve them," a soldier interjects, to which the Italian responds: "You can only kill them by doing that. You can kill them much simpler. But when you do that, you have failed. The man whom you must destroy, as the only alternative to his obeying you, that man has beat you."

On accepting the Nobel Prize, Faulkner would not likely have stopped to ponder that the award was for fiction he had produced before 1942, in private—fiction evocative and heroic by virtue of understatement, despite the effusive rhetoric that often escorted his characters into life. Nor could he have realized in 1950 that, with few exceptions, his future work would be distinctly characterized by ethical and political moralizing and preaching. As the prime example, he would create *A Fable,* which he brought to fruition after more than ten years and which, more than any other work, embodies the political, philosophical, and artistic tenets that had polarized during his Warner Bros. tenure. Yet, even had he been able in the early 1940s to predict his journey through the next two decades, Faulkner may still have opted to accept the questionable legacy of the Hollywood experience—especially since the culmination in the Nobel Prize and the attendant fame would mark the actual public acceptance and recognition that had eluded him for so many dispiriting years. At least evanescently, that pinnacled moment in Stockholm and its aftermath mediated a lifetime of disappointment.

Robert W. Hamblin
Louis Daniel Brodsky

1. Howard Hawks and William Faulkner at work on "Battle Cry" (Courtesy of Warner Bros.)

"Battle Cry"
Materials in the Brodsky Collection

(Items from the Warner Bros. Story Department files are designated by the initials WB; materials acquired from A. I. Bezzerides are labeled AIB.)

I. "Battle Cry." Out-take (opening scene) from original story treatment by Faulkner. Carbon typescript, 4 pages (1–4). Page 1 of this version was replaced by pages 1–1c of next item; pages 2–4 remained unchanged. WB

II. "Battle Cry." Original story treatment written by Faulkner. Carbon typescript, 144 pages (title page, [1], 1a–1c, 2–21, 21a, 22–87, "88–89" [one page], 90–140), in blue wrappers with brass clasps; dated on title page, "April 21, 1943." Laid in is Warner Bros. file memo by John O'Steen, dated September 30, 1943, identifying this treatment as "the basic material by Hawks as written by Wm. Faulkner." WB

III. Another carbon typescript of treatment described in item II. AIB

IV. "Mama Mosquito." Initial Chinese sequence by Violet Atkins and William Bacher. Carbon typescript, 46 pages ([1]–46); undated [late April 1943]. In red pencil in unidentified hand at top of page 1: "Return / to Mr Hawks / [rule]." Opening and closing of this version were slightly altered in next item. WB

V. "Battle Cry." Expanded story treatment incorporating Atkins and Bacher's Russian and Chinese sequences. Mixed ribbon and carbon typescript, 239 pages (title page, [1], 1a–1c, 2–17, 18 ["Diary of a Red Army Woman" begins on second half of this page], 2–10, 10a–10g, 11–12, 12a, 13–42 [end of Russian sequence], 19–21, 21a, 22–87, "88–89" [one page], 90–107, [1]–46 [Chinese sequence], 108–140), in blue wrappers with brass clasps; dated on cover in pencil, "6/2/43/" (title page repeats "April 21, 1943" date from earlier version). WB

VI. "Battle Cry." Retyped, renumbered copy of item V. Carbon typescript, 233 pages (title page, [1]–7, [8], 9–193, 193a, 194–231), in blue wrappers with brass clasps; dated in typescript on cover, "June 2, 1943" (title page repeats "April 21, 1943" date from earlier version).

Includes a few subsequent penciled revisions by Faulkner in "Mama Mosquito" section. AIB

VII. "Battle Cry." Revised, restructured version of expanded story treatment, signed on cover, "Howard Hawks." Carbon typescript except for Russian sequence by Steve Fisher, which is ribbon typescript; 245 pages (title page, [1]–19, 19a–19e, 20, title page to Russian sequence, [1]–62, 157–199 ["Mama Mosquito"], 75–136, 138–156, 200–231), in blue wrappers with brass clasps; dated in typescript on title page of Fisher's Russian sequence, "June 16, 1943." WB

VIII. "Battle Cry: The Russian Story." Carbon copy of Fisher's version listed in previous item, 63 pages (title page, [1]–62).

IX. "Battle Cry." "First Temp. Draft," with Fisher's Russian sequence, Faulkner's rewrite of "Mama Mosquito," and John Rhodes Sturdy's English sequence. Mixed ribbon and carbon typescript, 237 pages (title page, [1]–27, title page of Russian sequence, [1]–62, 28–32, 157–195 ["Mama Mosquito"], 33–44, 92a–92e, 92ee, 92f–92y [English sequence, renumbered 83a–83y], 45–63, [138]–156 [French sequence], 200–216 [conclusion of French sequence], 64–72), in brown wrappers with brass clasps; undated [late June 1943]. Contains Bacher's revised transitions between various sections. On title page the names of William A. Bacher, Violet Atkins, and Steve Fisher have been added (in orange grease pencil) to that of Faulkner.

X. "Battle Cry: French Episode." Faulkner's screenplay version of treatment from earlier copies. Carbon typescript (except for page "D-8," which is a ribbon typescript), 53 pages (D-1–D-53); added in ribbon typescript in upper left corner of page D-1: "By William Faulkner/ 6/26/43." WB

XI. "The French Story." Fisher's screenplay version of Faulkner's treatment. Ribbon typescript, 42 pages (title page, [1]–41); dated in typescript on title page, "June 28, 1943." Accompanied by two carbon copies, one of which carries the penciled notation, "NOT USED," on the title page. WB

XII. "Battle Cry." Faulkner's "Second Temporary Draft" of the desert episode. Ribbon typescript (with Faulkner's holograph corrections on page 31), 121 pages (title page, "Cast of Characters" page, [1], 1a–1d, 2–14, 14a–14k, 15–23, "24-25-26" [one page], 27, "Russian A-62," 28–31, 31a–31h, 32–35, 35a–35m, 36–41, 41a–41c, 42, 42a–42c, 43–49, 49a–49b, 50–58, 58a–58b, 59–74); undated [July 1–5, 1943]. This copy is comprised of seven separate sections, each of which is paper clipped together, apparently in the order that Faulkner submitted the material to the Story Department. Clipped to the section containing pages 18–27 is a penciled note in Faulkner's hand: "These are the substitute pages for the original which Mr Hawks already has." Laid in at back of script are three ribbon typescript pages (apparently out-takes) numbered "34," "35f," and "35g," the texts of which differ from the corresponding pages in this version. WB

XIII. "Battle Cry." Carbon copy of pages 1–17 of previous item. Added in ribbon typescript on page 1: "William Faulkner 'Battle Cry' 7/1/43 / Replacement Pages." WB

XIV. "Battle Cry." Carbon typescript of item XII, with Faulkner's holograph corrections on pages 1 and 31; in blue wrappers with brass clasps. Pagination duplicates number XII, except that "Russian A-62" and "35m" have been deleted (text is continuous) and the pages have been sporadically renumbered, in pencil, to "117." On front cover, in typescript: "recd 7/5/43 / pgs. 1–117 complete"; on title page, in pencil : "RECD / STENO / 7/5/43." In this copy the scenes have been blocked and numbered, in pencil, to "190." WB

XV. "Battle Cry: Russian Sequence." Faulkner's revised version. Carbon typescript, 40 pages (title page, Russian A-1–Russian A-39); dated, in ribbon typescript, on page A-1, "7/26/43," and on title page, "7/26/43 / 8/3/43." Recorded in pencil on title page: "REVISED," "COMP.," and "RECD / 8/3/43." WB

XVI. "Battle Cry: Chinese Sequence." Fisher's revision of "Mama Mosquito" segment. Carbon typescript, 30 pages (title page, Chinese B-1–Chinese B-25, Chinese B-25A, Chinese B-26–Chinese B-28); dated in typescript on title page, "7/31/43." WB

XVII. "Battle Cry." Faulkner's "Second Temporary Draft" of complete screenplay. Mimeographed typescript, except for Russian sequence, which is carbon typescript; 287 pages (title page, "Cast of Characters" page, [1]-9, "10–11" [one page], 12–39, title page of Russian story, Russian A-1–Russian A-39, 40–51, Chinese B-1–Chinese B-37, 52–73, 19–24, 36–40, 57–61 [three segments of Lincoln material], 74–78, English C-1–English C-27, 79–100, French D-1–French D-43, French 44-French 54, 101–112), in brown wrappers with brass clasps; dated on cover, "August 5, 1943." Number "72" stamped on cover. AIB

XVIII. "Battle Cry: Chinese Sequence." Faulkner's partial further revision of the "Mama Mosquito" section. Carbon typescript, 10 pages (title page, Chinese B-1–Chinese B-9); dated in ribbon typescript on page B-1, "8/4/43." On title page, in pencil: "RECD / 8/16/43 / INC." WB

XIX. "Battle Cry." Fisher's rewrite of one scene in the American sequence. Carbon typescript, 8 pages (1–8); dated on page 1, "8/8/43." WB

XX. Signed, mimeographed form contract between Faulkner and Warner Bros., dated August 16, 1943, 1 page, assigning ownership of "Battle Cry" to the studio. WB

XXI. Warner Bros. file listing of work submitted on "Battle Cry," April 21–August 16, 1943. Records 18 entries by Faulkner and Fisher; includes: "Wm. Faulkner st. 4/7/43 / Steve Fisher st. 5/31/43." WB

XXII. Synopsis of "Battle Cry" prepared by Judith Meyers. Carbon typescript, 1 page, dated in typescript, "12/13/43." WB

```
            BATTLE CRY            (Hawks)
   Wm. Faulkner st. 4/7/43
   Steve Fisher st. 5/31/43
                                        #1
   4/21/43 - 1-140 complete script(Faulkner)
   4/27/43 - 1-22 script(Faulkner)#2
   5/4/43  - 23-31 script
   5/11/43 - 32-88 script
   5/18/43 - 89-99 script
   5/24/43 - 100-107 script
   6/2/43  - 108-228(231)complete script
   6/16/43 - 1-62 Russ.seq.(Fisher)#A-3
   6/18/43 - 157-195 R.Chin.(Faulkner)#B-3
   6/21/43 - COMPLETE TEMP. SCRIPT #3
   6/24/43 - 1-53 R.French(Faulkner)#A-4
   6/24/43 - 1-41 French Seq(Fisher)#B-4
   7/1/43  - 1-17 inc.script(Faulkner)#C-4
   7/5/43  - 1-117 comp.r.script(Faulkner)
           ,(73 R.Pgs.)      #4 - R.Temp.
   7/31/51 - 1-28 r.Chin.(Fisher)#A-5
   8/3/43  - 1-39 R.Russ.(Faulkner)#B-5
   8/9/43  - 8 R.pgs. script(Fisher)#C-5
   8/16/43 - 1-9 inc.script(Faulkner)#D-5
```

2. Warner Bros. file record for "Battle Cry"

EDITORIAL NOTES

IN PREPARING "Battle Cry" for publication, the editors have been guided by the principles of clarity, consistency, and readability. Obvious typographical errors have been silently corrected; spelling, punctuation, capitalization, and indentation have been regularized; and the basic format of the scripts has been slightly altered to conserve space. In those cases in which the typescripts employ variant but equally acceptable forms, the most prevalent form has been adopted. The relatively few instances that have required substantive editorial interpolations and emendations have been duly noted in the textual collation printed at the end of the volume.

Faulkner

*A Comprehensive Guide
to the Brodsky Collection*

Volume IV: Battle Cry
A Screenplay by William Faulkner

WARNER BROS. PICTURES, INC.
CHANGE PAYROLL NOTICE

BADGE NO.

NAME   FAULKNER, WILLIAM   NO.

DATE EFFECTIVE   1/25/43   HOUR EFFECTIVE

OCCUPATION   Writer

OLD RATE $300.—

NEW RATE $350.—

FROM DEPARTMENT

TO DEPARTMENT

REMARKS   26 weeks - 6 idle.

FORM 67   APPROVED   R. J. OBRINGER

3. Change Payroll Notice for Faulkner

I

Battle Cry

Expanded Story Treatment

FADE IN

Railroad station sign as it is today:

SPRINGFIELD, ILL.

FULL SHOT of station platform. The time is early in 1942. A group of soldiers, with their equipment, in charge of a sergeant, is waiting for a train. There is a sign: SPRINGFIELD U.S.O. Women and girls are passing doughnuts, cigarettes, etc. A WAR BOND poster on the wall. At one side is a small group of newly drafted men about to leave. They are in civilian clothes, are boys of all types, with a flavor of the country on them. Their families have come to see them off.

One of the draftees is Fonda. (Beginning with the first battle scene, this character is referred to as "Flynn." But he is the Fonda type,[1] and his name will be changed to Fonda for reference). Fonda has come from a farm; he has a little of the look of Lincoln as a young man. His grandfather is with him. They are a little awkward; we realize that the boy dreads the ordeal of saying goodbye to his kin; he is glad his mother and father at least stayed at home and so didn't force the thing on him in public.

But the grandfather is excited and proud and even triumphant. This irks the boy a little; the old man seems childish to him and he is a little ashamed of this public display. He would

---

1. Henry Fonda (1905–1984), American stage and screen actor, began his film career in 1935 with the title role in *The Farmer Takes a Wife* and starred in twenty-seven movies over the next seven years. His portrayal of Abraham Lincoln in *Young Mr. Lincoln* (1939) may have contributed to his being considered for the part of Flynn/Lincoln in "Battle Cry." Actually, Fonda would have been unavailable had the movie been produced, since he had joined the Navy in 1942 and was serving as a lieutenant in the Pacific at the time Faulkner was drafting this script.

3

FADE IN

A theme from the Freedom Train cantata: music, the sound of the train on SOUND TRACK, a montage showing that Lincoln is dead, the funeral train starting with his coffin. But we begin to reveal here the legend that he is not dead actually. Perhaps his ghostly figure is among the mourners or hovers about the scene, or perhaps the recitative voice begins to reveal the legend. There will be just enough of this to plant the train and the legend that Lincoln is not really dead, the VOICE continues, the sound of the train, into DISSOLVE.

> VOICE (finishes in DISSOLVE)
> They were the people. He was their man. Sometimes you couldn't even tell where the people stopped and Abraham Lincoln began.

Sound of the train carries over   DISSOLVE to

Gunfire. A party of American soldiers, including an English corporal with two prisoners: an Italian officer and a German officer, are hurrying to get clear of the shelling. They are under command of a lieutenant, who has been wounded. They are carrying him, panting, running, grimly intent, the English corporal driving his prisoners ahead of him with his bayonet. The Italian is co-operative. The German is cold, obeying but shows contempt not only of his captors but of his ally-companion.

> ENGLISH CORPORAL (to German)
> Garn! Garn! Maybe these are your shells, but you're just meat to them, same as we are.

4. Out-take from Faulkner's original story treatment

like to send the old man back home, if he knew how to do it. But he realizes that the old man is not going, would not miss any of this.

FONDA   I bet you wouldn't feel so chipper if it was you that had to go.

OLD MAN   *(bristles) Had* to go? *Had* to go?

FONDA   Aw, I ain't against going. We got to, I reckon, and it ain't any use in fighting against it. But ain't nobody never told me yet just what I am fighting for.

OLD MAN   *(heated)* Fighting for?

FONDA   Hush, Grampaw! Everybody's watching you!

OLD MAN   Let 'em! If there's any more here so poor in spirit they don't know either. You're going to fight for the folks that ain't free, that have been enslaved. And this ain't the first time boys from this town left this very station to go and fight against slavery. Hell fire, there was a man from this very town—

FONDA   Hush, Grampaw! Hush, Grampaw!

OLD MAN   —that said, there ain't room in all North America for a nation to exist half slave and half free. And now we got the same fight on our hands that old Abe had, only worse, because we know now there ain't room even on this whole earth for people to exist half slave and half free—

FONDA   Hush, Grampaw! Hush!

OLD MAN   Aye, wrote it across the page of America, across the whole ledger of human bondage, in his own blood, so that no folks anywhere can ever forget it—

The old man's face is fanatical. Now Fonda's face becomes rapt, as if he has been moved despite himself by the old man's fire, since what the old man had seen and felt 75 years ago is in his, the young man's, blood somewhere too. In b.g. a theme from the "Cantata,"[2] covering the moving of the funeral train bear-

2. "Abraham Lincoln Comes Home," with music by Earl Robinson and libretto by Millard Lampell. Faulkner worked from a handwritten manu-

ing Lincoln's body with the beat of the train sound, begins and continues as he speaks:

> **OLD MAN** I was right here that day, on this same platform—a strange day, a quiet day—the war over at last, and all the four years of hatred and bloodshed, and we had thought . . . Right here on this platform, along with all the other folks that had come in from the farms and the hamlets and the villages and the towns, to stand waiting here in the road outside the telegraph office ever since that shot had sounded, and old Jake Wetzel that run the telegraph come out and he never had to say it though even then we couldn't seem to believe it: "Folks—folks. Abe Lincoln is dead—!"

The music is drowned by the train sound as the train comes in off scene and stops. Now the moment of parting has come. The draftees are going off to meet what they know only vaguely, to come back when, they do not know, if at all. The draftees and their families huddle for a moment like sheep, at a loss. The sergeant saves the situation. He enters. His manner is sarcastic, brusque.

> **SERGEANT** Well, *gentlemen.* This way, if you please.
>
> **A DRAFTEE** Us?
>
> **SERGEANT** Certainly. I understand you are going to be with us from now on.

Goodbyes are said. The draftees move toward the train with their luggage: the awkward, shabby luggage of country boys, etc.

> **FONDA** But that was in 1865. The world was smaller, folks seemed to know then. At least, they never had to go to the ends of the world to fight slavery.
>
> **OLD MAN** That's jest where we want slavery: right at the ends of the earth! Then we can shove it the rest of the way off! Go on, now. When the shoving comes, let the rest of them be late to it, but not my blood and kin! Go on!

script of this work, which was later published as *A Cantata: The Lonesome Train* (New York: Sun Music Company, 1945).

Fonda turns. CLOSE TRUCKING SHOT of him as he approaches. His civilian clothes become khaki, he carries his rifle, gunfire in b.g.; he is running in a group of other soldiers in the African desert—he and another soldier are carrying a wounded officer. In the group is an English corporal with two prisoners: an Italian officer and a German officer. They hurry, panting, stumbling, the English corporal driving his prisoners ahead with his bayonet. The Italian is cooperative, but in his every movement the German shows a sneering contempt, a disregard of the shells and a haughty contempt directed not so much at his captors but at his Italian ally.

> **ENGLISH CORPORAL** *(to the German)* Go on! Maybe these are your shells, but you're just meat to them, the same as we are.

At last they are clear of the shelling, which continues fainter in b.g. The party stops. The leader is now an old Regular Army sergeant. But the officer is still alive; the sergeant has merely taken over to get them clear of the battle. We learn later that the party is on a special mission, and no one but the officer knows what it is yet.

They put the officer down. The sergeant gives him a temporary field dressing, then orders a stretcher made from two rifles and shirts, tunics, etc. They prepare to go on again, two men giving their equipment to the others so they can carry the stretcher. The English corporal suggests that the prisoners carry the stretcher, since the rest of them are already loaded down with equipment. The sergeant thanks the Englishman, and agrees. The Englishman orders the prisoners to take up the stretcher. The Italian obeys. The German refuses. In excellent English he repeats the international article by which no captive officer shall be forced to do any manual labor. The Americans, harried, worried, react to this angrily.

> **ONE** Maybe you can quote another one that says you can't shoot Germans.

> **SECOND** There is one that says you can't shoot prisoners.

> **FIRST** I don't know it. I can't read.

The German faces them, sneering. The sergeant interferes. He says the German is right, orders two men to take up the stretcher. But the Italian officer will not turn loose.

> **SERGEANT** *(to the Italian; he is worried over his responsibility and their situation)* Come on! Turn loose! Geneva says you can't!

> **ITALIAN** Geneva also said we would never be here fighting one another. But we are. *(he looks around, picks out a husky soldier)* Will you, signore?

The soldier takes up the other end of the stretcher. The sergeant gives up, turns. The others follow. The German has watched this with his cold sneering contempt which is directed mostly at his ally, the Italian. The English corporal prods him with the bayonet.

> **CORPORAL** Get on. This bayonet can't read either.

CLOSE SHOT of the sergeant and two corporals at the head of the party. The sergeant holds his compass in his hand, and a map. We see some indication of the gravity of their situation, and how the sergeant feels the responsibility. They cannot return now if they wanted to. But we realize that the sergeant does not intend to, if he could. He knows the party is on a mission, though he does not yet know what. He wants to find cover where the officer can rest and come to and take over again. He decides on his direction, gives the order. The men obey. The party moves on.

The DISSOLVE begins. The sound of their feet becomes the sound of the Freedom Train; the theme from the "Cantata" repeats, the recitative voice above the music and the train sound.

> **VOICE** They were the people. He was their man. Sometimes you couldn't even tell where the people left off and Abraham Lincoln began.

As the DISSOLVE completes, the music and voice and train sound become a banjo, playing rapidly a rollicking gay tune, American and Negroid.

DISSOLVE TO:

Inside a house. The fighting has passed here, and the occupants had to leave the house quickly. It is not wrecked, but household goods which the owners did not have time to move are scattered about. In the house is an American soldier, a young white man, a Southerner, and a wounded Negro soldier. The Southerner has apparently saved the Negro, found him wounded and carried him into the house to safety. The Negro has been shot near the spine and cannot move, though so far he is not suffering much. The white boy is entertaining them both by playing on a dulcimer which he found in the house, playing the rollicking merry tune. But he is on watch, too. Watching through a window as he plays.

The sergeant and his party are crouching under the brow of a hill. Beyond the hill the house can be seen. The thin rollicking music comes from the house. The crouching men hear it; the sergeant and the two corporals look at one another in amazement at hearing that sound here, on a battleground in the waste of the African desert.

CORPORAL FLYNN   That's a banjo.

SERGEANT   A banjo? Here, in Africa?

FLYNN   It's a banjo tune, anyway.

CORPORAL RILEY   It's more than that. It's an Alabama tune. I know it.

The music breaks off short. They watch the house.

SERGEANT   Stay close, now.

FLYNN   Here! Let me—

The sergeant raises his head cautiously. As soon as he does so, a shot comes from the house; the bullet smacks nearby, the sergeant ducks.

SOUTHERNER   *(from the house)* It's all right. You can come on out. I ain't going to shoot no more. I done seen you. Ain't no Heinie or Wop neither got a face as ugly as that un.

The sergeant orders them on. They rise to go on. One of the

men with the stretcher calls the sergeant anxiously. He pauses, he and the two corporals return to the stretcher, the others gather quietly in b.g. The wounded officer is in a convulsion which is to be the beginning of his death. The men realize it. The English corporal advances, extends a flask.

ENGLISHMAN Here.

The sergeant takes the flask, raises the officer's head, gives him a little of the brandy. The officer rouses.

SERGEANT Hold on, sir. We're almost there. We can make you easy then. Hold on, sir. Hold on.

OFFICER O.K. I'll hold on.

SERGEANT *(rises; to bearers)* Easy now with him!

They go on.

They reach the house and enter it, where the wounded Negro lies paralyzed on the rough bed which the Southerner has made for him. The Negro is not suffering. He never admits he is. All through the picture, whenever anyone asks him about himself, he disclaims any hurt. He says each time, "I don't feel nothing. I'm all right. I feel fine."

The Southerner, Akers, is a devil-may-care young chap, whom nothing probably ever worries except being cold. He meets the sergeant's party with a good deal of aplomb. If he was worried about himself and the Negro, about how they were going to get out of the scrape alone, he doesn't show it. He looks at the wounded officer.

AKERS Well, well. So we got two of them now.

The sergeant pays no attention to him. He gets the officer settled comfortably. Then he looks at the wounded Negro, Akers beside him.

SERGEANT Can he walk?

AKERS If he can, he sho better not let me find it out. I done toted him five miles since I found him this mawnin.

SERGEANT *(examines Akers)* Where you from? Kentucky?

AKERS   Naw. That's up nawth. I'm from Alabama. *(he turns to the Negro)* But you're O.K. now, ain't you?

NEGRO   *(in his peaceful voice)* Sure. I'm all right. I feel fine.

AKERS   *(suddenly: to the Negro)* Where're you from? You was out of your head so much, you never told me.

NEGRO   *(motionless, peaceful, paralyzed)* America.

AKERS   Sure. What part? What's your name, anyway?

NEGRO   *(unchanging, peaceful)* America. *(others in b.g. listening)*

AKERS   America? That ain't . . . *(a take as he comprehends all the implications of what the wounded and perhaps dying Negro has said. He is ashamed, would try to apologize, doesn't know how, must cover up in the only way he can: by sardonic humor)* Yeah. So'm I. Too damn far from it.

Corporal Flynn and the English corporal, Loughton, are squatting beside the officer, others in b.g. They realize that he is dying. Loughton is putting a dressing on his wound. Loughton shows some skill at it. The others seem to have resigned the business to him. They watch, interested, respect his skill.

Flynn says something about what a good thing the sulphur drugs have been in this war. As he and Loughton work, we learn that they have known one another before they met in battle, in a quieter time perhaps, apparently in England.

LOUGHTON   *(busy)* Yes. They stood us well in France.

A SOLDIER   *(respectful; all the others listen)* Were you at Dunkirk?

Loughton does not answer. He seems not to have heard even. Flynn covers up for him by sending the questioner on an errand, stopping the interrogation. We realize that Loughton does not want to talk about Dunkirk, or perhaps France, and that Flynn knows it. Perhaps something happened to Loughton in France or at Dunkirk, which Flynn knows, which Loughton does not want to remember. He cannot forget it, cannot help but remember it, but he does not want to be reminded of it from the outside like this. The officer is trying to move, fumbling with one hand at his breast; his face shows agony. They think it is from pain.

> **LOUGHTON**   Better call your sergeant and give him some more morphine.

Flynn rises, turns to call the sergeant, pauses, shouts, springs up. The others react. The Italian officer is gone. The German remains as before where they had left him, haughty and contemptuous. The sergeant rushes up to him.

> **GERMAN**   (*sneering*) Certainly he's gone. Did you ever know a member of his race who didn't run from the sight of armed men?

The sergeant orders two men to watch the German. He and the others run out. Outside the house, the sergeant and his party see the Italian some distance away, running into the empty desert. The sergeant snatches a rifle from the nearest man, kneels, loops the sling, prepares to fire. As he does so, we can see the expert marksman's badge dancing on his chest as he works the bolt and aims. Flynn jerks up the rifle. The sergeant turns on him, angry, furious at this slip which he has made in command by letting the prisoner have a chance to escape. They struggle over the rifle. The sergeant shouts to the others to fire, but the Italian is safe. The sergeant wants to know what the hell. It's hard for Flynn to explain; the fact that the Italian carried the wounded officer is not enough for the old sergeant. At last Flynn says, "Let him go. He has no water; the desert will finish him." The sergeant is still angry, not so much at their carelessness in not watching the prisoners, but because of the same anxiety over the responsibility which he sees devolving upon him if the officer dies. He could send out a pursuit party after the Italian, but to do this will further deplete the party, which has already been reduced from the original 39 to 17. And, since the officer is still alive, the officer is still in command. He orders Flynn to leave a man as lookout to watch the desert. The others return to the house.

Inside the house, the sergeant, Flynn, Battson and Loughton hold a conference. They have no more morphine for the officer. The sergeant has already given the officer all he had, and the officer's first-aid kit was destroyed by the same shell fragment which hit him.

LOUGHTON   Put water in the hypodermic. I saw it work in France and at Dunkirk.

SERGEANT   Water?

BATTSON   Yes. Go on, Sergeant. It's better than nothing.

The sergeant fills the needle with water. They bend over the officer, the others watching in b.g. Now they actually realize how far gone he is. He is still trying to move his hand to his breast, to speak. They think it is pain. The sergeant prepares to use the needle. But when the officer sees it, he makes a supreme effort. They realize that he is trying to tell them something. They comprehend that he is trying to refuse the needle. It is as if he were not only refusing sleep but were holding death itself off by sheer will so he can say something.

FLYNN   The flask.

But Loughton has already produced it. They give the officer a sip; he revives, puts his hand to his pocket.

OFFICER   Pocket . . . pocket.

The sergeant takes from the officer's pocket the operational order under which the party set out. The officer's face is less strained now; he puts his hand out toward the flask; Loughton gives him another sip. He speaks, gasping, but strongly for the moment.

OFFICER   Yes. That's it. We are a liaison party. We should have met a machine-gun battalion of the __th here. They're not here?

SERGEANT   No, sir. Nobody here but us.

OFFICER   How many men are left?

SERGEANT   Seventeen, sir.

OFFICER   Seventeen. Out of 39. *(he rouses further)* You must get out of here. You must leave as soon as it's dark.

SERGEANT Leave, sir?

OFFICER Yes! Their attack will probably come here tomorrow. We were to hold this well until our support came
up—us, and the __ battalion. And they're not here?

SERGEANT No, sir.

OFFICER Then you must get out. As soon as dark comes—
(he suffers, writhes; the sergeant advances the needle) No! No!
Not now. Give it to me just before you leave. Then you
must get the men out of here—out of here—

He sinks into coma again as they watch him. Then they start, all
hear it as the faint sound of aeroplanes begins.

The Italian officer is crouching beside a knoll as the aeroplanes
pass. They are fighter-bombers, German, low and fast, in close
formation, obviously on reconnaissance. The Italian watches as
they pass and go on toward the house. His face shows his reaction as he watches them, waits to hear the machine guns and
bombs.

Outside the house as the aeroplanes approach, Flynn and the
sergeant are trying to hide all traces of their presence, but the
sentry they had put out fails to get hidden as the aeroplanes
pass overhead; they are sure they have been discovered. They
crouch, the aeroplanes pass over, bank, and return and go back
where they came from without dropping a bomb or firing a
shot.

The Italian is crouching behind his knoll. He reacts as he fails
still to hear any bomb or shot. He knows what that means. The
aeroplanes pass back over him. The pilot of one makes a jeering gesture down at him as they pass. Then they are gone. The
Italian rises, brushes the sand from his clothes, makes a gesture
himself, Latin and fatalistic, turns and walks back toward the
house.

Inside the house. The sergeant and the others kneel again
about the officer. He has roused now, is struggling while they
hold him.

OFFICER *(frantic)* They neither bombed nor strafed. Don't
you see what that means? They want this well, too. They

will be here maybe before night. You must get out—get out—get—

He falls back. The sergeant stares at him until Battson speaks.

BATTSON   Come on, Reagan. Get your damned water.

SERGEANT   Water?

BATTSON   The hypodermic, damn it!

The sergeant rises, goes to where he had put the needle on a ledge. As he takes it down, Akers calls him.

AKERS   Here. America claims he's got one.

The sergeant bends over the Negro. He lies as before, motionless while the sweat of his own pain beads his face. But his voice has not changed.

AMERICA   In my pocket. Pick me up easy.

AKERS   *(shows his own sympathy and suffering with the man he has saved by his harshness)* I thought you been bragging every time you opened that big mouth that you didn't hurt.

AMERICA   I don't. Pick me up easy.

They turn him gently as possible, while the sweat springs anew on his face. The sergeant takes a first-aid kit from his pocket. They let him down again. He lies gasping, panting, sweating, but still his eyes and voice have not changed. Akers opens the box and finds a hypodermic and morphine and prepares it. He hesitates, looking at America.

SERGEANT   It's yours. You ain't in this command. By rights, you ought to have it. But he's the only officer—

AMERICA   No. I don't need it. I feel fine.

SERGEANT   Maybe I can save a little of it for you.

AMERICA   I don't need it. I feel fine.

The sergeant approaches the officer. As he does so, he stops dead. Battson is just laying a tunic over the dead officer's face. The others rise too while the sergeant stares stupidly at them, the hypo in his hand.

BATTSON   *(harshly)* Go on. Give it back to the smoke. He can use it.

Reagan turns back to America. Akers squats beside him, anxious, still trying to hide the sympathy and pity which he considers weakness. Reagan prepares to give America the hypodermic. America can move only his eyes as he protests.

AMERICA   No! No, Sergeant! No!

REAGAN   Roll up his sleeve, Alabama.

AMERICA   No, Sergeant. Save it. Somebody might get hurt.

AKERS   *(turns furiously on the sergeant)* Can't you hear him tell you to put that durn thing up? He don't need it. He ain't going nowhere. *(turns to America)* Are you, nigger?

AMERICA   No. I'm all right. I feel fine.

Reagan turns slowly, baffled, finds the men watching him quietly. Reagan's manner changes. He is in command now; he takes command.

REAGAN   Flynn and Battson!

FLYNN   Yes, Sergeant?

REAGAN   Flynn's squad will take the first watch. Battson's squad will take over from then on.

A SOLDIER   From then on until when?

Reagan pays no attention to him.

REAGAN   Keep four men on post, one at each compass point, 300 yards out. Get going, Flynn.

Flynn turns, begins to call off the names of his squad as they rise, answer, take up their arms.

DISSOLVE TO:

Night. Reagan is making his inspection round, checking the sentries. He approaches one.

SENTRY   Who goes there?

REAGAN   America.

SENTRY   Pass, America.

Reagan walks on, tramps on. As DISSOLVE begins, we hear his feet; his feet become the sound of the Freedom Train, the cantata theme on the SOUND TRACK, recitative voice, etc.

DISSOLVE TO:

SOUND TRACK
(Music from "Cantata")

1st VOICE *(sings)*
They sent the news from Washington,
That Abraham Lincoln's time has come;
John Wilkes Booth shot Lincoln dead,
With a pistol bullet through the head!

2nd SINGER
The slaves are free, the war is won,
But the fight for freedom's just begun;
There are still slaves,
The hungry and poor,
Men who are not free to speak.

3rd SINGER
Freedom's a thing that has no ending,
It needs to be cared for, it needs
     defending;
A great long job for many hands,
Carrying freedom across the land!

(music stops)

1st SPEAKER
A job for all the people.

2nd SPEAKER
A job for Lincoln's people.

OLD MAN
Sam's right. A job for all people
everywhere, to send the word of
freedom across the United States and
across all America and across the oceans:
His people are there too. They are
wherever people want to be free and will
be free: Europe, Russia, China—

(music continues)

1st SINGER
A Kansas farmer, a Brooklyn sailor,
An Irish policeman, a Jewish tailor;

SCREEN

Sign over R.R. station:
SPRINGFIELD, ILL. Time is 1865.

WIPE TO:

FULL SHOT of station, draped in mourning; sorrowing crowd of 1865 waiting for the train bearing Lincoln's body.

CLOSE GROUP of a few people in crowd, looking out of scene and up the track where the train will appear.

FULL SHOT as before of crowd waiting at station.

2nd SOLO
An old storekeeper shaking his head
Handing over a loaf of bread;

1st SOLO
A buffalo hunter telling a story
Out in the Oregon territory.

2nd SOLO
They were his people, he was their man;
You couldn't quite tell where the people
    left off
And where Abe Lincoln began.

WOMAN
There was a silence in Washington town
When they carried Mr. Lincoln down.

CHORUS (*train sound in b.g.*)   SHOT of train moving, type of 1865.
A lonesome train on a lonesome track,
Seven coaches painted black.

SPOKEN
Mr. Lincoln's funeral train,   Superimposed on the moving train: the
Traveling the long road from   station signboards:
    Washington to Baltimore,   WASHINGTON
Baltimore to Philadelphia,   BALTIMORE
                                       PHILADELPHIA
CHORUS   NEW YORK
New York, Albany, Syracuse   ALBANY
Cleveland, Chicago,   SYRACUSE
to Springfield, Illinois.   CLEVELAND
                                         CHICAGO
CHORUS   SPRINGFIELD
A slow train, a quiet train,
Carrying Lincoln home again.

                                            DISSOLVE TO:
4th SOLO
It wasn't quite mist, it was almost rain,   Another GROUP on station platform, a
Falling down on the funeral train;   young soldier of 1865, another old man,
There was a strange and quiet crowd,   all looking up the track.
Nobody wanting to talk out loud.
Along the streets, across the square,
Lincoln's people were waiting there.
(*music stops*)

THE SOLDIER
You'd think they would have warned
him; even a rattlesnake warns you.

OLD MAN
This one must have been a copperhead.

CHORUS (*music again*)
They carried Mr. Lincoln down,   The scene begins to FADE.
The train started, the wheels went
    round,

You could hear the whistle for miles
    around,
Crying, Free—dom!
Crying, Free—dom!
(music stops)

OLD MAN'S VOICE
Across America and across the oceans, to
all the people everywhere that want to be
free and will be free: Europe, China,
Russia—

(music begins)

SOLO
These are the people, woman and man.
Sometimes you couldn't even tell where
    the people left off
and the will to freedom began.

The scene FADES completely while the old
man speaks, the screen is dark.

Slow FADE IN starts.

Diary of a Red Army Woman[3]

Music subtly segues to "International"[4] to hold under. DISSOLVE slowly to top of page of diary with date printed. His pencil becomes Tania's pencil as she rests it on the name of the town and repeats slowly.

    TANIA *(softly, like an echo)*—February twelfth, nineteen hundred and forty-two *(Tania's pencil begins to move)* I, Tania Doronin, on this twelfth day of February, 1942, begin a diary—a letter to the future of my son . . . I have just learned about you, my son. *(gentle voice; flash to her face, closeup, not writing now)* I am to have a child. Wonderful! *(soft happy little laugh, starts writing again; lifts head now and then)* I thought Semyon was enough to fight for—I thought Russia was enough . . . but now I know that to go up in a plane to fight the enemy for the sake of a child is as much

    3. This section of the expanded story treatment was written by Violet Atkins and William Bacher and represents an expansion of their Treasury Star Parade radio script (from a story idea by Isobel Donald). Faulkner's revision of this material was incorporated into the screenplay.

    4. After the Bolshevik Revolution the "International" replaced the traditional "God Save the Tsar" as the national anthem of the Soviet Union. In 1944 the "Hymn of the Soviet Union" became the national anthem, but the "International" was retained as the official song of the Communist Party.

happiness as a woman can bear. *(face lifts, exalted, then concentrates on writing again, a little half-smile on her lips)* But I must not let your father know—not yet. He might forbid me to fly. And I cannot stop—not even for you, my son! We are at war—and your father and I fly bomber planes over enemy lines!

Through next speech her head lifts. She stops writing. Hand rests, relaxes.

TANIA   *(softly, reminiscently)* But there was a time when there was no war—time for games—for fun-making—for falling in love, in Russia.

FADE OUT INTO SCENE.

Wide field with usual fair background . . . carrousels, stalls, peasants in heavy boots, colorful costumes, girls in traditionally quaint headdresses of various villages, white embroidered aprons over full wide skirts, full-sleeved embroidered blouses and white kirtles, heavy black boots . . . hawkers, vendors, barkers calling . . . main throngs at improvised airdrome, parachute-jumpers exhibition. Parachute jumping is the new sport in Russia. Shop people, clerks, city folk and peasants all take it up for sport. Planes flying overhead, curious peasants gaping . . . children losing parents, weeping, finding them again, being scolded . . . good-natured patrols keeping crowds from getting too close to plane, field . . . sparkling, sunny day . . .

CAMERA picks up Tania, a well built though slender girl, in peasant costume, hair tied with ribbons, standing in attitude of restrained impatience before Fedya, a stock peasant, full trousers tucked into boots, tunic with high collar, upstanding shock of hair, stolid, high-cheekboned face, not cloddish but unimaginative . . . uneasily rubs his hands up and down against his thighs, as Tania speaks:

TANIA   *(impatiently)* Fedya—Will you stop *following* me? *(quick but dogged negative headshake from Fedya)* Go away—go anywhere—go home, if you like—I'll go back home with Nina and her cousins! *(waits hopefully)*

FEDYA   *(stolidly)* I brought you. I will not go home without you. Your father would take off my ears.

TANIA *(exasperated)* I wish—*(stops, shrugs)* Very well—you brought me. You must take me home. Or my father will take off your ears. *(stares vengefully at Fedya's large, prominent red ears)* I should like to ring them! *(Fedya rubs the right ear uncomfortably as if she had. Tania relents at his discomfiture . . . smiles a little; trying another tack, begins to coax . . . bends forward a little, hands clasped behind her head to one side)* Fedya— they have very good vodka over there at the stand—you like good vodka—

FEDYA *(shakes his head stubbornly, steps backward as if finding it difficult to resist Tania; speaks with dogged repetitiveness)* I promised your father—

TANIA *(hands pressed to her ears)* Promised! Promised! *(whirls with her back to him, smiles in swift change of mood as she sights a small, pretty girl running across the grounds toward her)* Nina!

Nina comes up breathless. Both girls embrace as if they had not seen each other for years, yet both are from the same village. Nina is small, vivacious and merry, not intense like Tania.

NINA *(breathless and excited)* Such fun, Tania! The wooden horses—fell off, trying for the ring—*(giggles)*—you should have seen me! *(gale of laughter; Tania joins a little ruefully, half enviously)* Why didn't you come with us?

Tania makes a motion toward Fedya. Nina flashes a glance at Fedya, purses her lips. Fedya looks guardedly from one to the other as if with Nina's presence he anticipates difficulties.

NINA Look, Tania—what happened to my underskirt when I fell—

Turns her back on Fedya—lifts voluminous skirt a little. Tania makes a sound of sympathy. Both faces of girls are full of mischief, downbent so Fedya cannot see them.

TANIA You'll catch it if your aunt sees it, Nina—I'll sew it for you—*(turns to Fedya)* Wait here, Fedya—I'll go with Nina to the women's room—

Goes off with Nina before Fedya can speak. Fedya blinks after them uneasily. He suspects he is being tricked, but can do nothing about it, frowns. Dubiously shoves his shock of hair even further up on end as he watches them run toward the women's room. While he waits, stolid and patient, his eyes are drawn against his will to the stand where men are drinking vodka and swapping stories, but he drags his gaze from the stand and tries to concentrate on the door of the women's room, where women and children go constantly in and out. Meanwhile Tania and Nina have slipped out the back way, running toward the parachute jump.

TANIA   (breathlessly) That was—clever—Nina—

NINA   (gurgling) Poor Fedya—(stops for breath, still laughing) He will wait—

Pulls Tania to a stop near a group of boys fastening their parachutes under instructions from a broad-shouldered blond Russian in a flyer's uniform. Tania is entranced by the dipping, circling planes and the parachutes being strapped on the men and boys before them. There is something hungry and a little envious in her gaze.

TANIA   (half to herself)—The lucky ones—

The blond flyer hears her, turns and looks at her with an amused, superior look. A flicker of anger runs over Tania's face; she openly resents his look. He stops smiling, his attention caught by her beauty and spirited attitude. Their gaze seems riveted. Immediately there is the strong, powerful sex-antagonism which is sometimes felt by two people who are basically attracted to each other. Both have a kind of arrogant handsomeness. (He does not know that Tania's resentment is composed partly of her frustrated desire to fly.) In an obscure male desire to goad her, he turns to Nina.

SEMYON   Zdravstuite, little one!

NINA   (prim but confused . . . colors) I am eighteen!

SEMYON   (laughs heartily, throwing his head back; Nina joins reluctantly after a moment; Tania ignores them) So you are a woman!—and women believe in luck! (condescendingly) Do you believe in luck, Black-eyes? (Nina nods quickly) What is your name?

In all this the audience has the feeling he is addressing himself to Tania through Nina. She continues to ignore him.

NINA *(becoming saucy and self-confident)* Nina—Nina Federovskaya.

SEMYON *(loftily)* Very well, Nina Federovskaya—touch my parachute—for luck. If I win the twenty-five rubles for landing in the right spot, I will buy you a present!

He shoots a sly glance at Tania, whose eyes flicker for an instant to the parachute; her fingers tighten as if restraining herself from touching it. She looks swiftly away, but Semyon has seen. He laughs again. Nina, glancing sideways at Tania as if a little ashamed of seeming credulous, leans over and pokes a finger at the 'chute on Semyon's back, giggles self-consciously.

SEMYON *(hitches the straps on his shoulders)* Now—I'll land safe!

A whistle blows from the airfield. The men and boys with parachutes run to waiting planes. Crowd surges after, Tania and Nina with them.

TANIA I hope he lands in the dung-heap!

Nina makes a moue of distaste. Both girls strain to watch the rising planes. At the required height, the parachutists jump . . . crowd gasps and murmur as bodies hurtle toward the ground. Sighs of relief and cheers as 'chutes open and belly upward, and parachutists begin to drift toward the ground. Tania stands in attitude of strained attention until 'chutists are all on the ground. People push past the good-natured patrols, run toward 'chutists, laughing and pushing. Girls are drawn along.

NINA *(excited)* I must see—I must see where the blond one landed, Tania!

TANIA *(pretending lack of interest)* That one?

NINA What do you suppose he will give me, Tania?

TANIA *(scornfully)* Another story, perhaps!

A shout of warning goes up from the crowd. People surge toward the parachutists. One, blown by a gust of wind, erratic and strong, has been jerked toward a barbed wire fence at the edge of the fairgrounds. The crowd surges toward the spot, Tania and Nina in their midst, straining to see. It is the blond flyer. He is angrily trying to extricate himself, humiliated at his predicament, refusing good-natured proffers of help to disentangle him. Laughter from the crowd and good-natured gibing make him angrier.

TANIA　　*(slyly to Nina)* There goes your present, Nina! Look at him.

NINA　　*(crestfallen)* Let's go back to Fedya, Tania—

Nina starts away but Tania stays, pushing to the forefront of the crowd as it moves away. There is a little half-smile almost of triumph on her lips. It dies as a shout of laughter goes up from the crowd when Semyon's struggle with the 'chute and the barbed wire suspends him a little from the ground. Tania's face shows annoyance at them. They disperse, slowly, but she stays watching. He glowers at her. There is a peasant-like, naive, slumbering quality in her as she stands there, her hands clasped behind her back, making no move to help him since he refused all offers of help from the crowd. He throws her angry glances, that do not seem to dismay her. She bends her head this way and that, with an almost childish doll-like motion, following his movements as he seems to hopelessly entangle himself further in the cords and wire. Slowly, a gay, playful, girlish quality emerges as a smile begins to tug at the corners of her mouth. He gets more and more furious . . . His trouser leg catches on the wire. Tania tries to stop smiling but it proves too much for her. At his redoubled efforts, futile and angry, she finally loses control of herself . . . leans against a broad tree trunk, and shrieks of girlish laughter burst from her lips. He looks up at her, grimly, then with a tremendous jerk he pulls free. His trouser leg rips from thigh to ankle and a long gash appears on his leg, but it does not halt him. Rigid with fury, he strides toward Tania, like an angry bull . . . She is leaning against the tree trunk, laughing helplessly, her face half-turned against it, weak tears of laughter at the corners of her eyes. He jerks her upright, stretches her arms wide. Before she can move he kisses her, a furious, savage, insulting kiss . . . lifts his head and looks down at her, still holding her arms pinioned. A look of terror fills her eyes as he bends to kiss her again. She struggles but he kisses her . . . this time a longer kiss.

When he finally raises his head, Tania stares up at him mutely, the fear in her eyes turned to misery. The tears of laughter have become real tears. Semyon drops her arms . . . her head bows as she stands mutely before him, almost as if she had been beaten. There is a complete letdown of violence in Semyon, dismay at what he has done.

SEMYON (*blunderingly*) I—I didn't mean—

Tania's lips quiver. She keeps her head down. Semyon pulls out his handkerchief, thrusts it into her left hand. She raises hand with handkerchief a little, but does not use it. With clenched fist of right hand, she rubs her cheeks and eyes, with quick hard motions as if trying to wipe out the whole picture of what has happened—her mortification and shame at the wild emotions that surged within her from the moment Semyon touched her. A tremendous potential passion has been stirred in both by the violence of this scene, but as yet neither is fully aware of what is happening. When they speak, to cover their emotions, their words are completely irrelevant to their real feelings. The words they use are incompetent to express their inner violence and turbulence. We must show the contrast between their words and their feelings. This can be accomplished by having the words sound absolutely wooden.

SEMYON (*standing before her with arms hanging heavily; in reluctant apology*) I am sorry—you were laughing at me—

TANIA (*oblique glance down at his bleeding leg . . . tears still flowing . . . sobs in her throat . . . points a tentative finger*) You—are hurt—

SEMYON (*not looking at her*) It is nothing—

Tania looks up at him. His eyes lift shyly to her face.

SEMYON (*softly*) You are beautiful. (*Tania shakes her head slightly in negation, swallows hard*) But you *are* . . . (*pause*) What is your name?

TANIA Tania Nev—

Semyon's half-shy smile slowly turns to wide grin of friend-
liness as he stops her with a quick gesture.

SEMYON The second name does not matter . . . Mine is
Doronin—Semyon Doronin.

TANIA *(repeats it softly)* Semyon—Semyon Doronin—

She looks straight at him now, and the small pout of distur-
bance now turns to the beautiful smile of a woman for whom
the future holds great promise.

DISSOLVE TO:

TANIA *(writing in her diary . . . deep satisfied sigh as she
reads)*—Semyon Doronin . . . he was to be your father, my
son! *(little delightful laugh that stops as she goes on writing)* My
parents did not want me to marry Semyon—at first. He
was an aviation instructor. They wanted me to marry
Fedya—with a good farm and four horses and the new
litter of pigs and the cow soon to calve—and his grain crop
as good as my father's . . . But Semyon opened a whole new
world for me—a world of blue skies and freedom!—a
world of love—

Wedding of Tania and Semyon

DISSOLVE TO:

The one village street in Tania's village. Signs of great excitement. CAMERA PANS from house to house showing various
stages of preparations for some great event. On one hearth a
pig is roasting. Before another, great loaves of bread lie brown
and crisp. In a doorway a woman sits peeling a pile of potatoes.
Children run about, shrill-voiced and excited. A woman leans
from a window and calls a boy to gather more wood. Another
woman shoos a dog away from some hams cooling on a tray on
a broad window sill. CAMERA moves past all of this very slowly,
on to the last house on the street, somewhat distant from the
others, half hidden behind enormous gnarled trees . . . moves
through the doorway into the big kitchen. Tania's father is on a

ladder hanging festoons. Her mother is bending over a side table under the window, counting the smoked hams. CAMERA slows up as it passes, to take in the following action.

> MOTHER *(counting beneath her breath)*—fourteen-fifteen-sixteen—*(looks up at the father)*—Would you think that is enough, Anton?

> FATHER *(continuing to hammer a festoon of leaves against the top of the window, speaks absent-mindedly)* Enough—*enough*—

> MOTHER *(hands on hips, good-naturedly, as camera continues slowly toward Tania's room)*—And what would a man know about food except to eat, eh?

Both laugh a little, not because of what is said, but because they are happy on this great day. Sound picks up giggling girls off scene. CAMERA moves into Tania's room. Sounds in perspective to show Nina and the three village girls giggling and pointing at Tania, leaning against her window . . . the same kind of four-barred window that is in the kitchen. She is dreamy-eyed and lost in thought—her lips soft and tender.

> MOTHER *(outside—coming nearer)* Tania! *(closer)* Tanischka—*(in room)* Tanischka—what is this? *(shakes her head with a scolding motion, hands on hips)*—not begun to dress yet?

> NINA *(giggling)* She has been like that all morning! *(mimicking)* What petticoats, Tania? *(assumes Tania's abstracted manner, folds her hands on her kirtle and stares into space)* What stockings, Tania? *(repeats mimicry; girls double up with gay laughter)*

> TANIA *(a little ruefully, now thoroughly aware, comes over and gives Nina an affectionate little shove)* Be quiet, Nina—I did say—

Nina presses her cheek against Tania's. Rocks Tania affectionately in her arms.

> GIRL I *(laughing)*—she *did* say the yellow petticoats—

> GIRL II —and the black stockings! *(all giggle)* For a bride!

> MOTHER *(smiling at Tania's blushing face)* Go, all of you—go on—I will dress Tania—

Shoos them out, gay and giggling ad libs as they go. Shuts the door after them. Turns and looks at Tania, again looking out of the window. But now there is a look of tremulous excitement on her face. Mother comes up behind Tania. Sees the reason . . . Semyon is on the street, at some distance away. Now and then as he strides toward their house, people stop him with good-natured handclasps and slaps on the back. The four girls run gaily down the street toward him. This is the happy scene Tania sees through a four-barred window—the same street that her parents and Georg and Fedya view later with horror when the Nazis march in. Mother puts her hands on Tania's shoulder. In the gesture there is the evidence of the unaccustomedness of open sentiment between these practical peasant folk. But Tania turns and faces her mother. They both smile a little shyly at each other.

MOTHER *(softly)* Tanischka—you are happy—

TANIA *(nods quickly as if finding it hard to put into words)* Yes—yes—*(letting go quickly)* Oh, he is coming, Mother— Semyon is coming! *(gives her mother a quick hug and runs into the kitchen)*

MOTHER *(calling after her)* Tanischka—you will be late—

TANIA *(breathlessly to her father)* Semyon is coming, Father—

FATHER *(pretending not to hear her but smiling to himself)* Are the leaves straight, Tanischka? *(looks down at her as she does not answer. She is waiting for the door to open and Semyon to appear. Softly)* Tanischka—

Tania looks up at him. Laughs a little in delightful confusion and comes toward the ladder. Stands looking up at her father. Puts both hands on his boot.

TANIA *(gently)* You like Semyon, father?

FATHER *(taps his left palm with the hammer. Screws up one eye and purses his lips as if considering. His eyes are humorous. Lifts his shoulders a little)* If he beats you, I shall take off his ears. If he does not beat you—*(shrugs)*—what good is such a man?

Tania laughs outright. Her eyes are full of affection as she puts her cheek for an instant against her father's leg. Semyon's great laugh is heard outside the door as Tania's hand goes to her heart and she starts toward the door. Her mother comes hurrying into the kitchen and draws Tania back.

> **MOTHER**   *(half scolding)* Do you not know it is forbidden for the bride to see her husband before the wedding?

Tania casts one longing glance backward as her mother takes her out of scene. The father, still on the ladder, looks after them . . . laughs a little.

> **FATHER**   Ah, soon there will be music! *(claps his hands happily, a great laugh)*

> DISSOLVE INTO:

Wedding festivity with clapping of hands and playing of the fiddles, to start with a closed shutter to spread gradually to take in full scene of wedding in the big kitchen. Fiddlers in their places in the corner. Great long table at one end of the room loaded with food. Music, dancing, laughter, men drinking vodka and telling stories. CAMERA switches from dancers to dancers, picking up Nina and the other girls with their partners, until it picks up Semyon and Tania dancing together, breathlessly. Tania in her bridal veil laughing up into Semyon's face, her eyes ecstatic. One after another the village men catch hold of her and dance with her, and the village girls dance with Semyon. (NOTE: Establish Georg among wedding guests.) Fedya is the last to catch Tania, but he does not dance. He stands still, looking at her.

> **FEDYA**   You are very happy, Tania?

Tania nods, still breathing quickly from the dancing. Puts her hand on his arm gently, for a moment, then stretches on tiptoe and kisses his cheek. Before he can move, she turns, looking for Semyon. He is toasting with the men at the vodka table. She catches sight of her mother wiping her eyes as if she had been crying. Tania runs over to her, catches her mother and holds her close.

> **TANIA**   *(a little reproachfully)* Mother—

MOTHER *(wiping her eyes with the corner of her apron; usual scolding tone but gentler)* So I am crying—

They look at each other amidst the confusion and laughter and music as if there is much they would wish to say . . . all the unspoken things mothers and daughters have between them on such a day.

TANIA *(softly)* It—it isn't so far to Leningrad, Mother—

MOTHER *(takes a long breath and holds herself erect, folds her hands tightly over her stomach as peasant women do, nodding her head)* Not—so very many versts, Tanischka—*(lips quiver)*— and a wife should be where her husband is.

Tania hugs her quickly, hears Semyon calling her from the other side of the room. She half turns toward him.

TANIA I am coming, Semyon! *(hastily to her mother)* You will come to Leningrad, Mother—you and Father—

MOTHER *(shakes her head softly, her eyes misty)* Your father and I will never leave our land, Tanischka. We have lived on it—we will die on it. *(gives her a gentle shove)* Now go to him—

Watches Tania almost fly to Semyon. Semyon catches her, lifts her and twirls her around. Crowd around them gay and bantering.

SEMYON *(putting Tania down gently, his hands at her waist. Significantly)* The sun is going down, Tanischka—

It is as though the words had a special significance. Tania nods quickly, happily . . . a little fleeting expression on her face, as though the words were a signal. The two turn and walk out, leaving the music and festivity behind.

CAMERA picks them up on the hilltop in the field of tall rich grain waving in the slight wind. Tania stands with her head lifted, the wind ruffling her hair, outlined in the glow of the setting sun. Semyon stands a little behind her, looking at her. She turns and looks at him. Still looking at each other, they sink to their knees, almost in an attitude of prayer. He takes her gently in his arms. The angle of the CAMERA must be such as to show the slow, gradual, almost complete merging of these two people into one.

DISSOLVE TO:

TANIA *(writing in her diary, reading as she writes)* We went to Leningrad to live. We took Nina with us. Leningrad—the white city . . . the beautiful city. I had never been outside Bessarabia—never been to a big city, my son. It was like a new world. Libraries, with millions of books . . . universities where boys and girls studied together . . . art galleries . . . the Leningrad University . . . all in great white buildings that looked as if they would be there forever. *(camera on face as she writes)* But greater and more beautiful than all of them, for me, were the airfields, with hundreds of planes, where Semyon taught Nina and me how to fly.

DISSOLVE TO:

Great airfield, with planes taking off and coming down . . . great deal of activity. CAMERA picks up Tania, taxiing her plane to a standstill . . . the mechanic running up just behind Semyon, who pats her shoulder commendingly, then slips his arm around her as they walk toward the hangar, Tania pulling off her gloves and loosening her helmet.

TANIA *(gaily)* Well, Semyon—how did I do today?

SEMYON *(absently)* Fine—fine, Tania—

TANIA *(stopping and looking at him wonderingly)* What is it, Semyon?

The faint, almost unintelligible sound of a voice on the radio comes to them in the momentary silence. They walk on toward the hangar. Through the open door a few aviators and mechanics can be seen, bending over to listen. Their faces are serious and concerned.

SEMYON *(gloomily)* The news is not good, Tanischka—

They are at the entrance of the hangar now. As they come in, Tania is about to speak, but the voice of the commentator arrests her. (News commentator's voice comes over, brief, cryptic. He is recapitulating what Hitler has done in Europe.)

COMMENTATOR —and we observe that the German military machine has moved forward with fine precision. *(voice tinged with subtle edge of sarcasm)* First it was Czechoslovakia . . . of course, Germany had to protect her borders. Then came Poland—the Polish Corridor was very necessary to her. His armies sweeping across the lowlands was military strategy. France needed to be humiliated . . . Crete was stubborn . . . England remains still in the way. One after another of Germany's conquests have proven her great might. It is of much interest to us, at this time, however, that Herr Hitler has seized the Aegean Islands at the mouth of the Dardenelles where our entire Russian Black Sea Fleet is at this moment resting. Of course, all this may mean nothing. It is very interesting, however, to speculate on the thought—"Where will Hitler move next?"

One of the men leans over and clicks off the radio dial. They look at one another.

AVIATOR That Veloskaye—*(waving toward the radio)*—he looks at things black, always. We have a peace pact with the Nazis.

SEMYON *(grimly)* Hitler has kept his promise to no one. He will not keep his pact with us!

Music up with horn quality of loudspeaker. Blend in loudspeaker. Show great horns up on street post.

DISSOLVE TO:

Street corner in Moscow (to show Moscow, a shot of the Kremlin could be used). This is to be a double-exposed film. Background to be a map of Russia and the countries bordering her on the west, from Finland to Bulgaria, on a two-thousand-mile front. White circles to represent Finland, Eastern Prussia, Poland, Yugoslavia, Bulgaria and Greece. These white circles to turn black the moment they are taken over by the Nazis. All this in order to heighten the suspense of the Nazi strategy, against Russia, up to the moment when the declaration is made: "Germany attacks Russia along a two-thousand-mile front!" Yugoslavia does not turn black until after East Prussia and Poland.

Faces of crowd taken at an angle closeup from loudspeaker, showing heads lifted, listening. On these faces there is little concern and no fear.

LOUDSPEAKER Bulgaria joins the Axis—Nazi troops enter Sofia, heading for the Greek border!

DISSOLVE to street corner in Stalingrad with faces a little more concerned.

LOUDSPEAKER Germany attacks Greece and Yugoslavia! Russia and Yugoslavia sign a friendship pact!

DISSOLVE to street corner in smaller town of Novgorod or place like it. Faces show beginnings of fear.

LOUDSPEAKER Hitler concentrates infantry divisions, from France and Germany, in East Prussia and Poland!

DISSOLVE to Leningrad. This time the faces of Semyon and Tania are among those listening. There is tenseness and, in some faces of older women, real fear.

LOUDSPEAKER Nazi troops reported in Finland—

Quick move of CAMERA to pick up people on another street corner in Leningrad.

LOUDSPEAKER Finland mobilizes!

Long shot of backs of many people craning heads to look. CAMERA moves forward over heads until it comes to the billboard on which notice is posted.

NOTICE: JUNE 22ND, 1941—NAZIS ATTACK RUSSIA ALONG A TWO-THOUSAND-MILE FRONT FROM FINLAND TO BESSARABIA!

DISSOLVE TO:

DATE ON TOP OF PAGE: JUNE 22ND, 1941.

TANIA *(writing with rapid determined strokes)* It had come, my son—that which we had long expected . . .

Double exposure of all Tania describes, behind the diary.

TANIA *(writing)* The Nazis broke another pledge—and marched across another country's borders, moving swiftly

through Bessarabia, taking over railroads, cutting communications—stealing, robbing—and murdering as they
marched! *(camera on face, stern and fierce eyes)* Nazi tanks
rolled through the beautiful rich fields of Bessarabia—and
crushed the food of Russia into Russian earth—and the
helpless old and young of Russia with it! *(desperation in eyes
now)* There was no way of finding out what had happened
to my village. I was frantic with fear about my father and
my mother. Then, suddenly—one day—came one from
our village . . .

DISSOLVE TO:

Tania and Nina coming into their room. They show the effects
of weeks of fear and worry as they switch on the lights. Georg,
Fedya's younger brother, gaunt and tragic with the things he
has experienced, sits up, blinking dazedly at them. He had
fallen asleep while waiting for them. Nina runs to him, but
Tania cannot seem to move. No one speaks, as if the two girls
are fearful of questioning him, afraid of what they may hear.
Georg tries to stand, falls back exhausted. Tania moves slowly
toward him, kneels beside the couch. They look at each other
wordlessly. Then Georg lays his forehead against Tania's shoulder, and she puts her arm around him. As if the touch of her
hand released all the nightmare horror and suffering he had
experienced, the boy begins to cry—without tears, a desperate,
silent crying. Nina puts her face down into her hands. Tania
stares straight ahead, out of the window, as if she sees all he
cannot say, pressing his face against her shoulder. When he is
quiet, she gets to her feet.

TANIA You must eat . . .

GEORG I am not hungry.

TANIA Make the tea, Nina.

They go silently about the prosaic business of preparing food.
Georg tries to eat but his eyes stare straight ahead; now and
then he shuts them as if he wants to keep seeing what is invisibly
before him. Shoves food away. Tania comes behind him, puts
her hands on his shoulders.

TANIA Georg—tell me—*(long deep breath to steady herself)* my father—my mother—

Georg shivers. Tania's hands press harder on his shoulders, steadying him.

TANIA *(gently urgent)* It is better for us to know, Georg— then we will not—imagine—*(cannot go on)*

GEORG *(speaks very slowly)* We heard on the radio—that the Nazis were coming. We were told to put the torch to our grain. So Fedya and I—

Through the sunken eyes of the boy the picture comes, as he looks out of the window, with red flames leaping behind the pupils as the memory fills his eyes.

DISSOLVE TO:

Closeup of flames leaping among the rich tall grain that was Fedya's pride. He has thrown the torch on it, and watches as it ignites. On the face of Georg there is uncontrolled boyish anger, but on Fedya's usually stolid face there is a great sadness mingled with a fierce exultation. Beyond the hill on which they stand, there is the leaping of flames where other torches are being set to the wheatfields.

GEORG Instead of burning our wheat we should *kill* them—we should have guns, Fedya!

FEDYA *(with a peasant's acceptance of authority)* If it was for us to have guns, we would have been given guns. If we are not armed, they cannot say we resist them. So the old ones and the children will be safe. The worst they can do is to whip us for burning the wheat. *(catches Georg's arm, turns him about)* Now—you go, Georg—

GEORG I told you—

FEDYA *(sternly)* Am I your father and your mother, or not? Go to the hills—stay there for tonight—in the morning you may meet our soldiers—they will tell you how to get to Moscow—to Tania.

Georg plants his legs firmly, shakes his head.

FEDYA   *(shaking him exasperatedly)* Georg!

Again Georg shakes his head.

GEORG   If you go, I will go. Or I stay here with you.

FEDYA   *(giving Georg an impatient shove)* If I could go, would I not? Our wheat is gone—do I wish to stay to welcome the Nazi pigs? But can I leave Tania's old people—and her father sick? I promised her—

GEORG   *(stubbornly)* Then I will stay too.

FEDYA   *(anxious yet angered at Georg's resistance)* I tell you, nothing will happen to me—

GEORG   Then why do you want me to go away?

FEDYA   *(shouting)* Do you want the Nazi devils to ship you to Germany? Eh? *(Georg shakes his head)* Do I have to beat you to—

Georg makes a sound, stares down the hill to the far end of the village road. The Nazis are coming over the rise.

GEORG   *(hoarsely, pulling his brother's arm)* Fedya—*(pointing)*

FEDYA   *(whirling)* Here already—*(gives Georg an impatient though affectionate box on the ear)* Will you—

Realizes Georg will not listen. Both scramble down the hillside to the house of Tania's parents, a low house half hidden in old trees. It is the last on the village street, some distance from the others. They run into the house; Tania's mother is shoving her precious polished samovar and candlesticks into the blackened hearth, covering them with ashes. She whirls as they come in, terrified—begins to weep a little in relief when she sees it is Fedya and Georg. Tania's father, white and ill with fever, is sitting on the edge of the big double bed, wrapped in a shawl.

FATHER   *(quietly)* Let them have the brasses, mother—it may bribe them to leave us in peace.

MOTHER   *(grimly)* They belong to Tania, for her home. Why should a Nazi thief have them? *(wipes her hands on her apron, calmer now)* Get back into bed, Father. If they see you are sick they may—here, Fedya—help me—

Short series of quick shots. Stifled sound from Georg. They all turn to the window. Georg is there, face pressed against the pane. The mother and Fedya crowd behind him. Through the four-barred window, the whole length of the village street is visible. The gray mass of Germans pours down the street. Through the eyes of the watchers at the window, the whole tragedy of the village is seen. Nazi soldiers run in and out of houses, coming out laden with brasses and linens and foods, cramming food into their mouths. Wherever there is protest, a gun shot is the answer. Already five bodies lie sprawled at the distant end of the street. The three watchers are at first spellbound, as if in a horrible nightmare. Their staring eyes are seen through the window.

A woman tries to stop the Nazi soldiers from entering her house. As the Nazi lifts his bayonet, a boy of Georg's age leans out of an upstairs window and throws a heavy plantpot at the soldier. He is shot by another. A smaller boy, standing petrified at the window, is another victim. The mother is bayoneted.

GEORG *(hands over his mouth)* Gregor—Mitya—

Fedya, suddenly crazed by what he is seeing, starts for the door. Tania's mother holds him back with one hand, never taking her eyes off what is happening.

MOTHER Don't leave us, Fedya—

FATHER What is it? What are they doing? *(starts to pull himself up from the bed, holding to the posts)*

FEDYA *(dazed)* They are madmen—devils—*(more shots)*

FATHER *(repeating)* What are they doing? Why are they shooting?

The screaming and shouting of the soldiers and victims comes a little muted into the house with its closed doors and window, but it has an effect of nightmare-like unbelief. The father gets to the window, clings to the ledge, staring out with the others.

Older men and women are being pulled from houses, lined up. A little girl of seven runs out of one house, her mother running after her, calling her to come back. But the child runs this way and that like a terrified blind little animal.

TANIA'S MOTHER   Little Anna Wesyslaus—

A soldier kicks the child aside. The child screams. The mother tries to reach her, frantically calling her name. The child turns her fear-blinded face to the watchers; the CAMERA takes it in closeup of stupified terror. She pushes away the German soldier—he raises the butt of his gun, his body filling the camera as he bends to strike . . . The soldier follows other soldiers into the house as the mother gathers the dead child in her arms, rocking her to and fro in the middle of the street.

TANIA'S FATHER   *(trying to steady his lips)* For this they came from Poland—to be free—

Fedya steps back, pounds his temples with his fists, as peasants do, his eyes darting to find means of escape for them all.

FATHER   Where are they taking our neighbors, Mother? What—

Stops. The CAMERA in closeup of three faces pressed against the window, Fedya's a little behind, all watching with staring eyes the Nazi soldiers throwing long ropes over strong branches of the great trees behind the village houses, pulling on the branches, testing them. The line of older men and women is being shoved and prodded with bayonets toward the line of trees. Steadily closer comes the mob of Nazi soldiers, nearer to the house of Tania's parents.

The mother moves from the window, as if unable to look any longer. Takes her husband by the arm, leads him, a shaking, incredulous-eyed, shuffling man, to the bed. Sits down beside him, as if resigned to the inevitable. Their very incredulity is like an anaesthetic, dulling them to this unbelievable horror. Behind the house, the pigs begin squealing in the pen.

The soldiers are at the last house before theirs.

MOTHER   *(quietly)* The pigs should be let out—it will be harder for the Nazis to catch them.

FATHER   *(feeling his throat)* The pigs are safer than we.

Fedya throws a look back toward the pigpen. His eyes widen with a look of hope. He moves toward Georg. His eyes rove over the boy's head and hunched shoulders—and beyond to the men and women over whose head the nooses are being lowered by laughing Nazi soldiers in the trees above them. His hands begin to move up and down on his thighs. Slowly they begin to clench into fists.

> **FEDYA** Georg—*(his lips move but no sound comes; he wets his lips, tries again)* Georg—

Georg turns slowly. His face is drained of expression, his eyes are like those of a sleepwalker. The big red fist of Fedya comes up in a swift, paralyzing blow to the boy's chin. The two old people stare uncomprehendingly—they are already dulled by the enormity of what they have witnessed. The boy's eyes turn up, he slumps against the window ledge, but before he can fall, Fedya has picked him up. Holds the boy's head an instant hard against his breast, one hand against the boy's cheek, then slings him over his shoulder and runs out the back door to the pigpen. He opens the pen, lets the pigs run out, lays Georg down in the reek and mud of the pigsty, behind the little low mud hut. He covers the boy with mud, even his face, leaving his nostrils and lips clear. Georg is almost invisible.

(NOTE: Since in the telling of the story by Georg to Tania and Nina, this would be as much as he could reconstruct of his own experience, it seems to me that it would be wise at this point to dissolve to Georg's awakening. Georg would not know exactly what Fedya did after Fedya hit him, except as the boy sees what the Nazis had left behind them when he came to consciousness and went back to the house.)

(NOTE: Although formal religion was frowned on in Russia, peasants as a whole kept to their simple beliefs. It seems to me that Fedya would make a natural simple gesture of making the sign of the cross over his brother before he ran back to the house. However, this would be something again that Georg could not visualize. It makes a good touch, though.)

It is dusk when Georg comes to consciousness. There is still a dull red glow in the sky from the burning fields, and two or three barns that have caught fire are still burning. Georg gets to his feet, covered with the mud of the pigpen. Uncomprehending, he stares down at himself, shudders, his eyes stare numbly across at the house of Tania's parents, and he begins to recollect. Begins to run, zigzagging weakly, and gets to the doorway at the rear of the house.

The room is a shambles. The bed is ripped apart by bayonets as if the Germans had searched for things there—but the soot of the hearth still covers the brasses Tania's mother had hidden. Half hidden by the bed, Georg sees Fedya's body. Bends to turn him over. Takes a few steps backward, his hands out as if warding off an unbearable sight. Still moving backward, he comes up against the window ledge, turns swiftly as if to shut out the sight of the room. Then stands staring. Before his eyes, through the four-barred window, the whole tragedy of the village lies. Along the whole row of great trees behind the village houses, the bodies of men and women hang, silhouetted against the reddened sky. The two boys still lie on the window sill where they were shot. The mother lies huddled over her dead child in the street. Nothing is left alive in the village but Georg. As Georg watches, a kind of dumb-animal sound of suffering begins to rise in his throat—the wordless moaning of a stricken thing. The closeup of his face, his staring eyes, lit with the red of the flames.

DISSOLVE BACK TO:

Scene in Tania's room in Moscow.

> **TANIA** *(writing slowly, reading with hard determination as she writes)* That is how the Nazis waged war, my son. My father and mother fell in their burned fields, and the hot black ash that should have been their bread, pressed into their mouths—their wounds—*(voice breaks; controls herself; camera switches to her face)* But the peasants of Bessarabia will not forget! Russia will not forget! *(face has the look of someone taking an irrevocable pledge)*—and I will not forget, my son! Today, with hundreds of other Russian women, I took the oath of the Red Army Soldier. We stood before the Commander in the great square . . .

DISSOLVE TO:

Great public square in the center of the city. CAMERA PANS along, closeups of faces of women . . . students, with young, determined faces and stern young eyes . . . square-chinned, broad-cheeked mothers . . . old women with gaunt, wrinkled faces showing through the folds of their shawls, stand watching and listening . . . all with their eyes lifted to the Russian flag, floating on its standard above the commander, on a raised platform . . . all faces with the same inspired, uplifted, devoted expression. Roll of drum.

> **COMMANDER** Women of Russia, repeat after me—I, a citizen of the Union of Soviet Socialist Republics—

> **WOMEN'S VOICES** I, a citizen of the Union of Soviet Socialist Republics—

> **COMMANDER** —take the oath and swear to defend the Motherland courageously and with wisdom—

> **WOMEN'S VOICES** —take the oath and swear to defend the Motherland courageously and with wisdom—

> **COMMANDER** —in honor and in dignity—

> **WOMEN'S VOICES** —in honor and in dignity—

> **COMMANDER** —without sparing my blood and my life until complete victory is attained!

> **WOMEN'S VOICES** —without sparing my blood and my life until complete victory is attained!

CAMERA closeup of Tania and Nina at close of pledge.

> **NINA** *(stepping forward)* I promise not to yield a single foot of precious Russian sky or earth!

> **TANIA** *(stepping forward)* It is better for me to lie dead on my earth than to live and give it away to the enemy. If I break my promise—and if I am afraid in battle—I ask death to punish my crime and my shame!

Chorus swell with orchestra into "International." All the women gathered in the square sing it, CAMERA taking closeups of various faces.

DISSOLVE TO:

> **TANIA** *(writing, reading as she writes; camera on face, grim, bitter)*—and then, my son, I began to settle my account with the Nazis—

Orchestra into low plane theme.

DISSOLVE TO:

Tania, in plane, grim-faced and determined, firing at a Nazi plane. She scores a hit; there is a sudden sharp burst of flame, with a complete disintegration of the enemy plane. (This same flame burst is to be used a little later to show progression of planes brought down.)

TANIA   *(exultantly)* That for your grandmother, my son!

QUICK DISSOLVE TO:

Long shot of planes in battle . . . closeup of Tania in her plane, firing machine gun . . . burst of machine gun fire from Tania's plane . . . enemy plane hit . . . bursts into flame . . . as it plummets downward.

TANIA'S VOICE   That one for your grandfather.

QUICK DISSOLVE TO:

Two planes in battle . . . quick flash of Tania's face in her plane . . . machine gun fire from her plane . . . explosion from the other. As it plummets, the plume of black smoke spreading from its tail widens, fills the screen, becomes a blackboard with the other names shadowed, Tania's in bold relief showing date, city and number of planes she has brought down . . . evaporating into progressive numbers until seventeen has been reached . . . each number to be left on screen following fire flash with name of town in flash, i.e., Rzhev, Voronezh, Moshaisk, Mozdok, Kuibyshev, Rostov, Novorrossisk, Grozyny, etc.

Long room in barracks. Only a few of the aviatrixes are there . . . some reading, sleeping, etc. Suddenly the noise of incoming planes is heard. Alertness in the attitudes of those in the room . . . scene switches to airfield outside . . . planes taxi to a standstill . . . tired members of Tania's squadron climb out, walking slowly and with bent heads toward the barracks. One can see by the way they walk, in contrast to their usual brisk, swaggering, self-confident walk, that something has happened. Tania and Nina walk together, not speaking. Tania stops at the hangar, speaks quietly and briefly to a mechanic.

TANIA Number eight—Antonina—*(lifts her hands a little, a tired, sad, meaningful gesture)* We got five of theirs.

They walk on to the barracks, come in silently and quietly. The effect of this first loss—the "baby" of the squadron—on the rest of the flyers is shown in a swift series of closeups as the girls straggle into the barracks. One girl, unlacing her boots, stops as she pulls her boots off, sits on the edge of her cot, staring into space. Another looks at the empty cot with the imprint of the dead girl's head still in the pillow from her night's interrupted sleep. CAMERA stays on the pillow, rises a little to take in the picture of the dead girl and her sweetheart, smiling. CAMERA switches to an orderly, coming in with a letter. Hands it to Nina, who puts it on the dead girl's blanket. CAMERA full on name, "Antonina Dubova," with the number of her squadron. Then CAMERA follows hands of the girls as they silently gather all her things, put them in the center of the blanket, then fold the blanket ends over them all . . . all in silence, but with a feeling of tragedy and grief.

LENINGRAD, AUGUST, 1941

TANIA *(repeating date)* Leningrad—August, nineteen hundred and forty-one. *(writing, reading as she writes)* This is a day all Russia will remember, my son . . . a day you must never forget! The day when the music of Russia proved greater than the thunder of Nazi guns.

The dull pounding of guns begins in the distance . . . a constant booming sound that grows imperceptibly. Mingled with it is a kind of formless music, indeterminate yet surging and powerful, with the hint of the as-yet-unformed beat of the "Iron Rats" movement of Shostakovich.[5] The music always overlays the pounding of the guns, growing as it grows.

TANIA *(writing, reading as she writes)* You will hear that music one day, my son—the whole world will hear it—*(puts down pen, stares ahead as if steeped in memory, her eyes intense*

5. Dmitri Shostakovich (1906–1975), one of the leading Russian composers of the twentieth century, wrote the first three movements of his Seventh Symphony during the German siege of Leningrad in 1941. The work was first performed at Kuibyshev in 1942.

and concentrated, as if striving to remember every detail of a picture she has seen)—but not as we heard it . . . with guns blasting—shells screaming—buildings pulverized! The bursting bombs turning the ground into a blasting furnace, and overhead the planes locked in screaming combat! A million demons loosed upon the city! Yet in this inferno of sound and fury, Dmitri Shostakovich finished his greatest symphony—music born of suffering, written in fire!

Takes up pen again . . . writes with swift and inspired strokes. Double exposure of Shostakovich at a piano, the palm of his left hand bandaged, writing on sheets of music.

TANIA *(begins to write again here; fade her out . . . voice continues)* It was our music—and he wrote it for us! He wrote it with hands singed from the fires of Nazi bombs—he wrote it with cold eating at his fingers, my son!—with hunger gnawing at him, and the guns pounding at the gates of our beloved city! He wrote it—and finished it—yes, the music was finished, and it had to be played but there were no musicians to play it! Then—the call went out, my son—you should have heard—

The music and the booming of guns imperceptibly louder but held down behind voice from loudspeaker.

LOUDSPEAKER Attention! Attention! men and women of Leningrad! *(faces lifted in arrested attention; swift flashes of closeups of faces at different angles, listening)* One hundred musicians are needed to play the music of Dmitri Shostakovich! One hundred musicians—*(voice goes on behind action)*—are needed, etc.

Closeup of hand tapping shoulder of white-haired, elderly man with sorrowful eyes . . . looks up, deeply moved, nods eagerly, starts away.

Quick shot of a man reading notice posted on billboard, while echo of loudspeaker comes from distance: "One hundred musicians are needed to play the Seventh Symphony of Dmitri Shostakovich! Only fifteen men are left of the Leningrad Symphony Orchestra!" Man starts off, hurried, excited. Echo of loudspeaker always on the air.

CAMERA shifts to cobbler's shop . . . middle-aged man with heavily-lined face seated at cobbler's bench. Left arm folded on table before him, holding down shoe-last. Left hand is not seen. Takes small nail out of his mouth (as cobblers do) with right hand, places it on sole, hammers with right hand. As he places second nail on shoe, voice of newsboy heard. He pauses.

> **VOICE OF NEWSBOY** —musicians needed—one hundred musicians needed to play the music of Dmitri Shostakovich! *(fading)* One hundred musicians—

Almost as if some frustration drives him, the cobbler hammers the nail into the sole of the shoe. A hand taps him on the shoulder. He looks up, as if listening. Then very slowly he draws out the sleeve of his left hand with his right. With an expression of restrained anguish he lifts it. The end of the sleeve is tied at the wrist—his left hand is gone. He looks up, shaking his head.

Booming of guns and music always under. Echo of loudspeaker on the air as CAMERA shifts to—

Long shot of great room in munitions factory. Voice swells full.

> **LOUDSPEAKER** Workers in factories! Attention!

Hum of motors dies down . . . quick flashes of workers lifting heads from work to listen. Voice goes on behind following action. Closeup of hand tapping shoulder of girl at a lathe. Looks up, then down at her coarsened fingers. Nods quickly, gets up, eyes shining.

Quick shot of boy picking up handbill and reading same announcement as was printed on billboard. Voice of loudspeaker echoing in distance.

DISSOLVE TO:

Long shot of hospital ward. Voice of loudspeaker full.

> **LOUDSPEAKER** Attention, doctors and nurses of Leningrad! Attention!

Voice goes on. Faces of doctors, nurses, patients, all lifted . . . listening. Nurses wheeling patients, stop, heads lifted. One boy sitting in wheelchair with right leg amputated at the knee, crutches beside him. Hands grip arms of wheelchair as he leans forward, absorbed and listening. Closeup of hand tapping him on the shoulder. Boy looks up, face alight. Looks down at leg. Mouth sets in stubborn determination. Takes hold of crutches and starts to get up. CAMERA flashes to closeup of doctor bandaging a little girl's wounded hand. Hand taps his shoulder, doctor looks up, nods quickly, finishes bandaging hand, washes his hands, slips off hospital coat, reaches into cabinet and takes out a trumpet . . . Voice of loudspeaker continues behind—

DISSOLVE TO:

Trench with soldiers. All lift heads quickly as voice from the loudspeaker comes full.

VOICE FROM LOUDSPEAKER　Attention, soldiers of Leningrad, attention! One hundred musicians are needed—

Voice continues under action: Closeup of hand tapping shoulder of a young soldier. Looks up, nods eagerly, puts down gun and turns toward back of trench.

DISSOLVE TO:

Deck of destroyer. Sailors and officers with heads suddenly lifted in attitudes of listening. Voice from loudspeaker comes full.

VOICE FROM LOUDSPEAKER　Men of the Red Navy, attention! One hundred musicians—

Voice continues under action: Closeup of hand tapping shoulder of young sailor with bandaged head. Looks up with eager attention. Nods quickly. Starts down companionway.

As the music builds slowly behind above action, it seems to follow each of the following people. These are quick sharp italicized flashes, taken at varying angles:

Old man comes into his son's room. Picture of boy on dresser, playing the flute. Old man stands with his back to camera, holds it in his hands, reading inscription. Closeup of inscription on picture: "To my beloved father, who gave up his own dream that I might fulfill mine. May I be forever worthy." (Notice to director: Object is to show that the father's great dream of music for himself was never quite realized—and his great pride was in the greater accomplishment of his son, now dead.) Mirror shows the old man puts down the picture, opens a drawer, takes out the flute wrapped in a piece of felt . . . takes it carefully in his hands, grips it with fierce determination . . . goes out.

Soldier digging in dirt of trench, uncovers a box which he tenderly rubs clear of dirt, opens it, rubs his hands on his stained uniform, tenderly and carefully lifts out his violin . . . clambers up over the trench.

Sailor who runs down companionway, takes bassoon out of his bunk chest . . . runs back up companionway.

Girl from factory runs down into cellar of partly bombed house, pushes away heap of firewood, disclosing a rough box, very large, drags it out. With shaking hands she pulls one piece of wood away, disclosing a harp. Presses her cheek against the strings.

Boy with amputated leg, on his knees, crutches lying beside him, lifting bricks from hearth of a completely burned house with only the fireplace left standing . . . brings out a cello wrapped in old cloth . . . hugs it to him.

Voice of loudspeaker continues in background, fading under the indeterminate yet powerful music that surges upward as if propelling all these people to what they do. Music seems to pick them up with that same surging power now faintly beginning to hold something of the beat of the Shostakovich.

As the people begin to converge on the Leningrad Auditorium, through darkened streets, with the incessant booming of guns always in the background, the music, heard until now only as a formless sound, begins to take on the beat of the "Iron Rats" movement. The people come from all directions . . . soldiers, sailors, tired women with babies in their arms and children clinging to their skirts . . . wounded men, fire-fighters . . . anti-aircraft gunners . . . sweethearts holding to each other's hands, grasping at this brief moment of beauty . . . a blind man led by his daughter . . . an old woman guided by a girl of thirteen, trying to slow her pace to the older one but eager to get to the auditorium . . . the grimed faces of boys coming from building ditches . . . all different, but all with the same gauntness of hunger, the pallor and dark-circled eyes of sleeplessness and endurance, the sorrow for lost ones, and on all faces the same exaltation, fierce and hungry and beautiful.

The music and surging people seem to become one. They seem to dissolve into the orchestra on the stage of the auditorium. A quick long shot of orchestra showing uniforms of sailors, soldiers, fire-fighters, factory workers in their work clothes. Then closeups of two of the faces of those tapped by the hand—the old man with the flute lifts it to his lips. Tears brim into his eyes. One drops onto the flute, rolls along it like a shining bubble. Closeup of the boy with the amputated leg, his cello braced against his good leg, his downbent face arrested in a look of quiet ecstasy. Then the CAMERA, taking medium shot of audience, travels slowly around, every seat filled, people standing against posts and walls. CAMERA picks up Semyon and Tania against the wall, hand in hand. Closeup of Semyon and Tania, heads thrown back against the wall, faces turned toward the orchestra. Their two faces are the last the CAMERA picks up before it swerves to the stage and the uplifted baton of Shostakovich. The booming of the guns outside is a constant beat now, the occasional bursting of shrapnel, the dull thud of a bomb falling, all muted but unmistakable. (NOTE: The Shostakovich music gradually drowns them out so that at the end only the music is heard, powerful and triumphant.) The lights go down a little in the auditorium. Quick flashes of various groups of musicians with lifted heads, the moment of waiting for the baton to fall . . . and faces of audience waiting . . . and then the conductor's baton lifts and falls . . . the first strains of the pastoral begin—the first movement of the symphony with its feeling of quiet and peace . . . the delicate haunting notes of the "Iron Rats" theme are italicized against the background of the booming guns outside.

The CAMERA takes in group after group of instruments, picking out in each group the faces of those who were called to play by the tapping of the hand on their shoulders.

The great sweep of violins . . . the soldier, his violin nestled beneath his chin, his eyes half closed in a moment of supreme happiness.

The blare of trumpets . . . the doctor with his trumpet.

CAMERA swerves to audience . . . closeup of a mother pressing a baby's sleeping head against her shoulder.

The wood winds . . . the sailor with his bassoon. *The old man* with the flute. No tears now, only a grave exaltation, playing as if granted a great privilege.

CAMERA swerves to audience . . . closeup of a girl with her cheek pressed against the shoulder of the boy next to her. Closeup of a wide-eyed child of ten, holding to her grandfather's hand. Both thin-faced, but deeply moved and contented.

The harp . . . closeup of harpist who had come from her lathe in the factory . . . cheek pressed against her harp.

The bass viols . . . face of the boy with the amputated leg. Alight and glowing.

All this time the music is building, with the growing of the "Iron Rats" theme becoming menacing and overbearing. As the music approaches the feeling of climax, the CAMERA swerves to the drums and cymbals. For the first time the audience is made aware of the cymbalist. It is the cobbler. One cymbal is tied to his crippled left hand, the right hand holds the other. He stands straight and proud, courage and determination in his lifted head: his eyes are turned to the conductor as he waits for the cue, rapt and exalted. A quick flash of the CAMERA to the conductor . . . the baton moves. Flash back to the cobbler, and the moment toward which the whole music seems to have been building—the tremendous clash of cymbals by the crippled cobbler, which seems to be the triumph of this man over adversity—the symbol of the triumph of all this great orchestra over death and disaster and the devastating siege of their beloved city.

Through the above the flashes of audience faces must sufficiently punctuate the playing of the music, to give it balance.

By the time the music has reached its climax the guns are no longer heard, and it segues gradually into the icy music of Sevastopol—winter in Russia—as Tania continues her diary.

DISSOLVE TO:

TANIA *(writing, reading as she writes)* Sevastopol, December, 1941 . . . the first winter of the war, my son—with the Nazis blasting Sevastopol by air and sea and land. Forty degrees below zero—and homes blasted to rubble. Sevastopol became a city of caves, with men and women and children living like moles in the dark. But we could bear the bitter cold—they could not! The Nazis froze at their sentry posts . . . they froze as they ran with pillaged loot from Russian homes . . . they froze as they fell wounded by our bullets! They came to Russia to die—and our snow was their tombstone!

DISSOLVE TO:

Quick flashes of icy wastes of Sevastopol—mounds covered with snow . . . wrecked buildings covered with snow. Everything the CAMERA rests on is a dreary waste of snow and ice . . . a white city of death. But the planes still rise in the air . . . come down coated with ice. Shots of engines being heated with charcoal stoves so that motors can be started. Breath white on the air of the dawn as the dawn patrols take off.

Music segues to intimate romantic music of Tania.

DISSOLVE TO:

TANIA *(writing, reads the date as she writes it)* February 12th, 1942 . . . *(face lifts; closeup of happy, shining-eyed face)* I found out about you today, my son. I went to see a doctor . . .

DISSOLVE TO:

Tania looking at the physician with mixture of unbelief and growing happiness.

TANIA You are sure? There is no mistake?

DOCTOR *(smiling)* As sure as Russia will win!

TANIA *(laughs a little, then hugs herself)* Me, Tania Doronin. Me. It's happening to *me!* *(laughs in sheer delight, clasps the doctor and kisses him on both cheeks)* Oh, I must send word to Semyon. I—*(stops, both hands to cheeks; elation dies down a little)* No—no—*(as if talking to herself)* I mustn't let him know—not yet—

Dashes out of infirmary. Runs to barracks. Rushes past men and women pilots, bivouacked in same building. Smiles follow her as she runs into her own barracks. No formality in barracks. Rank is forgotten. Some of the girls are writing, some reading, a few attempting to sleep. Tania rushes to Nina, who is sleeping, nose pressed into the pillow. Shakes Nina gently, then more firmly as she does not awaken.

TANIA Nina—Nina, wake up—

NINA *(sleepily)* What—*(blinks, pushes Tania away)* Idiot—I was sound asleep—

TANIA *(pulls Nina upright)* I know—I know—*(laughs in tender excitement)* but I've got something to tell you, Nina—

NINA *(tries to lie down again, eyes closing in spite of herself)* Save it, for pity's sake, Tania—*(yawns)*—I'm *(yawns again, mightily)*—sleepy as—

Almost falls onto the pillow again. Tania pulls her upright. Gives her a little slap on the cheek to wake her up. Nina's eyes stay half shut.

TANIA Listen, Nina—what could be the most wonderful thing that could happen to a girl?

NINA *(crossly, eyes closing completely)* Forty hours' sleep at a stretch—and to blow Hitler to hell!

TANIA *(joining in the general laughter)* Guess again, Nina darling—

NINA *(pulls away, opens eyes with an effort; impatient and nearly angry)* Now listen, Tania—what—*(looks closely at Tania's shining eyes, really awake now; Nina's face softens, clears of irritation)* Semyon's here! Tania, how wond—

TANIA *(shaking her head)* No—but oh, how I wish he were, Nina—just for this minute . . . I wouldn't *tell* him, but . . .

NINA *(puzzled, frowning)* Tell him—

TANIA *(pulls Nina's head down, hugs her ecstatically)* Nina—Nina—darling, I'm going to have a baby!

Nina hugs Tania with unrestrained delight. Then becomes frightened . . . holds her gingerly away.

NINA Tania—I didn't mean to be so rough. I—*(jumps up on her cot)* Everybody—listen, everybody—Tania's having a baby!

Excitement. Comic situation when some of the men flyers come in to find out what is happening. Some with jackets off, shoes off, various phases of attire . . . some humorous, typically male comments, ad libs and fade out.

TANIA *(writing, reading as she writes)* Kuibyshev, June, 1942. Your father knows, my son . . . about you. *(tranquilly, tenderly)* I didn't tell him—he said he could read it in my eyes. I had not seen him for four months. Four—long—months, my son. When there is a war being fought as we are fighting it, husbands and wives do not see each other very often. It was like the breath of a new life to see him again—to know he was alive. *(tiny hint of delicate laughter)* But he was stern about you, my son!

DISSOLVE to Semyon and Tania in a room in Kuibyshev.

SEMYON You are not to go up again, Tania! Not till it's over! Someone else will command your squadron.

TANIA *(shaking her head, gently)* My squadron has never flown without me, Semyon.

SEMYON *(pleading)* I only ask that you do not fly again until the child is born, Tania. Promise me—

TANIA *(interrupting, tenderly, her eyes traveling over his face)* I love you, Semyon—

SEMYON *(insistently)* Promise me, Tania!

TANIA *(going on as if she had not heard; voice aching, low)*

Hold me, Semyon—it's been four months—*(presses close to him)* a hundred and twenty days since you held me like this—*(voice breaks)*

SEMYON *(passionately)* A hundred and twenty years, my love—

TANIA *(softly)* Every time I go up into the sky, I think—somewhere Semyon is going up too—like birds flying to meet each other—*(tenderly)* My pilots do not know why I always kiss my hand into space and wave. They don't know I'm waving to you . . . as if you could see—

SEMYON *(solemnly)* I saw you—*(begins to count on his fingers)* At Novgorod—at Moshaisk—Mozdok—

TANIA *(eyes shining with delight)* Oh, my darling—darling—

SEMYON *(still counting)*—Rostov, Frozny—

TANIA Semyon—I love you—I love you—I love you—

They embrace with fierce passion, as if holding time off.

SEMYON *(softly, as he puts her away from him)* Oh, Tania—Tania—take care of yourself—and him. God keep you both!

TANIA *(simply)* God keep us all.

Semyon looks at her yearningly. They melt into each other. Music takes on feeling of time, beautiful, lingering. Dark shadows fill the room—scene slowly fades.

Early dawn. He is outside the door. She leans against him, her eyes closed. They are now both helmeted, ready for flight. He looks at the watch on his wrist.

SEMYON *(gently)* I must get back to Moscow, Tania—

TANIA I know—I know . . . and I to Stalingrad. *(a little desperately)* Hold me again—kiss me, Semyon—

Semyon takes her face in his hands and studies it, feature for feature, as if he must remember it a long time. Then he gently kisses her eyelids, her cheeks, and finally her lips.

DISSOLVE TO:

Airfield. Semyon helps Tania into her plane. They smile at each other with steady courage, then Semyon runs back to his plane. They go up into the sky, their planes keeping close. The CAMERA picks them up at various angles . . . then long shot of them swaying together, like two great birds. They finally come close enough to see each other . . . though they [blank] as they stunt and dip and play about in the sky like two great birds. Their planes finally come close together. They dip their wings to see each other better. He waves his hand. Tania kisses her hand and waves back at him. Both planes draw away from each other in a spreading triangle, widening and separating to form the letter "V", with the CAMERA the apex of the letter, until both planes are lost in the distance.

(NOTE: Since this is the last time Tania sees Semyon alive, and this is truly goodbye, though neither knows it, there is a profound poignance to the playing of this scene. In all their lovemaking there is a kind of gallant defiance of the threat of death, but in the very nature of things, there is a tacit acknowledgment of its nearness in all they say and do.)

> **TANIA** *(writing, reading as she writes; tired voice)* Stalingrad, September, 1942. *(with bitterness)* Hell—at Stalingrad, my son. Our buildings are in ruins . . . so many industries have been put out of commission that thousands of workers have left the ruined factories and taken up guns. Nazi field guns fire with clocklike regularity into the heart of the city. Every man, woman and child knows there can be no retreat. We must live—or die—at our posts. Today the orders came through from Moscow . . .

> DISSOLVE TO:

Official sending announcement through loudspeaker.

> **OFFICIAL** Stalin orders all boats on the Volga to be removed! There is no escape by the river! *(flashes of faces listening, lips moving in echo of the words)* Stalin orders all bridges behind Stalingrad to be blown up or burned! There is no road back from Stalingrad!

> DISSOLVE TO:

TANIA *(writing, reading as she writes)* No road—no bridge—no boat out of Stalingrad. Remember those words, my son. Hear them as we heard them, with our backs to the Volga—knowing there was only one end—victory or death. But the skies were still ours! Yes, the skies! *(voice builds)* My squadron was ordered to take off and bomb the German supply lines south of Stalingrad. My pilots raced for their planes. I—I could not run with them, my son. I walked slowly, while I could hear them check their controls.

Revvying of motors and voices of pilots off scene.

WOMEN'S VOICES *(irregular, off mike)* Wheel chocks out right . . . out left . . .

VOICES DOWN B.G. Tail wheel unlocked . . . Brakes? . . Brakes locked . . . Magnetos? Checked . . . Engines? . . . Run up . . . Flight controls? . . . Unlocked and free . . . Generators? . . . On! *(voices go on ad lib)*

NINA *(other voices off scene)* Tania! Tania—wait!

TANIA Yes? What is it, Nina?

NINA *(breathless on mike)* Tania—you are ordered not to go up . . . So near—your time—

TANIA *(quietly)* I must, Nina—this once—

NINA *(half sobbing)* I'll take your plane, Tania! If anything should happen to you—

TANIA *(reassuringly)* Nothing will happen. I'll just drop this last load of bombs—

NINA *(pleading)* No, Tania—no—

WOMEN'S VOICES *(on mike, confusion of calls, motors louder)* Contact! Contact! Take off!

TANIA *(strong voice)* Contact! *(roar of motor)*

NINA *(through motor)* Tania—Tania, come back! *(motor swells over voice and fades to a steady drone down under)*

TANIA *(through subdued drone of motor)* My squadron was flying in formation . . . a beautiful sight, my son! I hope you will fly so with your own squadron—in times of peace. We climbed, ten thousand feet . . . twenty thousand feet. Far below we sighted the German supply lines . . . the bombs hurled from our planes. I could see the plumes of smoke where they struck! *(exultant)* And then—like angry vultures—the enemy planes roared toward us. *(motors louder)* We could hear their machine guns as we flew back toward our lines. Pain shot through me—I thought I had been struck. But then *(exultantly)* I knew! I knew, my son! My time had come—to see you—

Orchestra takes it away with surging sound of motors fading into faint cry of infant and Tania's low crooning of lullaby.

TANIA *(contentedly)* You are here, my son . . . born in a peasant's hut just inside the Russian lines. You are here—

NINA *(softly urgent)* Tania—you are well?

TANIA *(happily)* Look at my son, Nina—*(pause, fear in voice)* Nina—*(orchestra into love theme to hold under softly)*

NINA *(brokenly)* Tania—Semyon *(cannot go on)*

TANIA *(breathing the word)* Yes—?

NINA He—was coming—*(chokes)* . . . when two Messerschmidts—

TANIA No—no—*(refusing to listen)* Oh, Semyon! *(weeping; infant's wail in)* My little Semyon, you will never know your father now . . . *(breaks)* His great laugh, his big shoulders on which you were to ride . . . his tenderness and love for us both. Now Russia must be your father—and perhaps your mother too. For I must leave you, my son *(love theme segues to lullaby strain, softly crooning)* It is not easy, little one. It would be so sweet to stay—feed you—kiss you—and watch you grow . . . *(voice low and filled with yearning)* But I must go. I *must.* It is not only for Russia we women are fighting, my baby—Beyond Russia, beyond Stalingrad—there is a world of suffering people I must try to help. I cannot forsake them—even for you, my little one. *(baby cries a little)* Please do not cry. Do not be angry with me. I have no choice. I go perhaps to join your father—*(voice catches)* Someday, when you read these words I have written you, you will understand why I—had to put you in the arms of a kindly peasant woman and—*(struggles for control)*—and kiss your small dear face so like your father's already—*(voice breaks)*—and say—goodbye . . . *(sobs)* Goodbye, my little Semyon—goodbye—

Orchestra up softly as scene fades for transition to—

SOUND TRACK	SCREEN
The sound becomes that of the Freedom Train in motion, with the theme from the "Cantata."	FADE OUT begins.
	Screen is completely dark.
The sound of the Freedom Train becomes a measured tramp of feet. The music stops.	FADE IN begins.

FADE IN

Night. Four men are carrying the dead officer, wrapped in a blanket, out of the house. The others follow, save America and Akers, who remains with him.

(NOTE: From here on, "Flynn" is "Fonda.")

The German officer watches them pass. The sergeant and Loughton pass. An American soldier now stands guard over the German.

GERMAN *(to Loughton)* I will come too, nein?

LOUGHTON *(turns his head briefly)* Geneva.

GERMAN He is officer. Besides, he is now dead. We are civilized even by your American and English standards. We will always bury those of you whom we kill.

The others react to this. The sergeant looks at the German, at a loss. Apparently the German is not even trying to be offensive. He seems courteous almost: just arrogant and sneering and contemptuous, as if he and the others were of a different species of creature. Loughton looks at the sergeant.

LOUGHTON Well?

SERGEANT *(turns: to guard)* Bring him on then. Watch him.

The German and his guard follow. Akers watches them out.

AKERS *(to America)* I better go too.

AMERICA Yes.

AKERS *(rises)* You can holler for me.

AMERICA I'm all right. You go on.

Akers follows.

In the courtyard, night, moonlight. Two soldiers are just finishing digging the shallow grave in the sand as the others enter with the body and put it down.

During this scene, the Italian reappears. He simply walks in. Everyone is surprised to see him again. He has found an abandoned Italian machine gun. (Will have to verify this.) It is mounted on a light dolly; the Italian reappears dragging the gun behind him. Nobody knows why he came back. He has a reason. He intends to throw in his lot and fate with his late enemies. He read the meaning of the two German reconnaissance planes and he knows that the German officer knows what is up; and the Italian has returned, as it will appear later, to do what he can to disrupt the German officer's action. He knows he will in all probability not be able to save either himself or the Americans. He knows that he will die with them. But the Americans don't know his reason. They assume that he is the coward the German has called him and his whole race, that he was afraid of the desert, etc., and so returned. He carries the matter off in his fatalistic, sardonic Latin manner.

In this scene, playing the German officer against the American old-line sergeant, we will show the fundamental difference between Nazis and other people. The German himself will show why Nazis are dangerous, and there is no hope to change them, all to do is to destroy them. We will show a man, representative of a nation, who has really sold his soul to the devil: a clever man, no fool at all. At the end of the scene, during which the German has thought faster than the sergeant, has baffled the sergeant and all the others, a man states the fact: "They are monsters. There is no hope for them, no place in the world for them and us too. We will have to destroy them to save ourselves."

As the German talks his calm and insufferable arrogance, finally one of the Americans can stand it no longer. He draws his pistol. He is standing behind the German.

AMERICAN Turn around you _____, so I won't have to shoot you in the back.

The German turns, still calm, sneering at the pistol with which the angry American is obviously going to kill him. Battson steps forward quickly, knocks the pistol up.

BATTSON *(to soldier)* Stop it, you fool!

Reagan, a little slower to move, reaches the soldier, furious at this threat to discipline and the Articles of War.

REAGAN *(angrily)* Do you want to murder him?

SOLDIER *(angrily, as Battson holds him)* Why not?

REAGAN *(takes the pistol)* I don't care whether he is alive or dead either. But no man of mine shall murder a prisoner.

SOLDIER The Japs do it. Maybe the Germans do it too, for all you know.

REAGAN Maybe they do. They're Japs and Germans. That's why we are fighting them: because we ain't Japs and Germans.

They bury the American officer. The old sergeant has been trained all his life to be a good sergeant, to take command when his officer dies like this. But he has spent so many years training for this moment, that he never actually had time to believe the moment would come. But he is doing the best he can. But he is old, his habits and thinking are fixed and professionally military. The younger men, amateur soldiers, civilians who have had to become soldiers simply to save the world, and will stop being soldiers as soon as the world is safe, think faster than he does. But he is doing the best he can, and the others help him along.

Someone brings up the fact that there is no chaplain to bury the officer. All the sergeant knows to do is to read his manual to find out what to do about it. Finally Akers says his father was a minister in Alabama; he has had to listen to so many sermons that he can probably do one. He says defiantly that he has a Bible; is a little shamed of it.

> **AKERS**   I got a Bible. *(defiantly)* I ain't ashamed of it neither.

> **LOUGHTON**   *(quietly)* Why should you be?

Akers reads the service. The men begin to fill the grave; the Italian takes one of the shovels in his turn, insists on it. As the mound of sand grows on the grave, we PAN to the shovels; the sound of the shovels becomes the beat of the Freedom Train in—

DISSOLVE TO:

Clumsy shovels filling a grave in China. It is the grandson of Mama Mosquito, after a Jap air raid, Chinese peasants mourning about the graves.

We tell the Mama Mosquito story: the moving by hand of an entire munitions factory, piecemeal back into the hills where the Japs can't bomb it, on to where General Chiang decorates her.

FADE OUT.

As FADE IN begins, the rollicking, tinkling, merry sound of Akers' dulcimer is heard.

FADE IN

Several of the men are gathered about America's pallet, listening while Akers plays the dulcimer. The German officer and the Italian are in b.g. under guard now. The Italian is interested in the music, the method, tune, etc. The German is still cold, sneering, sardonic. Akers finishes his piece.

> **BATTSON**   *(interested)* I used to play a banjo, myself.

He takes the dulcimer, plays and sings "Porterhouse Sadie." The Italian is interested.

ITALIAN I could also play once. *(reaches for dulcimer)* You permit?

They let the Italian have the dulcimer. He begins to pick at a tune.

BATTSON *(to America)* The smoke here can probably beat us all. Can't you move your hands even?

But America cannot. Now they notice that the Italian is trying to play "Porterhouse Sadie." Battson helps him; soon they are all singing it as the Italian gets the swing.

In the middle of this, Reagan enters. He has just made another round of his sentries. He is worried. He shows it. He is not afraid; he simply wants to run his command as the Articles of War say it should be run; he is now involved with some men who at heart are civilians and who refuse to take the Articles of War as seriously as all Reagan's life has taught him they should be taken. He wants to know what they are doing, wasting their time with a damn banjo. Somebody, kidding him, suggests that he look in his book about the matter. He starts to do so before he realizes he is being kidded. (Perhaps at this point somebody asks when they are going to start back, get to hell out of here before the Germans come in.)

ANOTHER He'll have to look in the book for that too.

They ride him a little. He says he is still running the party, and in effect, if they want to waste their time playing a banjo, at least they can play something decent, that their mothers could listen to, etc. They take him at his word, Battson takes the dulcimer, all join him as he plays "When Johnny Comes Marching Home." This scene should build up to a definite lift; young men who may not even see tomorrow, playing the old tune about when they will march triumphant through the village streets of America. (One here will have a cheap tin flute; another simulates a drum.)

The tune ends.

A SOLDIER Well, that's what we'll do when the fighting's over. We all know that. But what I want to know is, what are we fighting for while the fighting still goes on?

They make different suggestions, half serious, half kidding. It is not that they don't know, but rather as if they were a little ashamed of being serious about it. They say, "Freedom," "Liberty," "Souvenirs," etc. One says he's waiting for the captured beautiful women, has seen none yet, though. Another says he didn't want to come to Africa at all, but since he is here, he would like to have a lion cub to take back home with him.

Battson is an intelligent man, a college man, who has traveled, read, etc. He turns to Akers.

> **BATTSON**   Folks in your country probably thought they were going to fight the Yankees again, didn't they?

> **AKERS**   Well, it ain't that bad, not this time. It happened in 1918 though.

He tells the story of the man who brought his son to the draft board in Vicksburg in 1918, the two of them having walked almost a hundred miles from the back swamps, and told the chairman how he heard they were fighting the Yankees again and he had brought his boy to help out.

> **A SOLDIER**   But sure enough, what are we fighting for?

> **AKERS**   *(shy, does not want to look soft, etc.)* Well, this is what I heard one night at home. I was possum hunting, it was night, in the woods, an old church—niggers—

SOUND TRACK

Sound of Freedom Train.
Music from "Cantata."

1st SOLO
They tell a story about that train,
They say that Lincoln wasn't on that
    train;
When that train started on its trip that
    day,
Abraham Lincoln was miles away.

SPOKEN
Yes, sir, down in Alabama
In an old wooden church,
Didn't have no paint,
Didn't have no floor,
Didn't have no glass in the windows . . .

NEGRO WOMAN
Great God Almighty, Lord.

SCREEN

DISSOLVE begins.

SHOT of moving 1865 train.

                                DISSOLVE.

SHOT of small, shabby Negro church.

1ST SOLO
Just a pulpit and some wooden benches,
And Mr. Lincoln sitting in the back,
Listening to the sermon,
Listening to the singing.   DISSOLVE TO:

Int. of church. Negro preacher and congregation, country men and women and children, Negroes, laborers, music from the "Cantata."

CONGREGATION   Amen, brother, amen.

PREACHER
You may bury me in the east,
You may bury me in the west,
But I'll hear that trumpet sound in the morning.

WOMAN   Yes, Lord, in the morning!

PREACHER   *(chanting)*
This evening, brothers and sisters,
I come in the holiest manner,
To tell how he died.
He was a-laying there,
His blood on the ground;
And while he was laying there the sun riz,
And it recognized him;
Just as soon as the sun recognized him
It clothed itself in sackcloth and went down!
Went down in mourning!

He was a-laying there,
And the sky turned dark,
And seven angels lepp over the battlements of glory
And come down to get him;
And just when they come near him, he riz,
Yes, Lord, he riz up and walked down among us,
Praise God,
Walked back down among his people!

WOMAN   Lord, he's living now!

PREACHER
We got a new land!
Ain't no riding boss with a whip,
Don't have no backbiters,

Liars can't go, cheaters can't go,
Ain't no deputy to chain us,
No high sheriff to bring us back!

WOMAN It's a new land!

PREACHER
You may bury me in the east,
You may bury me in the west,
But I'll hear that trumpet sound in the morning!

CONGREGATION In the morning, Lord! In the morning!

SOUND TRACK	SCREEN

1st SOLO
Down in Alabama,
Nothing but a pulpit and some wooden
 benches,
And Mr. Lincoln sitting in the back, away
 in the back.

DISSOLVE BEGINS.

CHORUS
A lonesome train on a lonesome track,
Seven coaches painted black,
A slow train, a quiet train,
Carrying Lincoln home again.

Montage of 1865 train running. Over it the station signs follow one another: Washington, Baltimore, Harrisburg, Philadelphia.

Washington, Baltimore, Harrisburg,
 Philadelphia,
Coming into New York town,
You could hear the whistle for miles
 around,
Crying, Free—dom!
   Free—dom!

Mourning and anxious crowd on station platform.

SPOKEN
From Washington to New York people
 lined the tracks.

CHORUS
A strange crowd,
A quiet crowd,
Nobody wanting to talk out loud.

SPOKEN
At lonely country crossroads there were
 farmers
And their wives and kids standing for
 hours;
In Philadelphia the line of mourners ran
 three miles.

CLOSE SHOT of an old Negro woman, decently dressed, but poor, in shawl and

OLD WOMAN
Mr. Lincoln! Mr. Lincoln! You ain't dead,
    Mr. Lincoln! You can't be dead!

COTTON SPECULATOR *(turns away)*
Well, boys, I'll buy the drinks.

widow's bonnet, at the coffin. Behind her,
a cotton speculator, a gambler type, in
frock coat, etc.

CHORUS
For there were those who cursed the
    union,
Those who wanted the people apart;
While the sound of the freedom guns
    still echoed,
Copperheads struck at the people's
    heart.

Montage of stations, train.

Battle SHOT, flag.

SPOKEN
I've heard it said,
I've heard tell that when that train
    pulled into New York town,
Mr. Lincoln wasn't around.

Montage: Lincoln's figure superposed on
train, stations, etc.

1st SOLO
He was where there was work to be
    done,
Where there were people having fun.

SPOKEN
When that funeral train pulled into New
    York

DISSOLVE TO:

1st SOLO
Lincoln was down in a Kansas town
Swinging his lady round and round!

A country barn dance, rustic, 1860–80,
two fiddlers, a triangle, a banjo; on crude
platform, dressed in Sunday clothes, a
caller. The dancers are farmers, young,
middle-aged, the old people sitting in
chairs or on benches along the wall. Lincoln's figure is superposed, or he is one of
the dancers maybe.

CALLER
Swing your maw, your paw,
Don't forget the girl from Arkansaw!

CHORUS *(off scene)*
When young Abe Lincoln came to dance,
Those Kansas boys didn't have a chance!

Lincoln as a young man, dancing, taking
the prettiest girl. Lincoln and Fonda here.

CALLER
Grab your gal and circle four,
Make sure she ain't your mother-in-law!
Now, promenade!
Feed your chickens, milk your cows,
Have all the fun the law allows!

CHORUS *(off scene)*
They were dancing people, you could
  see,
They were folks who liked being free,
The men were tall and the girls were
  fair,
They had fought for the right to be
  dancing there!

A couple, young man in remnants of
1865 uniform, with a pretty girl. The
man is Fonda.

CALLER *(points the couple out)*
Pretty little gal, around she goes,
Swing your lady for do-si-do!

The couple follow the caller's directions.

First to the right, and then to the left,
And then to the gal that you love best.

The young man surprises his partner,
kisses her before she can resist; the others
react, applaud.

Duck for the oyster, dig for the clam,
Pass right through to the promised land!

CHORUS *(off scene)*
Those Kansas boys didn't have a chance
When young Abe Lincoln came to dance.

Lincoln dancing. (Lincoln in this sequence is young, is Fonda.)

DISSOLVE TO:

Int. the house. Akers is banging out his merry tune on the
dulcimer, America lying on his pallet, others gathered around,
including the Italian and German, Loughton, Battson, etc.
Reagan enters. He is worried, realizes his responsibility, is trying to carry on as best he can, as his officer would expect of
him. He shows that he cannot understand how they can be so
carefree, etc. He thinks they should not be playing and singing
profane songs. They still ride him a little, kid him. Someone
suggests that he look in his manual, the official Articles of War,
to find out what to do. He takes the book out, realizes he is
being kidded. But there is one point on which he is right. He
examines his watch. It says a few seconds to twelve. He notifies
Battson to get ready to take over the guard with his squad.

Somebody brings up the matter of when they will go back, get
out of this possible and very probable trouble. Reagan says,
Never mind that, he is in command now, etc. Loughton says he
will take a spell as guard. Someone says he can't, he is a member
of another army, a foreigner. They are still kidding Reagan.
Someone tells him to get his book out and see what the answer
to this is. He is about to do so, remembers his watch again,
orders Battson to take his squad and relieve Fonda.

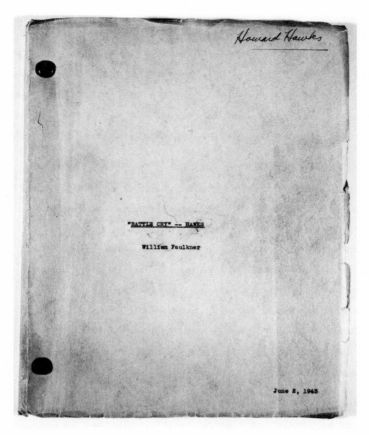

Howard Hawks

"BATTLE CRY" -- HAWKS

William Faulkner

June 2, 1943

5. Howard Hawks's copy of expanded treatment

Battson calls his men out, goes with them. Loughton goes along with them. Akers starts to play the dulcimer again. Reagan turns on him, tells him to shut up that noise. Akers reminds Reagan that he does not belong to Reagan's command and that Reagan has no authority over him. Reagan knows this to be true, is on the point of looking into his book again, finally says he has enough authority to stop the damn noise, anyway. Akers asks him what he can play then. They finally compromise on a tune which Akers begins to play, softly. Reagan departs to change the guard.

Never mind that, he is in command now, etc. Loughton says he will take a spell as guard. Someone says he can't, he is a member of another army, a foreigner. They are still kidding Reagan. Someone tells him to get his book out and see what the answer to this is. He is about to do so, remembers his watch again, orders Battson to take his squad and relieve Fonda.

Battson calls his men out, goes with them. Loughton goes along with them. Akers starts to play the dulcimer again. Reagan turns on him, tells him to shut up that noise. Akers reminds Reagan that he does not belong to Reagan's command and that Reagan has no authority over him. Reagan knows this to be true, is on the point of looking into his book again, finally says he has enough authority to stop the damn noise, anyway. Akers asks him what he can play then. They finally compromise on a tune which Akers begins to play, softly. Reagan departs to change the guard.

Exterior, night. Reagan relieves the sentries. Nobody takes it seriously but him; he is doing the best he can, doing the job that all his years of service as a professional soldier have trained him to do. At last the government is getting some return for the $125.00 per month they have been paying him ever since he became a top sergeant.

When the guard is relieved, Loughton and Fonda remain together. We DISSOLVE from them to

must know 2 things Loughton does not want to talk about English incident & woman in

6. Page 83 of Hawks's copy of expanded treatment

Exterior, night. Reagan relieves the sentries. Nobody takes it seriously but him; he is doing the best he can, doing the job that all his years of service as a professional soldier have trained him to do. At last the government is getting some return for the $125.00 per month they have been paying him ever since he became a top sergeant.

When the guard is relieved, Loughton and Fonda remain together. We DISSOLVE from them to—

England, 1941. Fonda and two other American privates are walking along the street. They have the typical new American soldier's reaction to England: a blend of astonishment and annoyance and a little contempt. They don't know the people yet, apparently never will, and don't want to. Traffic is on the wrong side of the street, going in the wrong direction. Bars are closed at certain hours of the day, there is no ice. You can enter certain restaurants only if you are an officer or wear a black tie, and the food is not much when you do. The town is choked with soldiers doing nothing. There are bomb craters which have been there for years; in America they would have been filled up and all traces removed in 24 hours. Now and then there are a few curling wisps of high thin vapor, which they are told are Spitfires shooting down bombers. But otherwise there is no war at all.

They have heard of a place called Bucktown, where something is going to happen at eleven o'clock this morning. They don't know what it is, partly because English people seem to want to tell foreigners little enough to begin with, and don't even seem to know how to tell even that little.

> **FIRST (FONDA)**   How can there be a place called a town in the middle of a city?

> **SECOND**   There's a place called Greenwich Village in the middle of New York City.

> **THIRD**   That's nothing here. The city of London is just a little square of land in the middle of London town, like putting Manhattan Island in the middle of Brooklyn and calling it New York.

SECOND   I'm going to ask this cop.

They are approaching a policeman, who is talking to an RAF officer, a boy of about 18. He doesn't look old enough to be an officer, and the single stripe around his cuff is so near the color of his uniform that they don't pay any attention to it. He doesn't look anywhere as near responsible and powerful as an American transport-line pilot, nor half as military as a hotel doorman.

> **SECOND AMERICAN**   *(to policeman)* Morning, officer. How do you get to Bucktown?
>
> **RAF OFFICER**   I'm going there. I'll show you.
>
> **FONDA**   Much obliged. What is it?
>
> **RAF OFFICER**   What is it?
>
> **FONDA**   Yes, Bucktown.
>
> **POLICEMAN**   *(scandalized)* What is Bucktown?
>
> **RAF OFFICER**   *(turns on)* Come along. We're already late.

They go along with him. He walks briskly on, leading them. Battson approaches. They know Battson. But he has been in England longer, has visited Europe before. He recognizes the officer's uniform, salutes smartly. The other Americans see this with amazement. For the first time they realize that the youth is an officer. Battson wants to know where they are going. They tell him to Bucktown. Now Battson is amazed, wants to know why they think they can get in. The other three Americans are amazed at this idea. The RAF officer tells them all to come along, it will be all right, etc. They all follow him now.

> **FONDA**   *(to Battson)* What is this Bucktown, anyway?
>
> **BATTSON**   No. I'm not going to tell you. It's going to be too good. Jesus, you wouldn't have believed it.

They approach Buckingham Palace. Fonda and the other two begin to get it, but they never quite until they actually are watching the investiture. But they are a little more sober as they see other British soldiers and sailors and airmen converging to enter, all looking too young to be veterans of a war, and many civilians: oldish men and women whom they do not know are the parents of men about to be decorated, and young women who are the widows of dead men.

FONDA *(to RAF officer)* Say, Lieutenant, what is this?

RAF OFFICER Mister'll do. It's a gonging.

FONDA A gonging?

BATTSON *(to Fonda)* Shut up, you fool!

The RAF officer goes on. They follow. They approach the gate with its Guards sentries, joining the entering crowd. Among the crowd is a couple, middle-aged, Albert and Mary Loughton. They are in their Sunday best, show grief and sorrow. When they see the Americans, Mrs. Loughton shows emotion.

MRS. LOUGHTON *(grasps husband's arm, stares at Fonda with painful intensity)* Albert! Albert!

He soothes her, restrains her from running forward, until the Americans have gone on.

The Americans did not notice the Loughtons. They follow the RAF officer on, seeing the Guards sentries, then the palace functionaries, and gradually realize where they are.

(Can we show a royal investiture, with the king?)

They are in a long hall, among the civilians, the mothers and fathers and wives and widows. The king enters, mounts dais, with aides, equerries, etc., behind him. The men receiving decorations enter, the citation for each is read, the decoration given, the man goes on. They are soldiers, sailors, airmen, civilians who have done extraordinary jobs as wardens, etc. The RAF officer advances and stops facing the king.

CHAMBERLAIN Pilot Officer Ackroyd.

On his right breast he wears also a set of U.S. Navy pilot's wings. The CAMERA PANS to the American wings.

DISSOLVE THROUGH TO:

The HORNET (WASP?) off Malta. It is ferrying a load of Spitfires to Malta. It sails up within the fighters' flying range, then the fighters take off from the flight deck to fly to the island to reinforce it; they are badly needed. One of the pilots is Ackroyd. The Spitfires take off. When he is airborne, Ackroyd discovers that he cannot switch from his take-off mercury-charged tank to his cruising tank. He cannot reach the island.

The Spitfire will take off from the carrier's deck, but it travels too fast to land on it. He radios back what has happened. The flight officer radios back to him to jump. If he does this, he will throw away the desperately-needed fighter. He radios back he is going to land on the carrier. They tell him not to be a fool, to jump. This time his radio does not answer at all. They realize that he intends to try to make the landing. They try to wave him off, but he is still coming in. The carrier picks up all the speed it can, into the wind, the asbestos crash crew stand to, etc. Ackroyd winds flaps and gear down, does everything he can to slow up the Spitfire, makes a miraculous spot landing just over the stern, locks his brakes and scoots up the short flight deck with the rubber burning off his locked tires, and stops inches away from the crash barrier at the bows. Thus he has saved his aeroplane. He gets out of the aeroplane cursing his clumsiness because he overshot the spot he intended to touch his wheels by at least eight feet. Then and there the American pilots on the carrier run up, one of them rips his wings off his tunic and pins them on Ackroyd.

DISSOLVE TO:

Ackroyd at attention facing the king while the aide reads the citation. As he reads it, we DISSOLVE to the action itself:

A freighter in the North Sea, in convoy, British. The British have begun to equip the flagship in each convoy with a fighter aeroplane on a catapult. When a German reconnaissance-bomber, a long-range Focke-Wulf with four engines and a big range from shore, appears, the fighter is catapulted off to meet and destroy it before it has time to guide a submarine or bombers to the convoy. The fighter of course cannot land on the ship again and is not expected to. The pilot simply bails out when his job is done and lets the fighter crash. The convoy cannot stop for him, so he takes his chances of parachuting near enough to be caught up in passing, or to float in his Mae West until someone else finds him, which usually doesn't happen.

This pilot is Ackroyd. When we dissolve to them, Ackroyd and the ship's officers are in a sort of caucus: the grizzled captain and mate, who know nothing about the damned aeroplane, and a junior officer and others. Ackroyd has something on his mind. He is not against going up, he doesn't want to, no sane man would want to. But it must be done, someone must fly the damned kite and the government sent him to do it, is paying him to do it, etc.

CAPTAIN What's the matter, then? Can't you fly the aeroplane?

ACKROYD Oh, sure. Anybody can fly a damned Hurricane—who is unlucky enough to be put on them.

Finally, and with a great deal of diffidence, and with what they realize is shame, something he hates to admit, he says that he doesn't want to get wet. They press him further; how did he expect to help that when he came to sea? Finally, he admits that he can't swim and is afraid of water. He has spilled the beans now, and might as well shoot the whole business. So he confesses. He was a boy scout, but never could make the first class because he never could learn to swim, was afraid of water. This time was only a year or so back, since he is now only 18. So he just doesn't want to get wet, find himself alone in a whole lot of ocean. Of course, he will do it if he has to, since that's what the Air Ministry has sent him to do. But he has been talking with the third officer and the bosun, and they thought—He bogs down here, while the grizzled captain and the mate glare at him.

CAPTAIN Thought what?

Ackroyd still hangs fire. The captain turns to the third officer, who seems a little readier to talk, or maybe just old enough to know what Ackroyd can't seem to say.

CAPTAIN What the hell is this, Mr. Clifton?

The third officer tells it. The bosun will help, and McKenzie, the third engineer, will help too. They wish to rig a platform, as large as they can, with crash barriers, nets, etc., and tow it behind the ship for Ackroyd to try to land on.

> **CAPTAIN** *Try* to land on? Don't you realize we haven't enough stuff in this ship to build a platform larger than about forty feet?
>
> **THIRD OFFICER** Yes, sir. We thought about that.
>
> **CAPTAIN** And that boy wants to try to land a damned aeroplane traveling 100 miles an hour, on a forty-foot platform towing behind my ship?
>
> **THIRD OFFICER** *(to Ackroyd)* Is that right?
>
> **ACKROYD** Oh, sure. A hundred, easy. I can slow it down to a hundred and twenty anyway. Then I won't have to get into the water.
>
> **CAPTAIN** Why, the thing will blow up and take fire.
>
> **ACKROYD** At least, I won't get wet.
>
> **THIRD OFFICER** *(to captain)* You see, sir, if it works, we can save the pilot every time, at least.

The captain sees this point, gives his permission but washes his hands beyond authorizing material, men to contrive the platform and the tow.

Ackroyd and the Third have plenty of help. The whole crew wants to volunteer. Between them and the engineer and the bosun, they contrive the platform and test it, let it over the stern and pay out cable, at the end of which the platform looks little larger than a postal card.

> **ENGINEER** *(dubiously)* It looks like an orange crate, doesn't it?
>
> **ACKROYD** Sure. I bet it's a good deal larger than just forty feet. And look here—I was rotten at match, but don't I remember something like this—that the area in which a traveling object must stop increases in direct ratio of traveling object's decreasement in speed?

They watch him.

    ENGINEER   What drivel are you trying to talk now?

    ACKROYD   *(eagerly)* Look—

                                                    WIPE TO:

Ackroyd, the Third, the engineer, bosun and crew are rigging an auxiliary flap on the aeroplane. It will work but once, and cannot be retracted, and it will have but one test and it may throw the aeroplane completely and irrevocably out of control for good, so that it will crash.

    ACKROYD   Well, if it does, I'll just get wet, which I'd do anyway.

    ENGINEER   But you'd jump first, then. My brother is a pilot; I know a little about these things. I know what happens to them when they strike water with that air-scoop open under the nose. They don't even stop to crash. They keep right on flying until they strike bottom land. And land's a good way from here—anywhere up to five miles. By that time you'll be a good deal more than just wet. Because if this thing don't work, you won't have time to jump.

They have him cornered. They are grave, sober, watching him as he hunts for a comeback, an out. He can't find one.

    ACKROYD   All right. Maybe so. But I'm not going to get in that damn ocean in a Mae West.

The Focke-Wulf is sighted, the alarm given, Ackroyd in the fighter is catapulted off the ship, engages and shoots down the German, returns to the ship. The platform is cast off and paid out, the ship turns into the wind and gets up as much speed as possible, Ackroyd makes the landing. His aeroplane goes crazy as soon as he puts down the homemade flaps, but he manages to control it and stops it on the platform. I imagine it will be a wreck when he does so, but with salvageable parts, instruments, guns, engine parts saved, which is better than to have let it crash into the sea. And the pilot is saved. The platform is pulled in, the aeroplane and Ackroyd are hoisted to the deck without having to stop or change course much.

DISSOLVE TO:

ALTERNATE: (TO BE USED IN PLACE OF PRECEDING SEQUENCE)

Ackroyd facing the king. We need not show the king: only Ackroyd at attention while the aide finishes reading the citation. A hand extends the medal, Ackroyd shakes the hand, steps back (if he wears his hat at an investiture, he will salute; otherwise he will right or left turn), and exits. The aide's voice calls: "Mr. and Mrs. Albert Loughton."

Mr. and Mrs. Loughton, the middle-aged grieving couple who were staring at Fonda, appear with a chamberlain. The aide's voice begins to read this citation. As he reads, we DISSOLVE through Mr. and Mrs. Loughton to the action:

It is their dead son. He was a sailor. The scene is at night, in an enemy harbor, perhaps Norway. A German warship lies in the harbor. An English destroyer is off the coast. An officer has volunteered to disable the German ship's rudder, so that it can be bombed or attacked by a British vessel large enough to handle it. He is an amateur, a reserve officer, not a professional. As we see his crew, we realize that they are just civilians who are serving their country in an emergency; not trained war-making men at all. One is an old man who ran a fishing boat with his son; a German fighter, for no military purpose whatever, strafed it one day and killed the son, and the old father went on the warpath. Another had been a lighthouse tender, another had been a Thames waterman, another a steward on a fine Atlantic liner, etc. John Loughton had been an apprentice shipwright. The officer had been an amateur yachtsman and a London architect.

They have only the crudest tools. They are a ship's dinghy and some dynamite. They load the dinghy, steal past the mine field and over the nets and into the harbor, approach the German ship to fasten the dynamite to the rudder and so disable it. The whole affair is timed. As soon as the dynamite explodes, the Germans will know something is up and they will bring up enough opposition to stop the British bombing attack before it ever begins. So, once the affair starts, it must go through, not only to destroy the ship, but to save the British bombers, which will have to fly from Scotland.

The architect-officer has made his plans to explode the dynamite at a zero hour. The dinghy has passed the mine field and the patrol boats, is approaching the warship when by bad luck it is discovered. They cannot turn back. Patrol boats and searchlights from the warship are hunting it. It manages to reach the ship. It is under fire now; any moment a bullet may strike the dynamite and the whole thing will go up. One or two men are already hit, the dinghy is sinking. Once under the counter of the warship they are reasonably safe from fire. But the dinghy will never float them away. They tie the dinghy to the rudder, cap and fuse the dynamite. The commander orders all the men to take to the water and try to swim ashore, to get as far away as possible before he lights the fuse. When the men have swum away, the officer finds that Loughton has not gone. Loughton says quietly that he can't swim, for the officer to go on and leave him to light the fuse. The officer refuses; Loughton says the officer can make it ashore, get the men out, and blow the rudder off another German warship some day. The officer orders Loughton to take an oar, leap as far as he can from the sinking dinghy and hold on until he reaches him. Loughton obeys. The officer lights the fuse, dives from the dinghy, swims to Loughton, tries to carry Loughton as far from the ship as he can. But he cannot go fast enough; Loughton realizes the explosion will get both of them. The officer is expecting nothing, so suddenly Loughton breaks free, kicks himself away into the darkness, shouts, "Go on, sir!" to the officer. The officer is still trying to find Loughton when the explosion goes off. After the turmoil of the water subsides, the officer comes to the surface, regains strength; as he is about to swim away, he finds Loughton's dead body floating. While he examines it, the sound of the approaching bombers begins. The officer waits to remove Loughton's identity disc, swims away, the bombs falling on the warship behind him.

DISSOLVE TO:

Mr. and Mrs. Loughton facing the king as the aide's voice finishes the citation. The hand extends the decoration. Mrs.

Loughton takes it, fumbling. The hand is still extended. Mrs. Loughton does not know what to do.

LOUGHTON   Come, Mary; shake it. *(to the king out of scene)* We ain't used to this sort of thing, sir.

KING'S VOICE   But we're doing pretty well under it, Mr. Loughton.

LOUGHTON   Thank you, sir.

Mrs. Loughton shakes the hand, then Loughton shakes it, bows clumsily. The chamberlain touches Loughton's arm; the couple move with him out of scene.

AIDE'S VOICE   Air Vice Marshall Simon.

(NOTE: This is the Gilpatric story, printed in *Collier's*.[6] I don't know who owns the rights, or if they are available. I include it here under condition that the story can be gotten.)

A figure begins to emerge facing the off-scene king. It begins as a ghost, diaphanous, solidifies into a man of forty-five or fifty, in uniform, a handsome man, a Jew, an aristocrat, member of one of the old Jewish families who have been prominent in finance, government, diplomacy, in England for generations. He wears an observer's single wing and ribbons from the Great War and from this one.

AIDE'S VOICE   Squadron Leader Levin.

A second figure materializes beside the first; a man of twenty-five or thirty, a younger Simon, of the same class, background. He wears pilot's wings and a D.FC. ribbon from this war.

AIDE'S VOICE   Flying Officer Lowenstein.

A third figure materializes beside the other two. He is twenty-five. He, too, came from the same class and kind as the others. He wears no wings, but a ribbon from this war.

AIDE'S VOICE   Pilot Officer Van Tauck.

A fourth figure materializes beside the others. He is maybe twenty. You would find him by the dozen at Oxford or Cam-

6. Guy Gilpatric, "A Bomber Goes Back Home," *Collier's*, 106 (February 8, 1941), 11ff.

bridge in peace time. He wears pilot's wings, but no ribbon. (Not in the Gilpatric story.) Now the aide seems at a loss. His voice falters, hems and haws.

> AIDE'S VOICE   And ah—ah—Mister ah—Ignatius Cohen, pawnbroker, Whitechapel—

The fifth figure materializes. It is a man of thirty-five, shabby, not very clean, a little fat; a stage Jew almost. We hold them for a while.

DISSOLVE TO:

The same five men in Simon's office. An orderly has just brought Cohen in.

> SIMON   *(to orderly)* Thanks. See that the door is closed, will you?

> ORDERLY   Yes, sir.

The orderly exits, sound of door. The three younger men look at Cohen while Simon re-reads a letter on his desk, then destroys the letter, looks up at Cohen too, who has been waiting quietly.

> SIMON   *(to Cohen)* How did you know about this?

> COHEN   *(with accent)* In my business, ve hear.

> SIMON   But do you talk? You understand what it would mean—

> COHEN   If ve talked, vould ve haf a business?

> SIMON   Yes. Quite.—Why do you want to go?

> COHEN   Look at my nose.

The Gilpatric story from here on, with the exception that Cohen is aboard. Intelligence knows that at noon on a certain day, Hitler's car will drive up to some public building in Berlin, and Hitler will get out of it and enter the building. The RAF have brought down a medium German bomber and rebuilt it. Under Simon's plan, with the Prime Minister's sanction, the bomber is at a hidden field. It is loaded to capacity with explosive. Secrecy must be observed, yet they can't risk being shot down by British planes before they can cross the channel. Thus the plan is a hair-trigger affair to get the bomber with its German markings clear of England. Nobody knows what they plan to do save the essential ones themselves, the Prime Minister, etc.

With his volunteer crew, and Cohen, Simon takes off from England, runs a gauntlet of British fire in which Van Tauck is wounded and Cohen spends the rest of the trip nursing him, and reaches France-Belgium, where German fighters take them to be what they seem. They reach Berlin at the time set, see the car approaching the point where it will stop. Levin, the pilot, points the nose of the bomber straight down at it.

> **SIMON** (*into interplane communication which the others all hear*) We're going down, my friends. Goodbye to you, and sleep well.

> **LOWENSTEIN'S VOICE** Valhalla tonight, Marshall?

> **SIMON** Apostate.

He switches off the interplane communication, turns to Levin, who is advancing the throttles, trimming the props out as the dive increases, and the speed, and the tiny figures below begin to take alarm and then to run for shelter.

> **SIMON** (*to Levin*) Right on in, Horace! Right on in, boy!

> **LEVIN** (*ruddering onto the scurrying frantic people, now quite near and growing larger at terrific speed*) Right, sir. Hold your hat, as the Americans say—

Crash, explosion; as it fades, we—

> DISSOLVE TO:

(NOTE: In the sequence of the dynamiting the warship's rudder, we will see why Mrs. Loughton was so moved at the sight of Fonda, the American soldier whom she had never seen before. Her dead son, John, looked like Fonda. He could be either identical and both of them could be Fonda, or the resemblance could merely be close enough for a grieving mother and father to see it, and no one else. I think this would be more effective.)

They have left Buckingham Palace. Again Mrs. Loughton is hurrying along, anxious, watching Fonda, while Loughton, who sees the resemblance, too, tries to restrain her, for decorum in public, and because there is nothing that can come of it, of the fact that a casual American soldier who may be gone tomorrow happens to look like their dead son.

LOUGHTON   Now, Mother. Now, Mother.

MRS. LOUGHTON   But he looks exactly like John! See!

LOUGHTON   I know. I know.

MRS. LOUGHTON   I must speak to him! He will get away.

Mr. Loughton restrains her, says he will do the speaking. She watches anxiously as Loughton overtakes the American soldiers; the strong, healthy young men from the western world which the war so far has not touched save from across the sea. He stops them. They look at him with surprise: a snuffy little man whom none of them would have looked at twice. He excuses himself, singles out Fonda, tells him what the matter is about, asks if he minds speaking to Mrs. Loughton.

Fonda's first reaction is, he doesn't want any of this. He is young, has seen little trouble, has a young man's dislike and distaste for what he thinks will be a tearful sentimental business. He is sorry for Mrs. Loughton, but just because she happens to think her dead son looks like him can't help her grief. But he is polite and courteous from his country breeding, so he agrees; best thing is to get it over with. His companions agree to wait for him while he accompanies Loughton back to where Mrs. Loughton is waiting.

But to Fonda's surprise, there are no tears, no sentiment to embarrass him. He merely sees a middle-aged woman who tells him quietly that he looks like their dead son; he is an ally whom they are glad to see. They would like to have him come and visit them, if he will. She tells him where they live: a village (will decide later just where) where her husband is the butcher. She says that maybe it will be dull for him, and perhaps he won't have time anyway, but just if he can and will, etc. (He recalls now having seen the couple when they received their son's medal this morning.)

When he returns to his companions, they want to know what it was. Fonda says, "Aw nothing. It's over now." He thinks he is relieved to have escaped the tears, and he has no intention whatever of going to see them and so risk the sentimentalizing which he was lucky enough to escape.

But as the next few days pass, he finds that he cannot forget the couple. He doesn't know why. He has learned a little more about England by this time, and apparently the whole little island is full of people like the Loughtons. Then suddenly it occurs to him that perhaps this is why he can't get them out of his mind. But he is still ashamed, feels a young man's shame over being considered sentimental, to tell his companions what he is thinking of. He just becomes quiet. They notice it, and that he is refusing to explain what is on his mind.

The same four of them have arranged to receive leave for the same weekend. They have made plans to go to London, have saved their pay for a big time. Fonda is acting more peculiar than ever. At the last minute he tells them he is not going. He will not lie, so he gives no explanation at all, but just ducks out, leaving them looking after him in amazed disgust.

He has already received an answer to his wire, saying the Loughtons will be glad to have him come; he has already packed to go and spend his leave with them. He goes to the little Sussex village. He sees the village which is typical of villages all over England. All the young men are gone as soldiers, all the surplus middle-aged men are in armament factories. All the young women above 18 are gone to factories. Only the necessary middle-aged men to keep the village going, and the mothers of children and the old, remain.

But nobody is downhearted about it, or even worried. They are too busy. Loughton is the village butcher. He had a good shop once. Now Fonda sees it with its cases almost empty and only the meagerest of rationed cuts necessary to life, in the ice boxes. The rear of it was once a warehouse, slaughterhouse. Now it is a factory, run by the women of the village. Mrs. Loughton works so many hours a day in it and she takes him there. He sees a dozen women's bicycles leaning against the wall, with baskets on the handlebars with packages in them where the owners have stopped to market. He passes an improvised nursery where the mothers leave their infants while they are working, in charge of a little girl of about twelve. He enters the factory.

It is a room containing pans and small boxes and a mixture of furniture: old garden chairs, deck chairs, broken pieces of once-fine furniture, and a tremendous pile of discarded rivets. He meets the manageress: a young woman whose name and picture used to be in all the smart papers and magazines as a horsewoman. She explains that the rivets have been gathered up from the floors of aircraft plants and are sent here to be sorted and cleaned to be used again, thus freeing skilled men for more important work. She explains how the women who do the sorting give as much time as they can; how they will put dinner on the stove to cook and then come to the shop to sort rivets until time to go back home and serve the meal.

He learns about the women whom he sees in overalls and old clothes, sorting the rivets. There is the rector's wife, the schoolmaster's wife, the wife of a local earl who is with the army in Africa, Mrs. Loughton, the wives of farmers, the postman, the local constable and the pub-keeper and blacksmith and garage owner and shopkeepers, etc. They are all ages: young women, mothers of the children in the nursery, middle-aged like Mrs. Loughton, and old. He is presented to one woman so old as to be deaf and almost blind.

> **MANAGERESS**   This is Mrs. Boggan. She's one of our best workers. She can't see any but the big rivets, so she never makes mistakes.

The manageress, Mrs. Wolfolk, is the wife of an RAF squadron leader now on duty. She is smart, attractive. She is sorting rivets, too, while she talks to Fonda. She asks him if he rides.

> **FONDA**   (*puzzled*) Ride?

She explains she means ride a horse. Fonda, the countryman, says he thought anybody could ride a horse, if he had to, didn't want to walk where he was going. Mrs. Wolfolk explains what she means. The local hunt will go out tomorrow morning; she invites him to come with them. He is still puzzled. She explains how it is one of the oldest hunts in England, that the men are all away and so the women are keeping it up: she is now temporary M.F.H.,[7] which, the idea of a woman being Master, probably makes the old founders of it turn in their graves. She explains how they are keeping up the hunt, the dogs and mounts, which means a lot of time and trouble and expense.

FONDA How can you afford it?

MRS. WOLFOLK We can't, really.

FONDA But you do?

MRS. WOLFOLK Of course.

She sorts the rivets; she seems to think she has explained it. Fonda is amazed. He is learning. He realizes that this, this preservation of a sporting club, is a part of the England which these people are fighting and suffering privation for, and that maybe this is one of the symptoms of what has made them tough, made them able, out of all western Europe, to resist the Germans. He accepts the invitation to go along.

He was wise enough to bring some of his army rations with him. Mrs. Loughton is pleased; they will save the good food for tomorrow's dinner: a celebration, because tomorrow her other son, Albert, Jr., will be home for a day's leave. She becomes suddenly diffident and shy, finally asks Fonda not to ask Albert anything about France or Dunkirk when they meet.

It is dusk. They are just finishing tea, the evening meal. A sound of aeroplanes begins. Mrs. Loughton pauses, looks up.

MRS. LOUGHTON Here they come.

They go outside and watch the evening bombing raid going over to bomb Germany. Fonda sees all along the street some of the women whom he had seen in the workshop, coming out to watch the bombers, too.

MRS. LOUGHTON There are 500,003 rivets in a Wellington. We always watch them pass and think that maybe some of our rivets are in them.

7. Master of Foxhounds.

When the bombers have gone, Mr. Loughton takes Fonda to the pub. Here he sees the men of the village and the surrounding farms, the men who are left, the little men, who have worked every day and had the hell bombed out of them every night and gone back to work the next day without enough sleep, who have seen the beer getting thinner and the tobacco more and more like hay and who haven't had all they wanted to eat at one time in three years and have got stubborner and stubborner and madder and madder and never will give up and their enemy knows they never will give up. The pub is 300 years old. A bomb struck it in 1940. There was not enough money to fully repair it, so the darts board is now turned around, outside the bar, with a shed built over it. Fonda hears the men talk after they have accepted him on Mr. Loughton's vouchment. He hears them criticize the government and the running of the war, talk atheism, anything they want to in freedom, and he realizes that this is democracy and that there is something in democracy, for all its waste and clumsiness in government, that can't be destroyed.

The next morning, Albert, Jr., is home. He is a corporal. Fonda seems to find a morose quality in him; apparently Albert anyway is not especially glad to see him. If Albert sees any resemblance in Fonda to his dead brother, it is something in Fonda's disfavor if anything. But Fonda remembers Mrs. Loughton's curious and troubled request that he not mention France, Dunkirk, etc., to Albert, and this may be partly it. But mostly it is the thing which Fonda and other American soldiers have already met with English soldiers, which was true in the other war: a bitterness due to the extreme difference in pay between American and British troops, and the feeling which English troops have that America stays out of the wars until they are practically won, and comes in just in time to divide the glory and the spoils. But Fonda has expected this. He has already determined that he will get along with Albert, whether Albert gets along with him or not; besides, he is the guest. So they are a little cold, distant, and quite polite to one another.

It is time for Fonda to meet the hunt. He asks if Albert is going, takes it for granted that Albert is. Albert says he doesn't belong to the hunt. In Fonda's country, when anybody went fox or coon hunting, anyone who wanted to or heard the dogs and horns went along. Albert tells him shortly that this is not America, that nobody but members and their invited guests ride with the Willingham Hunt. Mrs. Loughton stops the incipient trouble, tells Albert that this is not 1939 either and that he, Albert, knows he can go if he wants to. Albert quiets down, says he is not going, that he does not intend to spend a day's leave from riding a tank across country on such a busman's holiday as riding a horse across country. Mrs. Loughton says that at least Albert can go along and see the guest has a good mount.

The rest of this is the story of I.A.R. Wylie, in the *Saturday Evening Post*, title I forget, and date,[8] included under conditions that rights are optionable, as the Gilpatric story was included. The exception is the inclusion of Fonda in the story.

Fonda and Albert reach the meeting place. What Fonda sees is a curious enough sight to him, who had never seen a traditional Hunt meeting before, but it would be strange indeed to anyone who had, though Fonda misses the implications. A few of the horses are bred hunters, but most of them are farm and plow horses, and most of the riders are women, young women and middle-aged and old, whom he had seen in the rivet shop yesterday.

There are a few pink coats, but most of them wear anything and everything. The rector is there, in his dog collar. Mrs. Wolfolk is Master, one of the whips is a girl of 17, the other a boy of 12. Some of the older men who argued in the pub last night are there. Squadron Leader Wolfolk is present. Fonda is introduced by Mrs. Wolfolk, sees that Wolfolk has only one leg and wears a patch over one eye, but he still rides and flies combat with the artificial leg. (S/L Wolfolk is also added to the Wylie story.)

A slightly comic incident is Fonda and his horse. He has never ridden a flat saddle before; does not even remember ever hav-

8. I. A. R. Wylie, "A-Hunting We Will Go," *Saturday Evening Post*, 213 (July 27, 1940), 12ff.

ing seen one. He wants to know where his saddle is. Mrs. Wolfolk explains gravely that this is it, on the horse.

> **FONDA**   I thought that thing did look a little thin and lumpy for a blanket.

> **MRS. WOLFOLK**   A blanket? You ride under blankets in Illinois? Is it that cold there?

> **FONDA**   Nome. A blanket under the saddle.

> **MRS. WOLFOLK**   Oh. A pad.

> **FONDA**   Yessum. A saddle blanket.

He gets up. It seems to him that his knees are up under his chin. He looks soberly about at the others, who are grave and polite, courteous, not laughing at him. He sees their knees are the same way. But he is not used to it.

> **MRS. WOLFOLK**   *(to Albert)* If you please, Albert, will you lengthen the leathers for Mr. Fonda?

> **FONDA**   I'll do it. I expect I know better than Albert how I am used to them.

He gets down. He is careful, deliberate. They wait for him, courteously, while he stretches each leather against his arm, putting his finger tips against the slip-hook and measuring the leather against his arm (with that deliberation of Cooper taking the glare off his front sight with his wet thumb in *Sergeant York*[9]), then slipping the strap through the buckle and measuring again until he gets each one just right. Then he gets back up and sits in his country fashion, slack-rumped, his legs dangling practically, holding the reins in one hand as if he were holding a fishing pole. They ride off.

The Wylie story follows, in which this collection of war-harried people, trying to keep alive this part of England which this 500-year-old hunt represents, mostly women and old men and children and cripples, and the addition of the American soldier,

---

9. Gary Cooper (1901–1961), American film star, earned an Academy Award as the best actor of the year for his portrayal of Alvin York, an American World War I hero, in *Sergeant York* (1941).

without any arms at all, see a German parachute attack coming down and ride the armed enemy down one by one and capture them. We might play it that at first Fonda thinks this is what they have come out on horses for, and wonders for a minute at the folly of not bringing at least one gun, as at least one man in any fox hunt in America would have had. Then he is too busy. He does well. When the last German is captured, he is told that he has saved Squadron Leader Wolfolk's life, though he was too busy at the time to pay any attention. (Wolfolk's artificial leg gives way and he is thrown. A German with a Tommy gun is about to kill him when Fonda rides the German down.)

They return to the village with the prisoners. The village turns out, the wardens take charge of the prisoners. Albert is present when Wolfolk approaches Fonda.

> **WOLFOLK**   You did well. Let's hope this is an augur of your luck in this war. What's your branch?
>
> **FONDA**   Infantry, sir.
>
> **WOLFOLK**   A mistake. You don't need a rifle: all you need is a horse. Thanks, and goodbye, and good hunting to you.

Mrs. Wolfolk thanks him, too, as a man would, without sentiment. They depart, leaving Fonda and Albert.

> **ALBERT**   Come along, hero. Mother says dinner's ready.

Albert has expected Fonda to be a little blown up about the exploit. But Fonda is modest about it, almost dumb. As Albert realizes this, his attitude toward Fonda changes. But he still keeps Fonda on probation, waiting to see if Fonda will begin to throw his weight about. Fonda is not aware of this. He just acts his normal self. But suddenly he knows that things are all right between him and Albert; that is, Albert is no longer stiff with him. He realizes this when they enter the house and Albert says, "Come along to my room and we'll have a wash." Then he knows that things are all right between them.

They go up to Albert's room. Albert leads the way to a photograph on his dresser.

> **ALBERT**   There's still one member of the family you don't know yet. This is my sister. She's on Malta.

FONDA   On Malta? Can't she get home?

ALBERT   Get home? Why? She has a job there.

PAN to photograph of a young girl while they talk.

DISSOLVE THRU TO:

Malta. The same girl, about 20. She is working in an air raid shelter or a canteen or a hospital; hospital may be better. It is an underground shelter. An air raid is just over. Someone is putting a chalk mark on the wall, to keep the record of the raids. An argument starts that the marker has made a mistake. The argument is whether this is the 1526th or the 1527th raid. All join in it: the shelter women, wardens, patients who have been hurt, refugees, etc. An RAF pilot enters, still in flying kit, with Mae West, parachute harness, phone jacks, etc., dangling about him. He wants a cup of tea. He should know how many there have been; he has probably been in all of them, or he wouldn't be alive now. Someone asks him to settle the question.

RAF PILOT   Jesus, how do I know? Tea, please.

An American war correspondent (John Garfield type[10]) now comes creeping out of his hole. He is no more frightened than anyone else; he is clowning it a little. ("This is what you people call fun, is it? Then you can have it"—that sort of attitude.) He has been on the island (Malta) only a few days. As soon as he and Margaret Loughton saw one another, they were attracted. Garfield frankly went on the make for her. She knows it, but under the strain of war, bombing, life on Malta, this is all right with Margaret. She likes him, may love him in time. In any case, she is confident she can protect herself, or it will be all right anyway. He has persuaded her to give him the first date this evening, as soon as she is off duty. He hangs around, talking to the other people in the post, while she finishes her tour of duty. They will have a little time together before the next raid is due, if Margaret will just hurry and get done. If she will just hurry, he may have time to persuade and charm her to some remote

---

10. John Garfield (1913–1952), American screen actor, was under contract with Warner Bros. Pictures from 1938 to 1947. In 1943 he appeared in *Air Force,* a movie on which Faulkner worked briefly in September 1942.

privacy and maybe he can even lay her before the next raid. Of course he doesn't say this, but Margaret knows he is thinking it, she is excited somewhat herself. She teases him by seeming to delay, waste time. They have a short scene when she passes him, during which we know what Garfield is thinking and that Margaret knows it; there is a second, a touch, a look, and they know they are going to be really in love with one another and perhaps it will happen now, as soon as they are alone.

Margaret is through at last. Her relief comes, and she is free. She and Garfield leave, walking along the shore, while Garfield is hunting the private place which he desires. Now he realizes how densely crowded is this little island which the Luftwaffe has bombed month after month, three and four times a day, without being able to drive the people off it. Margaret knows what he is after, laughs at him, not to tease him but because she enjoys this pursuit which is an important part of the love which she realizes she is getting involved in, and is not sorry. There are people in sight, soldiers, peasants, etc. She stops, asks him, laughing at him, what he is waiting for. After a moment he comprehends, takes her in his arms, kisses her. She tells him the people on Malta don't mind them; the place is too crowded for anyone to be interested in anybody else's kissing. She is right. The people pay them no attention whatever; a little girl and an old man herding goats pass them and don't even look. Garfield looks at her; she watches him, still smiling a little but grave, too; he realizes she has surrendered.

 GARFIELD *(excited)* Come on. Let's go on.

She still taunts him a little.

 MARGARET There's plenty of time. The next raid is not due until ten after eight. You'll have plenty of time to run back to your hole.

 GARFIELD All right, damn it. I love you, then.

 MARGARET What do I do now? Thank you?

He takes her in his arms again; they kiss, then they go on.

They have found Garfield's private place. It is a cove in the hills above the sea. It is sunset. They are lying in each other's arms.

Margaret is still holding him off; there is plenty of time and she is enjoying her woman's right to being pursued before she surrenders. But they both know that the surrender is not far away.

Suddenly the air raid warning sounds through the island, an extra raid, an insult thrown in gratis; a raid two hours before the regular one is due. They are kissing. For a moment Margaret lies still. Then she flings Garfield back, strikes him across the face. While he watches in shocked surprise, she springs up, stands facing the sea across which the German bombers are already soaring, bombs falling, A.A. batteries firing. She has stood the 1527 regular ones, intends to stand the next 1527 regular ones. But this extra one is too much. She shakes her clenched fists at the passing bombers.

MARGARET   Damn you! Oh, damn you!

Garfield approaches her.

GARFIELD   Come on! Get under cover!

He takes her arm. She strikes him again, frantic, raging, crying, shakes her fists again at the bombers.

MARGARET   Damn you! Oh, damn you! I wish I were a man!

GARFIELD   Your men are doing all right! Get under cover!

MARGARET   I know they are! They're doing fine! But I would make one more! I could fly a Spit, too! *(to the bombers)* Damn you! Oh, damn you!

DISSOLVE TO:

Int. train compartment. Albert Loughton and Fonda are returning to London after their leave. They are friends now. Fonda knows that Loughton has accepted him. Loughton says something about France. Fonda realizes that Loughton is showing his friendship by giving a deliberate opening on this forbidden subject.

FONDA   I thought you didn't want to talk about France.

LOUGHTON   Mother warned you, eh? No, I don't. In 1938 I clerked in one of our branch banks in Paris. I knew a girl there. *(he stares out the window while he talks; talks in a dry, emotional voice)* She was a Midinette, worked for one of the big Rue de la Paix milliners. She was . . . no better than she should be. Had been. Poor, you know, had to. Before I knew her. But not after we . . . I was called up in '39, went back to France in Gort's army.[11] I went to Paris and saw her again. She had been . . . had waited for me, even poor, working for a few francs a week. I knew it. We were to be married. Then the break came and I got out at Dunkirk.

FONDA Oh. And she's dead now.

LOUGHTON *(stares out window)* I hope so.

FONDA You—what?

The train slows into the station. Loughton gets up.

LOUGHTON Here's Victoria. *(he turns to Fonda)* We're moving soon. You probably are too. Maybe we'll meet there—wherever we are going.

FONDA *(they shake hands)* Wherever we are going.

DISSOLVE TO:

The desert, a short distance from the house. Fonda and Loughton sit in the moonlight, talking. This is the first chance they have had to talk. They met hurriedly in the uproar of the battle, had only time to recognize one another. Then they were too busy getting out of the shellfire.

They had not expected to meet here, though one place is as good as another now, and for the next year or two, longer than that if it takes longer to get the fighting done so that young men can meet and talk in peace, with only work between the talks and decency and old age to look forward to and attain. They talk soberly and quietly; they know this is just an interlude and that tomorrow will bring danger and trouble, and in the future surely for both of them and for all here and for all the other young men about the world who are fighting to stay free, the

11. General John Standish, Lord Gort (1886–1946), was commander of the British Expeditionary Force in France in 1939–40.

chance (and for some the inevitability) of death. Fonda talks of England, the England which he had come to know by sheer chance, simply because a bereaved mother happened to think he resembled her dead son, which, except for that chance, he might not have known. He speaks of how he didn't know exactly what he was fighting for, even on the day he first put on uniform, and he says he believes that most people in his country still don't know.

> **FONDA** The country is so big. It's too big. Yours is different. It's easy for you to know what you are fighting for. You are fighting to keep an enemy out.

> **LOUGHTON** We are fighting for the same thing you are. For the same thing the Greeks died for without ever giving up, and that some of the French and Belgians and Poles and Scandinavians are still fighting for, and little hantles of starving men in the Balkans; Montenegro, Serbia; Croats and Slovenes. We are fighting for the right to keep on living in the way we want to live. Maybe that way is wrong, unjust to some, and will change later—

> **FONDA** *(interrupting)*—but you want to change it yourselves, without help. It was like a man of America's people, Joe Louis,[12] who said it about as well as I know, good enough, anyway: "There's a heap wrong with this world, but Hitler can't fix it."

> **LOUGHTON** Yes. That's right. We want to change it, make it better for all people. But while we are making it better for all, it suits us as it is, for all its folly and waste—

They talk on. Presently Loughton starts to tell Fonda about the French girl he loved, but before he can get into the story, a man approaches from the house calling Fonda's name.

> **FONDA** *(rises)* Here.

The soldier comes up. He carries an empty gas mask container.

> **SOLDIER** Reagan says to come on in. We're going to vote.

12. Joe Louis (1914–1981), popularly known as the "Brown Bomber," held the world's heavyweight boxing championship from 1937 to 1949.

FONDA Vote? On what?

SOLDIER On whether we stay on here or whether we pull out before daylight, while we can, and try to get back. He's waiting.

The soldier goes on.

FONDA *(to Loughton)* Come on.

LOUGHTON *(doesn't move)* Vote? The leader of your party is going to let his men vote on what they want to do next?

FONDA Why not?

LOUGHTON What sort of chap is he? I hope he shows brighter by daylight than he has tonight, or he'll never get you out of here.

FONDA *(quickly)* You're wrong there. He's a good man. Have you seen anything wrong with the way he has run this party since Lieutenant Whitesides died?

LOUGHTON *(rises)* No. Vote. By George, you're right. Maybe you Americans don't know yet what you are fighting for, and maybe you haven't quite learned yet how to do the fighting, but—No. That's wrong. I think you not only know what you're fighting for, whether you can say it or not, but you know the best way to do the fighting, too. Go on. Vote.

FONDA Aren't you coming? You're in this, too. That's right. I forget you don't belong with us. You can leave any time, can't you?

LOUGHTON So can you, apparently—if Reagan's going to let you vote on it. *(he goes on)* Come along. Let's cast a ballot. If it's too close, I'll make my two prisoners vote. That's good democratic politics, isn't it?

They go on.

The soldier with the gas mask container approaches the first sentry.

SOLDIER We're voting whether to stay or pull out while we can. Here.

He takes from his pocket two cartridges: a live shell and an exploded case, hands them to the sentry and holds out the gas mask container.

> **SOLDIER** If it's "Go," drop in the live one; if it's "Stay," drop in the hull. After I'm gone, you can throw the hull away. But if it's the live one, put it in your pocket because you'll need it.

The soldier shuts his eyes, turns his head aside. The sentry drops in one of the shells, the soldier shuts the container, goes on toward the next sentry. When he has gone, the sentry puts something into his pocket, resumes his watch.

Inside the house. Akers is banging away on the dulcimer, rapid and merry, playing "Black Market Sadie" beside America's pallet. The Italian and others are gathered around America as he lies on his back, his face sweating with pain but his eyes peaceful and quiet as he listens with rapt pleasure to the music. Fonda, Loughton, and Reagan enter.

> **REAGAN** (*to Akers—the strain of his responsibility showing more and more as the crisis approaches*) Stop that damn noise! How many times have I got to tell you?

> **AKERS** I don't know. I reckon until it finally gets through your skull that I ain't a member of your company and so you can't tell me to do nothing. Articles of War. Look it up. One of your corporals can tell you what page.

Reagan glares at Akers, marshalling words to speak. Battson interrupts.

> **BATTSON** (*to Akers*) Shut your trap. Since you don't belong to this party, we'll turn you out of here and you can walk around out there in the moonlight until you find Rommel.[13] Maybe he can tell you what page it's on. Put that damn thing down now, long enough for us to vote.

> **AKERS** Vote on what?

13. Field Marshall Erwin Rommel (1891–1944), the "Desert Fox," was the German commander in North Africa in 1941–42.

REAGAN On whether we stay here, or get out while we can and try to get back to the lines.

ITALIAN OFFICER *(eagerly)* Vote? Hah.

Nobody pays any attention to him.

AKERS What do we want to go anywhere for?

BATTSON *(to Reagan)* Why not tell them all at once?

REAGAN All right.

He turns. The men all face him, quiet, sober, attentive. Reagan unfolds his map. Battson and Fonda help him extend it.

REAGAN We are about here—

A MAN Sure. We all know that. We are right here. It's the American and British armies that're lost.

REAGAN Silence, there!

He glares about at them. They are quiet, watching him. He turns back to the map.

REAGAN The battle yesterday was somewhere about here. As far as I could tell, we were not winning it in a hurry. So the Heinies are still somewhere in here, and you heard Lieutenant Whitesides say when those two aeroplanes came and looked at us and went away, that the Heinies want this well. And they were German aeroplanes that came and looked at us—not ours—

BATTSON *(to Reagan)* Let me tell it while you get your breath. *(to the men)* We were sent here to meet a battalion of the __th and hold this well. Only, the __th never got here, and those two Jerries yesterday afternoon know it. Lieutenant Whitesides said for us to get out of here quick. But Lieutenant Whitesides is dead. So the question is, do we get out while we can and get back to the lines, or do we hold on here until the __th gets up?—if it's going to get up—

The soldier with the gas mask container enters.

BATTSON *(to the soldier)* Have Smyth and Hopkins and Shipp and Blount voted?

SOLDIER Yes.

BATTSON *(to the men)* Manning will give every man two shells: a live one and a hull—

SOLDIER If it's "Go," drop in the live one; if it's "Stay," drop in the hull. You can throw the hull away after the voting, but if it's the live one you still got, keep it because you're going to need it—

The Italian officer moves center, eager; they all look at him.

ITALIAN OFFICER Hah. Voting. That's American. But we too, once: the men of our Garibaldi[14] voted themselves death and glory too in their time. But that was many years ago, and now the world thinks that my race has forgotten that once it too produced free men, heroes—

BATTSON Sure. The bright flowers of bursting Italian bombs, shot through with flying black scraps of Ethiopian women and children, I think he called it in his book.[15] It must have looked more like caviar than corsages, though.

The Italian pauses and listens to Battson, courteous, quizzical, attentive. He shrugs.

ITALIAN OFFICER Perhaps you are right. Perhaps the world is right, and what we have left is merely that for which we bartered that old glory—

A SOLDIER And what you are going to get?—

ITALIAN —is only what we deserve. Yes. But I will tell a story. It happened among the race of the Herr Kapitan there. Perhaps he recalls it. If not, I will try to speak slowly and clearly enough so that he will hear it too.

An ANGLE favoring the German officer, cold and sneering and contemptuous still. As the Italian speaks, SLOW DISSOLVE begins.

14. Giuseppe Garibaldi (1807–1882), legendary Italian patriot and warrior, led an army of volunteer guerrillas, or "Redshirts," in support of various revolutionary causes.

15. Reference here is to the Italian-Ethiopian (Abyssinian) war in 1936, but the source of the quotation attributed to Mussolini has not been located.

ITALIAN This man was a Greek, who had lived in America and worked and saved his money so that he could return to his country and marry the woman who was waiting for him—a big man, bigger than your Louis or Dempsey,[16] who had fallen in love, not with a Greek girl but with a Serb, so that it was not to his Greek village that he returned, but to hers—a little village in the mountains, with little in it of note but this young girl and the bell—

DISSOLVE COMPLETES TO:

NOTE: The following is an adaptation of a story by Budd Schulberg, published in the *Saturday Evening Post*.[17] Will ascertain title later. Know nothing about present rights, as per the Gilpatric and the Wylie stories used in this treatment.

A tiny mountain village. It is very poor; you would wonder why an enemy should want it. There is a church, a priest, a few houses, the barest necessities for life for a few people who herd their sheep and weave cloth and till their tiny scraps of land. Thus the only thing in the village of any value is the bell. It is in the church belfry. It has been there 500 years and it has now become a living personality to the village. It has marked every event which has ever happened there. It rang to warn of the invasion of the Turkish hordes; it has rung for all the births and deaths, it rang dirges for famines and troubles, and rang joyous peals for all occasions when the village knew happiness.

A German company has occupied the village. The villagers accept the fact; there is nothing else they can do. They had only time to hide in the mountains the two or three guns and the 30 or 40 rounds of ammunition which they possessed. The Germans commandeer the food, but still there is nothing the village can do because they are poor, nowhere to go. So they work a little harder and have a little less to eat themselves, in order to feed the guests whom they did not ask for. So far, the village remains peaceful, though the sullen hatred is there.

---

16. Jack Dempsey (1895–1983) was the world's heavyweight boxing champion from 1919 until 1926.
17. Budd Schulberg, "The Bell of Tarchova," *Saturday Evening Post*, 215 (October 24, 1942), 12ff.

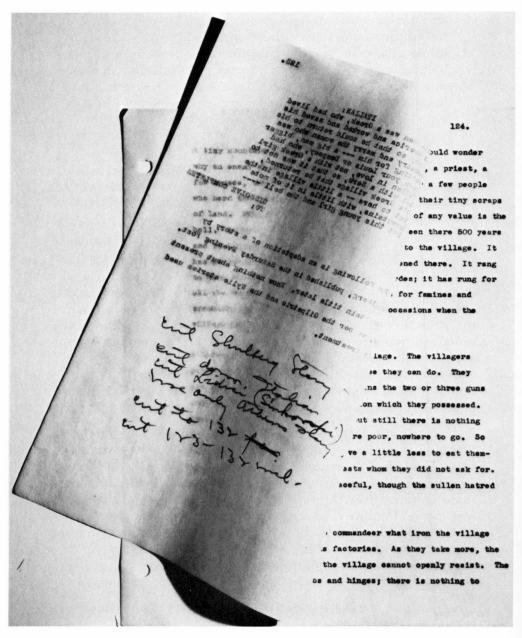

8. Pages 123–124 of Hawks's copy of expanded treatment

The German officer begins to commandeer what iron the village has, to send it to munitions factories. As they take more, the hatred grows, though still the village cannot openly resist. The Germans take the doorknobs and hinges; there is nothing to close the doors by against the mountain night cold. They take what plows can be spared, so that the people have to go back to plowing with sticks, as their remote ancestors did. The Germans take the fire irons, shovels, pokers. Still the priest keeps the people calm with his power over them and the power of God, who will not desert them who endure. The priest continues to conduct the services; the bell still rings on its occasions. At least they still have that; at least their village still exists, and will exist as long as the bell can ring. Meanwhile, the Greek, the stranger, works harder then ever, so that his sweetheart and her people may survive. He helps the priest keep the people in line; becomes a leader among them. Then one day the Germans demand the bell, to be melted down into a cannon.

This is the last straw. Now, even the priest condones what steps the village will take. He might even bless the plan. The Greek, the erstwhile stranger, is now the leader of the people, because of his physical strength, his proven love for the girl, and the other things he has constantly done to shield the village from the German occupants. The whole village watches sullenly as the Germans try to remove the bell from its hinge, beam. It is known that the Greek can move the bell alone. The German commander orders him to move it. Demetrios hesitates.

GIRL   (*screams suddenly*) Don't move it, Demetrios!

The German officer orders two men to catch the girl. They do. The girl's father starts forward. Demetrios removes the bell, helps to lower it. The tension eases. The villagers watch with sullen disbelief as Demetrios seems to help the enemy. The girl's father, one of the chief men, protests, is silenced.

That night, Demetrios and a few of the young men steal the bell. Demetrios, because of his strength, carries the bell on his back. They take it into the mountains to hide it.

The next morning the German commander arrests the girl's father as a hostage, to compel the young man to bring the bell back. He lets the girl go to tell Demetrios her father will die if the bell is not returned. While she is gone, her father tries to assault the officer. While the guard holds him, struggling, the officer shoots him in cold blood.

DISSOLVE TO:

The group of soldiers gathered about America's pallet, listening to the Italian, favoring the cold contemptuous German officer, who is also listening.

ITALIAN   So they voted perhaps, what to do, as you are about to vote, because this Greek who was in love, this Demetrios, had lived in America, where all men have a vote in what all are or are not to do—

BATTSON   All of them except America's folks. There are parts of it where America's folks don't have any say. Ask Akers.

ITALIAN   That's true. But that condition will change.

BATTSON   When? They will give America's father and mother and brothers and sisters a vote in exchange for that bullet in his back?

ITALIAN   I think it will be changed just as soon as the people outside that part of the country, whose concern it is not, stop trying to force them to give America's people a vote. When the people outside that part of the country have cleaned their own house a little, as they had promised to do on the first day of January, 1863—

BATTSON   So your name is Demetrios. You don't look to me as big or as handsome either as you make yourself out.

ITALIAN   No. I am not Demetrios. But I have lived in America too, for many years. *(he continues)*—clean their own house a little, who have herded America's people into tenements in Harlem and Chicago and Detroit—

BATTSON   They are free to leave, whenever they don't like it. They can go anywhere they want. They won't have to ride in Jim Crow cars to do it either.

ITALIAN   So can they leave the Jim Crow part of the country, whenever they like. If the rest of the United States' house were as clean as it should be, as it had given its promise to be on that first day of January, 1863, making them as welcome into it as that old promise implied, I think the Jim Crow people would need much more than just a vote to bribe America's people to remain in the Jim Crow land at all. But perhaps not. Perhaps it is not that simple, not that easy to turn your back on the land, the earth, where you were born and where the only work you know is and where your mother and father and sisters and brothers and children, too, are buried—even if it is only a tenement in Harlem or Chicago or Detroit or a farm in Jim Crow land—

BATTSON   All right, all right. Get on with your Greek.

ITALIAN   *(continuing)* Yes. This Greek. This Demetrios. So perhaps they voted on whether to bring the bell back or not. Or perhaps—

DISSOLVE TO:

The mountains above the village. The girl overtakes Demetrios and the men with the bell. She is terrified for her father's safety, tells them how her father is being held by the Germans. There is nothing to do but carry the bell back. They decide this quickly, following Demetrios' lead. They start back to the village with the bell. Just before they reach the village, Demetrios stops them; they are to wait there with the bell while he and the girl go on to the village and look the situation over; maybe there is still some way to save the bell. The girl divines that Demetrios perhaps has some intention of giving himself up to free her father. She does not wish to accept this, but she is worried about her father, and the whole village has learned to depend on Demetrios, the young men have, that is, and to let him lead them.

The others remain with the bell. Demetrios and the girl return to the village. Demetrios is arrested at once by the Germans. Then he and the girl learn that her father is dead. Demetrios is being held by two German soldiers. His strength is such that he breaks free, flings them aside as if they were sawdust dolls, breaks the German commander's neck with his hands. The two soldiers are trying to shoot him. The girl has snatched up the rifle of one of them when Demetrios knocked him down, strikes the other German with the rifle as he tries to shoot Demetrios. The other German officer, the junior, hearing the uproar, enters from an adjoining room, his pistol drawn.

GIRL *(screams at Demetrios)* Run! Run, Demetrios! The bell!

The girl flings herself against the other officer, keeping him from shooting. Demetrios escapes.

DISSOLVE TO:

The girl's voice carries over the DISSOLVE and becomes the Italian's voice.

SOUND TRACK	SCREEN
ITALIAN'S VOICE . . . the bell. Demetrios carried it as they ran, because no other man in that village could lift it, let alone carry it, carrying it faster than those who pursued them could run—	Demetrios carrying the bell on his back, his companions now with ancient clumsy guns, hurrying through the mountains, climbing, stumbling, going fast. WIPE TO: Demetrios, carrying the bell, and the others hurry on, while one of them remains lying behind a rock, aiming his gun over it. He fires, gets up, hurries after the others. DISSOLVE TO:
ITALIAN'S VOICE So that it still rang in the mountains, each day ringing in the mountains, for the Herr Kapitan's people to pursue it again. Because they could not ignore it, you see. There was the prestige, not to mention the dead German officer who had died not even from a treacherous knife in the back, but between the soiled hands of a peasant . . .	The village. The bell can be heard ringing in the mountains. All the Germans show strain. The remaining officer harshly details men to try to follow the sound. They don't show much enthusiasm. A sergeant barks harshly at them. They exit, pursuing the bell which they know once more they not only will not overtake, but will cost the life of at least one of them . . .
ITALIAN'S VOICE Ringing in the mountains just ahead of them, always just ahead of them who followed it . . .	In the mountains. The party of Germans crouching, trying to keep down yet still go forward, the bell ringing ahead. A shot

comes from ahead, a German falls. The
others look at him. The sergeant harshly
orders them on, kicks one. The bell rings
on somewhere in front of them. They go
on, reluctantly. A shot comes from behind
them now. Another German falls. The
sergeant shouts and kicks them on again.
The bell still rings.

DISSOLVE TO:

Int. of the house. GROUP SHOT as before, favoring the sneering
and contemptuous German, of the men gathered about America's pallet, listening to the Italian.

ITALIAN   . . . still ringing just ahead of them in the mountains until the sound of that bell reached to Berlin even,
and more troops were sent there and that village was
razed—that not even one stone should remain upon
another, and its very name should be obliterated from human speech[18]—

BATTSON   Yes. I can tell some of that, myself. The rest of
it's in America—

WIPE TO:

MAP of NORTH AMERICA. PAN SWIFTLY, too swiftly for actual location, to a spot on the map.

DISSOLVE TO:

Int. of a town hall, a meeting of an American village, men,
women. The chairman of the meeting is speaking, reading
from a paper while all listen soberly, intently.

CHAIRMAN   . . . since Hitler and his gang have declared
that the location and the name of the town of Cincovci shall
be forever obliterated from human knowledge and speech,
be it hereby resolved by us, the citizens and voters of the
incorporated town of Stevenson in general meeting assembled, that the incorporated town of Stevenson be from

18. This passage is based on the actual experience of the Czechoslovakian
village of Lidice, which was entirely destroyed by the Nazis in 1942. The town
was later restored as a national memorial.

now on known and recognized as the incorporated town of *(mispronounces it)* Sinkovski.

                                                    DISSOLVE TO:

Int. house. GROUP SHOT as before.

> **BATTSON** —so that the name of the village which Hitler thought he had obliterated from human speech will be mispronounced daily from now on until eternity begins. What became of the girl?

> **ITALIAN** *(shrugs)* Who knows? Why? Girls are cheap in Europe today. But I think that bell still rings in the mountains, a little ahead of those who pursue it, even though it is no longer the Greek who carries it. Because he went back to his own country, this Greek, this Demetrios, who had lived in America and had learned how men can vote on what all are to do. . . .

The DISSOLVE begins while he speaks, and COMPLETES TO:

From a short story, "The Weapon," by Georges Carousso, *Saturday Evening Post,* April 24, 1943.[19] Certain atmosphere, incidents, characters, are used here, as in Gilpatric and Wylie stories mentioned.

Athens. The city is slowly starving, the people creep about, grubbing for food in garbage, die of starvation and fall in the streets, are carted away by Italian and German squads. The Italian's voice continues on track.

> **ITALIAN'S VOICE** . . . Because there is one quality in human nature, in the nature of Southerners who have lived always near the sun, which is stronger than oppression, than ruthlessness and rapacity, than starvation and death itself even . . .

A street, starving people sitting weakly about, on steps in the sun, against walls, in b.g. carts are carrying away dead bodies. Two Italian officers enter, strut past. Behind them, strutting

---

19. Georges Carousso, "The Weapon," *Saturday Evening Post,* 215 (April 24, 1943), 23ff.

step for step, clowning and mocking them, are two ragged Greek boys about 10, aping the Italian movement for movement. Suddenly the two boys shout together.

BOYS Heil Hitler!

The two Italians stop, whirl about, their right arms already raised in Hitler salute, find the two ragamuffin, ragged boys facing them stiffly, their right arms raised. The starving people stir, sit up, watch. The two Italians react, the boys break and run, the Italians are about to chase them, remember their dignity in time. The weak people begin to laugh, the laughter passes from mouth to mouth until the whole street is filled with it while the baffled Italians glare about, helpless to do anything. They turn and go on, while the weak laughter sounds on all sides of them.

DISSOLVE TO:

SOUND TRACK

The Italian's voice tells about the fat German commander, who has commandeered all the food and has eaten it himself. It is a disease with him almost, a mental disease like dipsomania. The Italian tells how the very sight of the starving people all around him seems to give the German an ungovernable and constant appetite.

ITALIAN'S VOICE
He would even take the rations from his own troops. He was like a drunkard, who hates the very drink from which he cannot restrain himself, taking the meat and bread from his own kind as the drunkard pawns his wife's and children's clothing to buy drink with it, until his own men must have hated him too, as the drunkard's wife and children come in time to hate the husband and father for his vice . . .

ITALIAN'S VOICE
Until this Greek, this Demetrios, returned to his native city, who had loved the girl in the Serbian hills and lost her and so he had but one thing to live for now, but, being a Southerner, a Greek, he too still had the gift of laughing . . .

SCREEN

The fat, porcine German officer seated at the table, alone, eating.

German soldier-sergeant as he watches the gorging officer, with hatred and disgust.

The fat German at the table. He tucks his napkin in his collar, gloats on the bowl which the servant sets before him, begins to eat, drops the spoon, reacts in alarm, then anger, spits something out. It is a black marble, a black ball. The German

shows rage, dashes the soup from the
bowl, pauses, looks into the bowl, reacts.

CLOSE SHOT of inside of the empty bowl
Scrawled on the bottom of it is the Greek
word which WIPES TO: "NO."

DISSOLVE TO.

ITALIAN'S VOICE
A black ball, you see, a vote, as in America. And the soup was made by a German
soldier cook, and there was no one else
about the kitchen but one starving Greek
scullery lad, and no reason to lock this
starving Greek up in jail where he would
have to be fed, so he was fired and
another taken on because they were easy
to get; a man could get a prince or a
princess to do his scullery work for the
privilege of gnawing the scraps. Yet on
the next day . . .

The fat German seated at table. He
spoons food from a casserole onto his
plate, finds another black ball in it,
snatches off his napkin and finds the
word "No" scrawled on the napkin.

ITALIAN'S VOICE
Until presently he would not even have to
wait for the next day . . .

The German takes up his cap to go out, a
black ball falls from the cap and rolls
across the floor.

WIPE TO:

The German officer puts his hand into
his pocket, pauses, takes something out.
It is a tiny homemade Greek flag; when
he opens it, a black ball falls out. The German reacts in furious and impotent rage.

ITALIAN'S VOICE
Until at last, even on the street . . .

As the German officer opens the front door to go out, a marble
ball as big as a small cannon ball, big and heavy enough to have
dashed his brains out if it had struck him, daubed crudely with
soot, crashes down at his feet. It was wrapped in another
homemade Greek flag. He starts back. The weak, starving people are sitting and lying about the street in the sun. They begin
to laugh, the weak laughter traveling on up the street. The
German reacts to the flag, the black ball, the laughter. He
speaks to the German soldier behind him in German. The sol-

dier advances toward the nearest man, kicks him. But even the soldier is ashamed to kick a man that near dead. The laughter continues. The German officer shouts angrily at the soldier, who stands stiffly at attention, refusing to kick again. The officer speaks in German again to the soldier, strides on, the soldier following stiffly, the laughter continuing. Another black ball comes from somewhere, rolls past the officer. The soldier watches it soberly; as the officer whirls, the soldier whirls too, lowers his rifle threateningly. The laughter ceases. The German officer speaks again in German. He and the soldier go stiffly on. The laughter begins again.

DISSOLVE TO:

ITALIAN'S VOICE *(in dissolve)* And not only the laughter, but the flags. But that was our job . . .

The street is filled with tiny crude homemade Greek flags, on the walls, lampposts, etc. The starving people watch. The angry German officer, with his bodyguards, watching while Italian soldiers snatch down the little flags. As fast as they jerk one down, another one appears. In b.g. the weak constant laughter.

ITALIAN'S VOICE Until at last he could no longer eat—this man who lived for eating. He wished to leave, but he had no excuse to give to his superiors, for how could he confess that he could not prevent his own servants, this conquered and starving people, from putting children's marbles into his food and his cap and his coat pockets? But at last it was the flags which saved him . . .

The German officer is relieved and dismissed, sent somewhere else by his successor, in contemptuous disgrace.

ITALIAN'S VOICE But even that did not stop the flags . . .

Street. The weak starving people watch, while the new German commander orders the Italians to tear down the flags. As fast as they tear them down, other tiny crude homemade flags made of scraps of cloth, paper, anything, appear. The laughter continues in b.g. weak, steady, becomes the sound of the FREEDOM TRAIN in—

DISSOLVE TO:

Int. of the house. The soldiers gathered about America's pallet, listening to the Italian.

BATTSON   Well? Is that all?

ITALIAN   It will never be all, as long as they can laugh. How can you conquer people who can still laugh at you?

A SOLDIER   You can starve them.

ITALIAN   You can only kill them by doing that. You can kill them much simpler. But when you do that, you have failed. The man whom you must destroy, as the only alternative to his obeying you, that man has beat you.

BATTSON   *(turning)* Well, you should know.

ITALIAN   *(quietly)* Yes. We should know.

BATTSON   *(to Manning)* All right, Manning. Let's finish the voting.

Manning approaches with the gas mask container. It is full of votes now, heavy; the voting is nearly over. He hands a live shell and an exploded case to Akers.

MANNING   Here. If you vote "Go," drop in the—

Akers does not even look at the shells.

AKERS   I done voted. Me and America ain't going no-where.

MANNING   You got to vote. Everybody has voted but you—

BATTSON   *(takes the container)* Let him stay here, if he wants to. He don't belong to us.

He hands the container to Reagan. Now they become quiet; it is official now, as Reagan solemnly prepares to pour out the votes and count them. All gather near. Reagan pours out the votes. They are all empty cases. Nobody has voted to go.

A SOLDIER   Hell. Didn't anybody vote to go.

BATTSON   *(looks at him)* You're like everybody else. You thought everybody else would vote to go. So you would vote to stay, and just for the price of one empty 30 caliber hull you would buy a reputation for being brave.

There is a moment of dead silence. Akers breaks it.

AKERS *(forced jeering laughter)* Heh, heh, heh.

He begins to play "Porterhouse Sadie" on the dulcimer, quick and rollicking.

REAGAN *(angrily)* Stop that damn—

VOICE *(in b.g. to Reagan)* Ah, go on outside. Take a walk yourself in the moonlight. Maybe you can find Rommel and he will tell you what page to look for.

Akers plays the dulcimer. Fonda and Loughton have moved aside.

FONDA The girl . . .

DISSOLVE TO:

The dulcimer and the sound of the FREEDOM TRAIN carry OVER DISSOLVE. The FREEDOM TRAIN ceases, the dulcimer becomes the sound of a carrousel.

Paris. 1938. A street, night, a carnival: merry-go-rounds, booths, Punch and Judy, vendors, crowds of people enjoying it. Clemente Desmoulins and Albert Loughton have just met each other. Albert is in civilian clothes, a young Englishman clerking in the Paris branch of a London bank, a sober, solid young man, honorable and dependable. This is his attraction for her. Clemente is not only French, but Parisian: chic and smart in appearance even in the cheap clothes she can afford, gay, cheerful, vivid. This is her attraction for him.

They have just met. They both know they are falling in love, and that it will be for keeps. Clemente realizes it first; she enjoys the fact that Albert's English nature makes him a little ashamed to admit it so quickly. Also, in Albert's background there is a long line of solid, cautious, middle-class provincial ancestors warning him against the *femme fatale,* the worldly woman, the first and most dangerous of which is the Parisienne.

They have just met. They are attracted. Now they are learning to know one another, as a young man and a girl do. They have not quite reached the stage for confidences. It is apparent to Clemente that there is little about Albert that does not appear on his honest surface. She is still cautious. She has lived more than he has, she knows it, knows that her past might even shock him. But there will be time enough to cross that bridge when she knows how far their interest will develop.

The first thing Albert realizes is that he is having more fun, pleasure, than he has ever had, at the cost of almost no money at all. He had saved some money before being given the Paris job. He is willing to spend it on her. He not only discovers that she will not let him, is protecting his money from himself, but that she can choose for them cheap drinks and food and cheap amusements and at the same time give to them a glamour and excitement which should have cost ten times what she will let him spend. He gradually loosens up his reserve, finds that he is learning how to really enjoy.

She works for a swank famous Paris modiste, with many English and American wealthy clients. Thus she has managed to learn a little English. Albert had to learn French in order to get his present job. As the affair progresses between them, a part of it, a part of their loving one another, is teaching the other each one's own language.

Soon they know they are in love. Clemente is still light and gay about it, because she is hiding something. She does not care if everybody knows it, it means little to her, but she knows Albert's serious moralistic nature, and she is not certain how he will take it. And besides, there is no need to tell him yet. He knows what work she does, how little she is paid, is amazed that she can be so happy and carefree.

When Albert realizes he is in love, he becomes quite serious and sober. At last he admits, like a confession, that he loves her. She has known this all the time. She is light, gay, happy about it. She tells him so does she, which he certainly knows by now. She appears to think this is all of it, that they love each other and that is sufficient, enough. When Albert realizes that she takes it for granted that they will live together, if Albert wants to, or that he will come to her whenever he wants to, if he is afraid to live only with her, Albert is shocked. He says he means for them to marry. She says quickly, "No, no, we don't need to marry; being in love is enough." But she realizes that Albert is more and more shocked. She soothes him, knowing him well, with her gaiety, with warmth. She says, in effect, that Albert won't even sleep with her unless she promises to marry him? Albert, still sober and grave, says Yes. She says, all right, they will be married, after a while, when Albert is established better, etc.

They are lovers now. All Europe is about to explode, but for the time they are not even aware of it. Their life is idyllic; Albert is happier than he ever knew he could be. In a way, they are like two children together. She is learning his language much faster than he is learning hers. He tries from time to time to learn more about her background and life before he knew her, not out of curiosity, but because he loves her. She stills puts him off, learns from him without his knowing it more and more about his people. As she does so, she realizes more and more what will probably happen if Albert ever learns about her past. She knows that someday it will come, he will have to know and she will lose him. But she is determined to get what happiness they can before this happens. She has spells of gravity about it, but hides them from Albert. Now and then he suggests again the marriage, each time she puts it off, hides the reason from him.

A year passes. It is 1939. Albert's vacation is coming due, when he will go home to England for two weeks. Clemente is preparing to live without him for the two weeks. But he is preparing a surprise for her. He keeps it secret. He gets Clemente leave from her job to accompany him, makes reservations for the two of them, so his mother and father can meet his future wife. All she has to do is to get her passport. This will not take long. He keeps the secret until the last day, just time for her to get the passport. Then he tells her she is to go with him, and why.

She is dumbfounded and aghast. But she is caught; there is not time. If she tells him now why she can't go, she is afraid of what she knows will happen. She had planned to tell him when she had to, but at least there would be a last few days in which she could get the most possible out of loving him before the blowoff. So she agrees to go, to put it off; if she is careful, she can get through the visit and they can get back to Paris, where she will be safe. (She has no people, he has gotten her leave from her job; there is no reason she can give him for not going.)

She goes to get a passport. He wants to go with her. She nervously puts him off, makes an excuse, which he accepts.

She goes to the bureau. She knows that to get the passport she will have to produce the card which exposes her past. She is registered as a professional prostitute by the police. The official hesitates about giving her the visa. She pleads with him. She must have it, not because she wants to go to England, but if the visa is refused, she knows Albert will insist on knowing why and will learn the truth. She tells the official that she became a prostitute when she was young, because she had to, no people and no job then, that as soon as she got work and became able to live on her earnings, she stopped. And now she never will again, because she is in love, though she does not tell the official this. She just says she will work and support herself, is done with the other. The official is cold, cynical. She was registered once as a prostitute; as far as the police are concerned, until she is married and becomes respectable, she is still one. He is after information. He asks her questions; she admits because she has to that she has kept within the law, has gone for her police inspections at the proper time, even since she quit practicing the profession. He cannot deny the visa, since she has observed the law. He stamps the passport.

They reach England. It is July, 1939; the signs of imminent war are present here too, typical of that time. They go to the little Surrey village. Albert introduces Clemente to his father and mother as his future wife. Mr. Loughton would rather his son marry an English girl, thinks foreign girls are naturally unstable, etc., but is willing to accept it since it is apparent that Albert means business, is in love with her, and so there is nothing to be done.

But Mrs. Loughton, Albert's mother, is a different matter. As soon as Clemente meets her, she realizes that Mrs. Loughton has divined the truth about her: that this middle-class, middle-aged English woman who has passed all her life in this little quiet village has divined the truth about the woman her son is in love with. Clemente is terrified. She wants to get away, before Mrs. Loughton tells Albert. But she knows that even that may do no good. If Mrs. Loughton believes that there is real danger of Albert marrying her, she, Mrs. Loughton, will never let Albert return to Paris, where he might marry her, without telling him what she has divined.

So she not only has to keep Albert quiet, she must make Mrs. Loughton believe that she has no intention of ever marrying Albert. She acts the two parts, still fearing that at any time before the visit is up and they can return, Mrs. Loughton may decide to tell Albert. She realizes that Mrs. Loughton may be watching them, to see how much Albert is in love with her, to tell him the truth as soon as she, Mrs. Loughton, decides the matter may go as far as marriage. Clemente also has to play still another part to Mr. Loughton, who seems to suspect nothing of the tension in the house, who has apparently accepted her since Albert loves her, whether he approves of the marriage or not. Mr. Loughton is gradually coming to like her, so she knows that at least so far Mrs. Loughton has not told him.

Albert, of course, suspects nothing. His people had not definitely refused to accept Clemente, which was all he had expected anyway. He had not expected them to approve of her or even like her: the foreigner, from that modern Babylon, Paris. When he sees that his father is beginning to like her, that is so much velvet.

Now he reveals the next part of the plan which he has had in his mind all the time. He tells Clemente they are to be married now, in England. They will go to the French Consul, etc., have the marriage ratified and thus Clemente will become a British subject. Clemente realizes this will blow the whole thing. She is frantic, desperate, hides it, puts the marriage off, says she wants to be married in her own country, etc.: a feminine reason which Albert accepts simply because it is feminine.

So she has escaped again, if she can only keep Mrs. Loughton persuaded that she has no intention of marrying Albert. She tries this, cannot tell from Mrs. Loughton's sober and watchful manner whether she has succeeded or not. But the visit will be over soon, Albert's leave will be up; she just hopes she can keep things as they are, get them both back to Paris before Mrs. Loughton decides to tell Albert.

The war breaks. Germany invades Poland. Britain and France declare war; all British reservists, of which Albert is one, are called up. Albert cannot return to Paris; now Clemente, as long as she remains a French subject, must. Now Albert will not take no for an answer. The marriage must be performed at once. Clemente tries to protest, resist, but he carries her forcibly to his mother and tells her they will be married at once, before he has to report for service. Clemente believes this has blown the gaff. She recovers, asks Albert to leave her alone with his mother. Albert does so.

Clemente is quite calm now. She tells Mrs. Loughton about her past, how she became a prostitute because she had no money, quit it as soon as she was able to live without it, that she loves Albert and never will again. Mrs. Loughton listens, apparently still cold, grim.

> **CLEMENTE**   Believe me. I never will again, never.

> **MRS. LOUGHTON**   *(coldly)* But you were once. Do you expect the fact that you have quit to mean anything to me?

> **CLEMENTE**   *(gives up)* No. Of course not.

> **MRS. LOUGHTON**   And, since you love Albert, of course you have told him.

Clemente sees here one last desperate hope. She and Albert must part, perhaps forever, but at least maybe Albert will never have to know about her past; he will at least remember her with love and trust.

> **CLEMENTE**   Yes. I told him. We agreed never to speak of it again. He will be a soldier now, and I will be back in Paris. I hope you won't ever speak of it to him. I ask you not to. I beg you not to. I am giving him up; that's little enough to ask in return. There's a train today I can take, isn't there?

> **MRS. LOUGHTON**   *(still cold, watchful)* And Albert loves you.

> **CLEMENTE**   Yes! Didn't he forgive that? When does the train—

> **MRS. LOUGHTON**   *(turns)* Yes. I had thought of that myself; call Albert.

She crosses to a bureau. Clemente watches her as she takes something from a drawer and looks up.

MRS. LOUGHTON Did you call Albert?

Clemente goes to the door, opens it, stands aside, says nothing as Albert enters. He and his mother meet, Mrs. Loughton gives him her wedding ring, the one she and Mr. Loughton used, for Albert to give Clemente. Mrs. Loughton goes out.

Albert is happy. Clemente is in despair. Things are just as Albert had expected, only better. He tries to take Clemente in his arms to put the ring on her hand. She breaks free, runs out; Albert, puzzled, follows.

Mrs. Loughton is arranging flowers in the hall when Clemente runs up the stairs, and a moment later Albert follows.

In Clemente's bedroom. She is frantically preparing to pack her bag when Albert enters, wants to know what the hell. Clemente tells him about her past. Albert is shocked, too dazed to react. He listens quietly until Clemente finishes. She sees herself losing him. Then it is all over, she has lost him. He is too quiet. He puts the ring on the table, says quietly he will walk a bit, clear his head, will see her at dinner, etc. He leaves the room. She watches him out. Then she finishes packing, puts on her hat and coat, takes up the ring, exits.

She meets Mrs. Loughton in the lower hall.

CLEMENTE *(dully)* Goodbye. I'm going now.

She gives Mrs. Loughton the ring.

MRS. LOUGHTON So you lied. You hadn't told him.

CLEMENTE Yes. I lied. Goodbye.

MRS. LOUGHTON There is a slow train this morning. You can change for New Haven and cross there to Dieppe.

CLEMENTE Thank you.

She goes out.

Albert is walking briskly in a country lane, walking off his shock

and pain. As he rounds a corner, Mrs. Loughton is waiting
there. She tells him Clemente has gone.

ALBERT Gone?

MRS. LOUGHTON To New Haven. To cross to Dieppe. *(she
gives him the ring)* You can do it if you hurry.

ALBERT Then you know too.

MRS. LOUGHTON Yes. *(Albert stares at her)* But you must
hurry.

ALBERT New Haven. But how—

MRS. LOUGHTON My bicycle's around the corner there.

Albert catches her in his arms. She frees herself.

MRS. LOUGHTON Stupid, don't you realize you must hurry?

Albert runs out.

New Haven. The dock. The packet for France is about to sail.
Albert rushes among the passengers, finds Clemente, embraces
her. She is surprised, recovers, protests.

CLEMENTE No! No!

ALBERT *(embraces her)* It's all right. It doesn't matter. I just
had to get used to it. It's all past now. It doesn't matter. It
doesn't matter at all.

She gets on the boat to return to France. They will wait for one
another, until they can meet again.

DISSOLVE TO:

CLOSE SHOT of Fonda and Loughton. Others in b.g. As the
DISSOLVE completes, Akers is banging away at the dulcimer,
playing "Porterhouse Sadie."

LOUGHTON So she went back to Paris.

Then he describes the next year, until they met again.

LOUGHTON I was busy, learning to be a soldier . . .

His voice might continue in b.g. against a MONTAGE: shots of
Loughton drilling, learning to handle tanks, maybe shots of the

battle of Norway, attempts by British forces to invade: Narvik: naval fighting, etc., while Loughton's voice describes it, until the spring of 1940, and he is sent to France to the B.E.F.[20]

> **LOUGHTON** We wrote to each other. She was carrying on too, holding her job so she could live, and doing what war work she could, and still taking time to write me the sort of letters that would make me feel good. Until at last I got 24 hours' leave to go to Paris so we could be married. They were not giving leave then, because we knew it was coming at any minute, but my section commander got it for me, just long enough to go to Paris and be married. She had already the banns, so all we had to do . . .

> DISSOLVE TO:

Gare du Nord station, Paris. A train comes in, Loughton gets out, Clemente meets him; they meet again after almost a year, with 24 hours before they must part again. It is late afternoon.

This sequence has a passionate undertone, but it is tender and serious, too. They are to be married, which they have wanted to do for a long time; they have just 24 hours to be together before Albert must return to the front. Everybody knows that the battle will start at any minute, though nobody for one moment believes that the outcome will be what it is to be. They think that the British and French armies will hold, perhaps win a quick battle. But men will die in it, they realize that one may well be Albert. Albert reassures Clemente.

> **ALBERT** Not me. It's hard to kill a man when he has something to live for.

He says, come on. Where is the registrar?, etc. Clemente is suddenly shy. She tells him how she was a good Catholic when she was a child, until her old dead life intervened. Now, since that old life is past and forgotten and a new one is starting, she wants the blessing of her church on her new life. She stops, seems unable to tell Albert what is in her mind, because he might think it's silly. He insists. At last she tells him. She would like to spend this last night in Notre Dame, praying, not for her

---

20. British Expeditionary Force.

past to be forgiven but that their future might be blessed and that the saints protect Albert in the coming battle. She expects him to say Nonsense. He does not. He agrees, though he is not a Catholic.

They go to the cathedral. This is a little strange to Albert, yet serious to him, too. He follows her quietly as she crosses herself at the font, makes obeisance, enters, bows to the Host. They take an empty pew; a few people are scattered about the cathedral, though no service is in progress. Clemente kneels and prays silently. Albert sits quietly beside her. A priest is moving about, from group to group; a few are French soldiers, the others the wives and mothers of soldiers at the front. The priest approaches Clemente and Albert. Clemente tells him she and Albert are to be married tomorrow, asks the priest to bless the marriage.

> **PRIEST** *(notices Albert's uniform)* Monsieur is an Englishman. He is a Roman Catholic?

> **ALBERT** No, sir. I—*(the priest waits; perhaps Albert does not want the blessing of a Roman priest. Albert knows what the hesitation means)* Yes, Padre, if you please—

The priest blesses them. Clemente still kneels, Albert is standing. The priest goes on.

> **ALBERT** *(to Clemente)* Will it be all right if I pray here too?

> **CLEMENTE** Yes. He is just one God.

Albert kneels beside her.

WIPE TO:

Morning, they are still in the cathedral. The news comes that the Germans have invaded the Low Countries; the allied armies are already engaged; all soldiers to hurry back to their units. This will probably be a sacristan who enters and announces it. Clemente and Albert leave the cathedral. There is no question of marriage now. They have agreed without having to say it that Albert must hurry back to the front. As they hurry through the streets, we will see Paris on this first shocked morning. Soldiers, with their wives, sweethearts, are hurrying toward the station.

People are gathered excitedly in the streets, listening to radio broadcasts and news bulletins. They are excited, yet they are quiet too; they have expected this for months. They are not alarmed, some are triumphant almost; they will whip the enemy, now that he has come out into the open.

They reach the station, the same scene but intensified. A train is ready, soldiers being loaded into it as fast as they arrive. Albert is an Englishman, yet the officials hurry him onto the train just the same. Albert and Clemente have only a moment for good-bye, an embrace. He is not alarmed. She is worried over his danger, but is holding on for the sake of his morale. She will carry on, wait for him. He enters the train, leans down again from a window. They kiss, he holds her up as the train begins to move, releases her at last as she trots beside a moving train.

    ALBERT   After we beat them.

    CLEMENTE   Yes. Yes. After we beat them.

The train moves faster. Clemente cannot keep up. They are drawing apart. She stops, her face still courageous, waving. She grows smaller and smaller, the train noise louder and faster, into—

                                               DISSOLVE:

Albert's voice speaks in the DISSOLVE.

    ALBERT   Only we didn't beat them—

                                           DISSOLVE TO:

MONTAGE covering this part of the battle of France: the break at Sedan, the surrender of the Belgian king, the allied armies are split apart on the Somme, the British and a few French fall back to the coast, still fighting, retreat to Dunkirk.

The beach at Dunkirk. The British have abandoned everything but their rifles. They crowd down onto the beach, huddle along the beach, while German bombers and fighters bomb and strafe them. They wade out into the water, where the boats pick them up, still being bombed and strafed: boats of all sorts; dinghies from warships standing off shore, sailing yawls and power launches and tiny boats with outboard engines which civilians

have brought across the 20 miles of rough Channel from England.

DISSOLVE TO:

CLOSE GROUP SHOT of Albert and other soldiers standing waist-
deep in the water, waiting for the boats, while German fighters
strafe them, coming up in succession, low, ripping the water
with machine guns. Now and then a man is hit. As each aeroplane comes in, the men face it, shooting at it with their rifles as
long as they can. Then they duck into the water for what protection they can get, as the aeroplane shoots past. One comes in
quite low. This time, as the others duck beneath the surface,
Albert, still standing, draws a hand grenade from his pouch,
pulls the pin, times the throw, and hurls the grenade at the
aeroplane as it flashes over. Albert ducks beneath the water as
the aeroplane explodes.

DISSOLVE TO:

Albert's voice speaks in the DISSOLVE.

> **ALBERT** So I didn't go back. I went to England, as every-
> one who could escape from the Continent came to England
> then.

SOUND TRACK	SCREEN
	MONTAGE: People, soldiers, men and chil-dren and a few women, homeless, dazed with the sudden defeat, arriving in Eng-land.
VOICES De Gaulle. De Gaulle.	The figure of General De Gaulle, repudi-ated by his country, his life forfeit, arriv-ing in England with nothing but a clean shirt and a razor.
ALBERT'S VOICE There were no letters, of course. But peo-ple still came, and so maybe . . .	

A crowd of French refugees in a street. Their faces are anxious,
strained, but now there is the beginning of hope in them. Albert is moving among them.

> **VOICES** De Gaulle. De Gaulle.

Albert approaches a man.

> **ALBERT** From Paris, monsieur?

MAN   *(looks at him briefly, inattentively)* Lyons, monsieur.

He looks back toward CAMERA.

VOICES   De Gaulle. De Gaulle.

Albert approaches another man.

ALBERT   Paris, monsieur?

MAN   *(inattentive, like the other)* Yes, monsieur.

ALBERT   I don't suppose you happened to know . . .

DISSOLVE BEGINS.

VOICES   *(in dissolve)* De Gaulle. De Gaulle.

DISSOLVE TO:

ALBERT'S VOICE   *(as dissolve completes)* But at last one day . . .

Albert is on duty at his army post. A Frenchman comes to see him. Albert hurries to the Frenchman, greets him. He is a man whom Albert and Clemente knew in Paris, a friend. Albert can't speak. He doesn't dare to ask, yet he must ask. The Frenchman sees this, watches Albert with compassion.

FRENCHMAN   She said to tell you goodbye. That she will love you always, and goodbye.

ALBERT   Goodbye . . . Goodbye . . . Then you don't—

FRENCHMAN   *(quickly)* I do not know.

He puts his hand gently on Albert's shoulder.

FRENCHMAN   Do not ask, my friend.

Suddenly he claps Albert hard on the shoulder. His face is sardonic, indomitable, inscrutable, hiding what he thinks, or as if he did not care.

FRENCHMAN   My sister was in Paris also. So we do not ask. We do not wish to know, eh?

ALBERT   Yes. We do not wish to know.

DISSOLVE TO:

"MAMA MOSQUITO"

(THE FOXHOLE. . ALL MEN INTENT ON LAST STORY, WHEN SUDDENLY THERE IS A BURST OF SHELLFIRE A LITTLE TO ONE SIDE OF THE HOLE, AND A GREAT AVALANCHE OF MUD AND DIRT AND STONES FALLS ON THE MEN. AS HIS HAND WIPES OFF THE MUD, THE CAMERA EXPOSES THE STREAKED FACE OF THE CHENNAULT FLYER...HIS EYES COCK UPWARD FOR A MOMENT IN MOCKERY OF THE SHELL THAT HAD SO NEARLY DESTROYED THEM. A LITTLE CURVE OF HIS LIPS INDICATES CONTEMPT.

FLYER: The dirty b - - - - (TIGHTENS HIS LIPS ON THE LAST WORD. STOPS AND THEN GRINS WITH A LITTLE GRIM CHUCKLE DEEP DOWN IN HIS THROAT)

AMERICAN: (CASUALLY) Don't let 'em worry you, Jim.

FLYER: They don't - - (FACE TAKES ON AN ABSTRACTED LOOK) Y'know - I've been thinking about what you fellers been saying. Guess I've been doing my own share of wondering too . .but in the place I just come from, they don't have much time to wonder - why or what for - or even how long. . (GRIMLY) . . a great people, the Chinese! . . (BENDS FORWARD, POINTING HIS FINGER TO A SPOT ON THE MAP. THE SHADOW OF HIS FINGER FALLS ON IT) Here in Changsha, I saw - (OUT OF THE SHADOW HIS FINGER THROWS ON THE MAP, THE INCIDENT HE PROCEEDS TO TELL, BOILS INTO ACTION. VERY SUBTLY, THE LOW, MOANING MUSIC WHICH WE HAVE REGISTERED FOR THE FOXHOLE, CHANGES TO AN ALMOST IMPERCEPTIBLE, CHANT-LIKE QUALITY OF A MISERERE IN THE CHINESE IDIOM. . CAN BE BEST ACCOMPLISHED WITH A CERTAIN TYPE OF CHINESE FLUTE. THE MUSIC SHOULD HAVE A REED-LIKE QUALITY: AGAIN WE HAVE THE SENSE OF UNREALITY AS IN THE RUSSIAN SEQUENCE - VIOLENT ACTION IN RETROSPECT, MOODED WITH AN UNCHANGING, CHANTLIKE MUSIC THAT TYPIFIES THE PATIENCE AND ENDURANCE OF A PEOPLE. THE WHOLE

9. Page of Violet Atkins and William Bacher's story development

PATHETIC SADNESS AND MISERY OF A RACE IS IN THAT MUSIC,
BUT IT IS IN DIRECT APPOSITION TO THE VIOLENCE OF THE SCENE)
(NOTE: EACH SCENE BOILS INTO ACTION DURING DESCRIPTION AND
FADES BEFORE NEXT DESCRIPTION) (THIS PART OF THE PICTURE
IS LIKE A PICTORIAL NEWS REEL.)

FLYER: - I saw the Chinese, with only knives in their hands, going
over the top - half of 'em cut down by bombers - but you
couldn't stop 'em! Eleven times the Japs came - but they
never took that hilltop. (ACTION BOILS OUT). .and here at
Kaifeng - (FINGER MOVES TO ANOTHER PLACE. STOPS. SHADOW
BEGINS TO BOIL INTO ACTION) I saw three hundred Chinese
men and women lined up against a wall - their hands tied
behind 'em. .they had refused to tell where they'd hidden
one of our flyers.
(THROUGH SPEECH, A VOLLEY OF SHOTS - - ONE AFTER ANOTHER
THE ROW OF MEN AND WOMEN FALLS BENEATH THEM) (ACTION BOILS
OUT) . . and when it got so they couldn't hold out any
longer - they left their villages and towns - moving like
rivers over China - toward the west. . (SHADOW THROWN BY
FINGER NOW BECOMES A MOVING LINE OF PEOPLE) . .following
a voice that rang through China - (HIS VOICE SEEMS TO
DISSOLVE INTO A DISTANT VOICE THAT APPEARS TO EMANATE
FROM THE MAP) (VOICE HAS DIFFERENT PERSPECTIVES. .SEEMS
TO BE CARRIED BY THE WIND)

VOICE: "People of China - go to the west - TO THE WEST! Take
only what you can carry! Whatever you cannot carry,
destroy! Leave nothing behind but ashes for the enemy!"

10. Page of Violet Atkins and William Bacher's story development

The house in the desert, Fonda and Loughton, Akers banging merrily away at "Porterhouse Sadie" while the others gather around America's bed, listening, in b.g.

FONDA   I see. So that's why you hope—

LOUGHTON   Yes. That she is dead.

FADE OUT.

"Mama Mosquito"[21]

Very subtly, the low, moaning music which we have registered changes to an almost imperceptible, chant-like quality of a miserere in the Chinese idiom . . . can be best accomplished with a certain type of Chinese flute. The music should have a reed-like quality: again we have the sense of unreality as in the Russian sequence—violent action in retrospect, mooded with an unchanging, chant-like music that typifies the patience and endurance of a people. The whole pathetic sadness and misery of a race is in that music, but it is in direct apposition to the violence of the scene. (NOTE: Each scene boils into action during description and fades before next description. This part of the picture is like a pictorial newsreel.)

FLYER   —I saw the Chinese, with only knives in their hands, going over the top—half of 'em cut down by bombers—but you couldn't stop 'em! Eleven times the Japs came—but they never took that hilltop. (*action boils out*)— and here at Kaifeng—(*finger moves to another place, stops; shadow begins to boil into action*) I saw three hundred Chinese men and women lined up against a wall—their hands tied behind 'em. . . . They had refused to tell where they'd hidden one of our flyers.

Through speech, a volley of shots—one after another the row of men and women falls beneath them. Action boils out.

21. Like the Russian segment, this section of the expanded story treatment was written by Violet Atkins and William Bacher. It is based on a news feature by Dean S. Jennings: "Ma-Ma Mosquito," *Collier's*, 105 (April 13, 1940), 17ff.; condensed as "Mother of the Guerrillas," *Reader's Digest*, 37 (October 1940), 117–118. Faulkner revised this section of the script for the screenplay.

FLYER —and when it got so they couldn't hold out any longer—they left their villages and towns—moving like rivers over China toward the west. *(shadow thrown by finger now becomes a moving line of people)* . . . following a voice that rang through China—

His voice seems to dissolve into a distant voice that appears to emanate from the map. Voice has different perspectives . . . seems to be carried by the wind.

VOICE People of China—go to the west—TO THE WEST! Take only what you can carry! Whatever you cannot carry, destroy! Leave nothing behind but ashes for the enemy!

Entire mood of music begins to change. Building with each new river of people and pounding with the pulse of their marching feet and the dust and steam that rises from the path of their trek.

FLYER —and they followed the voice. *(new rivers start into action across map)*—from Canton—from Hangehow—from Nanking—Kiang and Shantung—Honan, Hopei and Hunan—a swollen flood of people flowing toward the west, carrying their pitiful possessions, leaving nothing but fire behind.

The whole screen is now filled with people carrying bedding, bits of machinery, looms, spindles, household furniture. Women with children, some with babies in their arms, marching in long endless streams that seem to overflow, one stream into the next, until the whole map seems like a huge swollen river. (NOTE: Keep all this going while showing isolated incidents in this whole group—flaming in various places.)

FLYER I saw kids whose homes and schools were shot to hell, go to school in caves—*(incident to stand out)*—I saw the Chinese people move whole factories, board by board, stick by stick—wheel and axel! *(incident to stand out)*—and in Shantung Province, they diverted the course of the Yellow River for hundreds of miles by blowing up the dikes—

The released waters of the river seem to engulf the people of that section of the map and the entire sequence fades out to—

DISSOLVE BACK TO:

Faces of men in foxhole listening intently. Closeup of flyer.

> **FLYER** *(passes his tongue over his dry lips as he watches them)*
> Big, huh?—well, China's a big place—takes lots of livin',
> and lots of dyin'. . . . Here in this village—*(points again, voice
> weighted and deep with the memory)*—I saw what the Japs left
> after 'em when they'd passed through . . . those that
> couldn't escape—the weak—the helpless—the old *(voice
> slows)*—the dead—

Shadow boils up. But this time it looms out of the whole map. A
closeup of a broken wall. Against it an old woman, sitting
huddled and motionless. Her clothes are torn, one slipper and
stocking off. There is a bleeding wound over her right eye. The
blood drips down her cheek, but she makes no move to wipe it
away. Her hair hangs matted in the blood. Her eyes stare
straight ahead with the dreadful, blank, unblinking look of a
woman who is in a state of complete shock. A hand touches her
shoulder. She does not look up. CAMERA moves to take in face
of a Chinese soldier, leaning over her.

> **SOLDIER** *(voice tired)* Old mother—come away—it does no
> good to stay—

She continues to stare before her. Slowly the staring blankness
of her eyes changes ever so slightly, like the eyes of a person
who is recovering consciousness after a dreadful nightmare.
The eyes do not blink, but they begin to focus. As they focus,
the CAMERA dollies back slowly, widening the scope of the scene.
Slowly, as if through her eyes, there unfolds the dreadful devas-
tation of the ruined village . . . houses still burning, wreckage—
and the dead. Near the old woman, two feet away perhaps, lies
the huddled body of a young woman, her face mercifully
turned earthward, the clothing stripped from her back. One
arm is flung out, half covering even in death the slight body of a
little boy of six, who seems asleep, until the CAMERA moves on,
and in passing we see the dark spot over his heart. Beyond
these two is the body of a boy of ten, curled up, still clutching in
his arms a mewing, frightened kitten—and near him, a boy of
fifteen on his back, arms wideflung, his face turned upward,
sightless staring eyes. The CAMERA focuses again on the face of
the old woman. In the wrinkled face there now begins a slight

motion—the quivering of muscles of the cheek, the soundless movement of her shaking lips. The Chinese soldier bends over her again, his hand on her shoulder.

SOLDIER Come, old mother—

She looks up at him blindly, then slowly her eyes go down again to her beloved dead. The tears begin to stream from her eyes, pouring down her cheeks. Her head moves from side to side in excruciating anguish. Her wrinkled old hand half-lifts, trembling, moving in a quivering half-circle to include those she speaks of.

OLD WOMAN They are all dead—all who belonged to me. See—*(looks up at the soldier through those sunken weeping eyes; his face is full of mute pity for her)*—this one was six—*(points to little boy with dead mother)*—this, ten—*(kitten mews pitifully; her eyes turn to the oldest boy)*—this one—fifteen . . . *(voice breaks; both hands go to her eyes, covering them)* They will not breathe again—nor speak—nor walk—nor run—

A moan follows her words. Her body rocks back and forth for a moment in unendurable suffering. Then, almost like a hurt animal, with her eyes still streaming tears, she drags herself on her hands and knees to where her daughter lies. Her wrinkled old hand touches the bare back gently, with a pathetic caressing movement. And slowly, anguished, her head droops until her forehead rests on that wrinkled hand. Completely motionless a split second. Then her hand slips out from beneath her forehead, to fall on the dark wet patch of bloodstained earth next to the body. A cold chill wind seems to pass over her. Her head slowly lifts, she turns to look at her hand. With a harsh, violent gesture she scoops up a handful of the wet soil, crushes it in her hand so that the dark ooze spreads over her fingers. Then her eyes lift to look full into the camera and a complete change comes over her. The eyes are different now. The blankness is gone. Grim and implacable, they seem to have sunk deep into her head as she stares straight before her. The quivering mouth is now a straight thin line. Her face has settled into an immutable mask. Now her voice is grim and weighted as she pledges vengeance for these dead.

OLD WOMAN All gone—but I—*(voice grows stronger)* I shall do all the things they would have done. A thousand men shall take the place of each, and I shall teach how we must harry those who murdered these!

Orchestra building under with the music of New China. Keep music building under following sequence.

DISSOLVE TO:

Quick long shot of Mama Mosquito in rice field, talking to three farmers. She is leaning toward them in an attitude of earnest appeal. They listen attentively, one leaning on his scythe, the other on his hoe, another on his rake. With quick nods they leave her, going in one direction with their implements, while Mama Mosquito goes in another.

(NOTE: While Mama Mosquito is going from one to the other of the groups, the voice of the flyer is heard in slow deep tones.)

FLYER —and these things came to pass—

DISSOLVE TO CLOSEUP OF:

Mama Mosquito in a blacksmith's shop. Her back is to the camera, her mouth to his ear, her head almost touching his. The blacksmith's eyes are darting beyond Mama Mosquito, out of the window and door. The blacksmith nods his head affirmatively and picks up his hammer. Mama Mosquito turns to go.

DISSOLVE TO MEDIUM SHOT:

Mama Mosquito in schoolroom, her profile and that of the teacher are silhouetted against a blackboard whereon is written: "The future of China is in the determined resistance of the people." The same gesture of whispering to the teacher, slow affirmative nod from him, and Mama Mosquito turns to go.

FLYER Thirty thousand men she trained—

DISSOLVE TO:

Darkened cellar—one candle illuminating the face of Mama Mosquito, the first time we see her face clearly since the time she looked at her dead daughter and grandsons. The candle-light picks out the new harsh lines as she stands before the men. A few of their faces are clear, the rest in shadow. Their hands

raised in the Chinese gesture of victory. One man stands halfway up the steps, head uplifted as if listening to sounds above,
one hand resting on the balustrade.

> **FLYER** Thirty thousand men came at the bidding of a
> sixty-year-old Chinese woman—

Music comes up strongly with the beginnings of a deep martial
beat.

> **FLYER** These became her voice!

DISSOLVE TO:

Sequence of marching group. The entire sequence to be done
in rhythm, each group taking only a part of the screen, coming
in and fading out with an effect like the opening of a Pathé[22]
newsreel, to build toward the climax in the glen. Each group
has its own voice. As one group fades into another, the words of
the next group follow without a break in their rhythm or their
marching. Each group carries either the implements of their
calling—pitchforks, scythes, rakes, hoes, axes; or any object
which can be used as weapons—bludgeons, obsolete guns,
lengths of pipe—crude weapons for the beginnings of China's
guerrilla army.

SEQUENCE OF MARCHING GROUPS

NOTE: Each voice becomes more vibrant, building to Mama
Mosquito's voice.

Group of coolies marching. One voice is heard—

> **VOICE** —they cannot stop us, and one day they will no
> longer try—

From another part of screen, group of farmers marching. One
voice is heard—

> **VOICE** —we will be the air they breathe—

Group of merchants marching.

---

22. Charles Pathé (1863–1957), French industrialist and film pioneer,
headed an international film production empire from 1901 to 1929. In 1908
Pathé's company introduced the "Pathé-Journal," the world's first weekly
newsreel.

VOICE   —the sod they walk on—the silent voices that they cannot hear—

Group of students marching.

VOICE   —the echo of our footsteps in the night will be their blight—

Group of laborers marching.

SCHOOL TEACHER   We will be all about them—and one day we will strangle them with the dust of those whom they strangled!

Mama Mosquito's voice picks up as we DISSOLVE newsreel effect into tremendous gathering of men and women in great clearing nearly filling the screen. Just beyond is seen a cemetery. Mama Mosquito stands on a slight rise. Her voice follows that of the foregoing voice without interruption:

MAMA MOSQUITO   —for we are the voices of the dead they slaughtered! The women they enslaved—the children driven mad!

Closeup of blacksmith, still in his apron, hammer in hand.

BLACKSMITH   —the guerrilla fighters—the invisible army marching from the sea to the mountains of the west!

Shot of Mama Mosquito pointing to the cemetery.

MAMA MOSQUITO   How many—how many of you for one of these who lie here dead?

VOICES   *(building, coming from every direction, with the hands of men lifted in the gesture of victory)* I! I! I! I! I!

Voices raised in a mighty chorus, swelling full with the music of New China. Slowly the entire scene fades out with its climactic music, into a long shot of a quiet village with thatched houses and dirt streets. In view of CAMERA, a vegetable cart stands near a house. As the camera moves forward, we see a great well with wide stone coping, over which hangs a great cherry tree. A detachment of Japanese soldiers is marching up to the well.

A few pathetic-looking villagers are grouped a little distance away. The CAMERA is now focused on the well. Out of scene we hear a Japanese command to halt. At the well a soldier draws up a bucket of water. Rests it on the coping.

CAPTAIN *(coming into scene, motions to another soldier)* Bring the twelve here to drink—

Soldier goes over to small group of villagers and prods them forward with his gun butt. They are stopped near the well. They stand stolidly as the captain dips the dipper into the bucket and holds it out to the nearest one.

CAPTAIN Drink—

The dipper passes from one to the other. The captain watches each face keenly as the dipper goes to the next. The water drips a little from each one's mouth but the faces remain impassive, stolid, unmoved. The captain nods as if satisfied, when the last of the twelve men and women has taken his drink.

CAPTAIN *(to soldier)* These twelve will be here each morning to drink. *(to villagers)* You go now!

The villagers shuffle stolidly away. Laughing and pushing, the tired dusty Japanese soldiers crowd around the well and drink, thirstily, the water sloshing over their clothes and dripping from their mouths.

FADE OUT.

FADE IN.

The well. One Japanese sentry walks slowly around the well, guarding it. Others are lolling idly, watching an old wizened man who is spraying the trees with a hand spray. As the old man sprays, he moves backwards. His foot touches that of the sentry, and the Japanese shoves him roughly away with his elbow, a contemptuous gesture. The old man sidles away, hunching his shoulders as if against an expected blow. He goes on spraying. The sun catches the fine sheen of the liquid as it falls from the leaves. The spray empties. The old man fills it from a small can. Goes on spraying the great branch overhanging the well. The CAMERA now concentrates on a few of the leaves on this branch, and we notice that the liquid surface is slightly gray in tone. Slowly DISSOLVE but only partially, as if there has been a change in the time of day. Our CAMERA now becomes the microscope under which the changes in the leaves are disclosed. Our tones are darker now, and we notice myriad changes—first the edges curl slightly—the leaves have dried—a slight brownish tone is evident—then the leaves gradually turn almost into parchment-like texture, like the leaves in the fall of the year. All of this is to be performed by the camera with the suggestion of the passage of time. It might be six hours—it might be six days—it might be six weeks—there is a slight rustle of wind. Slowly one of the leaves detaches itself and flutters gently to the ground, falling just outside the well. A stronger breeze comes up. We notice that the leaves at the furthest edges of the tree are still green, but from the branch directly over the well flutters slowly a second brown leaf—then a third—falling outside the well. Then one leaf falls to the coping of the well. The next leaf flutters gently in the breeze and spirals downward so we know its course will take it directly into the well. CAMERA now focuses at the top of the well, shooting down to the dark blot of water beneath. The eye of the CAMERA seems to make a glistening patch on the water, towards which, through the light, the leaf spirals until it flutters and falls like a lily pad on the surface of the water. Very slowly the water covers this brown leaf with a thin film until it slowly turns gray.

Next shot is outside the well, now almost covered with leaves. Heavy Japanese boots trample the leaves, and CAMERA PANS upward to take in the twelve Chinese, being given the dipper to drink. Now there is a definite gauntness and grayness on their impassive faces.

We flash to the fourth face in line, which is that of an aged Chinese woman, with a face like parchment. Obliquely, while the dipper is being passed to her right, we get a cross shot across her face, to show the dipper passing down the line, so that all we see are the mouths of the Chinese as they are drinking. Her eyes are obliquely raised toward the topmost line of the cherry tree, from which gently flutters one of the dried leaves. Apparently idly, her oblique glance registers the falling of that leaf right into the center of the well. At that moment, her hand goes up with the dipper, which has reached her, and with a slow inscrutable smile twisting the corners of her mouth, she puts the ladle to her lips and drinks deep.

DISSOLVE TO:

Uneven, lagging footsteps now treading on a heavy mass of leaves outside the well. Coping of well is covered with seared leaves. We see the bottom itself filled with leaves . . . Japanese soldiers dragging water in low slung pails, their boots seeming weighted to show the weariness that comes from accumulative poison.

DISSOLVE INTO:

Dead bodies of dozens of Japanese soldiers lying about, with the twelve Chinese drinking hostages fallen where they stood. As we see these dead bodies, CAMERA slowly moves to the cherry tree and we find the branches over and around the well completely denuded, as if by a blight. The rest of the tree is covered with healthy foliage.

DISSOLVE TO:

House of Japanese colonel. Closeup of small heap of brown dried leaves on a table. Scene expands to take in full table at which is seated the heavy-lidded, fleshy Japanese colonel. Behind him stands an orderly. Two guards at the door and a Japanese captain standing before him a short distance from the table.

COLONEL Fools! (*sweeps the leaves from the table with an angry gesture*) You should have known—! Why should the leaves be falling in the spring? (*leaves flutter to the floor*) What else have you found?

CAPTAIN Nothing, Excellency—only an old woman down on the road pulling her vegetable cart—

COLONEL (*barking*) What was an old woman doing out on the hills at night? Bring her in.

CAPTAIN Yes, Excellency. (*moves quickly to door, opens it, motions to guard*)

GUARD (*off scene*) Get up, you—the officer wants you—

MAMA MOSQUITO *(shaking old voice; coming in through the door. Camera moves to take in her frightened old face as she hunches one shoulder defensively against the threatening attitude of the captain. It is the old woman we first saw sitting against the broken wall of her devastated house)* I have done nothing— *(continues chattering before anyone can stop her)* I am a simple old woman—I harm no one—

CAPTAIN Silence!

MAMA MOSQUITO *(unheeding)*—and I appeal to your celestial majesty to spare a harmless old woman—

JAP COLONEL *(exasperated)* Be quiet and answer my questions!

MAMA MOSQUITO I know nothing, I swear—I was as a reed in my parents' garden—they were poor—they could not send me to the school—

CAPTAIN *(shouting)* Stop chattering and answer his Excellency's questions—what were you doing out on the road tonight? *(looms threateningly over her; she shrinks away, her hands going up in a defensive gesture)*

MAMA MOSQUITO I was on my way to my second granddaughter's house, but Your Excellency—I am old—and as a child my feet were bound and I walk slowly, and it was late and the moon had risen when I started back with my vegetable cart—

COLONEL *(glaring at her)*—Did you hear any shots?

MAMA MOSQUITO *(shakes her head; a little, almost senile smile flutters over her lips)* No—but—*(as if imparting a great secret she leans toward the colonel; the captain and the colonel both lean forward expectantly)*—there is much to hear at night—the singing of the crickets—*(the captain tightens his lips grimly; the colonel glares at her, his mouth opening to speak)*—and once a night-bird called—I—I do not hear as well as I—

COLONEL *(snarling)* Enough! *Enough!* Take her out! Why do you stand there, idiot? Get her out of here.

Captain grabs her arm and roughly pushes her toward the door while she continues talking over her shoulder to the colonel. Last shot of her face with its almost senile look before—

DISSOLVE TO:

Japanese sentry facing up and down near a cliff at some distance from the hut. The old woman stops to peer up at him.

JAP SENTRY *(shoving her roughly with the butt of his gun)* Get along there, old woman! What are you waiting for?

MAMA MOSQUITO I am afraid the marching years have dimmed my sight almost to utter darkness—the path is so steep—one false step up and I would fall to my death—

JAP SENTRY *(grinning)*—and good riddance!

MAMA MOSQUITO Oh, I know how steep it is—*(seems to stretch her neck a little to see over the rocky ledge)*—in my youth I played among these rocky cliffs—and looked down upon the beautiful village far below—*(sighs gently)*—have you seen its lights tonight, young soldier of Japan?

JAP SENTRY *(harshly)* I have seen nothing, old woman.

MAMA MOSQUITO *(gently)* Ah—you must lean out a little and peer down—though it is a trifle dangerous—

JAP SENTRY *(contemptuously)* A soldier of Japan fears nothing—

But he stretches his neck to peer down. The old woman goes on a few steps. In the black night she seems to melt into the darkness past the cliffs. The young sentry leans further over the cliff, glancing back to make sure the old woman does not observe him, when suddenly a shadow from the other side seems to pass behind him—and a high, sharp, keening scream, taken up and extended by music, cuts the air as the sentry hurtles over the cliff.

DISSOLVE TO:

The old woman, trudging between the shafts of her vegetable cart, bent forward almost animal-fashion. Now and then she stops for breath. Suddenly, her wheels strike an obstacle. She rests the cart and comes to the front wheels, peering down. A shapeless human bundle lies there, motionless. She turns it over. Sees it is a boy of about twenty, apparently lifeless. Puts her ear to his chest. By a quick flicker of her lids we know he is alive. As she tries to lift him he begins to moan—half opens his eyes. His face is gray with agony. His arms hang curiously limp and disjointed looking.

> **BOY** *(pushing the words out)* They—broke—my arms—at— at the shoulders—*(falls back, losing consciousness as the old woman bends over him)*

DISSOLVE TO:

Old woman pulling her cart along, stolidly. But her eyes seem to peer ahead as if trying to see through the darkening night.

> **JAP SOLDIER** *(appearing suddenly out of a side path)* You— stop!

Old woman stops suddenly, stiffening as she does so. Her hands hold tightly to the shafts of the cart. She stares straight ahead. The Jap comes closer. Peers at her.

> **JAP SOLDIER** *(contemptuously)* Ah—it is *you*, old one!

Bends over the cart. Sees the ripe peaches. Smacks his lips. Calls in Japanese to others behind him. Grinning, their bayonets held ready, five others run up to the cart, jabbering in Japanese. The first sentry snatches a peach. Two of the others spear ripe peaches with the points of their bayonets while the old woman keeps a stiff mask of indifference to her face. Only every so often her eyes flicker sideways to the center of the pile of hay, fearful of what they might find if they searched it. The first Jap sentry, who has rested his bayonet against the cart, now picks it up, waves her on, part of the peach still in his hand.

> **JAP I** Get on with you, old one—

Relieved, she begins to move forward—CAMERA on her and the front part of the cart. She has escaped with her burden . . . but suddenly the sound—

> **JAP II** Wait!

—and she freezes in her tracks. A Jap walks into scene, leering.

JAP II You are sure it is only fruit and vegetables you carry, old woman?

Old woman nods quickly. Continues to try and pull her cart forward but now the Japs press closely, intrigued with the promise of game.

JAP I We will see for ourselves.

Lifts his bayonet and plunges it quickly into the hay. The old woman stiffens sharply, and for an instant her eyes close as if she herself had been stabbed. The Jap laughs aloud as he draws out his bayonet, only to plunge it in again. The others follow suit, grinning and talking as they plunge their bayonets into various points of the hay. The fruit and vegetables are sheared and spoiled by the bayonets. The old woman's face seems to grow gray and marble-like. Little beads of sweat appear on her upper lip. But her face stays immobile.

JAP II *(motioning her to move)* Get on, now, old woman— there is nothing there—

The old woman moves slowly away from them, hearing their laughter and mockery behind her. CAMERA picks up her face, close-up, the eyes grim and bitter. Her eyes turn once to stare toward the middle of the cart. The CAMERA follows her glance. Almost imperceptibly the straw in the middle seems to settle, ever so slightly . . . CAMERA closeup of a few strands of hay—it assumes an almost translucent, dark-red, burnished quality. As the CAMERA concentrates on it, a tiny, blood-red drop of liquid rolls down one strand, like a little rivulet, and drops off. CAMERA back to closeup of old woman. Her eyes, fastened on the drop, enlarge with a look of dread.

DISSOLVE TO:

Old woman rolling the cart into her back yard. Looks guardedly around. Calls softly to someone in the house.

OLD WOMAN Lu Ping—Lu Ping—come quickly—

Old woman runs to back of cart. With desperate haste she shoves the hay and vegetables away from the center. The boy is not there—but where he lay is a small pool of blood. Her hand comes away wet. She looks at it, wipes it on her skirt. A small woman, with a girlish figure but gray hair and a skin almost as gray as her head, comes running to the old woman.

LU PING What is it? What has happened, Grandmother?

OLD WOMAN *(frantically shoving the hay around)* He was here—he was here—the devils have killed him—

LU PING *(bewildered)* Who?

A low moan issues from the front of the cart. The old woman runs between the shafts. Bends down to peer under the seat where the boy has evidently rolled or pushed himself. One arm, speared by the Jap bayonet, hangs over the edge of the cart. He almost falls into the old woman's arms.

OLD WOMAN *(guardedly)* Lu Ping—here—quickly—help me—

Between them they prepare to take the boy into the house.

DISSOLVE TO:

Kitchen. Early morning. Mama Mosquito and Lu Ping are in the kitchen. Mama Mosquito stirs broth on the stove, fills a bowl and hands it to Lu Ping. She goes to a small door, opens it and walks carefully down the stairs into a cellar room. The boy is lying on a cot against the wall. CAMERA moves closer to boy. He is lying on his back, the empty left sleeve hanging over the edge, his right arm strapped to his side. CAMERA closeup of his face. His eyes are staring straight upward, the tears welling in them and slipping down his cheeks onto the pillow. Lu Ping comes to the side of the cot, sits down on a low chair. The boy's eyes go obliquely to the empty sleeve and avert quickly, half closed.

LU PING *(pityingly; low voice)* It had to be done . . . My grandmother found you on the road to Suchen and brought you home . . . She had to cut it off.

His head rolls to the right side and an oblique look takes in the strapped right arm.

LU PING The right one will heal—

The boy continues to weep, shaking his head from side to side in negation.

BOY I am like a dead tree in a forest—

OLD WOMAN (*camera picks her up as she speaks from the door-way*) A tree still lives, though one limb is gone. Feed him, Lu Ping—

Lu Ping rises. The old woman takes her seat and with her left arm half-lifts his head so that Lu Ping can feed him. As she does so, the old woman's hand begins the soft massaging movement of the boy's right arm, with which we become familiar as the picture progresses.

SCENE DISSOLVES TO:

Peaceful mountain top with swiftly flowing stream of water. All quiet and seemingly deserted until CAMERA moves to a piece of camouflaged leafage that seems to move gently from one spot to another. It settles beneath a great tree, in a clearing. Then a birdcall is heard, clear and high, repeated a second time. Almost without movement, shadowy figures begin to come out of secluded places. They move silently to the tree as the birdcall continues. Then suddenly it stops. The CAMERA moves closer. Slowly the disguise of leaves lowers and a boy of thirteen is disclosed. He brushes leaves from his hair as he talks to the assembled men. They are all in clothes that blend with the green and brown of the surroundings.

BOY I am from the village of Chuwo-You.

GUERRILLA CAPTAIN She sent you?

BOY (*nodding*) Aye.

GUERRILLA CAPTAIN (*squinting along the barrel of his rifle*) We have heard that a noble son of the Emperor was shot on the hill road to Suchen—

GUERRILLA I —and a sentry fell foolishly over a cliff seeking a lost village—(*laughter among them, that has a touch of grimness*)

GUERRILLA CAPTAIN (*grinning but speaking with mock solemnity*) Aie—if a man seek what lies beyond his sight—one small misstep may well cost him his life. *(grins and nods are cut short when boy takes out a slip of paper)*

BOY *(holding it out to the captain)* She ordered me to bring you this—

GUERRILLA CAPTAIN *(takes the paper and opens it, reads it aloud)* "The west patch of ground between the first and second hills is to be newly planted in furrows with a good crop of apple seeds. Six carts of rice should be a good yield from the north."

He looks up with a wry grim twist of his mouth. Plucks a pencil out of his pocket and begins to write Chinese characters beside those already written (characters to be written from top to bottom of page as Chinese is written). When he has finished the words translate to English:

"The Shensu Province in the west—between the mountain defile

"The west patch of ground between the first and second hills

is to be mined in between the railroad tracks with grenades.

is to be newly planted in furrows with a good crop of apple seeds.

Six trains of Japanese are a good yield."

Six carts of rice should be a good yield from the north."

Shot of guerrilla faces leaning over captain's shoulder as we read it. Captain then strikes a match and watches paper burn. Lifts his gun and settles it in the crotch of his arm. Then puts his hand on the boy's shoulder.

GUERRILLA CAPTAIN *(kindly)* You may go back now—and say it will be done.

BOY *(wistfully)* Let me go with you—

GUERRILLA CAPTAIN *(kindly)* You are too young—

BOY *(jealously)* In Chianghaien the children's unit fought for a whole night and day throwing hand grenades—and in Sinshui they—

GUERRILLA CAPTAIN *(silencing him)* I know what they did at Sinshui, boy—my nephew Yang was killed there. Who would bring us our orders if we let you children fight our battles? *(pats him on the head)* Now go—

Boys shrugs disappointedly. Crouches down and becomes one with the grasses again as he moves away. The guerrillas watch him a moment, then they turn, one by one, going in different directions. They disappear into the woods, their camouflaged clothing seeming to melt into the trees.

DISSOLVE TO:

A narrow pass between two hills. A railroad track. A train is heard in the distance. It is almost dark. The CAMERA moves near enough to pick up men laying small round objects in the ground between and around the tracks, covering them lightly with dirt and moving silently away. The rumbling of the train is close. The music becomes the humming of the rails—the headlights round a bend. The men seem to melt into the shadows. As the train approaches the pass, a high birdcall is heard, answered by another, the same birdcall that was heard on the hilltop when the boy brought the message to the guerrillas. Only this time it seems to take on the quality of the whistle of the Freedom Train. The train enters the pass, roaring between the walls. Music sweeps in with it. Hold entire effect for a moment of suspense, ending with a tremendous explosion that seems to lift the entire pass into the air. Rumble and debris.

DISSOLVE TO:

House of colonel in Suchen village. Colonel pacing up and down in helpless rage.

COLONEL   *(continuing a tirade)*—Last week it was the supply train near Mukden—two days ago they blew up the dam at Kiangsu—*(tightens his lips)* Last night a trainload of our soldiers blown to bits—and this morning four sentries killed by a bomb on the road to Suchen—*(glares at the soldiers as if they were responsible)*—and you have found nothing!

SOLDIER I   *(apologetically)* Excellency—at Kiangsu they found only a bent old grandmother who walked through the woods seeking sticks for her fire—

SOLDIER II   *(as if eager to corroborate that)*—and at Mukden they said a young woman was seen running toward the hills—

COLONEL *(snarling, stops them with a motion of his hands)* Stupid! Idiots! How can an old woman become young! How much reward is offered now ?

CAPTAIN Twelve thousand yen, Excellency—

COLONEL *(barking)* Offer another for fifteen thousand!

QUICK DISSOLVE TO:

Bridge over swirling stream. Explosion. Quick flash of woman's body bent double, clambering up side of bank. DISSOLVE into huge poster: "REWARD OF TWENTY THOUSAND YEN FOR INFORMATION LEADING TO THE CAPTURE OF WOMAN KNOWN AS MAMA MOSQUITO! ALIVE OR DEAD!" Poster explodes, showing tangle of communication lines. Figure of Mama Mosquito crawling through ragged hole in a wall, dressed in trousers and shirt like a man. DISSOLVE to marching Jap column . . . exploding land mine . . . cries . . . confusion . . . Out of explosion huge poster: "REWARD OF THIRTY THOUSAND YEN FOR THE BODY OF THE WOMAN KNOWN AS MAMA MOSQUITO!"

DISSOLVE TO:

Mama Mosquito placidly sitting in her kitchen, writing in her ledger. (NOTE: The guns, ammunition, grenades, etc., and Japanese killed, are to be entered as vegetables. This will be appended.) Near the window, Li Wen is seated. Lu Ping is massaging his arm. CAMERA shows profile of Li Wen against the window, and full face of Lu Ping as she watches the despondent face of the boy. In spite of the grayness of her hair and skin, her eyes seem young.

LI WEN *(looking wistfully toward the hills)* Perhaps even now she is up there in the hills—

LU PING *(rubbing his arm)* Of whom do you speak, Li Wen?

LI WEN Mama Mosquito. They say she shoots like a man—and dresses like a man, in trousers and shirt—*(turns his head slightly toward Lu Ping)* Have you ever seen her, Lu Ping?

Mama Mosquito's hand pauses. She lifts her head ever so slightly as if awaiting Lu Ping's answer.

LU PING *(evasively, eyes down)* Her pictures are every-where—

LI WEN *(with pride in his idol)* They will never take her—she is too clever with her disguises—

He looks out of the window again. Lu Ping and Mama Mosquito exchange a secret little smile. Then Mama Mosquito begins again to write. Li Wen turns to watch Mama Mosquito writing in her ledger.

LI WEN What book is that you write in, old Mother?

MAMA MOSQUITO *(placidly)* The book that says what one man owes another, my son—

Stops, listens. From outside the door a low moaning sound is heard. Mama Mosquito motions to Lu Ping. She rises. Goes to the door. Stands for a moment listening, then draws back the bolt. A little thin Chinese boy runs by her into the room, staring around with terrified eyes. Then rushes with a great sobbing cry to Mama Mosquito. Clings to her, hiding his face in her dress. A great racking sob escapes him.

MAMA MOSQUITO *(gently stroking his head)* What is it? What has happened, Ching-pau?

CHING-PAU *(through gulping sobs)* My sister—Mei Lan—*(Mama Mosquito stiffens; Lu Ping's hand goes to her throat)*—the Japanese soldiers were passing—*(begins to moan again)*

MAMA MOSQUITO *(flatly, as if making an effort to control her voice)* Hush—hush, little one—

CHING-PAU *(looks up at her face, his own streaked with tears)* They put their hands over Mei Lan's mouth and carried her—*(begins to sob again)*—there was no one to help—

Mama Mosquito presses his face into her dress again as if to stop the horror of his narrative. Lu Ping shivers. Li Wen tightens his lips, moves his head from side to side in helpless misery.

MAMA MOSQUITO *(echoing heavily)* No one to help. *(she disengages the child's clinging hands, goes to the cupboard and takes out a rice cake and a peach)* Here—take this rice cake and this peach. Go home, Ching-pau—*(sounds of commotion off scene)*.

LI WEN *(glancing out the window; sharply)* Japanese soldiers—through the garden—

The little boy sends a hunted glance around and runs into the corner, huddling his little thin body against the walls. His eyes are like those of a little frightened animal. Mama Mosquito motions to Lu Ping to take her former position near Li Wen. She obeys. Sits down. Begins to massage his arm. There is an almost maternal protectiveness as she leans toward him. A harsh knock at the door, and Mama Mosquito moves toward it. Her face is grim and set, but as she opens the door it assumes the placid untroubled blankness of a simple peasant. She stands with her hands folded in front of her as one Japanese soldier stamps into the room. The others loll just outside the door.

JAP SOLDIER   I wish water to drink.

Mama Mosquito motions with her head toward the pails of water at the other side of the room. The Jap marches toward it. The little boy shrinks further into his corner. The Jap stops for an instant as he sees Lu Ping massaging Li Wen's arm. Imperceptibly Lu Ping's hand slows as the Jap stops a little behind her, her body tense. The Jap sneers as he looks slantwise down at the boy and sees one arm is missing. He goes on, takes a dipper of water and drinks it down, wiping his mouth with the back of his hand. Mama Mosquito stands quietly, only her eyes moving. As the Jap comes back toward the door, he makes an unexpected swerve around Lu Ping. Deliberately he pushes Li Wen off his chair, watches him topple over. A burst of laughter from soldiers at door. Li Wen shuts his eyes in agony as his sick shoulder hits the floor. The Jap, grinning, kicks him, then continues toward the door. Li Wen's eyes open, filled with violent frustrated rage and hatred. Lu Ping rises, half bent toward him as if to help him. A quick, warning headshake from Mama Mosquito stops her. The little boy cowers back with a stifled, frightened sound as the Jap passes him. The Jap goes by Mama Mosquito, still grinning as if at a great joke. Joins his laughing companions. They go out. Mama Mosquito stands stiffly for a moment, then closes the door, leaning against it for an instant. Her face is grim and thoughtful. CAMERA picks up little boy, who, now that the soldiers have gone, is nervously beginning to nibble his rice cake. But his eyes are still full of fear. Mama Mosquito walks over to Li Wen, whose eyes meet hers with rage and pain and humiliation. Lu Ping, weeping with pity for Li Wen, slips to her knees, sobbing, her hand touching Li Wen's freshly bruised shoulder with the familiar massaging movement. She slips her arm under his shoulder to raise him. There is a fiercely-repressed protectiveness in her gestures. Mama Mosquito stands looking down at them.

> **MAMA MOSQUITO** (*purposefully*) I must go out, Lu Ping— there is work to be done.

CAMERA moves with her as she slowly descends the cellar stairs. CAMERA back to room. Little boy comes a little way out of his corner, moving toward Lu Ping and Li Wen. He is still cowering but less frightened. His hand with the rice cake goes to his mouth as he watches them.

> DISSOLVE TO:

Mama Mosquito in cellar, dressed in trousers and shirt, standing before a hidden cache, pulls aside some bricks, takes out a revolver and some bullets. Fills the revolving chamber. CAMERA closeup of her determined face. Puts revolver in holster. Replaces bricks and goes up the cellar stairs to kitchen, pulling a dark cloak over her to hide her costume. As she enters the kitchen she sees that Lu Ping has helped Li Wen to his feet and they are both absorbed in each other. Li Wen stares at Lu Ping with a look of complete amazement on his face. Mama Mosquito stops beside Lu Ping, who is wiping her tear-stained face with the edge of her wide sleeve. Li Wen continues to stare at her as the gray ash-dust slowly disappears from her face.

> **MAMA MOSQUITO** (*touching Lu Ping's arm*) Lock the door after me, Lu Ping—I will be back soon—

Lu Ping seems not to hear her, for she has become conscious of Li Wen's intense gaze. Mama Mosquito goes on to the door and closes it after her. CAMERA closeup of little boy, his eyes staring at these two, munching his rice cake absorbedly, all the fear now gone from his face as he watches them. CAMERA closeup of Lu Ping's face, the ash completely removed, revealing the young loveliness of an eighteen-year-old girl. As she now becomes fully conscious of his rapt gaze, a slow flush softly suffuses her face and neck, and her eyelids lower shyly. CAMERA moves to Li Wen's face. There is a new look in his eyes now, no longer despairing—but a dawning manliness, as if the realization of her youth and beauty has now made him her protector. Something of a slow smile, with a quality of tenderness and humility, begins to light his face as Lu Ping stands motionless before him. CAMERA moves to face of little boy as he stands staring at them, abstractedly munching his rice cake, watching them, his eyes going from one face to another in absorbed interest.

DISSOLVE TO:

Guerrilla hideout, with men huddled around a campfire. Late afternoon. The fire carefully bedded down so as to be nearly invisible. They are cooking a meal over the fire. Highlights of grim faces, young, middle-aged and old, all with the taut, watchful look of men who live dangerously. A young sentry paces back and forth in the rear.

There is the sound of a birdcall (heard earlier among the guerrillas)—and they stiffen in their attitudes. The call is repeated again. The guerrilla captain answers. The call comes once more. Then noiselessly, Mama Mosquito, clad in trousers and shirt, a soldier's cap on her hair, comes into the circle. It is the only time she is seen with the guerrillas. In the way each man gets to his feet, stands before her with a mixture of pride and respect and humility, and the affection in his eyes, is revealed the measure of their feeling for her. She is so little and frail looking, yet she appears strong and capable and calm.

She looks from one face to the other, but her gaze lingers on the young sentry. He is on the outer edge of the group. She speaks to the group in a low voice that does not carry to the sentry.

MAMA MOSQUITO   The village of Suchen has known more trouble—

The faces of the men grow hard. The guerrilla captain murmurs something beneath his breath. Jerks his head toward the sentry with a motion of warning. Mama Mosquito nods as if she understands. But the young sentry has caught the name of the village. He pushes through the circle. His eyes go swiftly from face to face.

SENTRY Did someone speak of Suchen? *(eyes evade his; he looks with desperate appeal at Mama Mosquito)* Tell me, good mother—what happened in my village?

MAMA MOSQUITO *(slowly, looking at him with pity)* Mei Lan was taken by the soldiers.

Avoid face of sentry but show faces of other men in the circle. As CAMERA shows faces of the men, Mama Mosquito's voice is heard:

MAMA MOSQUITO She chose to go to her forefathers, Lee Kim—she cut her wrists.

There is no sound from the men, whose faces we are still watching. A stifled sob from the sentry, out of scene. CAMERA moves to Mama Mosquito, moving quickly toward him. She stops after a few steps.

CAPTAIN *(hard)* There is a thing that must be done—

MAMA MOSQUITO Tonight. I need volunteers.

Guerrillas make quick offers. Flash for first time to Lee Kim's face. Grim, granite-like.

LEE KIM (SENTRY) It needs only one man—

MAMA MOSQUITO *(hard and swift as a man)* There can be no return.

LEE KIM *(emotionlessly)* I know.

MAMA MOSQUITO You must crawl right up to the house. There must be no warning.

LEE KIM Not a leaf will move in my passing.

MAMA MOSQUITO Choose your own time.

LEE KIM *(grimly)* I have already chosen it.

He salutes. Turns and disappears into the night. Men's faces and firelight dissolve into the outside of the big house as the almost unseen figure of the sentry crawls through the neglected garden of the house of the colonel. Laughter and high-pitched voices come through the window. The CAMERA creeps up . . . as if through Lee Kim's eyes we see into the room where the colonel is drinking with his officers. For an instant, the CAMERA moves for closeup of the grim young face of the Chinese sentry, seen through a screen of leaves. He wriggles into a kneeling position close to the window, his face twisted with hate. As he raises his arm—

DISSOLVE TO KITCHEN OF:

Small house of Mama Mosquito. At the kitchen fireplace the usual massaging of the boy's arm is going on. Only now the young boy's eyes rest on Lu Ping's disguised face with love. He sits straight as she massages his arm. She is young and shining with love in spite of the ash dust over her face and hair. They do not speak. The grandmother writes in the ledger. As the brush moves over the paper, there is a blinding explosion far off, and a burst of flame makes the night red. The brush poises above the page as the heads lift. Lu Ping's hand stops in its motion. Involuntarily she presses close to Li Wen. All turn to the window, where flames are lighting up the place where the colonel's house was. Then the old grandmother turns back to her ledger. Closeup of her face, nodding ever so slightly, as she puts down another entry.

DISSOLVE TO:

Scene in office of high Japanese official. Commandant and captain in room.

> COMMANDANT *(clipped)* This time there must be no mistake. The woman known as Mama Mosquito must be found. Here are her latest pictures—*(hands some pasteboards to the captain)*—have every suspect rounded up—men *and* women—

> CAPTAIN Yes, Excellency—

> COMMANDANT Search the villages of Suchen and Chuwo—

> CAPTAIN Yes, Excellency—

> COMMANDANT —and increase the reward to fifty thousand yen!

DISSOLVE to quick series of shots of old men and women being herded in various places. Closeups of frightened old faces turned this way and that by rough hands, with the picture of Mama Mosquito held up beside each face. Each suspect pushed away to make room for another. Picture shows Mama Mosquito in man's trousers and shirt, among a group of guerrillas. The picture is blurred as if caught in action, her face turned a little sideways, her cap pulled over her forehead. There is little or no resemblance to Mama Mosquito as we have seen her in the foregoing scenes.

Another shot of colonel's house. Captain is standing before him.

COLONEL   Have you found her?

CAPTAIN   Not yet, Excellency—but we know now definitely that she hides in Suchen.

COLONEL   Then we must destroy every man, woman and child in the village of Suchen!

DISSOLVE TO:

Destroyed village . . . smoke drifting up through tree branches. Shot of bodies hanging from trees. CAMERA comes down along these bodies, to show a few bodies on the ground. A small distance away, the guerrilla captain and the school teacher stand among a few guerrillas, with grim, bitter faces.

SCHOOL TEACHER   *(bitterly)* We are too late—

There are sounds of a scuffle off scene, and they turn. Four Japanese prisoners, hands tied behind them, are pushed into the circle. Three are insolent, but the fourth, looking up at the hanging bodies, shivers as if with a chill. The blacksmith moves forward, addressing one of them.

BLACKSMITH   How many were in your company?

Jap soldier, grinning insolently, murmurs something beneath his breath. From behind the Japs, comes a grim, implacable voice.

MAMA MOSQUITO   You must speak louder—*(there is a quick startled flash of surprise from all as they turn to the voice)*—it is difficult for them to hear—*(camera flash to hanging bodies, back to frightened faces of the Japs and the grim faces of the guerrillas surrounding them)*—and it is they who sit in judgment here.

CAMERA PANS to a body lying on the ground. The head has been resting sideways. As we watch it, the head suddenly rolls downward as if passing quick judgment, and the force of the fall continues in a gentle nodding movement before settling in the last rigidity of death. Quick flash to the guerrilla captain. He jerks his head sideways, and the jaws of the Japs drop in real fear. Guerrillas grab them in implacable hatred.

DISSOLVE TO:

Garden of Mama Mosquito's house. Li Wen is kneeling on the earth. It is early dusk. Lu Ping kneels before him, making furrows. As she draws them, Li Wen, with his weak right hand, drops seeds along. She smiles with tender encouragement as she watches. Their eyes meet now and then with a supreme, almost sublime contentment. Lu Ping is exquisite without her gray makeup. Pausing to let his eyes rove over her face, he does not speak, but she flushes and becomes starry-eyed beneath his look. To break the silence, she speaks.

LU PING *(shyly)* Grandmother will be angry with me for leaving off the ash dust.

LI WEN *(simply)* The anger of all the world would melt, could it but look upon your face, Lu Ping.

She drops her eyes and continues with the furrowing. He drops the seeds, looking at her. She turns her hand upward and one of the seeds falls into her palm. They both stop and observe it. Her hand gently closes over the seed.

LI WEN In the tale of Chang Tao there was a truly remarkable man whose ears were filled constantly with celestial music, and who sought many ways to find the cause of it.

LU PING *(breathlessly)*—And did he find it?

LI WEN Yes—and she was beautiful.

LU PING *(her hand opens, turns, the seed falls into the open furrow, lip trembles)* It is easy to love where beauty is—

LI WEN   Where love is, there is beauty.

They pause and gaze at one another for one long, tender moment, she grateful for his words. Then her eyes droop and his mood changes, quickly becomes mischievous.

> **LI WEN**   Look you, Lu Ping, I am a worthless son of illustrious ancestors. When I was but a boy, my honorable parent warned me I would come to no good end, because it was my habit always to go on in advance both of my feet and of my head.
>
> **LU PING**   *(falling in with his mischievous mood)* I have not found it so, Li Wen. *(a little merry look in her eye as she swiftly glances up, then down again)* I have found yours a very steadfast nature.
>
> **LI WEN**   *(watching her)* As the mountain rises, so the river winds—
>
> **LU PING**   *(merrily)* Your father taught you many things, Li Wen—
>
> **LI WEN**   To speak with humility of one's ancestors—to love China fervently—and to kneel with reverence before her beauties. *(a merry twinkle in his eye)*
>
> **LU PING**   *(delighted with him)* He taught you well, Li Wen. What more?

Li Wen and Lu Ping laugh delightedly. Their foreheads almost touch as they lean toward each other. As they laugh, their laughter is seemingly echoed in an ugly, loose kind of laughter. A man's thick shadow falls across them. Closeup of their faces, startled, the laughter dying. Li Wen looks up . . . the Jap captain is standing behind Lu Ping. Lu Ping keeps her face down. He looks scornfully at Li Wen's left sleeve and grins.

> **JAP CAPTAIN**   Lame pig of a diseased mother!

Li Wen bows his head in futile shame. Lu Ping's face lifts in swift anger and the Jap sees her for the first time. He gives a grunt of amazement, bends down, takes her by the hair, pressing her head backward to see her better. Li Wen, making a strangled sound in his throat, lifts himself to a crouching position; but contemptuously, without looking at him, the Jap captain kicks Li Wen back. Li Wen falls. The captain's face is now a mask of ugly passion, the eyes glazed, the mouth loose, with animal passion. Lu Ping covers her face with her hands and cowers back. The Jap clutches at her, tearing her dress from shoulder to waist, pulls her violently into his arms and puts his lips to her throat. There is a muffled, half-choked sound behind them. Suddenly an arm comes between Lu Ping's face and the Jap. It goes around the Jap's throat, stiffens, tightens. CAMERA picks up choking strangulation of the Jap's face—his desperate efforts to release himself, unavailingly. Then CAMERA shoots over shoulder to reveal Li Wen's face, pressed tightly against the Jap's head—a strange, grim, granite-like face with beads of perspiration on it, his lips drawn back from his teeth with the terrible effort he is making. The muscles of the arm stand out like cords. The Jap's eyes roll up in his head, and he goes limp. As his body relaxes, drops, Li Wen drops with him. CAMERA moves to Lu Ping's face, her eyes staring in fascinated horror. Behind them the voice of Mama Mosquito is heard.

    MAMA MOSQUITO *(grimly)* Let him fall—

The body rolls from the relaxed arm of Li Wen. CAMERA moves to Li Wen, staring down at his right arm (now hanging limp) in almost uncomprehending amazement. He looks up at Lu Ping. She is smiling tremulously. She moves toward him, touches his arm almost reverently, stands close to Li Wen as if she knows now that he will always protect her. Li Wen straightens up, dignity and pride in his bearing. Then he turns to Mama Mosquito. He stares at her, looking her up and down. She is in the man's costume. There is a puzzled frown on Li Wen's face, but only a grim, warning look in Mama Mosquito's.

    MAMA MOSQUITO You must get away to the hills, Li Wen— the soldiers will be here soon. Every house is being searched—

A quick startled glance from Lu Ping to Mama Mosquito. Li Wen looks from one to the other, then at Mama Mosquito's costume, with a dawning realization in his eyes.

    LI WEN *(enlightened)* Mama Mosquito—you are she—*(with deep reverence)* Mama Mosquito—

As if before a saint, he drops to his knees before her, bowing his head. She looks down at him with tenderness that does not erase the grimness of her face.

> **MAMA MOSQUITO** Take Lu Ping with you—it will not be good for her to be found here. She will show you the road to the guerrilla camp. They will take care of you—(*Li Wen looks up*) You are ready to join my army now, my son—

Her hand rests on his head for a moment as if in a blessing. Then she puts her hand to her holster. Li Wen rises. Mama Mosquito gives him her gun. He hefts it in his palm for a few seconds, then slips it into his pocket. Lu Ping stands close to him. His arm goes around her shoulders, holding her strongly to him. There is a beautiful light on their faces. The faint chugging of motorcycles is heard far off. Their heads lift to listen.

> **MAMA MOSQUITO** They come.
>
> **LU PING** (*motioning to the body*) The body—
>
> **MAMA MOSQUITO** I will take care of it.

As they fade away into the night, Mama Mosquito listens with her head raised for a scant second—then kneels and begins to drag the body through the shrubbery.

FADE TO:

Jap detachment coming down the road on motorcycles. Roar of motorcycles up full. Chugging fades as scene fades back to—

Mama Mosquito in her kitchen, once again dressed in woman's clothes. The chugging grows louder. She holds herself erect at the door. As motorcycles roar up to door and stop outside, she droops her body into the attitude of a frightened, dumb old peasant—the same attitude she had when the sentries accosted her on the road after the explosion of the troop train. A pounding on the door. Mama Mosquito opens it, shrinking timidly back as a Japanese captain and soldiers crowd into the room, with a wizened Chinese merchant shoved before them.

> **JAP CAPTAIN** (*barking*) Well—is this the old woman?

YEN TANG   *(peering)* Lift the lantern that I may see her well—

Lantern is flashed into the face of Mama Mosquito. She shrinks sideways against the wall, seeming shrunken and aged. Turns face in sudden gesture away from light as lantern flashes on her.

YEN TANG   *(triumphantly)* It is she—the old devil! She goes with her cart to the hills—the only one who leaves our village.

MAMA MOSQUITO   *(quavering)* I do not understand—

YEN TANG   It is she who sends word to the guerrillas!

MAMA MOSQUITO   *(old quavering voice)* He tells lies, honorable ones—*lies*. How could an old woman like me get up into those hills?

YEN TANG   *(shouting to stop her)* The dead man who threw the bomb was betrothed to Mei Lan! It was you who sent word to the hills!

MAMA MOSQUITO   *(cannily, peering up into the captain's face)* Aie—and how would that one know—unless he too were there? And how could he be there and still be faithful to you?

Jap captain looks uncertainly from her to Yen Tang. Yen Tang's face is suffused with fury.

YEN TANG   *(shaking)* I told you she would lie—

JAP CAPTAIN   *(curtly)* Be still. *(to Mama Mosquito)* I will take you to sit awhile in a locked place, old woman—until you tell us the truth. How did you get word to the guerrillas?

MAMA MOSQUITO   *(whining)* Why should I get word to them, Excellency—and kill those who buy my vegetables? Was not the Honorable Colonel one of my best customers—and did he not always pay me well—nay, better than any other? Just as he paid this one—this traitor—to bring him news of the Chinese? *(voice rises a little)*—just as the Chinese pay Yen Tang for news of the Japanese!

YEN TANG *(moves forward, lifting his arm to strike her; she shrinks back)* It is not true! Lies—all lies—*(the soldiers stop him)*

CAPTAIN A traitor wears two coats—*(roughly)*—But why should I believe *you*, old woman?

MAMA MOSQUITO *(again half-whining)* Because I have no reason to lie, Excellency. I am only a poor old woman who has harmed no one and wishes only to be let alone with my garden—but this Yen Tang would kill even his children for money. It was he who took word to the guerrillas and was well paid for it.

Yen Tang breaks away from the Jap soldiers. Face contorted, hands clawing at the old woman. Jap captain strikes him with his hand. He turns with a howl on the Jap captain, screaming: "Lies—lies—I have done nothing!" Soldier hits him on the head with the butt of his gun. Yen Tang falls. Captain looks closely at Mama Mosquito and then points quickly to unconscious body of Yen Tang.

CAPTAIN *(curtly)* Take him—

They go. Mama Mosquito locks the door after them and leans against the doorjamb wearily. Orchestra in softly to mood.

MAMA MOSQUITO *(bitter sarcasm)* Fools! Stupid fools!

VOICE *(speaking from the other side of the room)* So it *is* true!

(The stranger is the same flyer who is telling the story in the foxhole, but he is in shadow so it is not too apparent until we see him in next scene.) Orchestra hits sharp chord and holds ominous. Mama Mosquito's head comes up startled, with the first moment of terror we have seen. She stares into the darkened corner of the room from whence the voice came, and barely breathes the words.

MAMA MOSQUITO Who are you?

CAMERA is now on the shadowed face of a man moving toward her.

STRANGER So you *are* the woman known as Mama Mosquito—

(Cont.)   191.

Orchestra hits sharp chord and holds ominous.
Mama Mosquitos head comes up startled, with the
first moment of terror we have seen. She stares
into the darkened corner of the room from whence
the voice came, and barely breathes the words.
another ragged yet hard and capable Chinese
The stranger is ~~the same flyer who is telling the~~   *querilla,*
~~story in the foxhole but he is in shadow so it is~~   *a new face*
~~not too apparent until we see him in next scene.~~   *which we*
                                                             have not
                              MAMA MOSQUITO: *seen before*
           Who are you?

~~Camera is now on. The shadowed face of a man moving~~
~~toward her.~~

                                    STRANGER: (*Comes forward*)
           So you *are* the woman known a s Mama
           Mosquito -

Flash to Mama Mosquito's face. Pale - resigned -
lips barely moving.

                              MAMA MOSQUITO:
           How did you get in?

                              STRANGER:
           The others came the front way - I used
           the back. My orders are to bring you
           to Chung King! Come!   DISSOLVE

~~Music rises minutely. Scene changes~~ to corridor of *palace,*
~~of a large, well-furnished dwelling...~~ Music carries   *with*
theme of new China. We see the drooping tired figure *soldiers*
of Mama Mosquito hobbling along slightly behind the   *on guard.*
~~figure,~~ bewildered.
stranger
                              MAMA MOSQUITO:
           What place is this?

                              STRANGER:
                  (smiles)
           Come this way, please.

Door opens showing a large hall filled with people,
all standing at attention, looking toward the door
through which Mama Mosquito is to pass. She looks
to her guide with a startled expression. He nods and
smiles.. and now we know it is the flyer.. takes her
arm and leads her gently down the aisle between the
long lines of Chinese Dignataries and the military,
all gathered as if at a function. They make way for
her and the stranger, Mama Mosquito glancing in growing confusion to the right and left. Then slowly as
she sees what is ahead of her, her little, tired,
shriveled body straightens up. The guide has moved
aside, leaving her standing before a raised dais,
before Chiang Kai Shek and his retinve (CONTINUED).

11. Page of Faulkner's revision of Chinese sequence

(Cont.)

Chinese B —
192.

STRANGER:
Your Excellency - I have brought
you Madame Chau Yutang.

CHIANG KAI SHEK:
Welcome, Madame Chau Yutang - we
have been waiting for you.

Mama Mosquito kneels before him, head touching the
ground, hands outspread. Chiang motions ~~to a stranger~~, *Soldiers*
~~who~~ gently raises her.

CHIANG KAI SHEK:
We have heard much of the glorious
exploits of your guerilla fighters
against the enemy, Madame Chau Yutang.
(twinkle in his
eye)
How many have you ~~disposed of~~ *slain?*
.... eight hundred and sixty-three?

MAMA MOSQUITO:
(humbly)
Sixty-five, Excellency. I shot two
more soldiers on the Chu Yen Bridge
last week.
~~(a grin visible goes
around the room)~~

*Voices in bg.,
muted, repressed.
Sheng Li!*

CHIANG KAI SHEK:
(smiling)
Madame Chau Yutang --

MAMA MOSQUITO:
(voice quavering
a little)
~~Please, sir~~ *Excellency* - there is another
name they call me in the hills.
I should like you to call me by
that name too -
(proudly)
Mama Mosquito.

CHIANG KAI SHEK:
(gently)
Very well, then, Mama Mosquito.
I have brought you here to offer
you a commission in the mountain
forces. An angel of liberty like
yourself should be in my army.

(CONTINUED)

12. Page of Faulkner's revision of Chinese sequence

Flash to Mama Mosquito's face. Pale—resigned—lips barely moving.

MAMA MOSQUITO   How did you get in?

STRANGER   The others came the front way—I used the back. My orders are to bring you to Chungking! Come!

Music rises ominously. Scene changes to corridor of a large, well-furnished dwelling. Music carries theme of New China. We see the drooping tired figure of Mama Mosquito hobbling along slightly behind the flyer, bewilderedly.

MAMA MOSQUITO   What place is this?

STRANGER   (*smiles*) Come this way, please.

Door opens, showing a large hall filled with people, all standing at attention, looking toward the door through which Mama Mosquito is to pass. She looks to her guide with a startled expression. He nods and smiles and now we know it is the flyer. Takes her arm and leads her gently down the aisle between the long lines of Chinese dignitaries and the military, all gathered as if at a function. They make way for her and the stranger, Mama Mosquito glancing in growing confusion to the right and left. Then slowly, as she sees what is ahead of her, her little, tired, shriveled body straightens up. The guide has moved aside, leaving her standing before a raised dais.

STRANGER   Your Excellence—I have brought you Madame Chau Yutang.

CHIANG KAI-SHEK   Welcome, Madame Chau Yutang—we have been waiting for you.

Mama Mosquito kneels before him, head touching the ground, hands outspread. Chiang motions to stranger, who gently raises her.

CHIANG KAI-SHEK   We have heard much of the glorious exploits of your guerrilla fighters against the enemy, Madame Chau Yutang. (*twinkle in his eye*) How many have you—er—disposed of? . . . eight hundred and sixty-three?

MAMA MOSQUITO   (*humbly*) Sixty-five, Excellency. I shot two more soldiers on the Chu Yen Bridge last week. *(a grim chuckle goes around the room)*

CHIANG KAI-SHEK *(smiling)* Madame Chau Yutang—

MAMA MOSQUITO *(voice quavering a little)* Please, sir—there is another name they call me in the hills. I should like you to call me by that name too—*(proudly)*—Mama Mosquito.

CHIANG KAI-SHEK *(gently)* Very well, then, Mama Mosquito. I have brought you here to offer you a commission in the mountain forces. An angel of liberty like yourself should be in my army.

MAMA MOSQUITO Excellency—you would think me a foolish and stubborn old woman—and you are right. But you see—I know the only kind of war I can fight against the Japanese.

Pause. Voice deep with bitterness and repression. CAMERA goes close to her to take in each graven line of her face, as she slowly draws from the neck of her dress a small bag. She bends down and pours the contents of the bag on the edge of the dais, then sinks slowly to her knees and smoothes out the rough clumps of soil. Her hand touches it with a fierce kind of reverence. She seems absorbed to the exclusion of those around her. They move a little forward to look. Chiang Kai-shek bends closer.

MAMA MOSQUITO Here is a little of the earth of China, Excellency. *(her eyes look up with a deep glow in them)* From this earth, fed with the blood of her youth, will grow the New China—but this earth will not be planted again until the invader has been driven from our land forever. I have made that pledge—and all my thousands of guerrilla fighters with me! *(through the above line her hand clutches the earth with that same fierce gesture we saw once before, then slowly, tiredly, the hand goes limp; tiredly)*—but I am a poor, sick old woman who talks too much. I have not many days left to fight. May I go back to my people?

CHIANG KAI-SHEK *(gently)* You may indeed—and the blessing of all China goes with you.

Mama Mosquito slowly rises, straightens her frail body, and

suddenly she raises her hand with the two fingers in the "V" sign . . . utters the Chinese victory cry.

MAMA MOSQUITO   Sheng Li! Sheng Li Chiang Shi Women Di!

VOICES ALL OVER THE ROOM   Sheng Li Chiang Shi Women Di!

Through the effect of voices comes the eerie sound of the Freedom Train far off as scene fades and we find ourselves back to the original scene.

FADE IN

Paris. It is now occupied by the Germans. The order has gone out to round up all the prettiest young unmarried girls, so that German soldiers can choose them to get children and so improve the French race. The girls are rounded up by police, but no physical force is to be used on them to make them take soldier lovers. It is a little more subtle than that. A bribe, rather, is offered: if the girls acquiesce, behave, they will get more and better food, their families will be freer from molestation, etc. Clemente is one of these.

The other girls don't yet realize what is going on. Clemente does. One of the girls is the sister of the man who took her goodbye message to Albert in England. Clemente is trying to protect her. She is already struggling, protesting, to save all of the girls, but in particular this one whom she knows. At last the officer in charge has to order two soldiers to subdue Clemente and hold her by force.

With the usual cold-blooded German thoroughness, the officer has before him all the information about the girls. Clemente's papers show that she was once a registered prostitute. The officer informs her brutally that she is not fit to mix her blood with the German race. He orders the two soldiers to hold her until he gets through here; he indicates that he will keep her for himself. Clemente is taken out, struggling. The officer orders the business to get on.

The frightened huddle of young girls is taken in charge by some German women, police or some women's official Nazi organization, army, etc. They are forced to strip practically naked except for alluring negligee garments taken from the Paris shops. They are then paraded where the chosen young German soldiers can examine them and choose.

The officer returns to Clemente. He sends the guards out, tells Clemente she will now be his mistress, approaches her. She fights back fiercely. The German shouts for the guards to return. Four enter. The officer gives them an order in German. They approach Clemente. Clemente tries to fight them all while the officer watches. They begin to subdue her. She still struggles.

> **OFFICER** Careful, you dogs. I do not wish her hurt nor disfigured.

They subdue Clemente, hold her while the officer rapes her.

DISSOLVE TO:

Holland. The Battle for Britain is going on. Clemente is in Holland now. She is now a symbol of France itself: conquered, debased, prone and dazed and for a time apathetic beneath the conqueror's heel. She seems to have given up. She has gone down the ladder. The officer has deserted her, she probably took another one, a lesser one, in order to eat, get food and shelter and, since she has been debased and fouled, because she has given up and no longer cares. Now she is a camp follower, the easy intransigent mistress of any man, soldier, quisling, who will give her a little food or money or a tawdry scrap of finery. Her pride and hope are gone; she is no longer even physically dainty and clean.

One day she sees on the street the Frenchman, Henri Ballin, the brother of the girl she had tried to protect that day in Paris, and who had taken her goodbye message to Albert in England. He is disguised, but she recognizes him anyway, and he recognizes her. He tries to escape before she can speak to him. He is a De Gaullist spy working in Holland. Through his own organization he knows Clemente's history; that she has apparently taken up with the Germans. But it is mostly her present appearance that he distrusts. He knew her character before. He doesn't think that it has changed and that she has sold out, will be a spy for her seducers. But she is shabby and even dirty. Her present life is obvious. Her whole air is passive; not even embittered, but lost, as if she has given up, no longer cares about anything, France or herself either, that she might expose him by chance, without even meaning to, to any intransigent lover among the German troops or to the German police, who of course keep a checkup on her, as on all civilians, particularly the ones who seem to be willing to go along with them.

But she overtakes him. To escape now would only draw her attention to him more. He must conceal from her what he is actually doing. He intimates that he is like her; he has given up, just wants to live and keep clear of the police. For the moment a sort of hope has waked in her, but his air has discouraged it; it seems to die again. He tells her he has changed his name, now has a job in German-run factory.

CLEMENTE   You mean there's nothing to do about it?

Henri shrugs, passes it off: Not him, anyhow. He just wants to get along. She agrees; the hope, if it was hope, dies again. If this is the way French men feel about it, what can a woman do? The unspoken knowledge of his sister is between them. They both know it. Clemente hesitates to tell Henri. He almost asks, stops.

HENRI   (*as he has spoken to Albert*) No. Don't tell me. I don't want to know.

CLEMENTE   I tried . . .

HENRI   (*roughly almost*) I thank you. I don't wish to know.

He wants to get away now; this is already too dangerous; perhaps he should leave Holland, send another who is not known to anyone in his place. But there is something in Clemente's mind, that she is trying to say. At last she does so, humbly, clumsily. If he has a room, maybe she could come and live with him. She would not bother him, she would sleep on the floor. Then she could quit the way she now has to live. He has a job; maybe he could get her one too . . .

But Henri realizes this will not do. He pities her, but he can do nothing. This is one of the reasons why he must get away; not to see a countryman, a girl whom he had known in happy times, brought to this pass. He says he's sorry, he can't; he is being transferred to another town, anyway, says goodbye, stops, takes what money he has from his pocket and offers it to her. She refuses it quietly.

> **CLEMENTE**   You are poor, too. I don't need it. I can always earn enough.

> **HENRI**   Goodbye, then.

> **CLEMENTE**   Goodbye.

He goes on.

DISSOLVE TO:

Some time has passed. One day Clemente is picked up by two Gestapo agents. She offers to show her police card; it is in order. They don't answer. They take her on to the police station, and in to the same man who raped and then cast her off. The officer sends the two policemen out, leaving only Clemente and his orderly. He shows Clemente a photograph of Henri, asks if she knows him, watches her face, realizes that she does. Clemente has just time to remember that Henri has changed his name, and will get in trouble if the Germans find it out, denies that she knows the man.

> **OFFICER**   Come, come. When you asaulted two of my men that day in Paris to defend his sister, you do not know the brother?

Clemente still denies she knows him. The officer has a copy of the photograph. He gives it to Clemente. He tells her that the man is now in Holland, probably disguised and under a false name. Clemente from now on is to spend her time looking for him. As a guarantee of good faith, her police license to practice her profession and her food card will be taken from her and held until she finds the man.

> **CLEMENTE**   But how will I eat?

The officer says his orderly will see to that, that once each day

Clemente can return and receive some food. But she knows what will happen if she is caught practicing her profession. He dismisses her.

Now he tells the orderly that Henri is a De Gaulle spy, is up to something. That is, the orderly knows this; he and the officer have already planned the plot, which is now in operation. Just enough dialogue here to tell the audience what is up. At last the officer tells the orderly: "Wait three days. Let her get good and hungry."

Now Clemente can neither earn money, nor buy food with it if she could. Each day she returns to the police station, joins a queue of hungry people while the orderly watches, receives a bowl of thin soup, a scrap almost of bread, nothing else. She is slowly starving. She protests to the orderly, who puts her off.

On the third day, there is hardly anything in the bowl. While she looks at it, the orderly approaches, asks her if she wants to eat. She says, "Yes." He says, "Come with me."

WIPE TO:

The garret room where Clemente has been given permission to sleep. Clemente sits on the tumbled bed, her clothes disarranged. The orderly has obviously just gotten up and has given her a plate of food. She is gaunt, bedraggled, crouching over the food which she has bought with her body, wolfing it like a starved dog while the orderly watches her. The orderly takes the empty plate from her. She is still hungry; she watches the plate as he takes it and sets it aside.

    ORDERLY   You are not looking hard enough for this man.

    CLEMENTE   Why do you want him?

    ORDERLY   Never mind that. But you can see what will happen to you if you don't find him.

    CLEMENTE   Maybe if I knew why you want him, I would know where to look.

This is reasonable. At last the orderly tells her that Henri is a De Gaulle spy; if that knowledge can help her, to get out now and look. Clemente rises, rearranges her clothes, prepares to leave. The orderly takes her in his arms, intends to kiss her.

CLEMENTE I thought I had already paid for the food.

ORDERLY You may need some more—if you don't find him pretty quick.

Clemente submits to kiss, goes out.

Now she is both terrified and overjoyed. If Henri is a De Gaulle agent, maybe he can get her to England. She knows she is lost to Albert for good now, but maybe she can work, earn a living. Now she has some idea about where and how to hunt for him. But she also knows that now the police will follow her, since they know she knows what Henri is, and therefore they will not trust her. If she doesn't find and turn him in, she will starve; if she can dodge the police and find him, she can get to England and be saved.

She is about to find Henri, though she doesn't know it. She believes she has lost her police spies, though she has not. But Henri's people know the situation; that she is getting closer and closer, with two police spies following her. At last, in self-defense, they kidnap her, snatch her suddenly into a doorway, gag her and blindfold her, and escape from the police.

When she has a chance to find herself, she is in a secret underground headquarters of some sort. She doesn't know what it is and she doesn't care. She has found Henri now; all she wants is a chance to get out of Holland, off the continent; she believes of course it will be to England, hopes so. But just so she can get away from the Germans who are starving her. She is thinking only of herself. She has been degraded until pride and all are gone now; she is simply an animal that wants only enough to eat. Therefore, although there are others in what she already recognizes to be an organization of some sort, Henri is the only one she pays any attention to or even looks at. She does not care what they are up to, just so Henri helps her get away. She is ravenously hungry. They give her food, watch her wolf and gnaw it like an animal.

She is a problem to them. They escaped the police by the skin of their teeth; they cannot let her go; to keep her hidden until they accomplish their plan is the lesser risk. So they keep her in the basement. They give her a place to sleep, a heap of rags on the floor, and food. She seems content, is not interested in anything. Then, as her hunger and terror subside, she begins to notice the men, but still without much interest. There is an old man, a Dutchman, one or two other Dutchmen, a Belgian, Henri, a few others. They are making plans for something. The place is too small for them to be private from her. They realize this. Perhaps Henri, in his anxiety to get on with the plan, which they all share, tells them not to mind her, he knows her, she is a Frenchwoman, was once straight and honorable, and she can't get out anyway. Clemente pulls herself up, backs up what Henri has said, tells them that all she wants is to get away; if they will take her to England with them, she will swear never to reveal it, do anything to harm their plan. They see her sincerity in this, and besides they don't intend to let her escape, so they take the risk of talking before her, as if she were the forlorn dirty homeless stray mongrel dog which she resembles.

So they go on making their plans. She is present but seems to pay no attention to what is going on, waiting apparently only for the next meal. Once Henri makes an attempt to get her to clean herself up. She says she will do that when she gets to England; just get her to England, is all she wants.

So she learns the plan without wanting to, caring, without even listening. (This anecdote is based on a story in the *Saturday Evening Post*.[23] I don't remember title nor author nor date. Will find them later. The Dutch captain is taken from the story, and the incident of towing the barges loaded with German invasion troops is taken from the story. The climax of the story is an original idea of mine.)

The old Dutchman is a boat captain, owner and operator of a tugboat which hauled barges of goods up and down the rivers, the Meuse into France, the Rhine and the Maine into Germany. He has made many friends among Germans in his trading days. After his country and France were occupied, it was too late for him to get away. Besides, he was old, his life and business were here, and since, after the first horror of the bombing and battles, the Germans apparently intended to let business go on as

23. C. S. Forester, "The Dumb Dutchman," *Saturday Evening Post*, 215 (July 11, 1942), 16ff.

before, he continued. He was not a quisling; he was simply trying to earn his living as he had always done, without any subservience to the conquerors, as he would have carried on a business which a new owner had bought, whether he liked the owner or not. So he still ran his boat, with the two young Dutchmen in his crew, and presently a refugee Belgian, all of whom he kept quiet, actually saved them from getting in trouble by resisting the conquerors, by his age and calm sense and the force of his will.

But he soon sees that things are neither as he had believed nor even hoped. He sees his country being ruined, bled white of men and women to work in German factories; all the food is taken, some of the Dutch still resist, against the old man's judgment, and are killed for it; other innocent people are taken as hostages and are murdered for the deeds of others. But outwardly, he shows no feeling about it. He still goes on, running his boat, for the Germans now, doing his work despite his country's grief, keeping his crew quiet. One of the young Dutchmen is his son, who would someday inherit the boat and the reputation for probity which the old man has built up. The son has wanted to resist, but the old man overrules him, keeps him in line. Soon the Germans realize how dependable he is, reliable in doing what they command. They are outwardly friendly with him. He is still stolid, quiet, accepting their amicability and apparently returning it, or that is, never giving any trouble. They ask him to do more things of a responsible and important nature as they come to trust him. He always does them. Presently they begin to offer him extra pay, privileges, etc. He always refuses them. The Germans are only momentarily surprised. They soon come to think that here is a stupid Dutchman who does not even need to be bribed to serve his country's conquerors.

One day he is sent for by the town commander. The commander asks him if he can sail his tug across the Channel in a fog, to a given point on the English coast, towing a string of barges, and land the barges at the given point. The old man is inscrutable, imperturbable. He says he can do it. He asks when? The commander reiterates: is he sure he can strike the point in fog? He says yes, asks again, when? The commander says he will tell him later, to get his boat in shape, say nothing to his crew or anyone else. (In the writing of this scene, the German will tell him as little as possible, of course, since the Germans do not trust even their traitor subjects. But the German will have to tell him enough for the Dutchman to answer the question. Thus he learns that he will have a long tow of barges, and will go in fog. When the Germans dismiss him, they have no reason to believe that his manner is at all different.)

But he has divined the meaning which they did not tell him. There is no reason for the tugboat to cross the Channel with a string of barges in a fog, unless the barges contain invasion troops bound for England.

He sets about the next step, in his stolid, phlegmatic way. He has always opposed what he considered the useless resistance of the imprisoned Dutch. The ones who still resist know this, and cannot trust him. So he has trouble even getting in touch with the people he seeks. He knows they are avoiding him, but he does not give up.

There is a widow, whom he has known for years, whose son has mysteriously disappeared, to whom he has been giving food. She is not sorrowful enough about her missing son, so he knows the son is not dead. And if the son is not dead, then he is engaged in the secret resistance to the Germans. He goes to her, asks where the son is. She has known him of old, knows he is a good man. He says no harm will come to the boy or his friends; he simply must get in touch with them. She is overjoyed.

WOMAN *(eagerly)* Then you have changed too!

He says nothing. His manner shows no change. Her hopes sink again. Yet he must have some reason like that for wanting to see her son. But she realizes he will not admit it. But she believes his word; he has been feeding her. She tells him how to find her son.

Thus he makes contact with the Dutch patriots. There are Belgians and French among them; Henri Ballin, as a De Gaulle agent, is their contact with the Dutch, French and Belgians in England. He tells them what is going to happen, and their plan is set, which is: to have British destroyers waiting in the fog on the day the tugboat with its loaded barges sails.

It is at this point that Clemente is flung into their laps by what they consider sheer bad luck. They have to talk before her, because there is nowhere else for her to go. But it seems safe to talk before her, because they can't release her now, and she seems only to want food to eat. She does not even seem to be listening until she hears the words "boat" and "England." Then she wakes from her stupor, begs them to take her. The old Dutchman hesitates.

> **DUTCHMAN**   It will be dangerous.

> **HENRI**   She can go as a crew member, in disguise, hair cut off, men's clothes.

> **DUTCHMAN**   I don't mean that.

Now all but Clemente realize he means what they all know: that maybe the boat itself will never reach England. Henri tells Clemente to leave the room for a moment. She goes out. Henri reminds the old Dutchman what will happen to Clemente after they leave and she has to go back to the Germans, with no food card nor police license to make a living; that she will be better dead anyway than to remain here. The old Dutchman agrees that she can go. Henri calls her back and tells her.

So her last worry is settled; all she has to do now is wait for the day. She even seems to have stopped listening to their talk. She is like a dog which has been trained to cook and wait on them.

The plan is complete but for one thing. Henri has made a secret trip to England and arranged for the destroyers to stand by. But as the expedition depends on fog and weather, they will have only a last minute in which to warn the destroyers what day and hour. At last they evolve a plan for this, the only one they can think of. When the word comes to the old Dutchman to stand by to sail, a fake broadcast will be made from a Dutch station. The broadcast will be all right, authentic, issuing apparently from the Gestapo headquarters, but it will contain a phrase which will give the destroyers the time. They can arrange through a spy in the Gestapo chief's combination apartment and office for the faked script to go out to the station. But the chief at the station may find something funny in the code phrase. If he does so, he will insist on having the Gestapo chief O.K. it. The question is, to keep the radio station from contacting the Gestapo chief until the expedition has left. Clemente has been moving about or sitting quietly in the b.g. Now she stops and is listening, though they do not notice her.

> **HENRI** We won't send the broadcast until just before we sail. If we could just keep the Gestapo chief incommunicado for an hour, say.

> **THE BELGIAN** That will be easy. We will keep him quiet forever.

But to kill the Gestapo will be too risky; it might be discovered at once. They argue the matter while Clemente listens quietly. They can arrive at no better plan; they will have to chance it. Of course, whoever does the killing will probably be caught, but no one considers that, as they know that the man who does the job will not consider the fact. So they let it go at that, and break up. Clemente has stopped listening, continues what she was doing.

The day arrives. The old Dutchman, who has lived on that coast and sailed boats on it for sixty years, knows that the fog and weather will be right tomorrow, even before the message comes. Henri gets Clemente some men's clothes, tells her to cut off her hair.

The message comes to the old Dutchman to stand by to sail at a certain hour. The fake message has been planted, to issue from the Gestapo chief's house. Henri sends for Clemente to come in. When she enters, her hair is still long. She has not changed her clothes. The others are busy talking. They must risk killing the Gestapo chief; they have thought of nothing better— Clemente interrupts. They look up in surprise at this dirty, slovenly tramp. When she speaks, she gives up forever her chance to get away. Her air has changed; it is reckless, devil-may-care, hard and tough.

> **CLEMENTE** Give me a cake of soap and some scent. I'll keep him quiet for two hours.

DISSOLVE TO:

We might show a scene where the Gestapo chief, unsuspecting, enters his bedroom and finds Clemente, in a negligee, beautiful now, waiting for him.

WIPE TO:

The closed door to the chief's bedroom, a sentry before it. A man enters from the radio station, wants to see the chief to confirm the strange broadcast. The sentry says he has orders that the chief is not to be disturbed, winks, indicates he has a woman, something extra, with him.

SENTRY I just wish I was in there myself, not to be disturbed for two hours.

ORDERLY But what about this broadcast?

SENTRY Broadcast it. The chief ain't interested in radio right now.

The orderly returns; the broadcast with its concealed message will be sent.

DISSOLVE TO:

The old Dutchman tows the barges, loaded with invasion troops, into the foggy channel. He contacts the waiting destroyers over his radio. His message of course will be picked up ashore; he knows he will not have much time, as the destroyer commander also knows. The Dutchman gives the position of the barges.

DESTROYER Good. We've not much time, you know. We'll give you a minute to cast the barges loose and get clear.

DUTCHMAN You will lose them in this tide in that time. Range on me. We are clear. Commence firing.

DESTROYER (*after a moment*) Right. (*a pause*) Are you there?

DUTCHMAN Yes.

DESTROYER Thanks. And good luck.

The Dutchman (is this possible?) switches his wireless over so that it sends a beam for the destroyers to range on. The firing starts, shells fall among the barges.

WIPE TO:

A destroyer's wireless room. The beam from the tugboat sounds in the receiver. The destroyers are firing rapidly. The sound of the beam cuts short off as the tugboat itself is hit. The firing continues, becomes the sound of the FREEDOM TRAIN in—

FADE OUT.

FADE IN

The house in the desert. Dawn. The men are all sleeping at last, during these last few minutes. Even America is asleep, with Akers snoring beside him. The two prisoners are asleep, the two guards sleeping beside them, their rifles lax across their knees. The rest of the rifles are stacked in a corner. Thus the soldiers are unarmed. Even the pistol holsters are hung in a bunch on the wall. The sun is just rising.

A sentry post outside the house. The sentry has seen something. He crouches, peering through his binoculars.

A shot through the binoculars: a cloud of dust far away on the desert, movement in the dust. Gradually we discern tanks, motorized troops. A tank emerges from the dust. It bears a swastika.

The sentry rises, fires his rifle as an alarm, pumps the bolt and fires again.

Inside the house. The men have heard the shots. All have waked. They hurry to the windows to look out. For a moment they are disorganized, waked suddenly from sleep like this. Reagan and the corporals shout orders, get them under control. The men respond, turn and hurry toward the stacked rifles.

GERMAN OFFICER'S VOICE   (*off scene*) Achtung!

All the Americans pause, look back.

ANOTHER ANGLE. The German officer now stands behind the Italian machine gun, covering the clump of Americans with it, as they halt for the moment in helpless surprise. He seems to read their thoughts.

> **GERMAN** *(still taunts them)* That is true. One or perhaps even two of you could reach your arms. Perhaps one of them would even be able to fire. But—*(he swivels the gun slightly, to show how it will traverse)*—the rest of you will be dead. In fact, two of you hold arms just beside me here. Why do they not shoot?

> **REAGAN** *(to the two guards, who are motionless too, from surprise at the German's quickness)* You, Humphries and Jewett. Don't move.

> **GERMAN** What? A few lives are not worth the destruction of an enemy? Well, perhaps you are wise. To an American, a bad trade is worse than no trade, eh? *(to the Italian: his voice changes, becomes sharp and harsh)* You there! Disarm those two guards.

> **ITALIAN** *(mildly)* I?

> **GERMAN** Yes, Garibaldi, you!

The helpless Americans glare with impotent rage. The Italian shrugs, goes to the two helpless guards.

> **ITALIAN** *(politely)* You permit, signores?

He takes their rifles. The German still watches the others who face him, holding the machine gun ready. He speaks to the Italian over his shoulder.

> **GERMAN** Lay them against the wall there. *(the Italian does so)* Now, the other rifles. The pistols too. Then gather up the grenades.

The Italian goes and gets the stacked rifles and the pistol holsters and returns to lay them down. His air is still quizzical, Latin. The German watches the men who face him. The Italian puts all the rifles down. Then he moves rapidly. He puts the pistols down, draws one from its holster, pulls back the slide to see there is a live shell in the chamber, all in one rapid movement. He is now slightly behind the German.

ITALIAN   Herr Kapitan. *(the German turns his head; as he does so, the Italian continues rapidly)* I too would have you looking at me, even though the bullet does go into your back.

He fires as he speaks. The German slumps forward, dead. There is a take for a second. Then the Americans rush toward the Italian. Before they can reach him, he snaps the safety on, spins the pistol on his finger and tosses it toward the Americans. Battson catches it, not because he intended to or had time to, but because the Italian threw it right into his hands.

BATTSON   You murdered him!

ITALIAN   So what? Between us we have murdered all Europe. What is one more little stain of blood on the hands of either of us—especially our own.

FONDA   On your soul, then.

ITALIAN   *(in mock amazement)* What? Is there still a man anywhere who still believes we have souls?

Reagan, a little slower than the others as usual, but efficient enough when he does catch up with what is going on, takes command, brings them back to order. The sentry who had first given the alarm runs in.

REAGAN   *(to sentry)* All right, Franklin?

The sentry, excited, starts his report. Reagan interrupts:

REAGAN   *(continuing)* Do you know they're Heinies?

SENTRY   Yes, I saw the cross—

REAGAN   Hold it. *(to Battson)* Take four men. Reinforce each of your sentries. If they're coming in from all directions, we want to know it. As soon as you know what direction they are coming from, and how many, as near as you can tell, bring your men back to the house. Don't wait too long.

Battson calls out his four men; they run out. Reagan now lets the sentry report. As soon as the sentry has told the gist, Reagan stops him again and begins to place the men at the windows with their rifles and ammunition. Akers doesn't move. He is beside America's pallet.

AKERS *(to Reagan)* What about America? We can't leave him—

AMERICA Don't leave me here, Sergeant. I can—

REAGAN *(impatiently)* I'll tend to you in a minute.

He goes to the Italian machine gun and examines it.

REAGAN *(to all)* Any of you guys know how to work it?

ITALIAN I.

Reagan and Akers look at him; others turn from their positions at the windows.

AKERS *(slightly hysterical)* How in hell do we know who's the next one you'll decide to shoot in the back? Your Heinie buddy couldn't trust you; do you expect us to?

They all watch the Italian, wait for his answer. He looks quietly about at them, Latin, sardonic, mild and courteous.

ITALIAN You can't. I am now twice apostate, even for an Italian. In fact, if you were to trust my simple word, I would doubt not only you, but my own five senses. An Italian of this day and time believes in nothing else, but he does believe in his five senses. When once he doubts them—*(he shrugs)* So I do not waste your—our—time protesting to you my good faith. I only say that I can operate this gun—*(he slaps the breech of the gun, looks about at them)* Well?

They watch him, then they watch Reagan. Reagan stares at the Italian as though he were trying to stare through the Italian's skull and read what is there. The Italian has looked at Reagan for only a moment, but he has read Reagan.

ITALIAN I would suggest in the door there, where there will be room to traverse it. To cover your outside party when they fall back, if necessary.

REAGAN *(quietly—turns)* All right. Give us a hand here, Franklin.

Franklin, Reagan, and the Italian set the machine gun in the door. The Italian takes charge of it, prepares it for action. Reagan and Franklin turn back, Franklin to his former post. Akers is still beside America.

> **AMERICA** *(to Reagan)* Don't leave me here. I can—

> **AKERS** *(hysterically)* You durn right we ain't! *(to Reagan)* At least we can lay him close to the wall, where a stray bullet won't—

> **AMERICA** No, no. Up there at a window, where I can see out. I can shoot the pistols.

> **AKERS** You durn right you can! *(he turns to the others)* Come on, you guys—

> **REAGAN** *(to Akers)* Will you shut up a while? *(to America)* Can you move your arms all right?

> **AMERICA** Yes. *(he moves his arms and hands and turns his head to prove it—the sweat of the pain beading his face again)* I can shoot.

> **REAGAN** All right. *(he turns)* Four men here.

Four men join them. The six prepare to pick America up.

> **AMERICA** *(sweating)* Easy now. Pick me up easy, please.

> **AKERS** Durn it, you better be easy with him!

The six men raise America, as gently as they can. But the pouring of sweat on his face shows the agony of movement, though his calm face and his eyes do not change; only the increased sweat.

> **AKERS** *(panting)* You durn clumsy sons, can't you be easy?

> **AMERICA** *(sweating)* They're easy. I'm all right. I feel fine.

They lay him on a ledge, where he can look out the window.

> **REAGAN** *(to Franklin)* Bring all the pistols here. Akers can shoot from this window, too, and load for him.

Franklin gathers up the pistols and returns. Akers bends anxiously over America. He is almost crying.

AKERS You durn black son, what did you want to get shot for? Are you all right now?

AMERICA *(peacefully, a pistol in his hand; he draws back the slide to see the live shell)* I'm all right. I feel fine.

A volley of firing sounds from outside. The men become alert. Through the open door, where the Italian crouches behind the machine gun, Battson and his men can be seen retreating, stooping, running. The firing continues. Battson and his men enter. The firing outside increases.

BATTSON *(to Reagan)* Here they come.

REAGAN How many?

BATTSON *(laconic)* Plenty.

A SOLDIER *(turns from his window)* You mean *enough*, don't you?

BATTSON Naw. I just said plenty.

REAGAN All right. Place your men.

Battson places his men at windows. The firing outside increases.

A SOLDIER Manning? Where's Manning?

MANNING Here. Whataya want?

SOLDIER Ain't it about time to make another vote whether to leave or not? We'll get a good majority this time.

ANOTHER SOLDIER *(fires through his window—ejects the empty case)* Yeah. The same majority. There won't be nothing for Manning—*(he fires again, ejects the empty; others begin to fire)*— to pick up to vote with but hulls.

Now they are all firing, America too, as Akers fires, drops his rifle, loads another clip for America, picks up his rifle and fires again. The firing outside increases.

Outside SHOT, German tanks, swastikas, as they approach, firing. As DISSOLVE begins, the sound of the tanks and the firing becomes the sound of the FREEDOM TRAIN.

DISSOLVE TO:

SOUND TRACK	SCREEN

CHORUS from "Cantata"

A lonesome train on a lonesome track,
Seven coaches painted black;
The train started, the wheels went
    around,
On the way to Cleveland town,
Poughkeepsie, Albany, Utica, Syracuse,
    Cleveland.
You could hear the whistle for miles
    around,
    Crying, Free—dom!
        Free—dom!

The train, 1865, moving.

MONTAGE of mourning crowds at the stations, the station names superposed as the VOICE repeats them.

SPOKEN

In Cleveland the crowds were there;
Two hundred and fifty came from
    Meadville, Pa.,
Five hundred with two brass bands from
    Detroit,
A million people came from northern
    Ohio,
They came to mourn,
And some went home to celebrate.

Some in the north and some in the west,
And some by the president's side;
Cursed him every day that he lived,
And cheered on the day he died!
Some went home to celebrate!

The MONTAGE CONTINUES, following the NARRATIVE.

1st SINGER

When that train rolled into Cleveland
    town,
Mr. Lincoln wasn't around;
Lincoln sat in a hospital ward, far from
    the funeral train,
Lincoln sat in a hospital ward, talking to
    quiet a soldier's pain.

Station sign "CLEVELAND" DISSOLVES TO:

Lincoln sitting beside a wounded soldier's bed.

LINCOLN'S VOICE

Where were you wounded, son?

2nd SOLO

Lincoln said,
Standing by the soldier's bed.

SOLDIER'S VOICE

At Bull Run, sir, and Chancellorsville.
I was shot when we stormed the hill;
And I've been worried since
    Chancellorsville,
About killing, sir, it's wrong to kill.

Lincoln beside the soldier's bed.

2nd SOLO
Lincoln said,

LINCOLN'S VOICE
That's been bothering me;
How to make the war and the Word
  agree.

2nd SOLO
Quiet and tall by the side of the bed.

LINCOLN'S VOICE
There is a reason,

2nd SOLO
Lincoln said.

CHORUS
Until all men are equal, and all are free,
There will be no peace.
While there are whips and chains,
And men to use them,
There will be no peace;
After the battles,
After the blood and wounded
When the chains are smashed
And the whips are broken
And the men who held the whips are
  dead!
When men are brothers and men are
  free,
The killing will end, the war will cease.
When free men have a free men's peace!

SOLDIER'S VOICE   Lincoln beside the soldier's bed.
I'll be going home soon,

4th SOLO
The soldier said.
Lincoln turned from the side of the bed;   Lincoln turns.

LINCOLN'S VOICE
I'll see you there,

2nd SOLO
Mr. Lincoln said.   DISSOLVE to moving train.

CHORUS
A lonesome train on a lonesome track,
Seven coaches painted black;
The train started, the wheels went
  round,
On the way to Joliet town,
You could hear that whistle for miles
  around,
Crying, Free—dom!
    Free—dom!

SPOKEN
Lincoln's people came;
Farmers from over in the next county,
Shopkeepers and shoemakers,
Men who'd hired him for a lawyer,
Men who'd split rails with him;
They came from Mattoon and Salem,
Fellows who'd swapped stories with Abe
    Lincoln during those long Illinois
    winter nights;
Lincoln's people were there.

MONTAGE to follow NARRATIVE.

CHORUS
A slow rain, a warm rain,
Falling down on the funeral train.
While the sound of the freedom guns
    still echoed,
Copperheads struck at the people's
    heart!

MONTAGE: the moving train. Gunfire in b.g. DISSOLVE TO: the box in Ford's Theater; as Booth fires, Lincoln falls, Booth leaps to the stage, flourishes the pistol, runs out. Pandemonium follows, DISSOLVE TO:

SPOKEN
When that train pulled into Joliet, you
    know where Lincoln was?
He was standing with his friends in the
    back of the crowd!
Yes, sir!

"JOLIET" DISSOLVES to crowd on platform, Lincoln tall among them.

CHORUS
Standing tall, standing proud,
Wearing a shawl instead of a shroud!

SPOKEN
Abe Lincoln was with his friends, telling
jokes!

LINCOLN'S VOICE
I presume you all know who I am. I am
humble Abraham Lincoln. My politics
are short and sweet, like the old woman's
dance.

(appreciative laughter from the crowd)

MONTAGE follows.

CHILD'S VOICE
Mr. Lincoln, how does it feel to be
President?

Child speaks to Lincoln.

LINCOLN
Well now, it feels sort of like the man
they ran out of town on a rail: if it wasn't
for the honor, I'd just as soon walk.

(crowd guffaws)

MONTAGE follows.

WOMAN
Mr. Lincoln, isn't it right that some men should be masters and some men should be slaves?

LINCOLN
Ma'am, if God intended some men to do all the work and no eating, He would have made some men with all hands and no mouths.

MAN'S VOICE
I say, America for Americans! What happens on the other side of the ocean ain't no skin off our backs!

LINCOLN
The strongest bond of human sympathy, outside the family relation, should be one uniting all working people, of all nations, tongues and kindreds. (Can't vouch authenticity of this)[24]

WOMAN'S VOICE
Somehow I wouldn't expect the President of the United States to be such a common man!

LINCOLN
I think God must have loved the common people; He made so many of them.
(If I remember correctly, Lincoln said, intent humorous, "God surely must love the poor people; He made so many of them." Am a little inclined to think the author stopped being a musician at this point in order to insert a little foreign matter.)

CHORUS
They were his people; he was their man;
You couldn't quite tell where the people
    left off and where Abe Lincoln
    began.

A lonesome train on a lonesome track,

A woman speaks to Lincoln.

A man speaks generally.

Lincoln in the crowd.

Lincoln's train leaves Joliet.

The train roars up the track toward CAMERA.

---

24. In a memorandum to Howard Hawks dated July 15, 1943, Earl Robinson took exception to this and the following editorial intrusion by Faulkner. Robinson insisted that he and Lampell had verified all of the Lincoln quotations used in the cantata.

Seven coaches painted black;
Coming into Springfield town,
You could hear the whistle for miles
        around,
Crying, Freedom! Freedom!

(the train sound increases)

The train LAPS to a modern locomotive as it roars past the CAMERA and the cars follow.

CHORUS
Abe Lincoln had an Illinois face,
And he came of a pioneer race;
He had power, he had drive,
And he liked the idea of being alive!

As the train roars past, we see the windows filled with the cheering faces of American troops.

His heart was tough as a railroad tie,
He was made of stuff that doesn't die;
He was made of hopes, he was made of
        fears,
He was made to last a million years!

The sound of the train and the cheering soldiers drowns the "Cantata" as CAMERA PANS the last car with its line of young cheering faces. On the car is scrawled in huge letters:

BERLIN   TOKYO   OR   BUST

FADE OUT.

THE END

II

Battle Cry
Second Temporary Screenplay

FADE IN

MAIN TITLE

Music theme from "Cantata" begins. As the Main Title fades out and the CREDIT TITLES appear on the screen, Music from "Cantata" continues OVER. SUPERIMPOSED OVER CREDIT TITLES, we see:

1. FULL SHOT   HEAD-ON

The locomotive of troop train, smoke and steam streaming. The CAMERA HOLDS on the locomotive as the landscape streams past. As the titles fade out the train FILLS the screen. MUSIC from "CANTATA" continuing OVER.

> VOICE   Battle cry is that which rises out of man's spirit when those things are threatened which he has lived by and held above price and which have made his life worth the having and the holding: the integrity of his land, the dignity of his home, the honor of his women and the happiness of his children;—that he and they be not cast into slavery which to a man who has once known freedom is worse than death.

2. CLOSE SHOT   THE TRAIN   BROADSIDE

—rushing PAST CAMERA. MUSIC continues OVER SCENE.

> VOICE   When these things are threatened, there rises from the throats of free men everywhere, even from beneath oppression's very heel, a defiance, an affirmation and a challenge against which lust and fury shall not stand and before which tyrant and oppressor each in his ephemeral and bloody turn shall vanish from the earth.

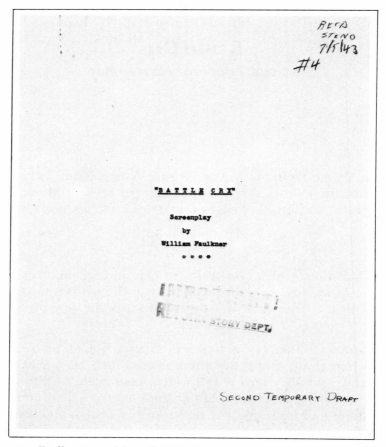

13. Faulkner's revision of American sequence

CAMERA HOLDS the last car as it passes, SHOWING huge scrawled letters:

BERLIN   TOKYO   OR   BUST

Above the letters, the windows are filled with cheering and waving soldiers. CAMERA PANS the last car as it passes and begins to recede swiftly down the track. The SOUND of the WHISTLE floats back as DISSOLVE begins, blowing the two long blasts, then the two short ones:

WHISTLE   Free—dom! Free—dom!

CAST OF CHARACTERS

IN DESERT EPISODE

FIRST LIEUTENANT WHITESIDES........	AGE	23
FIRST SERGEANT REAGAN..............		50
CORPORAL BATTSON...................		45
CORPORAL RILEY....................	DRAFT AGE 21 - 35	

1)	PRIVATE MANNING....................	"	"
2)	" FRANKLIN...................	"	"
3)	" LEVINE.....................	"	"
4)	" FINNEGAN...................	"	"
5)	" FONDA......................	"	"
6)	" TWO HORSES (A SIOUX INDIAN)	"	"
7)	" KOLINSKI...................	"	"
8)	" SMYTH......................	"	"
9)	" SHIPP......................	"	"
10)	" HOPKINS....................	"	"
11)	" BLOUNT.....................	"	"
12)	" GOMEZ (MEXICAN)..........		
13)	" WO HONG (CHINESE)........		
14)	" GRADY......................		
15)	" JANSSEN (SWEDE)..........		

PRIVATE AKERS (A straggler from another regiment)	19
" AMERICA (NEGRO, from another regiment)	25
CORPORAL LOUGHTON (BRITISH)........	28
GERMAN CAPTAIN (Loughton's prisoner)	37
ITALIAN MAJOR " "	35

* * * * * * *

14. Cast of characters in revised American sequence

During the DISSOLVE the WHISTLE becomes ROBESON'S[1] VOICE, completing the two short blasts of the signal:

ROBESON'S VOICE   Freedom! Freedom!

DISSOLVE TO:

3. EXT. FRONT PORCH OF A CABIN   MED. CLOSE   DAY

It is shabby yet neat. An old Negro man, with a fringe of white hair and a white chin whisker, in neat, worn, mismatched clothes, with a homemade stick, sits on the top step. Robeson stands leaning against the gallery post. Three small Negro children stand about the old man's knees, looking up at Robeson with rapt faces.

FIRST CHILD   *(eagerly)* Again, Uncle Paul! Go like a train again!

ROBESON   *(staring off, his face grave as he makes the whistle sound again, singing it, giving it the lonely quality of train whistles heard at night)* Free—dom! Free—dom! *(with a dying fall, as a train draws rapidly away)* Freedom! Freedom!

CHILDREN   Again, Uncle Paul! Do it again!

Robeson doesn't answer. He leans against the post, staring off.

OLD MAN   *(sarcastically, in his old quavering voice)* No. That's all you gonter get. This is Saturday. Your Uncle Paul got to go to town and tend to his Saturday frolicking. Thank God I done got too old to need to worry any more about whether I'm gonter have as much fun tomorrow as I never quite had yesterday—me and you chillen, too. Because you chillen done already forgot it if you never had enough fun yesterday. *(he speaks to Robeson over his shoulder, without moving his head even)* Go on to town. Do your frolicking.

Robeson doesn't move, leaning against the post, staring off.

OLD MAN   *(his voice quiet again)* That's it. Freedom.

---

1. Paul Robeson (1898–1976), black actor and singer, began his stage career in 1933 in Eugene O'Neill's *The Emperor Jones.* As a singer he was best known for his bass baritone rendition of "Ole Man River."

The children look at him now. They move toward his knees as he talks. Robeson stares off into space. As the old man talks, Robeson's face becomes rapt, calm, with a dignity in it, as if it were mirroring the invincible hope and belief which the old man talks about.

> **OLD MAN** *(continuing)* Abraham Lincoln gave it to us, offered it to all the people, black and white and yellow and brown. Because he was one of um. That's why he could speak for um, and all the people this side of the Big Water and the yuther side of it too, could understand him. Because he was the people. He was their man. Sometimes you couldn't even tell where the people left off and Abraham Lincoln began.

4. ANOTHER ANGLE   FAVORING OLD MAN AND CHILDREN

The children stand at his knees, watching him, waiting, intent and quiet and rapt, while the old man muses.

> **A CHILD**   Yes, Pappy. Tell it. Tell it again.

> **OLD MAN** *(rouses)* Again? When I done been telling it to you since fo' you was even big enough to listen?

> **CHILDREN**   Tell it again, Pappy. Again.

> **OLD MAN** *(stares off)* Yes. They told it to me too, in the old days, fo' I was big enough to listen too: that lonesome train on that lonesome track, seven coaches painted black, and the folks coming in from miles around to see it, hear it hollering . . . *(deepens his old voice in quavering imitation of Robeson's)* Free—dom! Free—dom! Freedom! Freedom! *(in chanting singsong now)* Washington, Baltimore, Philadelphia; New York, Albany, Cleveland, Chicago, Springfield, Illinois, hollering across the fields and the woods and the towns for the people to hear it: Free—dom! Free—dom! Freedom! Freedom!

The old man looks at the children now. As CAMERA begins to PAN to ROBESON'S FACE, MUSIC begins. Old man's VOICE continues OVER.

> **OLD MAN'S VOICE** *(over)* Because Lincoln was freedom,

and freedom wasn't dead. So Abraham Lincoln wasn't on that train.

5. CLOSEUP   ROBESON'S HEAD

SUPERIMPOSED over HEAD-ON SHOT of the FUNERAL TRAIN, small 1865 locomotive with bell-shaped stack, running toward Springfield. "CANTATA" MUSIC in b.g.

> **ROBESON**   *(sings)*
> A lonesome train on a lonesome track,
> Seven coaches painted black;
> Carrying Mr. Lincoln home again,
> —Only Mr. Lincoln wasn't on that train.
>
> Freedom's a thing that has no ending,
> It needs to be cared for, it needs defending;
> A great long job for many hands,
> Carrying freedom across all the lands.
>
> *(speaking)*
> New York. Albany. Syracuse.
> Cleveland. Chicago to Springfield,
> Illinois, crying—

As he begins to sing, the locomotive whistles the two long and two short blasts of the signal. Steam puffs from the whistle. Robeson sings with the blasts, drowning the whistle; we hear only Robeson's voice.

> **ROBESON**   *(singing)* Free—dom! Free—dom! Freedom! Freedom!

Robeson stops, motionless, his face grave and rapt, gazing off, as the CAMERA PANS PAST the train. It whistles again as FADE OUT begins.

> **WHISTLE**   Free—dom! Free—dom! *(fainter)* Freedom! *(very faint)* Freedom!

FADE OUT.

FADE IN

6. CLOSE SHOT   RAILROAD STATION SIGN

SPRINGFIELD, ILL.

LAP DISSOLVE TO:

7. FULL SHOT   STATION PLATFORM

Signs on the wall:

BUY WAR BONDS NOW:
We Must, We Can,
WE WILL—
SPRINGFIELD U.S.O.

A group of soldiers in f.g., in charge of a sergeant. They are veterans, are easy in manner, smoking as they wait for the train, while girls and women in canteen and women's service organization uniforms move among them with coffee, doughnuts, cigarettes, etc.

8. ANOTHER ANGLE   ALONG PLATFORM

—to show civilians coming and going, either women and girls or older men.

CAMERA PANS to another group. These are draftees, with their suitcases. They are young, sober; they have a country look about them. They seem to huddle already, in the face of the imminent future which is presently to sweep them away, where they do not know, to return or not to, they do not know.

Their parents and kin are with them: mothers, fathers, sisters, kid brothers, who have started before dawn perhaps from lonely houses about the countryside, to see them off.

CAMERA PANS TO:

9. CLOSE SHOT   FONDA AND HIS GRANDFATHER

Fonda is a country boy. He has an old-fashioned carpetbag. He is rugged, gawky; he has the look of Lincoln when Lincoln was that age. He is obviously ill-at-ease—wishes the train would come on so he can get away. The reason for this is his grandfather.

The grandfather is nearing 90: gnarled and bent yet still hale looking, and at the moment he is in the grip of a tremendous excitement.

Other family groups huddling in b.g.

GRANDFATHER   'Taint long now. Jest hold your hosses, now.

FONDA   I bet you wouldn't feel so chipper if it was you that had to go.

GRANDFATHER   *(bristles) Had* to go? *Had* to go?

FONDA   Aw, I ain't against going. We got to, I reckon, and it ain't any use in fighting against it. But ain't nobody never told me yet just what I am fighting for.

GRANDFATHER   *(heated)* Fighting for?

FONDA   Hush, Grampaw! Everybody's watching you!

GRANDFATHER   Let 'em! If there's any more here so poor in spirit they don't know either. You're going to fight for the folks that ain't free, that have been enslaved. And this ain't the first time boys from this town left this very station to go and fight against slavery. Hell fire, there was a man from this very town . . .

FONDA   Hush, Grampaw! Hush up . . .

GRANDFATHER   . . . that said, there ain't room in all North America for a nation to exist half slave and half free. And now we got the same fight on our hands that old Abe had, only worse, because we know now there ain't room even on this whole earth for people to exist half slave and half free . . .

FONDA   You've told me about that a dozen times . . .

GRANDFATHER   Aye, wrote it across the page of America, across the whole ledger of human bondage, in his own blood, so that no folks anywhere can ever forget it.

Grandfather's face is fanatical. Now Fonda's face becomes rapt, as if he has been moved despite himself by the old man's fire, since what the old man had seen and felt 75 years ago is in his, the young man's, blood somewhere, too.

10. EXT. STATION PLATFORM   FAVORING GRANDFATHER AND FONDA

In the distance a THEME from the "CANTATA," covering the moving of the funeral train bearing Lincoln's body with the BEAT of the TRAIN SOUND, begins and continues as he speaks.

GRANDFATHER I was right here that day—on this same platform—a strange day, a quiet day—the war over at last, and all the four years of hatred and bloodshed, and we had thought . . . Right here on this platform, along with all the other folks that had come in from the farms and the hamlets and the villages and the towns, to stand waiting here in the rain outside the telegraph office ever since that shot had sounded, and old Jake Wetzel that run the telegraph come out and he never had to say it though even then we couldn't seem to believe it: "Folks—folks. Abe Lincoln is dead!"

The MUSIC has been growing louder as the grandfather's voice rose. Both are now drowned out by the SOUND of the TRAIN as it roars up into the station and stops.

11. GROUP SHOT   DRAFTEES AND THEIR FAMILIES

Fonda and his grandfather in f.g. The moment has come. All have stopped talking now, are looking anxiously, the mothers with something like terror, at the sergeant who enters and stands facing them.

SERGEANT (*with sarcasm; he saves the tense situation in which these country people who must part don't know how to do it*) Well, *gentlemen.* This way, if you please.

FONDA Us?

SERGEANT Certainly. I understand you are to be with us from now on.

He turns and exits. The mothers cling to the boys; now they are restive to get the matter over. They release themselves, begin to pick up their clumsy suitcases.

12. TRUCKING SHOT   FONDA AND HIS GRANDFATHER

—as they walk toward the train in b.g. The grandfather is still trembling with excitement, Fonda sober again, thoughtful.

FONDA But that was in 1865. The world was smaller then;

folks seemed to know then. At least they never had to go to the end of the world to fight slavery.

GRANDFATHER *(wildly)* That's jest where we want slavery; at the end of the earth! Then we can shove it the rest of the way off! Go on, now! Let the rest of them be late, but not my blood and kin!

CONDUCTOR'S VOICE *(off scene)* Bo-o-ard!

The grandfather stops. Fonda walks on, increasing his pace a little. His face is rapt again, calm.

GRANDFATHER *(shouting now)* Go on! Whup them! They can't never beat folks that have ever once tasted being free!

SOUND OF STARTING TRAIN begins. Fonda starts to run.

13. CLOSE TRUCKING SHOT FONDA

—running faster and faster. SOUND of train increases, "CAN-TATA" MOTIF enters, grows swiftly louder with BEAT of train. SOUND of train and MUSIC becomes GUNFIRE, as we—

LAP DISSOLVE TO:

14. CLOSE TRUCKING SHOT FONDA

—in uniform, dirty, with pack and rifle, running. CAMERA DRAWS BACKS to DISCLOSE Fonda in a party of American troops in the African desert. Shells are falling around them. Leading the party are Lieutenant Whitesides and Sergeant Reagan. They run, stumbling, panting, ducking instinctively as the shells burst, trying to get clear of the barrage.

15. MED. LONG SHOT EXT. DESERT

A shell bursts, obscures Whitesides and Reagan. When the smoke clears, Whitesides is down. Reagan stoops over him; the others stop.

16. CLOSER SHOT GROUP

Fonda is nearest to Reagan.

REAGAN *(to Fonda)* Give me a hand! Jump!

Fonda passes his rifle to the nearest man. He and Reagan lift Whitesides, draw his arms about their shoulders, and run on. The others follow, CAMERA MOVING with them. The shelling continues.

17. GROUP SHOT

—as the party comes to a halt. Reagan and Fonda are supporting Whitesides, who hangs limp between them. Facing them are a German officer and an Italian officer, disarmed, battle-stained. Behind them, his bayonet at their backs, is an English corporal.

18. FLASH   GERMAN OFFICER

Despite his condition, he is still haughty, cold, sneering.

19. FLASH   ITALIAN OFFICER

Contrary to the German officer, he is looking at Whitesides with quick Latin concern and even pity.

20. CLOSE SHOT   FONDA

—staring at the British corporal. Shelling in b.g.

21. MED. CLOSE   GROUP   FAVORING FONDA AND LOUGHTON

Shelling in b.g. continues.

>FONDA   *(suddenly—to the British corporal)* Albert! Albert Loughton! What are you doing here?

>LOUGHTON   *(looks at Fonda briefly)* Hullo, Hank. Same to you. *(to Reagan)* Mind if I join you? Do you know where you're going? I don't.

>REAGAN   *(after a moment)* All right. Come on.

He and Fonda go on, carrying the officer. The others follow. CAMERA STAYS on Loughton and his two prisoners who are left behind. The German looks after the party with his sneering contempt. A shell bursts close behind them. The German does not even flinch. The Italian is nervous, flinches at the burst.

>ITALIAN   *(to Loughton)* We go too, eh?

>LOUGHTON   Yes. Get on.

He prods the German lightly with his bayonet. The German turns his head and stares at Loughton with that haughty sneering contempt.

> **LOUGHTON**   Get on! Maybe this is your barrage, but you're just meat to it, the same as we are. Get on!

The German moves deliberately on, the Italian ahead and Loughton following.

22. MED. CLOSE   GROUP

Whitesides is lying on the ground, unconscious. Reagan and the two corporals, Battson and Riley, are kneeling beside him, putting on a temporary field dressing. The others are in b.g., including Loughton and his prisoners. Fonda and Levine enter, naked to the waist now, carrying a stretcher, made by buttoning their two shirts about their two rifles. They spread the stretcher down beside the officer. They prepare to lift Whitesides onto the stretcher. The SOUND of the BATTLE is fainter now: they are clear of it.

> **REAGAN**   Easy, now.

They lift Whitesides onto the stretcher.

> **REAGAN**   *(rises)* Four men here.

Four men hand their rifles to others, start forward.

> **LOUGHTON**   What about my two chaps giving a hand?

Reagan, a little slow, has to think it out. He looks at the prisoners, and at Loughton. CAMERA PANS to the Italian, watching eagerly, like a dog waiting for permission to move. CAMERA CONTINUES PANNING to the German, who is still arrogant, detached, sneering, looking contemptuously at Reagan.

23. MED. SHOT   GROUP

> **REAGAN**   *(to Loughton)* Thanks. All right.

> **ITALIAN**   *(quickly—moves forward)* But yes.

The German does not move. Loughton prods him slightly with rifle butt.

LOUGHTON You too. Step along.

GERMAN *(turns his head to Loughton)* I quote your—not our—Geneva to you. Regulations regarding the treatment of prisoners of war: No captive officer shall be forced under any conditions to perform manual labor of any kind. I will also request that you keep that rifle out of my back.

24. CLOSE SHOT   THE MEN

They all stare at him. The Americans begin to react. Franklin reacts fastest.

FRANKLIN *(to the German)* Maybe you can quote another one that says you can't shoot Germans.

LEVINE *(quickly)* Let it go, Franklin. There is one that says you can't shoot German prisoners.

FRANKLIN *(he and the German stare at one another)* I don't know that one. I can't read.

REAGAN *(catches up at last)* Shut up, Franklin. *(to all)* All right. Four men.

25. WIDER ANGLE   TO INCLUDE STRETCHER

The four men come out. The Italian has already taken his place at one corner of the stretcher. The four men pause, at an impasse again.

REAGAN *(to the Italian—he speaks gently, but he is worried, impatient, with the growing weight of his responsibility)* You heard him. He's right. Get out of the way.

ITALIAN *(courteously)* With your permission, no.

REAGAN *(sharper)* Turn loose! Geneva says you can't!

ITALIAN *(calmly)* Geneva also said we would never be here fighting one another. But we are. *(he looks at the four waiting men)* Signores?

Reagan gives up, watches, baffled. Three of the men take the other three corners of the stretcher. They go on, the others follow. CAMERA STAYS ON Loughton and the German for a moment, SHOWING the German looking after the party with his same expression. Loughton prods him in the back, this time with the point of the bayonet instead of the rifle butt.

> **LOUGHTON** *(harshly)* Get on. This bayonet can't read either.

The two quickly join the party and start moving with them across the desert—CAMERA MOVING with them.

26. MED. SHOT   GROUP

—as the party come to a halt. Reagan is spreading out a map, Battson and Riley help hold it while all three examine it. Reagan holds a compass in one hand.

27. SHOT OF THE THREE

—studying the map.

> **BATTSON**   What's there? Why are we going there?

> **REAGAN**   I don't know. Whitesides has the order. All he gave me was, if he was hit, we were to go back.

> **RILEY**   What do you call it then, if he hasn't been hit?

> **REAGAN**   *(puts the compass in his pocket and begins to fold the map)* He ain't dead yet though. *(he sticks the map into his pocket, takes out the compass again)* Forward!

28. TRUCKING SHOT   THE PARTY

—moving across the desert; their feet pick up a rhythm, not quite parade marching. DISSOLVE begins. The SOUND of the FEET becomes the FREEDOM TRAIN, the SOUND of the TRAIN rises toward a rapid crescendo, becomes the SOUND of the DULCIMER playing a rapid, rollicking, tinkling gay tune, as we—

DISSOLVE TO:

29. CLOSE SHOT   AMERICA

—lying on a crude pallet. He is a Negro soldier. He has been shot through the spine, is paralyzed from the waist down. He is not suffering, or if he is, it does not show. His face is peaceful,

raptly interested as he listens to the quick gay tinkling of the
DULCIMER.

30. MED. CLOSE   AKERS   BENEATH A WINDOW

He is a private soldier, about 18 years old. He is gawky, devil-
may-care: a country boy. He sits on a stone ledge just beneath a
window. His rifle lies in the window, ready to be picked up
quickly. He is playing the DULCIMER while he keeps watch on the
desert.

31.   MED. CLOSE   REAGAN AND THE TWO CORPORALS   EXT.
DESERT

—lying behind a ridge of sand facing the Moorish house set in a
small grove of palms. The SOUND of the DULCIMER comes from
the house, faint now, rapid and gay and tinkling. The three
men listen in amazement, Reagan especially.

   RILEY   It's a banjo.

   REAGAN   A banjo? Here, in Africa?

   RILEY   It's a banjo tune, anyway.

   BATTSON   It's more than that. It's a country tune, from
   Alabama or Georgia or somewhere. They dance to it. I've
   seen them.

The MUSIC STOPS suddenly.

   RILEY   Now what?

   BATTSON   *(draws down quickly)* He saw one of us. Get your
   head down.

Riley obeys but Reagan still peers cautiously over the ridge.

   BATTSON   *(anxiously)* Come on, Sergeant . . .

   REAGAN   You two lay close. *(he begins to raise his head, cautiously)*

   RILEY   *(quickly)* Here! Let me . . .

A shot comes from the house.

32. CLOSE   REAGAN

—as the bullet kicks sand in his face.

33. MED. CLOSE   THE THREE

Battson and Riley grab Reagan by the belt and jerk him down.

>   **VOICE**   (*from the house—a flat Southern voice*) All right. You
>   can come on out. I ain't going to shoot no more. I done
>   seen you. Ain't no Wop nor Heinie neither got a face as
>   ugly as that un.

>   **BATTSON**   (*rises*) Let's go.

Reagan and Riley rise.

>   **VOICE**   (*off scene—concerned*) Sergeant . . .

34. MED. SHOT   GROUP

Reagan and Battson are kneeling beside the stretcher, where
the Italian and the bearers also squat.

35. CLOSE   WHITESIDES

—writhing in the beginning of a convulsion.

36. MED. SHOT   GROUP

Loughton thrusts through the watching men, extending a flask.

>   **LOUGHTON**   Here.

Battson glances up, sees the flask, takes it. He and Reagan raise
Whitesides' head and pour a little of the brandy into his mouth.
He chokes, swallows, rouses, opens his eyes.

>   **REAGAN**   Hold on, sir. We're almost there. You can lay
>   down then. You'll be all right then. Just hold on, sir. Hold
>   on.

>   **WHITESIDES**   (*gasping*) Yes. All right. I'll hold on.

>   **REAGAN**   (*rises—to the bearers*) All right. Easy now.

The bearers take up the stretcher. They go on.

37. INT. HOUSE

It has been evacuated because of the war. Its owner was apparently well-to-do. It was vacated hurriedly, though the fighting

has not actually reached it yet: no signs of pillage. This is obviously where Akers found the dulcimer. Open cabinet doors, disarranged rugs and curtains show how the owner cleared out in haste, taking only the valuables which he and his family and servants could carry.

38. MED. SHOT AKERS

—standing beside the door, his rifle negligently in his hand, as Reagan and the two corporals enter. SOUND of the BEARERS' FEET, then the bearers enter with Whitesides on the stretcher. Akers looks at Whitesides, devil-may-care, too young for pity.

AKERS Well, well. We got two of them now.

They pay no attention to him. The bearers go on, the men follow. Akers looks at each face with his reckless air.

39. INT. HOUSE MED. FULL SHOT

—as the men spread a rug, roll up a curtain for a pillow. Whitesides lies unconscious on the stretcher. Reagan stands supervising the making of the bed, though no supervising is needed. Akers approaches, watching. Battson, Levine and Janssen stoop to move Whitesides.

REAGAN Easy, now.

They shift Whitesides to the pallet. Reagan stoops over him for a moment, rises and turns.

40. CLOSE SHOT AT AMERICA'S PALLET

Reagan and Akers standing over him. America looks up at Reagan, his face peaceful, his eyes wide and calm.

AMERICA Evening, Sergeant. Look like we got almost a quorum now, don't it?

REAGAN *(to Akers)* Can he walk?

AKERS If he can, he sho better not let me find it out. I don toted him five miles since I found him this mawnin.

REAGAN *(examines Akers)* Where you from? Kentucky?

AKERS Naw. That's up Nawth. I'm from Alabama. *(he turns to America)* But you're okay now, ain't you?

AMERICA   *(in his peaceful voice)* Yes. I'm all right. I feel fine.

AKERS   *(suddenly—to America)* Where're you from? You was out of your head so much, you never told me.

AMERICA   *(motionless, peaceful, paralyzed)* America.

AKERS   Sure. What part? What's your name, anyway?

AMERICA   *(unchanging, peaceful)* America.

41. WIDER ANGLE   TO INCLUDE OTHERS

They are listening.

AKERS   America? That ain't . . .

A take as he comprehends all the implications of what the wounded and perhaps dying Negro has said. He is ashamed, would try to apologize, doesn't know how, must cover up in the only way he can: by sardonic humor.

AKERS   Yeh. So'm I. Too damn far from it.

42. MED. CLOSE   GROUP   AT WHITESIDES' PALLET

Battson, Fonda and Loughton squat beside it, others watching in b.g. Loughton is putting a fresh bandage on Whitesides. He shows so much deftness and skill at it that the others have drawn back, even Battson, leaving Fonda to give Loughton what help he needs. Loughton is using the sulphur derivative against tetanus. Whitesides is unconscious.

BATTSON   Great stuff, those sulphur things. This war'd be pretty bad without them—granted that anything can improve war.

LOUGHTON   *(busy with dressing)* Yes. They stood us well in France. Dunkirk, too.

FINNEGAN   *(quickly, respectfully)* Were you at Dunkirk?

The others all listen with that same interested respect for a veteran of Dunkirk. Loughton does not answer. He seems not to have heard.

FONDA   *(quickly—to Finnegan)* Look. Why don't some of you guys empty the canteens and fill them with fresh water from the well?

FINNEGAN Sure. O.K. *(to Loughton)* Were you at . . .

FONDA *(to Finnegan—quickly again)* Why not do it now, while we ain't busy. I'd like a drink of fresh water myself.

43. ANOTHER ANGLE   FAVORING WHITESIDES

—as he moves, groans, opens his eyes, tries to sit up. Fonda and Loughton grab him, hold him down. Battson moves quickly in. Whitesides pants, shows pain, raises one hand and fumbles at his breast pocket. Fonda, Battson and Loughton all three have to hold him.

> **LOUGHTON** *(rapidly)* Call your sergeant. Give him some more morphine.

> **FONDA** Yes.

He rises, turns, stops, looks out of scene, reacts, shouts.

44. REVERSE ANGLE

All the Americans are poised in astonishment. The German faces them across the room, standing easily, contemptuous. The Italian is gone.

> **GERMAN** *(sneering)* Certainly he's gone. Did you ever know one of his race who wouldn't run at the sight of armed men?

Battson recovers first, runs toward the door, others begin to follow.

> **REAGAN** *(shouts)* Janssen and Wo Hong! Watch him!

Janssen and Wo Hong stop to guard the German. Reagan follows the others out, the German watches them out with contemptuous amusement.

45. MED. LONG SHOT   EXT. DESERT

—as Reagan and Battson run in and stop, followed by others with their rifles. The Italian can be seen, about two hundred yards away, running into the empty desert. Reagan glares after the receding figure, snatches the rifle from the nearest man, kneels and aims.

46. CLOSE SHOT   REAGAN'S SHIRT-FRONT

—as he kneels, aiming the rifle, works the bolt to be sure of a live shell, steadies for the shot. Above his pocket are the campaign ribbons of 25 years: Mexico, France, Philippines, the Asiatic station. Beneath them the worn expert marksman's badge which he has held for 25 years jerks glinting in the sun as he takes a deep breath and holds it to squeeze off.

47. WIDER ANGLE

—as Battson snatches the rifle up so that the shot goes high into the air. Reagan rises, he and Battson face each other.

48. MED. CLOSE TWO   BATTSON AND REAGAN

The others in b.g. Reagan is raging, panting. He tries to jerk the rifle from Battson. Battson holds to it; they wrestle the rifle between them while Reagan watches again the fleeing Italian.

    REAGAN   *(jerking at the rifle)* Shoot, somebody! Shoot him!

Nobody moves, watching Reagan and Battson.

    BATTSON   Stop it, Sergeant! Stop it!

    REAGAN   *(panting, furious)* Yes! Got clean away. Just because he insisted on carrying Lieutenant Whitesides for a mile or two!

    BATTSON   Look. You couldn't hit him now.

Reagan looks out of scene, calms down, still breathing hard. He slowly releases the rifle.

    BATTSON   That's right. Let him run. He hasn't got any water. The desert will finish him.

    REAGAN   *(turns, calm now, grim with his constant worry about being in command)* Back to the house, everybody. I'm going to organize a little order around here.

He goes on, the men follow, sheepishly—CAMERA MOVING with them. Reagan continues to talk, walking on.

    REAGAN   Prisoners walking out any time they decide they don't like being captured . . .

49. FULL SHOT   INT. HOUSE

America on his pallet in f.g., Akers sitting beside it. Whitesides' pallet beyond it, Loughton still kneeling beside it. Akers and Loughton are both looking at the door, from beyond which comes the steady TRAMP of heavy soldier-shoes. The Americans are not trying to keep step; it is as if the shoes themselves, the whole military system into which they are temporarily regimented, produce the SOUND. Reagan enters, the others follow. The German and his two guards are exactly as Reagan left them. As they enter, the German watches them again with that quizzical contemptuous amusement.

> **GERMAN**   So. You did not catch him. That is good luck, no?

Nobody answers. Reagan's face is grim, hiding the worry which he feels. He passes the German.

> **LOUGHTON**   (*to Reagan—with sarcasm which Reagan misses, as usual*) Perhaps you can spare a moment now, then.

50.   CLOSE   A PAIR OF HANDS   (LOUGHTON AND BATTSON LEANING IN)

One hand holds a hypodermic needle, the other the phial which contained the morphine tablets. The phial is being tilted over the palm. Nothing comes out. CAMERA DRAWS BACK TO DISCLOSE Reagan as he taps the open end of the phial on his palm, to dislodge the tablets which he still cannot seem to believe are not there. Nothing comes out. He turns the phial up, raises it as if to peer into it, assure himself with his eyes of what he cannot believe.

> **BATTSON**   (*impatiently*) It's empty, Sergeant. Is that all you've got?

> **REAGAN**   Yes. I didn't know I had given him that much. But I must have . . .

CAMERA DRAWS BACK FURTHER to SHOW they are near Whitesides' pallet.

> **LOUGHTON**   Put water in it. I saw it work in France.

> **REAGAN**   Water?

BATTSON *(handing canteen to Reagan—his mouth open)* Loughton's right. Come on. Fill it.

Reagan clumsily fills the hypodermic from the canteen.

51. MED. CLOSE GROUP AT WHITESIDES' PALLET (FAVORING WHITESIDES)

Reagan, Battson and Loughton kneeling over Whitesides. He is conscious, suffering, still fumbling with one hand at his shirt. When Battson starts to roll up his sleeve so Reagan can use the needle, Whitesides opens his eyes, sees the needle, tries to resist it, repulse Reagan's approaching hand. He is panting, trying to speak. Again Loughton seems to have had the most experience in such.

LOUGHTON *(to Reagan)* Wait, Sergeant.

He procures his flask. Battson helps him raise Whitesides' head while Loughton pours a little brandy into his mouth. Whitesides chokes, gasps, tries to sit up. His hand now definitely fumbles at his shirt pocket.

LOUGHTON In his pocket.

WHITESIDES *(gasping—eagerly)* Yes . . . Yes . . .

Reagan unbuttons the pocket, his hands clumsy and gentle, and draws out a folded paper. Whitesides is watching; he rouses further, his face becomes strained, urgent.

52. CLOSE TWO SHOT WHITESIDES AND REAGAN

Whitesides' voice is strong now, as if he knows he has only so much strength to say what he must say.

WHITESIDES *(gasping)* Yes. That's it. Operations. We are a liaison party. We were to meet an anti-tank battalion from the 209th here. They're not here yet?

REAGAN No, sir. Nobody here but us.

WHITESIDES How many men are left?

CAMERA ANGLE WIDENS TO INCLUDE the others in the room.

REAGAN Seventeen, sir. Two corporals: Battson and Riley.

WHITESIDES *(reacts)* Seventeen . . . seventeen. Out of thirty-nine. *(he rouses again, urgent)* You must get out of here. You must leave as soon as it's dark.

REAGAN Get out, sir?

WHITESIDES Yes! They will be here tomorrow! They want this well too. That's why we were sent here to hold it—us, and the battalion from the 209th. And the anti-tanks are not here?

REAGAN No, sir. Just us.

WHITESIDES Then you must get out of here. They will probably attack about sunup. Get out of here. As soon as dark comes.

Whitesides is suffering, writhes, fighting it off until he can finish. Reagan advances the needle.

WHITESIDES *(tries to repulse it)* No! No! Not now. Give it to me just before you leave. Then you must get the men out of here—out of here—out . . .

He stiffens, a convulsion starts. Battson and Loughton hold him, Reagan still kneeling with the unused needle. The three pause, look up and out, as the FAINT SOUND of AEROPLANES can be heard.

53. EXT. DESERT   CLOSE SHOT   ITALIAN   (PROCESS)

—half-crouching, tense, watching as the two aeroplanes approach. They are fighter-bombers, flying low and fast in tight formation. The Italian follows them with his eyes as they roar up and flash past, with German crosses on the wings.

54. EXT. THE HOUSE   A SENTRY   (PROCESS)

—facing the house, flinging himself flat on the ground for concealment or to simulate death if seen, as the two aeroplanes roar past, zoom over the house, bank, dive down across the house again, circle it and straighten out and roar over the prone sentry again, returning as they came. The sentry raises his head, looks after them.

55. EXT. DESERT   THE ITALIAN   (PROCESS)

—crouching again, looking up as the aeroplanes pass him, going back where they came from. As they flash overhead, the pilot of the second one leans out and makes a jeering, contemptuous gesture at the Italian. The aeroplanes go rapidly on, the SOUND dies away.

56. MED. CLOSE   ITALIAN

He relaxes, sits down, fumbles in his breast pocket, produces a single cigarette, looks at it with quizzical fatalism, breaks it carefully in two, puts one half back into his pocket, takes a pin from his lapel, sticks the pin into the half-cigarette to hold it by, produces an expensive jewel-crusted lighter and lights the cigarette, tilting his head to one side to keep from burning his lashes and brows off. He sits smoking, holding the cigarette delicately by the pin.

57.   INT. HOUSE   GROUP   ABOUT WHITESIDES' PALLET

Loughton and Battson holding Whitesides down as he struggles. Reagan, still kneeling with awkward helplessness, the needle in his hand.

> **WHITESIDES**   *(struggling, frantic with urgency)* They neither bombed nor strafed! Don't you see what that means? They may be here before night, even! You must get out of here! Get out—get . . .

He gasps, struggling while Loughton and Battson hold him.

> **BATTSON**   *(sharply)* Come on, Reagan. The water!

> **REAGAN**   Water?

> **BATTSON**   The needle, damn it! Come on!

Reagan approaches the needle toward Whitesides' arm.

> **AKERS' VOICE**   *(off scene)* Wait. America says he's got some.

Reagan turns, rises, exits toward America's pallet.

58.   MED. CLOSE   REAGAN, AKERS, AMERICA   AT AMERICA'S PALLET

Akers and Reagan squat beside it. America lies peacefully, looking at Reagan.

AMERICA   In my hind pocket. Turn me easy, now.

AKERS   I thought you been bragging every time you opened that big mouth of yours about how good you feel, that
you don't hurt.

AMERICA   I don't. Turn me easy, now.

They turn him gently as possible. Akers is anxious, concerned.

AKERS   *(to Reagan, savagely)* Durn it, do you call that easy?
What was you before Uncle Sam give you them stripes? A
blacksmith? Hold his leg, like that. I'll get it.

Reagan does so. Akers slips the first aid kit quickly and gently
out. Reagan takes it, rises, turns, stops at what he sees.

59. REVERSE ANGLE

Loughton is just drawing the blanket over Whitesides' dead
face. Other men in b.g. watching. Battson rises, sees Reagan
standing, gaping, still not quite up to first base. Battson glances
past Reagan. Loughton rises.

BATTSON   Give it back to the smoke. He looks like he could
use it now. Look at his face.

60. MED. CLOSE   AT AMERICA'S PALLET

Akers bending anxiously over America. America's expression,
his peaceful eyes have not changed. But his face is beaded with
sweat now and he is panting faintly. Reagan squats again beside
him, holding the needle.

AKERS   Durn it, we hurt you!

AMERICA   *(sweating)* No. I'm all right. I feel fine.

REAGAN   Sure. You'll feel all right in a minute. *(to Akers)*
Roll up his . . .

AMERICA   *(sees the needle)* No, Sergeant! No!

REAGAN   Roll up his sleeve, Alabama.

AMERICA   No, Sergeant! Save it. Somebody might get hurt
and need it.

AKERS *(turns furiously on Reagan)* Can't you hear him tell you to put that thing up? He don't need it. He ain't going nowhere! *(he turns to America, takes his dirty handkerchief, tenderly mops America's face while the sweat springs out)* Are you, boy?

AMERICA *(sweating, peaceful)* No. I'm all right. I feel fine.

61. FULL SHOT   INT. ROOM

Reagan standing, baffled, holding the useless needle, the men watching him quietly. Reagan wakes up, pulls himself together. He is in command now; he takes command; the men recognize it: that despite his slowness, the years of training which he has had will serve them now and he will take care of them competently.

REAGAN *(sharply, forcefully)* Battson and Riley . . .

BATTSON Sergeant.

REAGAN Riley's squad will take the first guard-watch. Battson's squad will take over from then on.

FRANKLIN *(in b.g.)* From then on until when?

Reagan pays no attention to him.

REAGAN Post a man north, south, east and west, 300 yards out. Relieve every two hours. Get going, Riley.

Riley comes forward with his rifle, faces the men, calls out four names. The four men take their rifles and follow Riley out. TRAMP of FEET dies away, as we—

FADE OUT.

FADE IN

62. EXT. HOUSE IN DESERT   FONDA   NIGHT

—walking his beat at one of the outposts. He walks slowly AWAY from CAMERA, reaches the end, and turns. APPROACHING CAMERA now, his face is quiet, musing, reminiscent, lifted, as he hears again his grandfather's voice speaking on the Springfield platform. When he reaches CLOSE SHOT, CAMERA TRUCKS with him for a second, then HOLDS as Fonda stops, listening to Grandfather's voice.

18.

these are the
substitute pages
for the original
which Mr Howler
already has.

NIGHT

s. He walks slowly,
turns. APPROACHING
reminiscent, lifted,
ice speaking on the
CLOSE SHOT, CAMERA
DS as Fonda stops,

VOICE:

... ies, just where we want slavery:
right at the end of the earth, where
we kin shove it the rest of the way
off . . .

The VOICE CEASES. Fonda stands, waiting for it to go on,
rouses, remembers where he is, looks about to see that all
is well, turns.

CLOSE TRUCKING SHOT   FONDA

walking again. FAINT MUSIC THEME from CANTATA has entered.
Fonda's face is rapt again, his feet moving unconsciously
to the beat of the MUSIC as the SOUND of FREEDOM TRAIN
grows definite and slightly stronger.

GRANDFATHER'S VOICE:
(OVER)
... and I was here, right here that
day in eighteen-sixty-five, right here
on this same platform with all the other
folks that had come in from the farms
and the towns, that had been coming in
and coming in, in wagons and buggies and
a-horseback and some a-walking in the
rain and the mud, a-coming in and a-coming
in ever since that shot had sounded a
thousand miles away in Washington.
Standing here waiting outside the
telegraph office, and the old Jake
Wetzel come out ...

FONDA stops again, listening, CAMERA STOPPING with him.

(CONTINUED)

15. Section of Faulkner's revision of American sequence

> **GRANDFATHER'S VOICE** *(over)* . . . Yes, just where we want slavery: right at the end of the earth, where we kin shove it the rest of the way off . . .

The VOICE CEASES. Fonda stands, waiting for it to go on, rouses, remembers where he is, looks about to see that all is well, turns.

63. CLOSE TRUCKING SHOT   FONDA

—walking again. FAINT MUSIC THEME from "CANTATA" has entered. Fonda's face is rapt again, his feet moving unconsciously to the beat of the MUSIC as the SOUND of FREEDOM TRAIN grows definite and slightly stronger.

> **GRANDFATHER'S VOICE** *(over)* . . . and I was here, right here that day in 1865, right here on this same platform with all the other folks that had come in from the farms and the towns, that had been coming in and coming in, in wagons and buggies and a-horseback and some a-walking in the rain and the mud, a-coming in and a-coming in ever since that shot had sounded a thousand miles away in Washington. Standing here waiting outside the telegraph office, and then old Jake Wetzel come out . . .

Fonda stops again, listening, CAMERA STOPPING with him.

> **GRANDFATHER'S VOICE** *(over)* . . . and he never had to say it, though even then we couldn't seem to believe it . . . "Folks," he said, "folks, Abraham Lincoln is dead . . ."

Fonda's face wakes. He whirls sharply, brings his rifle to challenge position. SOUND of several feet in sand, off scene.

> **FONDA**   Halt! *(the sound of the footsteps stops)* Who goes there?

> **RILEY'S VOICE**   *(off scene)* America.

> **FONDA**   Advance, America, and be recognized.

64. WIDER ANGLE

—as Riley and three men with rifles enter scene.

> **RILEY**   Corporal of the guard.

Fonda lowers his rifle.

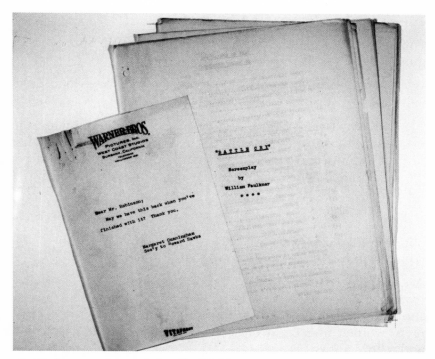

16. Review copy forwarded to Earl Robinson

RILEY Number Two: relieve.

Two Horses steps out, takes the post over from Fonda. Riley and the other two go on to the next post. Fonda turns away and returns to the house.

65. CLOSE TRUCKING SHOT FONDA

—relieved, his rifle at trail now, walking slowly, his face rapt as he has already resumed his trance, his dreaming, once more back in Springfield. FREEDOM TRAIN motif and TRAIN SOUND faint in b.g., in rhythm with Fonda's feet.

> **GRANDFATHER'S VOICE** *(over)* . . . and all of us here again on that other day, standing here in the Illinois rain so that you couldn't tell which was the tears and which wasn't, jest as they was a-standing and a-waiting at all the other stations with the same rain falling on them too like all the sky and all the earth was weeping . . . *(he begins to chant, BEAT of FREEDOM TRAIN increases)* Albany. Syracuse. Cleveland. Chicago. Joliet . . .

Fonda stops, CAMERA STOPPING with him, his face lifted. It begins to light, raptly.

> **ENGINE WHISTLE**   Free—dom! Free—dom! Freedom! Freedom!

> **GRANDFATHER'S VOICE**   *(over)* . . . except one old man; the rest of us standing there in the grieving rain, knowing what all the little people on the earth had lost but not even yet realizing how great that loss: except one old man, an old Negro . . .

> DISSOLVE TO:

66. SPRINGFIELD PLATFORM, 1865   MED. CLOSE   GROUP
FONDA'S SHADOWY FACE   SUPERIMPOSED

An old Negro man sitting easily on a box. His face is untroubled; if anyone is dead that he should grieve for, he doesn't show it. He is quite calm. About him stand a group of people, men, women and children, staring at him, puzzled, amazed, and a little angry.

> **A MAN**   *(angrily)* After what he did for you and your people, you ain't even got one tear for him?

> **OLD NEGRO**   *(calmly, unshakable)* No. Lincoln was freedom. Freedom ain't dead. I don't know what folks been telling you, but Abraham Lincoln ain't on that train.

The GROUP FADES OUT, leaving Fonda's lighted musing face on screen. Gradually CAMERA ANGLE WIDENS to show Battson standing behind Fonda, watching him.

> **ROBESON'S VOICE**   *(only Fonda hears it)*
> Freedom's a thing that has no ending,
> It needs to be cared for, it needs defending.
> A great long job for many hands,
> Carrying freedom through all the lands: *(chants)*
> America. Europe. Asia. Africa, crying *(sings)*
> Free—dom! Free—dom!
> Freedom! Freedom!

Robeson's VOICE CEASES. Fonda doesn't move. Battson watches him.

FONDA Freedom . . . Freedom . . . Yes. That's it. To all the people everywhere that want to be free . . .

BATTSON You could sleep a lot more comfortably lying down in the house.

Fonda turns quickly.

67. MED. CLOSE TWO SHOT   BATTSON AND FONDA

Battson offers a pack of cigarettes.

BATTSON Smoke?

FONDA I don't smoke.

BATTSON Yes, I'd noticed that. A soldier that don't smoke?

FONDA I just never got around to starting yet, I reckon.

They start walking toward the house, CAMERA MOVING with them.

BATTSON Then if I were you, I wouldn't rush it. There'll still be tobacco when this is over—I hope.

FONDA Yes, sir.

BATTSON *(lighting cigarette—pauses)* I've noticed that, too. You say "sir" to me. You don't say it to Reagan. *(watches Fonda keenly)* He's older than I am.

FONDA *(fumbles)* He's . . . You're different from Reagan. You're educated . . .

BATTSON Meaning, what am I doing here too?

Fonda doesn't answer, embarrassed, even alarmed that Battson should have read his mind. Battson watches him, then lights the cigarette, speaking through puffs.

BATTSON Couldn't help overhearing a word or two of your monologue.

FONDA *(embarrassed, kicks at something in his path)* . . . Just thinking out loud, sir—some tale my grandfather used to tell—keeps running through my head—

Battson looks at Fonda sideways with a quizzical smile. Fonda is aware of the look.

FONDA *(continuing)* . . . some story about the Freedom Train . . . the one that carried Lincoln's body to Springfield—

BATTSON —and they say he wasn't on it.

FONDA *(surprised)* You know it too?

BATTSON *(nods his head)* A lot of us know it. I've heard parts—here and there. I guess if we all got together, we could piece the whole thing in one somehow, and maybe have the answers to a lot of questions.

FONDA *(lets go for the first and last time)* What I want to know is what am I doing out here waiting for some guy's dirty bullet, when I ought to be home in bed? What have I got to do with all this?

BATTSON *(looking at him quietly)* Some of us are going to know—Remember that newspaper correspondent that was with this outfit?

FONDA Clyde?

BATTSON *(beginning to unbutton the breast buttons of his tunic)* Well—*he* knew—before he died . . .

Battson stops; Fonda halts a step behind him, watching as Battson reaches into an inner pocket and draws out a thin book with crumpled edges, its cover stained brown and torn. Methodically, Battson buttons his tunic again.

FONDA *(mystified)* What've you got there?

BATTSON —*one* of the answers.

68. INSERT: CLOSE SHOT   BOOK

—in Battson's hands. A bullet has gone through it. Battson opens it to FLYLEAF, smoothes out the ragged edges of the bullet hole until the writing on FLYLEAF can be read.

"Three gangsters got together and took over half of the world—and they made a plan . . . for years their plan worked . . . and there was one victory after another. Then—suddenly—for no reason they could see, they began to lose, so they called in their Wise Men and said— 'Look—we're bigger and stronger now than ever—we've got more gangsters working for us—and we've got half the peoples of the world enslaved, turning out guns and ammunition and planes . . . we have more tanks and guns and planes than we had before . . . how come we're losing?'"

69. CLOSE   BATTSON AND FONDA

Battson looks at Fonda who is watching him closely. Fonda makes a slight motion with his head as if to say "Go on." Battson looks down at book again.

70. INSERT: CLOSE SHOT   FLYLEAF

"I don't know what the Wise Men answered—but if those three gangsters could read what's in this little book— maybe they'd have some idea why they're losing—and why they can never win again!"

71. CLOSE   BATTSON AND FONDA

FONDA   (*curiously*) *Clyde* wrote that, huh?

BATTSON   Yes—so *he* must have known before he died . . .

FONDA   (*gulps once*) What's—in the book?

BATTSON   (*very slowly, touching the book almost reverently*) It's a bloody scrawl—in a woman's hand—and it's called— "The Diary of a Red Army Woman."

DISSOLVE THRU ABOVE INTO:

Russian Sequence

INSERT: THE DIARY

(Background music is a war motif, to fit the date, motif from the SHOSTAKOVICH SYMPHONY.)

The book is new, unstained, the bullet hole is no longer there.

TANIA'S HAND opens it to the first blank page. Her hand enters with a pen, begins to write:

"I, Tania Doronin, on this twelfth day of September, 1941, begin a diary—a letter to the future of my son. I have just learned about you, my son. I thought that Semyon was enough to fight for, vengeance on the slayers of my father and mother and on the despoilers of Russia was enough. But now I know better. I know now that it is you, my son, and all your unborn generation, that Semyon and I and all our Russian people are fighting for: that you and all your generation and all your generation's children's children may inherit the Russia which the men and the women of mine and Semyon's fathers' generation created with their blood and suffering; that you and your children's children may hold it in peace and forever."

CAMERA DRAWS BACK to DISCLOSE:

TANIA

—seated at a wooden box which serves as a desk, in a barracks room, with crude cots, flying clothes, etc., hanging on the wall. She wears a heavy leather flying overall, with boots, etc. A helmet with goggles and gloves lies on the desk beside the diary.

CLOSE SHOT   TANIA

She sits paused, the pen poised over the diary, her head lifted, listening as a loudspeaker blares.

> **VOICE FROM LOUDSPEAKER**   *(over)* Gull Squadron, stand by to take off in twenty minutes. Gull Squadron, stand by to take off in twenty minutes.

The LOUDSPEAKER CEASES. Tania bends over the diary, writes again.

INSERT: THE DIARY PAGE

—as Tania's hand writes:

"But I must start further back than today to tell you what I wish you to know. I must go back two years, to a time when there was no war but only the threat of it, when, even beneath the shadow of that threat, there was still time to enjoy in peace the Russia our fathers had gained and bequeathed us, to work and to love;—that Spring of 1939 . . ."

DISSOLVE THRU TO:

FULL SHOT   TO ESTABLISH THE RUSSIA OF PEACETIME, 1939

(Background music: the PASTORAL THEME from the SHOSTAKO-VICH SYMPHONY.)

A tremendous plain, fat white clouds of Spring drifting across the sky, fruit trees in bloom, a slow tremendous river busy with commerce in b.g., small villages about the plain in the distance, on the horizon the smoke from a factory which is the new Russia. In f.g., a man and his wife and their child with a plow, the man driving the plow, while the wife with an infant in a basket on her back, such as American Indian women used, and the half-grown boy sowing the seed.

LAP DISSOLVE TO:

EXT. COUNTRY SECTION

Frantic SQUEALING of a pig OVER scene.

MED. SHOT   GEORG

—as he dives at the frantic squealing pig. The pig escapes, leaves Georg lying in the mud for a moment. Then Georg rises, reacts ludicrously to the mud on him, follows the squealing pig, CAMERA FOLLOWING with him.

EXT. A SMALL LOT   WITH PIGSTY AND TROUGH

Georg, Tania, their father and mother are trying to hem up the frightened pig and catch it. The mother alternately holds her voluminous skirts spread and shakes a broom at the pig. Tania is young, quick, almost as active as Georg, but she is trying to keep from getting muddy. The father is crippled, limps with a stick. They are all intent. It is almost like a game; they are actually enjoying the contest, though they are not aware of it. They are intent now, cautiously driving the pig into a corner, the four of them closing in.

MOTHER   Soo, now. Soo, now. That's a good pig.

GEORG   (*muddy, closing in grimly: to the pig*) That's right, Ivanusha. Stand still. We ain't going to do anything to you but make sausage out of you.

FATHER   We are not going to do even that until we catch him. (*to Georg*) Go on. Grab him. When I was your age . . .

ANOTHER ANGLE   GEORG AND TANIA

Georg makes a rush at the pig. He almost has it, when it whirls and rushes toward Tania, who has closed in too, holding her skirts spread. Georg plunges again into the mud as he misses.

GEORG   (*to Tania*) Catch him! Catch him!

Tania holds the pig hemmed for an instant by her spread skirts. But the pig continues to rush at her. At the last moment she jerks her skirts aside to keep them from getting muddy, and the pig passes her, leaving a long smear of mud on her skirt.

GEORG   (*angry, frantic*) Why didn't you catch him?

TANIA   (*wails*) He's muddy! (*holds out her skirt*) Look at my dress already!

GEORG   (*rises again, muddy, angry and ludicrous*) Look at me, if you think a little swipe of mud . . .

TANIA   I don't want to look at you. You're filthy.

GEORG   All right. Just remember that when he's roasted on the table.

TANIA   I won't be there. I'm not a cannibal. I'm not going to eat Ivanusha.

GEORG   (*turns*) Ain't none of us, if we don't catch him. (*he starts out, happens to look up, stops*) Look.

Tania looks up. Her face reacts to the sight of the parachute mass jump; she and Georg have completely forgotten the pig.

THE SKY   THEIR ANGLE   FAINT SOUND OF AEROPLANES

The sky seems to be full of aeroplanes in formation, from which the tiny specks of human beings begin to fall. Then the parachutes open, others following, until the sky is filled.

AT PIGPEN

Georg begins to run, Tania follows. The father and mother have the pig hemmed, are waiting for the other two. They are looking up at the parachutes also, when Georg, followed·by Tania, passes them. They react.

MOTHER   Georg! Where are you going?

Georg doesn't answer. He runs to the fence, scrambles over it, runs on.

MOTHER   Georg!

MED. SHOT   TANIA   AT FENCE

Tania reaches the fence, holding her skirts up to her knees to run, climbs over the fence also, her skirts flying.

MOTHER'S VOICE   Tania! You, Tania!

Tania doesn't answer, crosses the fence and runs on.

MOTHER'S VOICE   Tania!

Tania runs on. Georg is far ahead now.

MED. LONG SHOT   IN A FIELD

Tania has stopped, Georg is far away across the field, running toward where a parachute is coming down. A second one is coming down some distance from the first. Tania hesitates only a moment, then she runs toward the second parachute.

CLOSE SHOT   SEMYON   ON THE GROUND

—kneeling, folding up his chute. He has landed in a secluded glade among trees. He is a big, handsome young man, a splendid animal, ruthless in his strength and his pride in his chosen vocation and his skill in it, in being an integer in the defense of his native land. He is a peasant too. From his helmet a long red streamer hangs. He gathers up the chute, rises, turns, stops.

REVERSE ANGLE   TANIA

—standing beside a tree, looking at him.

SEMYON   (seeing a pretty girl alone) Where did you come from?

TANIA From our field there. I saw you come down. I . . .

SEMYON Will a young woman pop up out of the earth wherever the others land, too?

TANIA The radio last night told us you would jump today and asked all the people to help you.

SEMYON And you chose me.

He begins to walk toward her.

MED. CLOSE   THE TWO

Semyon looks down at Tania, smiling, confident. Tania watches him, gravely, not quite alarmed yet.

SEMYON *(drops the chute)* Let me thank you, little comrade.

He takes her by both elbows and begins to draw her toward him, smiling and confident. Tania watches him, draws her face back a little. Semyon, smiling, leans nearer. As he does so, the red streamer swings over his shoulder. Tania looks at it. Semyon sees the movement of her eyes, follows it, sees the streamer.

SEMYON Oh, that.

He swings the streamer back behind him, a little self-consciously yet with an arrogant pride, too. He looks at Tania again, holding her, smiling.

SEMYON So that's why you chose me. So much the better for me then, even if there are a thousand airmen in Russia entitled to wear it.

He draws her face toward him, smiling. Tania resists faintly, grave, not quite certain of this. With a jerk of his head Semyon flicks the streamer forward again, smiling at Tania, confident, not to be resisted.

SEMYON Come now. Must I charm you all over again?

He draws their faces together. Tania does not resist, but at the last moment she turns her head so that the kiss falls on her cheek.

SEMYON Ah, bah, grandmother.

He takes her face in his hand, holding her pinned with the other arm, and turns her face up, and kisses her lightly on the mouth. Then suddenly, before she can move, he kisses her violently, with passion, holding her as she tries to struggle. As soon as he frees her, she tries to run. He catches her, she stumbles, is falling. Semyon, laughing with triumph, falls with her, turning himself to fall beneath her and save her from the shock.

CLOSE SHOT   TANIA AND SEMYON

—lying on the ground. Semyon laughing with triumph, Tania struggling. But he holds her.

> **TANIA**   No! No! No!

> **SEMYON**   Yes. Yes. Yes.

He holds her, kisses her, smothers both their voices in the kiss while Tania still struggles. But he holds her, is mastering her; she is helpless, is about to give in.

> **GEORG'S VOICE**   *(off scene)* Tania! Tania!

Semyon reacts, jerks his head up. This is Tania's chance. She frees herself, rolls away, gets quickly to her feet, breathless, panting, as she recovers. Semyon rises too as Georg enters, stops, staring at Semyon.

CLOSE   GEORG

—staring with dawning recognition and then awed admiration.

SEMYON   GEORG'S ANGLE

—the red streamer hanging from his helmet.

WIDER ANGLE

Semyon facing Georg, who still stares, as Tania, saved now, crosses quickly to Georg and takes his arm.

> **GEORG**   *(stares at Semyon)* You're Semyon Doronin.

> **SEMYON**   *(glances quickly from one to the other)* Do I know you?

> **GEORG**   Naw. She's just my sister. But we know you. You

flew an aeroplane from Moscow, across the North Pole, to
America.

SEMYON   Oh.

He approaches. Tania watches him, shrinks back beside Georg,
holding Georg's arm.

SEMYON   For a minute I thought maybe she was your wife.

CLOSE SHOT   THE THREE

Tania watching Semyon as she shrinks back, holding Georg's
arm. She turns, drawing Georg away. Georg is reluctant, staring
at Semyon with hero worship.

TANIA   We must go. Papa and Mama are waiting for us.
Ivanusha . . .

SEMYON   So the husband's name is Ivanusha, then.

GEORG   Ivanusha's our pig. We were trying to catch it.

TANIA   *(pulls at him)* We must go.

SEMYON   *(to Georg)* That's right. Go catch your pig.

MED. SHOT

Tania drawing Georg on, Semyon watching them. He holds the
rolled-up chute now.

SEMYON   Wait.

They stop, look back.

SEMYON   *(to Tania)* Come here.

Tania watches him a moment, gravely. Then she releases Georg
and comes back, watching Semyon. He holds out the parachute.

SEMYON   Touch my chute.

CLOSE SHOT   THE TWO   FAVORING TANIA

—as she stares at Semyon, gravely.

SEMYON   *(softer)* For luck, little comrade.

Tania stares at him. Then she lays her hand on the chute.

SEMYON *(softer yet, bringing all the charm to bear)* For better luck next time, eh?

Tania withdraws her hand, turns.

SEMYON Wait.

She stops. He jerks the streamer from his helmet and, before she can move, loops it about her neck. He turns to go.

SEMYON Go to your pigs then, and I to mine.

He exits.

CLOSE   TANIA AND GEORG

Tania looking out of scene, gravely, Georg in amazed exasperation.

GEORG Semyon Doronin. And you let him get away! You never even asked him to dinner!

TANIA *(rouses, turns, takes Georg's arm again; her face is serene)* He'll be back. Come on. Let's finish catching Ivanusha.

CLOSE TRUCKING SHOT   TANIA AND GEORG

Tania, holding Georg's arm, walking toward CAMERA. Her VOICE OVER, reading the DIARY:

TANIA'S VOICE And he returned, who had come that first time without warning out of the sky itself, the sky which guards Russia, wearing the red streamer in his helmet which marked him not only as a leader in the parachute school but as a leader among all the young men who were to keep our Russian skies safe to shield us . . .

LAP DISSOLVE TO:

CLOSE TRUCKING SHOT   TANIA AND SEMYON

Tania holding Semyon's arm. Wedding party following, villagers in their best finery, Semyon's two groomsmen in uniform, airmen like himself.

LAP DISSOLVE TO:

MED. SHOT   SEMYON AND TANIA   IN REGISTRAR'S OFFICE

—facing the table, signing the book which marries them. Wedding party in b.g., Tania's face gravely ecstatic, happy, Semyon proud and happy too. Nina, Georg, the mother and father in b.g.

LAP DISSOLVE TO:

THE WEDDING FEAST

A long table beneath an arbor.

LAP DISSOLVE TO:

EXT. CLOSE TRUCKING SHOT SEMYON AND THE TWO GROOMSMEN

—dancing a wild, fast dance from the Steppes, the fiddlers playing, the wedding party watching.

LAP DISSOLVE TO:

SAME SCENE LANTERNS AND TORCHES LIGHTING SCENE EVENING

—as the dance continues. CAMERA PANS from dancers to dancers, picking up Nina and the other girls with their partners, until it picks up Semyon and Tania, dancing together, breathlessly.

CLOSE MOVING SHOT TANIA AND SEMYON (DANCERS IN B.G.)

Tania laughing up into Semyon's face, her eyes ecstatic. CAMERA PULLS BACK A LITTLE, showing one after another of the village men coming up to catch hold of Tania and take her away from Semyon and dance with her, while the village girls dance away with Semyon.

EXT. GROUP SHOT (LIGHTS, MUSIC, FESTIVITY IN B.G.) NIGHT

Five young men, one of them Semyon's groomsman, shadowy, carrying tin pans and other noisemaking objects, squatting before Ivanusha's pen. Working swiftly, they draw from the pen one by one three small pigs, tie a pan or a can to each one, the pigs squealing in protest, Ivanusha herself protesting. They exit with the pigs.

THE GROUP AT A DARK WINDOW NIGHT

—as they open the window. One climbs in, the others pass him the pigs one by one, working quietly and rapidly. SOUND of dance, music, festivity in b.g.

DISSOLVE TO:

EXT. FRONT OF HOUSE   GROUP SHOT

The dance is over, the torches have burnt down, the fiddles are still. Semyon, Tania, the father, mother and Georg stand on the stoop, the wedding guests facing them, drinking a last toast to the bride and groom.

COMMISSAR   *(raises cup)* Happiness and long life, to Doronin and Doronina.

FIRST GROOMSMAN   And little Doronins for Russia.

SEMYON   I will drink that too. Fill for me, Sergei.

The groomsman fills the cups again. Semyon raises his cup.

SEMYON   Russia.

FATHER   And Termanskaya also. We will all drink it.

SEMYON   And Termanskaya also.

COMMISSAR   Russia is big. It is bigger than two Termanskayas even. But it is not bigger than all the Termanskayas because it is the Termanskayas which make Russia. And the Doronins and Doroninas which make the Termanskayas. So . . . *(raises his cup)* . . . Doronin and Doronina and the little Doronins.

All drink, the commissar holds his cup out bottom-up with a flourish.

COMMISSAR   Commence them, and goodnight.

Semyon turns toward door, his arm around Tania. The mother, father and Georg are turning also.

SEMYON   Goodnight.

MED. SHOT   AT DOOR

Father, mother enter the house. Tania and Semyon about to enter, pause. Semyon looks back.

VOICE   *(off scene)* Commence.

Tania shows confusion. Semyon leads her into the house, the door closes.

EXT. HOUSE   GROUP   AT WINDOW

The two groomsmen, Georg, and all the young bachelors of the village, with pots and pans, crouching beneath the window. It is lighted now.

INT. BEDROOM   CLOSE SHOT   THE BED

The covers are lumped, something is moving beneath them, heaving and surging. CAMERA PULLS BACK to a:

MED. SHOT   INT. BEDROOM

—as Semyon enters, jerks back the covers. The pigs are revealed, break out, the pans clattering. CAMERA SHOOTS THROUGH WINDOW to outside, where the shivaree party sets up a din of banging on the pans, shouting and whistling.

The pigs are still running and squealing, the pans banging behind them, as an undertone to the uproar from the shivaree outside the window. The SOUND from the shivaree STOPS, raggedly, then abruptly, leaving the FAINT RAPID RINGING OF A BELL from the village. The bell bangs and bangs, punctuated in the abrupt silence of the shivaree, by the squealing and clattering of the pigs.

LAP DISSOLVE TO:

CLOSE SHOT   AN OLD PEASANT

—ringing the village bell. It will not be in a church, but perhaps on a post on the village green, or before the commissar's office or house.

The peasant in his smock is pulling the rope steadily and rapidly. Tania's voice is HEARD OVER.

TANIA'S VOICE   . . . the same bell which his father had pealed that day in 1917, which he himself had knelled when Lenin died and on which he rang out the tocsin on this night when Hitler broke another promise . . . The bell which was ringing at that same hour in all the villages

throughout Russia . . . the voice of Russia herself demand-
ing that her children come to her defense . . .

CLOSE SHOT   SEMYON AND TANIA

—as Semyon holds her in his arms, their faces raised as they
listen to the alarm bell which means that Germany has invaded
Russia. The BELL RINGS steadily. In b.g. to the SOUND of the BELL
is the SQUEALING and CLATTERING of the little pigs.

FADE OUT.

FADE IN

LONG SHOT   TANIA AND NINA   ON A HILL

—standing, looking down upon the plain, with its burning
wheat fields and the burning village. They wear rough men's
clothes, have just escaped. CAMERA MOVES IN to a:

CLOSEUP   TANIA'S FACE

—as she looks down upon her destroyed country, the burning
village where she was born and grew up, and where her mother
and father have been killed by the invaders along with other
townspeople, friends and kin. CAMERA DRAWS BACK to INCLUDE
Nina, standing beside Tania, her face grim. At last she touches
Tania's arm, rouses her.

    NINA   Let us start then. It is far.

Tania looks down at the village a moment longer, then turns.
Nina turns also. They walk away as DISSOLVE begins. Tania's
voice over DISSOLVE as she reads from the DIARY:

    TANIA'S VOICE   It was far. Six hundred miles, from Ter-
    manskaya to where we hoped to find your father, who
    could tell us how to do what we wished to do. We walked.
    We saw all of Russia, the motherland, that Russia which
    they believed they could conquer, which to those who knew
    no better, who were not Russians, perhaps looked as
    though they were conquering it, though not to us. But
    sometimes we rode . . .

DISSOLVE TO:

MED. CLOSE TRUCKING SHOT   TANIA, NINA, A SOLDIER

—riding on the end of an artillery camion as it jounces along. Ruined village in b.g., signs of battle.

SOLDIER Termanskaya? I knew the commissar there. He is. . . ?

TANIA *(stares ahead)* Dead.

SOLDIER Ah. There were others, perhaps. Your mother, father . . .

TANIA Dead.

SOLDIER So. *(to Nina)* And yours?

Nina shrugs, staring ahead.

SOLDIER Good.

NINA *(reacts)* Good?

SOLDIER Yes. If our mothers and fathers and brothers and sisters and sons and daughters must have died, it is good for us to know it. Better still, for us to have been there and seen. Then we will fight.

LAP DISSOLVE TO:

LONG SHOT   ROAD   LONG LINE OF PEASANTS

—men, women, children, carrying sections of a factory, in ox-carts, perambulators, barrows, on sleds and by hand. They are indomitable, cheerful almost, not downhearted, determined.

MED. SHOT   TANIA AND NINA

—facing a halted line of men carrying a long drive shaft on their shoulders. In b.g. the peasants pass steadily, carrying the factory.

NINA From Termanskaya. Georg Matov, a boy sixteen. He killed a German sergeant and escaped.

FIRST MAN *(shakes his head)* I'm sorry. I don't . . .

ANOTHER MAN Matov? Georg Matov? That tiger? Yes, I know of him, as who in our district does not. Killed a sergeant, did he? That's nothing to what he has done since. He commands troops now.

TANIA Commands troops?

THE MAN He is the oldest, you see. His next is only six-teen. His youngest is thirteen, and that one is not even a boy. But I must go. Goodbye to you, sister of Matov, and good luck.

NINA And good courage.

THE MAN Bah. Let the Hitlerites wish for good courage. They will need it. As for us, we need only to hold them a little while. Then Russia will finish them.

NINA Russia?

THE MAN Yes, Russia. The snow. The cold.

He goes on. The steady indomitable stream of peasants with their burdens continues to pass.

LAP DISSOLVE TO:

GROUP SHOT   TANIA, NINA AND FIVE SOLDIERS

Tania and Nina show signs of travel, ragged, dirty, etc. In b.g. are the ruined walls of a destroyed village, burned fields, bro-ken carts, signs of battle, etc.

FIRST SOLDIER Bread? Certainly.

He produces a loaf, breaks it. Tania and Nina begin to eat, hungrily.

FIRST SOLDIER Where do you go?

NINA (*chewing*) To Moscow. To learn to fly.

FIRST SOLDIER To fly, eh?

NINA Yes. We learn to fight the Hitlerites. We have a friend there who will teach us—Semyon Doronin.

FIRST SOLDIER Semyon Doronin?

NINA Yes. (*indicates Tania*) This is his wife.

FIRST SOLDIER (*salutes Tania*) Salute, then, wife of Doro-nin! Ah, he will teach you. Kill them all, blow them all up: boom! eh?

SECOND SOLDIER No, we do not wish to kill them all. When this is over . . . *(with a sweep of his arm he indicates the ruined houses and fields)* . . . some of them must return to Russia and work.

NINA *(chewing)* True, Tovarish. Some of them must come back here and work.

DISSOLVE BEGINS.

Tania's voice in DISSOLVE, reading from DIARY:

TANIA'S VOICE So we reached Moscow at last. But he was not there. He was at the front. But we could still do what he would have had us do, whether he was there or not . . .

DISSOLVE TO:

EXT. GREAT PUBLIC SQUARE IN THE CENTER OF THE CITY

CAMERA PANS along the line of women, stopping for a moment on each face: students with young, determined faces and stern young eyes—square-chinned, broad-cheeked mothers—old women with gaunt, wrinkled faces showing through the folds of their shawls—all stand watching and listening.

CLOSER SHOT   CROWD OF WOMEN   AROUND THE COMMANDER

All have their eyes lifted to the Russian flag, floating on its standard above the commander, on a raised platform. All faces with the same inspired, uplifted, devoted expression. We HEAR the ROLL of a DRUM.

COMMANDER Women of Russia, repeat after me—I, a citizen of the Union of Soviet Socialist Republics . . .

MED. SHOT   CROWD OF WOMEN   CAMERA CENTERING ON TANIA

—as they all repeat with her:

TANIA I, a citizen of the Union of Soviet Socialist Republics . . .

COMMANDER'S VOICE . . . take the oath and swear to defend the Motherland courageously and with wisdom . . .

TANIA . . . take the oath and swear to defend the Motherland courageously and with wisdom . . .

COMMANDER'S VOICE . . . in honor and in dignity . . .

TANIA . . . in honor and in dignity . . .

COMMANDER'S VOICE . . . without sparing my blood and my life, until complete victory is attained!

TANIA . . . without sparing my blood and my life, until complete victory is attained!

DISSOLVE TO:

CLOSE TANIA IN COCKPIT OF AEROPLANE IN FLIGHT

Her VOICE OVER.

TANIA'S VOICE And so we learned to fly.

Tania watches her target. VOICE CONTINUES.

TANIA'S VOICE And to fight. We flew a dive bomber, Nina and I;—Nina, your godmother already, even though you were not here yet, even I did not know about you yet, but only dreamed of you and willed you to be, because still your father and I . . .

Tania adjusts mike, speaks into it.

TANIA I'm on, Nina. We're going down.

NINA'S VOICE Going down.

Tania sets diving flaps, puts nose down, feathers out prop and sets the throttle as dive begins.

EXT. SHOT THE DIVE BOMBER

—diving. Tania's VOICE OVER.

TANIA'S VOICE Because we had not found each other yet; he before Leningrad with his fighters, I before Moscow. Because there was Russia to be saved first, more important than you even, since if Russia were not saved, you would be born a slave. But each time . . .

ANOTHER ANGLE THE BOMBER

—as it makes run on its target, drops bomb, explodes target, flashes on. Tania's VOICE OVER.

TANIA'S VOICE   That was for my father.

ANOTHER ANGLE   THE BOMBER

—dives on, explodes a locomotive with machine guns, flashes on. Tania's VOICE OVER.

TANIA'S VOICE   That was for my mother.

CLOSE   NINA   IN REAR COCKPIT

—Tania's gunner, shooting machine gun.

CLOSE   GERMAN FIGHTER

—diving in. It explodes. Tania's VOICE OVER.

TANIA'S VOICE   And that one for your father. One less of them between us, between us and the day, the hour . . .

CLOSE   ANOTHER GERMAN FIGHTER

—diving in. It explodes. Tania's VOICE OVER.

TANIA'S VOICE   And another, until at last . . .

LAP DISSOLVE TO:

INSERT: CLOSE SHOT   DIARY PAGE   SOUND OF BOMBARDMENT IN B.G.

It reads:

"Leningrad. August, 1941. This is a day all Russia will remember, my son—a day when a single piece of Russian music drowned all Hitler's guns . . ."

SUPERIMPOSED we see Tania's face, as it slowly appears behind page of diary. Her VOICE OVER—BOMBARDMENT continues.

TANIA'S VOICE   You will hear that music someday, as all the world which believes in the will of a people to be free, will hear it, not because it is a formal pattern of musical sound but because it is the voice, the affirmation, of an indomitable city in the travail of refusing forever to be enslaved . . .

The DIARY PAGE FADES OUT, leaving TANIA'S FACE on screen as she speaks. BOMBARDMENT continues.

TANIA But you will not hear it as we heard it, under the shells and the bombs and the bursting and collapsing walls; and not only as we heard it, but as he wrote it, who, a musician, should not have been in battle, but was, because he loved freedom too and believed in the inviolable dignity of man—wrote it with his hands singed and blistered by the fires he helped to fight, sleepless as all in that beleaguered city were sleepless, hungry as all were hungry, yet with one blistered hand still on the pulse of that city which endured, and his ear still listening to the single voice of the men and women who refused to relinquish it, until he had done all to his symphony that he could do. Because he could not finish it. He could only write it. To be finished, it must be played, heard—but there were no musicians to play it. So the call went out, from Leningrad to all Russia, south to the Crimea, west to the Caucasus, north to Siberia . . .

DISSOLVE TO:

EXT. STREET   CROWD   AROUND A LOUDSPEAKER

The MUSIC and the BOOMING of GUNS imperceptibly are louder, but held down behind VOICE from LOUDSPEAKER.

VOICE FROM LOUDSPEAKER Attention! Attention! Men and women of Russia!

Faces are lifted in arrested attention.

MED. CLOSE SHOT

A hand taps the shoulder of a white-haired, elderly man with sorrowful eyes. He looks up, deeply moved, nods eagerly, and starts away. VOICE from LOUDSPEAKER continues OVER.

VOICE FROM LOUDSPEAKER One hundred musicians are needed to play the music of Dmitri Shostakovich! One hundred musicians are needed . . .

CLOSE SHOT   MAN

—reading notice posted on billboard, while ECHO of LOUD-SPEAKER comes from distance.

LOUDSPEAKER VOICE   . . . to play the Seventh Symphony

of Dmitri Shostakovich! Only fifteen men are left of the Leningrad Symphony Orchestra!

The man starts off, hurried, excited.

INT. COBBLER'S SHOP

A middle-aged man with heavily-lined face seated at a cobbler's bench. His left arm is folded on the table before him, holding down a shoe-last. His left hand is not seen. He takes a small nail out of his mouth (as cobblers do) with right hand, places it on sole, hammers with right hand. As he places second nail on shoe, the VOICE of a newsboy is heard.

    VOICE OF NEWSBOY . . . musicians needed . . .

The cobbler pauses in his work.

    VOICE OF NEWSBOY . . . One hundred musicians needed to play the music of Dmitri Shostakovich! *(voice fades into distance)* One hundred musicians . . .

Almost as if some frustration drives him, the cobbler hammers the nail into the sole of the shoe. A hand taps him on the shoulder. He looks up, as if listening. Then very slowly he draws out the sleeve of his left hand with his right. With an expression of restrained anguish he lifts it. The end of the sleeve is tied at the wrist. His left hand is gone. He looks up, shaking his head.

                          DISSOLVE TO:

GREAT ROOM   IN MUNITIONS FACTORY

BOOMING of GUNS and MUSIC always under. Room is full of workers, and air is filled with HUM of motors.

    LOUDSPEAKER VOICE Workers in factories! Attention!

HUM of motors dies down.

SERIES OF QUICK FLASHES WORKERS

—lifting heads from work to listen, with VOICE going on OVER action.

CLOSE SHOT   GIRL   AT A LATHE

A hand taps her shoulder. She looks up, then down at the coarsened fingers. She nods quickly, gets up, her eyes shining.

CLOSE SHOT   A BOY

—picking up handbill and reading same announcement as was printed on billboard. VOICE of loudspeaker echoes in distance.

> **LOUDSPEAKER VOICE**   Attention! One hundred musicians are needed . . .

DISSOLVE TO:

HOSPITAL WARD   FULL SHOT

> **LOUDSPEAKER VOICE**   Attention! Doctors and nurses of Russia!

Doctors, nurses, patients, all lift their heads, listening.

> **LOUDSPEAKER VOICE**   Attention!

Nurses wheeling patients, stop, heads lifted. In f.g. nearest CAMERA is a nurse wheeling chair with boy whose left leg is amputated at the knee. His crutches are beside him.

> **LOUDSPEAKER VOICE**   One hundred musicians are needed . . .

CLOSE SHOT   BOY   IN WHEELCHAIR

His hands grip the arms of the wheelchair as he leans forward, absorbed and listening. A hand taps him on the shoulder. He looks up, face alight. He looks down at his leg. His mouth sets in stubborn determination. He grasps his crutches and starts to get up.

> **LOUDSPEAKER VOICE**   . . . to play the music of Dmitri Shostakovich!

CLOSE TWO SHOT   A DOCTOR AND LITTLE GIRL

The doctor is bandaging the little girl's wounded hand. He stands still listening. A hand taps his shoulder. The doctor looks up, nods quickly, finishes bandaging the hand, slips off hospital coat. He reaches into a cabinet and takes out a trumpet.

> **LOUDSPEAKER VOICE**   Attention! One hundred musicians are needed . . .

DISSOLVE TO:

EXT. TRENCH

—filled with soldiers. All lift heads quickly as VOICE from loud-speaker comes in full.

LOUDSPEAKER VOICE   Attention, soldiers of Russia, attention! One hundred musicians are needed . . .

CLOSE SHOT   A YOUNG SOLDIER

A hand taps him on the shoulder. He looks up, nods eagerly, puts down his gun and turns toward back of trench.

LOUDSPEAKER VOICE   . . . to play the music of Dmitri Shostakovich!

DISSOLVE TO:

EXT. DECK OF DESTROYER

Sailors and officers with heads suddenly lifted in attitudes of listening.

LOUDSPEAKER VOICE   *(comes in full)* Men of the Red Navy, attention! One hundred musicians . . .

CLOSE SHOT   YOUNG SAILOR

—with bandaged head. A hand taps him on the shoulder. He looks up with eager attention, nods quickly, and starts down companionway.

LOUDSPEAKER VOICE   Attention! One hundred musicians are needed . . .

The MUSIC BUILDS slowly behind this action. It seems to follow each of these people.

DISSOLVE TO:

FLASH   A SOLDIER

—digging in dirt of trench. He uncovers a box which he tenderly rubs clear of dirt. He opens it, rubs his hands on his stained uniform, then tenderly and carefully lifts out his violin. He clambers up over the trench.

FLASH   A SAILOR

—who runs down companionway. He takes bassoon out of his bunk chest, runs back up companionway.

FLASH   BOY WITH AMPUTATED LEG

—on his knees, crutches lying beside him, lifting bricks from hearth of a completely burned house with only the fireplace left standing. He brings out a cello wrapped in old cloth, hugs it to him. VOICE of LOUDSPEAKER continues throughout in background.

DISSOLVE TO:

TRANSPORT   IN FLIGHT

> **TANIA'S VOICE**   . . . so we brought them in—flew them in, the musicians, from all over Russia . . . seamen from Murmansk and Sevastopol, soldiers from the front lines, doctors and wounded from the hospitals who could play instruments, workers in the factories, from Moscow and Stalingrad, Siberia and the Caucasus and the Crimea . . .

LAP DISSOLVE TO:

EXT. LENINGRAD AUDITORIUM   LONG SHOT

—showing people beginning to converge on the auditorium, through darkened streets, with the incessant BOOMING of GUNS always in the b.g.

INT. AUDITORIUM

CAMERA TRAVELS across the audience, showing the faces: all kinds of people: soldiers, civilians, old, young, men and women, the faces intent, quiet, waiting. SOUND of BOMBARDMENT is fainter. The CAMERA MOVES ON to the WINGS, HOLDS, as Shostakovich enters, approaches podium, walking quickly.

FULL SHOT   INT. AUDITORIUM

The faces turning as he passes, watching him, making no sound as Shostakovich reaches podium, raises baton. TANIA'S VOICE OVER.

> **TANIA'S VOICE**   They made no sound, no ovation, nothing. They just watched him: the quiet eager faces watching the

man who was about to evoke into sound all our suffering, endurance, grief and indomitable spirit . . .

Shostakovich brings the baton down. The symphony starts.

MED. FULL SHOT   ORCHESTRA

Shostakovich facing it, leading, music playing.

CLOSE   TANIA

—moving through seated audience, moving like a sleepwalker, staring ahead as she approaches Semyon. Music OVER.

CLOSE   SEMYON   TANIA'S ANGLE

—as he approaches her, same look in his face. Music OVER.

CLOSE SHOT   THE TWO   MUSIC OVER

—as they reach one another. They do not speak nor touch. They turn together, side by side, and walk away from CAMERA, toward exit, pass through it as MUSIC RISES toward a climax point.

FULL SHOT   ORCHESTRA

—playing. CAMERA PANS ALONG different sections to show the various musicians whom we saw when the call went out:

> BOY WITH AMPUTATED LEG, playing the CELLO
> SOLDIER with VIOLIN
> SAILOR with BASSOON
> DOCTOR with TRUMPET
> MECHANIC with OBOE
> BLIND BEGGAR at PIANO
> CRIPPLED GIRL at HARP, etc.

EXT. AN ALLEY NEAR AUDITORIUM   TANIA AND SEMYON

The alley is sandbagged, soldiers moving in b.g. The MUSIC is fainter, still loud, SOUND of SHELLS and BOMBS. Semyon and Tania have stopped, listening as the MUSIC SWELLS, almost drowns out the bombardment. Semyon stops Tania.

> **SEMYON** Listen. Hear it? They can never beat us. You can never beat men who believe in man's fate enough to fight for it. You can kill some of them, but you never beat them.

TANIA Yes. They can never beat us. *We* have known that all the time.

SEMYON *We?*

TANIA Yes. We women. *You* can only preserve man's fate. We women can renew it. How can you beat people who believe in his fate enough to supply new generations of flesh and spirit for that fate to continue in?

CLOSE SHOT   TANIA AND SEMYON

—facing each other, not touching. BOMBARDMENT AND MUSIC in b.g.

SEMYON Tania . . . That night—do you remember? We stood at the door while they drank the toast: Doronin and Doronina and Doronins, and we turned to go in, and the voice that spoke again out of the crowd of them—the single word: do you remember? . . .

TANIA *(meets his gaze—quietly)* Yes. It said, commence.

FADE OUT.

FADE IN

AIR SHOT   TANIA AND NINA   IN THE BOMBER IN FLIGHT

They are attacked by fighters.

NINA *(over interphone)* Coming in on your left! your left! Rudder off; I can't bear my guns . . .

Tania sees the fighter coming in. Instead of ruddering off to give Nina the shot, she puts her diving flaps down quickly, stalls the bomber, pulls up so that the fighter passes beneath, pulls the flaps up again and turns onto the fighter, a perfect no-deflection shot.

CLOSE   INSERT: THE FIGHTER   IN THE CROSS HAIRS

Tania's thumb on the gun button. She slowly removes her thumb without firing. The fighter escapes.

EXT. AIRFIELD   TANIA AND NINA

—walking away from the bomber. Tania wears a curious serene expression. Nina is angry.

NINA   *(angrily)* You had that M.E.[2] dead. Why did you let it go?

TANIA   *(serenely)* There was a man in it.

NINA   A man? A Hitlerite!

TANIA   *(serene)* Yes. But he was a little boy once. And before that, a child . . .

Nina stares in amazement as Tania walks serenely on. Suddenly Nina stops, takes Tania by both shoulders, stops and turns her.

NINA   You're going to have a baby.

TANIA   *(serenely)* Yes. I'm going to have a son.

CLOSE   A RUSSIAN FIGHTER

—on the ground on tarmac of an aerodrome.

CLOSE TRUCKING SHOT   TANIA

—carrying helmet, gloves, chute, etc., as she approaches the door to her barracks room. She opens the door, enters, stops, still holding the doorknob.

REVERSE SHOT   INT. BARRACKS ROOM   SEMYON

—standing facing the door as Tania looks at him.

CLOSE SHOT   TANIA AND SEMYON

—in each other's arms.

CLOSE TWO SHOT   FAVORING SEMYON

SEMYON   I had twenty-four hours. I've already spent half of it flying. The other half will just about get me back.

ANOTHER ANGLE   FAVORING TANIA

Semyon holding Tania by both elbows, looking at her.

SEMYON   Tell me.

TANIA   Then you have not slept.

SEMYON   No. Tell me.

2. A Messerschmitt Me 109, a fast, heavily-armed German fighter plane.

TANIA And you must fly back tonight, still without sleeping.

SEMYON Yes. Tell me.

TANIA Yes. We have a son.

DISSOLVE TO:

CLOSE SHOT   SEMYON AND TANIA   ON A HILLTOP

In the valley below, a battle is going on in distance.

SEMYON Listen. Can you hear it? Not just the guns, not just that . . . *(indicates the distant battle with one hand)* The other. Listen.

TANIA Yes. I can hear it.

SEMYON The music. Our music. It was born of the guns—theirs and ours, too. So how can they beat us, when we can make music out of the very uproar and din of their impotent fury, when in the midst of their fury we can create another generation to bear our fate and destiny, as if all that . . . *(indicates the battle again)* . . . did not even exist, were no more than wind . . .

ANOTHER ANGLE   THE TWO

Semyon holds Tania by both elbows.

SEMYON We are Russia, Tania. Not you and I, the individuals, but because in our son we will have become a part of the long cavalcade of man's immortality, coming from where, he does not know, going where, he doesn't know either, except that he has a destiny, to have so endured. So we are more than Russia. We are Man.

TANIA Yes. We are Man.

CLOSE   RUSSIAN FIGHTER   IN FLIGHT

It goes swiftly on, grows smaller and smaller in—

DISSOLVE TO:

INSERT: DIARY PAGE   THICK SNOW FALLING   GUNFIRE IN B.G.

(NOTE: Snow may be a liberty with climate and time of battle. Will verify.)

"Stalingrad. 1942. It is not hell, unless you can call all birth hell. Because if they fail here, they will have failed everywhere, and Russia, peace, will be born again. And they will fail. The order came through from Moscow today . . ."

LAP DISSOLVE TO:

BULLETIN

It reads:

"ALL BOATS ON THE VOLGA TO BE REMOVED. ALL BRIDGES BE-HIND THE CITY TO BE DESTROYED. LET THERE BE NO ROAD FOR US TO RETREAT OR FOR THEM TO ADVANCE."

LAP DISSOLVE TO:

CLOSE   TANIA   AT CRUDE DESK IN BARRACKS ROOM

—writing. Her VOICE OVER.

TANIA'S VOICE   No road, no bridge, no boat, out of Stalingrad. Remember those words, my son. Hear them as we heard them on that day, with our backs to the Volga, knowing, as the enemy did not know, that there was only one end: victory . . .

VOICE FROM LOUDSPEAKER *(Tania pauses, raises her head to listen)* Gull Squadron, man your planes! Gull Squadron, man your planes!

Tania rises. We notice pregnancy now, in her slow, stiff motions. She puts the diary quickly away, takes up gloves and helmet, turns as Nina enters, carrying helmet, chute, etc.

NINA   You're not going today. I've seen the doctor and the commander. Petrovna Olenya will take our ship.

TANIA   *(serenely, moves toward the door, swiftly as she can)* Will they?

NINA   Don't be a fool!

Tania goes serenely on. Nina looks after her, hurries out.

EXT. FIELD   TARMAC   AEROPLANES WAITING   SNOW ON GROUND

Mechanics busy, women and men together, SOUND of engines. Women pilots carrying chutes, hurrying toward planes.

CLOSE SHOT   TANIA

—clumsy, as she climbs into her cockpit.

INT. COCKPIT   TANIA   AT CONTROLS

She closes the canopy, snaps on radio.

> **VOICE FROM RADIO**   Switch off. Lock controls.
>
> **TANIA**   Switch off. Controls locked. Chocks in?
>
> **VOICE FROM RADIO**   Chocks in. Lock brakes and tailwheel.
>
> **TANIA**   Brakes and tailwheel locked.
>
> **VOICE FROM RADIO**   Contact.
>
> **TANIA**   *(switches on)* Contact.

SOUND of ENGINE begins, mounts. Nina and the doctor appear suddenly outside the canopy, clinging in slip-stream, while Nina shouts at Tania, beats on canopy. Tania runs up the engine, shakes her head to indicate she can't hear, increases throttle until Nina and the doctor are practically blown back off the wing. Slowly Tania pushes the throttle further open.

LAP DISSOLVE TO:

LONG SHOT   FIELD

—as squadron takes off, becomes airborne.

AERIAL SHOT

Squadron flying in formation.

> **TANIA'S VOICE**   *(over scene)* My squadron was flying in formation . . . a beautiful sight, my son! I hope you will fly so with your own squadron—in times of peace. We climbed, ten thousand feet—twenty thousand feet.

GERMAN SUPPLY LINES   (SEEN FROM PLANE)

> **TANIA'S VOICE**   *(over)* Far below we sighted the German supply lines . . .

SHOT OF SQUADRON

—as bombs drop from planes.

> **TANIA'S VOICE** *(over scene)* The bombs hurled from our planes . . .

GERMAN SUPPLY LINES   (SEEN FROM PLANE)

Bombs hit and explode.

> **TANIA'S VOICE** *(over)* I could see the plumes of smoke where they struck!

Her VOICE is EXULTANT.

AERIAL SHOT   SQUADRON OF BOMBERS

A.A. bursting around it.

CLOSE SHOT   TANIA   AT CONTROLS OF HER PLANE   (PROCESS)

—as it lurches violently. Her face reacts to pain.

> **TANIA'S VOICE** I thought I had been hit. But then I knew . . .

Tania wrestles the ship back level, her face showing pain.

> **NINA'S VOICE** *(over mike)* Are you all right? Where are we going?

> **TANIA** *(gasps)* Down.

> **NINA'S VOICE** I told you! I told you not to . . .

MED. SHOT   TANIA'S PLANE   ON GROUND

—in small snow-covered field.

SHOT OF ANOTHER PLANE

—as it comes in, lands; two women get out.

SHOT AT DOOR OF SMALL PEASANT HUT   THE TWO WOMEN

From inside the hut comes the CRYING of a CHILD. The door opens. Nina stands in it. CHILD'S VOICE is louder.

> **NINA** Hear him? You're too late now. But come on in anyway . . .

Her voice stops. She stares at the two women, who are watching her. Her face reacts.

NINA   What is it? Is it . . . ?

FIRST WOMAN   Yes. The message came this morning.

NINA   *(quickly)* But no flyer got him: not Doronin!

FIRST WOMAN   No. It was flak from the ground.

INT. SMALL HUT   GROUP SHOT   AT BED

Tania in bed, the child beside her, old peasant woman in b.g. Nina and the two pilots beside the bed.

TANIA   *(quietly)* It's Semyon. He got it, then.

NINA   But no pilot got him! I told them so! No German, nor any other pilot, could ever outfly him to get him! It was flak, and anybody . . .

She ceases, watching Tania as Tania looks quietly up at her.

TANIA   Semyon? Semyon dead? Here's Semyon. *(indicates the child)* We are both Semyon, as all three of us are Russia, mankind. So how can Semyon be dead?

DISSOLVE TO:

CLOSE   TANIA   IN COCKPIT

Her VOICE OVER.

TANIA'S VOICE   So of course you will know him—his great laugh which will be your laugh, his big shoulders which your son will ride on in his time, when all this death and destruction and grief and fury are over and there is peace and freedom for all. Because we are Russia . . .

Tania begins dive, sets flaps, props, throttle, noses down.

THE TARGET   FROM TANIA'S ANGLE

—the ground increasing rapidly, A.A. and tracer outside, noise building up. Tania's VOICE OVER.

TANIA'S VOICE   We are Man.

WARNER BROS. PICTURES, INC.
CHANGE PAYROLL NOTICE

BADGE NO.

NAME FAULKNER, WILLIAM   NO.

DATE EFFECTIVE July 26, 1943   HOUR EFFECTIVE

OCCUPATION Writer

OLD RATE $350.

NEW RATE $400.

FROM DEPARTMENT

TO DEPARTMENT

REMARKS 52 weeks - 12 idle.

APPROVED R. J. OBRINGER

FORM 67

17. Change Payroll Notice for Faulkner

Ground increases, SOUND of GUNFIRE AND ENGINE takes up BEAT OF FREEDOM TRAIN until TRAIN SOUND drowns the guns. Tania's VOICE OVER.

> TANIA'S VOICE   We are Man.

TRAIN SOUND CARRIES OVER—

FADE OUT.

SOUND of FREEDOM TRAIN carries through FADE OUT, becomes a measured tramp of feet, as we—

FADE IN

72. INT. HOUSE   IN THE DESERT

Four soldiers are carrying the dead officer who is wrapped in a blanket. The others are following, save the German officer, who has risen, stands now, his watchful guard with rifle standing beside him. His contemptuous demeanor has not changed, but now there is something also in his attitude. It is that purely automatic and formal respect required by strict military habit, from a live officer toward a dead one, regardless of nationality. In the German's case, there is just the formal attitude: nothing whatever of pity, of grief or anything else in it. The four men pass on, followed by Reagan and the others, Loughton among them.

GERMAN *(to Loughton—as he passes)* I will come too, nein?

LOUGHTON *(shortly, not pausing)* Geneva.

GERMAN He is officer. Besides, he is now dead. We are civilized even by your American and English standards. We will always bury properly those of you whom we kill.

They all stop, look at the German. They are waiting for Reagan to speak. As usual, he has not quite caught up with first base, though they know that in a moment he will. The others look at the German with that mounting anger which must be repressed, which he never fails to arouse in them. Now he seems courteous almost. Apparently he is not even trying to be offensive. He is merely arrogant and sneering and contemptuous, as if he cannot help it, or did not need to try, since he and all the others are of different races, species, as if either he or all the others had come from the moon. Loughton looks at Reagan.

LOUGHTON Well?

REAGAN *(catches up now, turns to go on)* Bring him on. Watch him, though.

They go on. The German and his guard follow. The slow tramp of the feet begins again.

73. CLOSE   AKERS

—beside America's pallet as the tramp of feet grows fainter. He is looking toward the sound. The feet cease. He turns to America.

AKERS I better go too.

AMERICA Yes. You better go too.

AKERS *(gets up)* You can holler for me. I'll listen out for you.

AMERICA   I'm all right. You go on.

Akers exits.

74. EXT. COURTYARD   (MOONLIGHT) NIGHT

Two soldiers are just finishing the grave. They stand waist-deep in it, shoveling the sand out, as the four men enter with the dead officer in the blanket, followed by the others. The two soldiers climb out of the grave, brushing the sand off themselves, as the four men lay the blanketed figure beside the grave. The German officer is in the rear. Without stopping, he shoves on to the front, his guard following alertly, the others making way to let him through out of surprise more than anything else, until he stands over the body, looking down at it, the others all watching him, too surprised for the moment to move. Reagan faces the German across the grave.

The German looks down at the dead officer, without pity, a little quizzical. He does not even seem to know that he is sneering. It is as if what is sneering to the others is not even sneering to him, as if they belonged to the two separate species of living creatures.

GERMAN   *(looking at the body)* His name?

A SOLDIER   *(in b.g.)* What's that to you, Fritz?

BATTSON   *(to the soldier)* Shut up, Franklin.

The German seems not to have heard either of them. He looks at Reagan.

GERMAN   His name?

REAGAN   Whitesides. Lieutenant Whitesides.

GERMAN   *(looks down at the blanket; in a musing tone, still heavy with contemptuous insult)* And so young. To die here, in a foreign land—3000 miles from home—in a waste of sand which nobody wants, save an Italian, since nothing remains but sand for an Italian to carve his empire from. *(he looks at Reagan)* He has beaten you.

FRANKLIN   *(in b.g.)* So you think *you're* going to get out of this alive?

BATTSON   Shut up, Franklin.

The German turns his head deliberately and looks at Franklin. Then he looks at Battson. All stare at him.

BATTSON   You heard him. Do you want to answer?

REAGAN   *(again he catches up with first base, with the authority and command which are now his—to Battson)* And you can shut up, too. *(to the bearers)* All right, Levine. You and Kolinski and Finnegan—and Two Horses—

GERMAN   *(looks at Reagan)* I will answer. No. I neither expect nor deserve to live any longer than you live. Because I was not strong enough. I failed: else I would not be here.

BATTSON   *(in mock amazement)* What? Ain't one German stronger than just seventeen—no, eighteen—*(to Loughton)* . . . excuse me—ordinary mongrel democrats?

GERMAN   *(looks at Battson)* I will answer that too. Yes. Because I am not afraid to die. *(he turns his head again, speaking to all and looking at no one while they stare at him)* You have been worrying ever since you got here, not about dying, but about your courage, how afraid you might be. Because you don't know what you are fighting for. You don't know why you are here. Why this young man . . . *(with his toe he flicks a little spurt of sand against the blanket)* . . . had to die here in this waste which six months ago neither he nor you had ever expected to see. So you are looking backward, toward the hundred million little identical dens, on the ten million village back streets, which you call "home" because a parent dinned the word into your ears before your mouths could repeat it . . .

REAGAN   *(clumsily, trying to hold his and his men's own)* I see now. I get it. Yeah. That's why you are supermen. You never had to bother with no mother and father; you just sprung full-sized out of a laboratory, without having to have no place called "home" to clutter your courage up . . .

GERMAN   *(calmly—to Reagan)* The German of my generation needs no home. He has all Europe for his domicile. And, if that is not large enough, the world . . .

75. ANOTHER ANGLE   GERMAN AND REAGAN   OTHERS IN B.G.

The German looks at nobody, holding them quiet without effort, by the cold contempt of which he does not even seem to be aware, speaking as if he were alone.

> **GERMAN** In 1918 I was twelve years old, too young to have had any part in my country's collapse or in its subsequent betrayal. But my father did. He was of what they called the common people then: an artisan. Then he became a soldier, and after 1918 he still remained one, though misled, since the strength and the will still remained which even betrayal and debasement could not destroy. And my mother, too: their blood ran red together in the same Berlin gutter on the same afternoon in that summer of 1919. So I was parentless and homeless, too.

76. ANOTHER ANGLE

He has raised his head a little, his voice rings, louder.

> **GERMAN** But not for long. There already existed among us a power, a force, capable of changing the world. That had never lacked, even in our degradation. But now even the pattern of our destiny had begun to appear, in the person of the man who . . .

> **REAGAN** A Ginney paper-hanger.

> **GERMAN** *(looks at Reagan)* Austrian, if you please.

> **VOICE** *(in b.g.—not loud)* Geneva.

The German turns his head deliberately and looks back. It is Akers who spoke. They stare at one another, Akers reckless, defiant, devil-may-care. The German looks at Reagan again.

> **GERMAN** Pah. If Hitler did not exist, our need would have invented him. We did not need leaders: we needed only a voice, any voice, to remind us of our strength and our old glory which all the power of Rome and all the decadent spawn which Rome's collapse scattered over Western Europe could not conquer nor even dim. We had it: the pattern which could take the homeless and parentless like me, and in exchange for simple absolute fidelity and obedience, offer them in return a concept of power, of will, of force, whose reward would be the world . . .

77. ANOTHER ANGLE

The desert can be seen now, stretching away, vast, still, illimitable in the soft moonlight. The German indicates it with a sweep of the arm.

> **GERMAN** *(to Reagan now)* It looks something like your West. Let us imagine it is, for the moment. Let us imagine that you and I are standing now on some peak of your Rocky Mountains, in Canada or your United States, looking out upon America from the backbone, the roof-peak, of your hemisphere. So. There it lies, then. What do you see there, Sergeant? Come. Tell me.

Reagan stares at him puzzled, watchful. The German looks at Reagan, prompts him.

> **GERMAN** Come, man. Timber. Rivers for power. Railroads. Mines. Factories. Farms for food.

> **REAGAN** Yes. That's right.

> **GERMAN** Good. For what, then?

> **REAGAN** For what?

> **GERMAN** For what purpose? What end?

Reagan stares at him.

> **GERMAN** *(continues)* I will tell you. For money. To buy the radios, the electric stoves with which to equip your dens which you call "home," the cars, the rich food which you neither deserve nor need, with which you try to drug yourselves into believing that ease is the same thing as security.

> **REAGAN** We're going to make it secure. That's why we're here. *(quickly now)* Yeah, you said a while ago we didn't know what we are doing here . . .

> **GERMAN** *(quizzically)* What? A security so tenuous that you must come all the way to Africa to defend it?

Reagan stares at him, stopped for the moment. The German turns his head toward the desert again, raises his hand again.

> **GERMAN** *(continuing)* I have said you are looking backward. *(contemptuously)* Timber! Mines! Electric power! Bank accounts! Radios, cars, ice cream and picture shows!

Pah. Let me tell you what I see. Power: the sinews of strength, the reins to control the force which only the strong dare handle—not for the moiling worthless mass of mankind, but for the power and glory of that race which has the strength to declare its own godhead, and so becomes godhead. America. An empty continent waiting for its master as a woman waits for hers. No wonder your hold on it is so tenuous that you have had to come to this African desert to defend it. The wonder is that she suffered you at all . . .

VOICE   *(out of scene, harsh and loud)* Turn around, you, so I won't have to shoot you in the back.

78. ANOTHER ANGLE

The German has turned his head, looks calmly at Franklin, who holds a pistol pointed at him. Battson is leaping forward. He knocks the pistol up, grapples with Franklin. Another man moves at last to help him.

BATTSON   You fool!

FRANKLIN   *(struggling)* Kill him! Kill him, somebody! They're mad! They're monsters! There ain't any hope for them! We got to kill them all! There ain't room in the world for them and us, too! We got to kill them all to save ourselves!

REAGAN   *(entering)* But you can't murder him! Stop it!

FRANKLIN   *(quiets somewhat while they still hold him; Battson takes the pistol)* Why not?

REAGAN   *(takes the pistol from Battson)* I don't care whether he's alive or not either. But no man of mine shall murder a prisoner.

FRANKLIN   The Japs do it. Maybe the Germans do it, too, for all you know.

REAGAN   Maybe they do. But they're Japs and Germans. That's why we are fighting them: because we ain't Japs and Germans . . .

A VOICE   *(sudden—loud—off scene)* What the . . .

A take as all turn.

79. ANOTHER ANGLE   OFFICER'S BODY IN F.G.

—beside the grave, as the Italian officer approaches, pulling something on wheels behind him.

A VOICE   It's a baby carriage.

ANOTHER VOICE   Hell it is. It's a wheelchair.

REAGAN   *(catching up again at last)* Guard, there! Jump!

The second of the pair of guards from whom the Italian escaped moves quickly toward him. The Italian pays him no attention. The Italian has seen the blanketed shape beside the grave. He has comprehended. His face changes, is sober and quick with pity as he comes on to the grave, drawing the thing behind him. We now see that it is a heavy Italian machine gun mounted on a dolly. He drops the handle, stops beside the dead officer, glances at Reagan, his face quick with pity.

ITALIAN   The officer?

REAGAN   Yes.

ITALIAN   Ah. The poor lad. So far from home. *(he clicks his heels slightly, salutes the body)*

REAGAN   How in hell did you get here? Weren't you challenged?

ITALIAN   *(to Reagan)* Do not be alarmed. Your sentry is a good man. I was challenged, quickly. He would have shot me very quickly and very dead if I had not stood. You do not need to worry about your sentries, Sergeant.

REAGAN   *(takes command again)* All right, you guards, pull your prisoners back a little.

The guard nudges the Italian with his rifle butt. The Italian withdraws to where the German and the other guard stand.

REAGAN   All right, Levine.

The four bearers come forward—a Jew, a Pole, an Irishman and an Indian: Americans too. They take up the officer and lower him into the grave.

REAGAN   Shovels.

Men with shovels come forward as the bearers move back.

A SOLDIER   Ain't we going to fire a volley?

BATTSON   Sure. We're going to shoot off guns every half hour. We don't want to leave the Heinies wandering around out there, lost too.

SOLDIER   But ain't we going to do something? Whitesides was all right, even if he was a durned lootenant.

They wait, Battson looks at Reagan.

BATTSON   What about it?

REAGAN   *(catches up again)* Anybody here got a Bible?

The men look at one another, a little sheepish. Battson looks from face to face. Reagan waits.

AKERS   *(suddenly)* I got one. I ain't ashamed of it, neither.

ITALIAN   *(to Akers)* Why should you be?

BATTSON   *(to Akers)* All right. I bet you can even read it, too. Get it, then.

AKERS   I know what to read. My pap preaches on Sundays. I've heard him.

REAGAN   All right, Alabama.

Akers advances, tugging a small Bible from inside his shirt.

80. AKERS   AT HEAD OF GRAVE

Bible open in his hands. Others quiet in b.g., bareheaded, as Akers, his helmet clasped under his arm, reads:

AKERS   *(reading)* "I am the resurrection and the life, saith the Lord; he that believeth in Me, though he were dead, yet shall he live; and he that liveth and believeth in Me shall never die."

He closes the Bible, steps back.

REAGAN   *(puts on helmet)* Shovels.

Four men with shovels come forward and begin to fill the grave.

VOICE   *(off scene)* Here, where are you . . .

The Italian enters, the guard quickly behind him. The Italian approaches one of the shovelers, touches his shoulder, extends his hand for the shovel.

ITALIAN You permit, signore?

The soldier surrenders the shovel to the Italian. Other Americans follow his example, so that the burying of the officer has, as of its own accord, stopped being a military affair and has become civilian, as when the neighbors of a small community in America bury one whom they have known all their lives and respected and loved. The shovels continue to throw the sand steadily into the grave as the mound mounts. The rhythm of the shovels becomes the BEAT of the FREEDOM TRAIN as DISSOLVE begins, increases, faster, louder. SOUND of DIVING AEROPLANES, machine gun fire, begins. The FREEDOM TRAIN and BATTLE SOUND very loud, SOUND of FREEDOM TRAIN is drowned out, BATTLE SOUND very loud in—

LAP DISSOLVE TO:

81. CHINESE PEASANT MEN

—hurling dirt frantically upward as aeroplanes dive roaring down at them and zoom on; rattle of machine guns, spurting of bullets along the earth as another plane roars down, the Chinese looking up as it approaches, still hurling their frantic and puny earth. Another aeroplane roars down, the Chinese spring up as if to intervene their bodies in one last desperate defiance, are cut down by the raking bullets. The SOUND of aeroplanes dies away, as we—

DISSOLVE TO:

Chinese Sequence

FADE IN

A CHINESE VILLAGE   FULL SHOT   DAY

The village is being savagely and viciously blitzed by the Japanese advance. There is something almost contemptuous about it: in this vicious assault by dive bombers on a collection of mud huts and peasants armed only with scythes and axes. But even then, the people are resisting. We see FLASHES of groups of unarmed men springing up and flinging their bodies into the blasts of the diving aeroplanes as if the men are holding the rampart of the village against an assault by other mere men, instead of vicious machines.

Then the uproar and noise passes on, leaving only scattered dead bodies and the smoke of burning houses. As it fades, CAMERA HOLDS for the first time on a recognizable person. It is an old woman, a peasant, frail-looking. She is crouching in the midst of the desolation, dazed, a streak of blood on her cheek. She looks as completely alone as an abandoned child.

MED. SHOT   OLD PEASANT WOMAN

—as Lu Ping enters SHOT. She is a young girl, disheveled. She runs frantically to the old woman, kneels beside her.

    LU PING   Grandmother!

The old woman rouses, wakes, looks about as Lu Ping clings to her, sobbing.

    MAMA MOSQUITO   Lan and Kyo?

    LU PING   *(sobbing)* Dead! Dead!

The old woman turns, faces CAMERA, then looks up, as if watching the sky. Her face is awake now, grim.

    LU PING   Aihe, dead!

    OTHER VOICES IN B.G.   Aihe, dead! Aihe, dead!

The child still cries. The old woman stares steadily and grimly at the sky, the blood still running down her cheek.

                                   DISSOLVE TO:

CHINESE VILLAGE   DAY

FULL SHOT   MAMA MOSQUITO, OLD MEN AND WOMEN, CHINESE SOLDIERS, AND YOUNG MEN

Mama Mosquito and a few other old men and women are sitting in a group while a few ragged Chinese soldiers and the young men of the village bury the dead.

MED. SHOT   GROUP   FAVORING MAMA MOSQUITO

Mama Mosquito still has her grim look. The other old people are dazed and quiet. The young women are keeping up a steady chanting wailing as the men bury the bodies hurriedly. The chief of the soldiers enters SHOT and approaches the old people. He pities them too, but there is no time for that now.

SOLDIER   Who is chief among you now? Who is oldest?

An old man dumbly indicates Mama Mosquito.

SOLDIER   Come, then, old mother. We must go.

MAMA MOSQUITO   (rouses) Ay. We must go. Bring me my bowl.

CLOSE SHOT   MAMA MOSQUITO

—sitting with her feet in a fairly good porcelain bowl of water. She wears a shawl, ready to start. In b.g. the soldiers and villagers are loading household goods into carts and paniers. Lu Ping approaches.

LU PING   Come, Grandmother. We are ready.

She stoops and takes the bowl away, wipes Mama Mosquito's feet with a cloth and sets her sandals down. Lu Ping empties the bowl and puts it into the cart. Mama Mosquito watches her.

MAMA MOSQUITO   Careful, there.

LU PING   I will place it well.

Mama Mosquito steps into her sandals, rises. Then she stoops and scoops up a handful of earth. It is bloodstained. She stares at it, squeezes it in her hand. Her face is grim and implacable now, yet still calm. She folds the lump of earth into her shawl and turns toward the cart.

MAMA MOSQUITO   (harshly) Come then. Let us go.

LAP DISSOLVE TO:

THE VILLAGE

—in motion, carrying its sorry possessions. Lu Ping draws a

cart, Mama Mosquito walks beside it, grim-faced. Slowly the
MAP of China is SUPERIMPOSED. A voice begins to speak.

LAP DISSOLVE ON MAP TO:

OTHER CROWDS OF PEASANTS

—carrying bundles, until we get the effect of rivers of people
from everywhere.

> VOICE   People of China! Go to the West! Go to the West!
> Take everything you can carry!

LAP DISSOLVE ON MAP TO:

A CROWD OF MIXED SOLDIERS AND PEASANTS

—men and women and children, as they dismantle a factory,
take it down stick by stick to carry with them.

> VOICE   Whatever you cannot carry, destroy! Leave noth-
> ing but ashes for the enemy!

LAP DISSOLVE ON MAP TO:

PEASANTS

—setting fire to crops in the fields and barns, until at last the
MAP is hidden by smoke.

FADE OUT.

FADE IN

A GUERRILLA HEADQUARTERS IN THE MOUNTAINS

The homeless people from several districts have gathered here,
where at least they are safe, dazed and apathetic because, although they are not satisfied to have lost their land, they don't
know what to do about it. The general sense among them is of a
people who would do something about it if they just had a
leader to tell them how. But at this point, with safety just
reached, they do not know where a leader will come from.

DISSOLVE TO:

GUERRILLA HEADQUARTERS   NIGHT

The chiefs and heads of the different villages have gathered in
a council with the guerrilla captain. Mama Mosquito sits among

them, her feet in her porcelain bowl. She has every right to be there, since she is not only one of the oldest, but her dead husband was head of their village. But it was she who called the council. The old people are there. A fire is burning nearby.

GUERRILLA CAPTAIN Well, old mother. What do you want?

MAMA MOSQUITO My land.

A MAN We have all lost land.

SECOND MAN And our houses.

THIRD MAN And don't forget our dead.

FOURTH MAN And our daughters whom they ruined and our children whom they have enslaved.

MAMA MOSQUITO A house can always be rebuilt, as long as there is a wall or a chimney left. Or a new house.

While they watch, she produces from her shawl the lump of bloodstained earth.

MAMA MOSQUITO *(continuing)* This is the blood of my daughter and my grandson, soaked into the earth on which they were born and died. I want that land back.

The faces of the others have lighted up.

VOICES Aihe! Aihe!

The guerrilla captain reacts. He extends his hand, almost humbly.

CAPTAIN Will you, old mother? I had land too, with my blood in it, before you did.

Mama Mosquito gives him a tiny scrap of the earth. He puts it carefully away.

OLD MAN And I Chau Yutang? I did not think of that—

Mama Mosquito gives him a fragment.

SECOND MAN And I?

Mama Mosquito gives him a scrap. There is only a scrap left. She offers it to the next man.

MAN   Keep some for yourself, Chau Yutang.

MAMA MOSQUITO   I have plenty more.

She looks at the earth for a moment. Her face is grim and in a way terrible. She tosses the earth into the fire. The man who received a scrap looks at her a moment, then tosses his into the fire.

MAN   I, too.

A second stoops, scoops up dirt from beside his feet and tosses it into the fire.

SECOND MAN   This represents that which I forgot.

THIRD   *(doing the same)* And I.

CLOSE SHOT OF FIRE

—as others do the same, the clots of earth falling on the fire rapidly.

VOICES   And I. And I. And I.

LAP DISSOLVE TO:

FULL SHOT   GUERRILLA HEADQUARTERS   NIGHT

The guerrilla captain and various chiefs of the different villages are there. Mama Mosquito is standing near the fire, the old people gathered around her.

FIRST MAN   *(to Mama Mosquito)* We have our scythes and pitchforks and axes.

SECOND MAN   Did they save us yesterday?

FIRST MAN   Some of us have guns, too. And there are the guns of the men of Captain Mu here.

MAMA MOSQUITO   No. That is not enough. *(she gropes for words)* The steel birds which destroyed us. The guns on them. That are like an old man who cannot stop his tongue. I saw. When the bird shot at me, the little red eye of the gun winking faster than the tongue of a lizard—

GUERRILLA CAPTAIN   Machine guns, old mother.

MAMA MOSQUITO   Ay. That is what we need.

FIRST   But where shall we get them?

MAMA MOSQUITO   From those who have them. *(they comprehend, react, stare at her)* We will go back.

FIRST MAN   *(quietly)* Yes. We will go back.

FADE OUT.

FADE IN

ROADSIDE   DAY

Mama Mosquito and her party have halted. Mama Mosquito sits with her feet in the bowl, the others have all halted while she rests them. Lu Ping and the other young women are now disguised to look like old women, with ashes and dirt in their hair and on their faces. They have their carts and paniers, just as they left. On Mama Mosquito's cart is a basket of chickens. Yo Ming, an old man, stands beside Mama Mosquito. The others are grouped respectfully about, waiting for Mama Mosquito to decide to go on.

YO MING   How far will we go? To our village?

MAMA MOSQUITO   Perhaps. We will go on until we meet them.

YO MING   That may be anywhere.

MAMA MOSQUITO   Yes. But we want only ones with guns which do not stop. *(to Lu Ping)* Come, lazybones!

Lu Ping kneels, wipes Mama Mosquito's feet and puts the sandals on and puts the bowl back into the cart. They go on.

ANOTHER ROADSIDE

They have stopped again, almost as before, Mama Mosquito with her feet again in the bowl. But they look anxious now, they are near their village and they are concealed in the bushes.

A boy enters, panting, goes to where Mama Mosquito and Yo Ming wait.

MAMA MOSQUITO   Well?

BOY They are there—many of them.

MAMA MOSQUITO How many of them?

BOY I don't know. They have guns. There are many of them.

MAMA MOSQUITO Come, then.

The wiping of her feet and putting the bowl away is almost automatic between her and Lu Ping, though this time Mama Mosquito wipes her feet and dons her sandals while Lu Ping is putting the bowl away.

MAMA MOSQUITO Maybe these will have the guns. Then we can stop in our village again.

YO MING Aihe. In our own homes again.

They go on.

VILLAGE STREET

They have been halted by a party of Jap soldiers. Mama Mosquito's manner has completely changed. She seems senile, stupid. The Japs are in a playful mood rather than fierce. None of them can speak Chinese. They jabber among themselves, push the Chinese about a little for sport. Two or three of them carry Tommy guns. They start to prod into the baggage, discover Mama Mosquito's crate of chickens. They jabber again among themselves while the Chinese watch. Then one smashes the crate, the chickens leap into the air, two of the Japs shoot at them with the Tommy guns.

MAMA MOSQUITO Yes. We will stay here.

EXT. YARD BEFORE HOUSE

Mama Mosquito and Lu Ping draw the cart up before the door and stop. Mama Mosquito looks about. Her face is still grim, but it is calm now. She stoops slowly and scoops up another handful of the earth. The blood has now dried from it. It crumbles as she lets it run through her fingers.

MAMA MOSQUITO (*quietly*) Yes. We will stay here.

FADE OUT.

FADE IN

WELL IN VILLAGE SQUARE   MAMA MOSQUITO AND CAPTAIN

A few pathetic-looking villagers are grouped a little distance away. The CAMERA is now focused on the well. Out of scene we hear a Japanese command to halt. At the well a soldier draws up a bucket of water. Rests it on the coping.

> **CAPTAIN**   *(coming into scene—motions to another soldier)* Bring the twelve here to drink—

Soldier goes over to small group of villagers and prods them forward with his gun butt. They are stopped near the well. They stand stolidly as the captain dips the dipper into the bucket and holds it out to the nearest one.

> **CAPTAIN**   Drink—

The dipper passes from one to the other. The captain watches each face keenly as the dipper goes to the next. The water drips a little from each one's mouth, but the faces remain impassive, stolid, unmoved. The captain nods, as if satisfied, when the last of the twelve men and women has taken his drink.

> **CAPTAIN**   *(to soldier)* These twelve will be here each morning to drink first. *(to villagers)* You go now!

The villagers shuffle stolidly away. Laughing and pushing, the tired dusty Japanese soldiers crowd around the well and drink, thirstily, the water sloshing over their clothes and dripping from their mouths.

LAP DISSOLVE TO:

MAMA MOSQUITO   THE WELL

One Japanese sentry walks slowly around the well, guarding it. Others are lolling idly, watching an old wizened man who is spraying the trees with a hand spray. As the old man sprays, he moves backwards. His foot touches that of the sentry, and the Japanese shoves him roughly away with his elbow, a contemptuous gesture. The old man sidles away, hunching his shoulders as if against an expected blow. He goes on spraying. The sun catches the fine sheen of the liquid as it falls from the leaves.

The spray empties. The old man fills it from a small can. Goes on spraying the great branch overhanging the well. The CAMERA now concentrates on a few of the leaves on this branch, and we notice that the liquid surface is slightly gray in tone. Slowly DISSOLVE but only partially, as if there has been a change in the time of day. Our CAMERA now becomes the microscope under which the changes in the leaves are disclosed. Our tones are darker now, and we notice myriad changes—first the edges curl slightly—the leaves have dried—a slight brownish tone is evident—then the leaves gradually turn almost into parchment-like texture, like the leaves in the fall of the year. All of this is to be performed by the CAMERA with the suggestion of the passage of time. It might be six hours—it might be six days—it might be six weeks—there is a slight rustle of wind. Slowly one of the leaves detaches itself, and flutters gently to the ground, falling just outside the well . . . A stronger breeze comes up. We notice that the leaves at the farthest edges of the tree are still green, but from the branch directly over the well flutters slowly a second brown leaf—then a third—falling outside the well. Then one leaf falls to the coping of the well. The next leaf flutters gently in the breeze and spirals downward so we know its course will take it directly into the well.

CAMERA now focuses at the top of the well, shooting down to the dark blot of water beneath. The eye of the CAMERA seems to make a glistening patch on the water, towards which, through the light, the leaf spirals until it flutters and falls like a lily pad on the surface of the water. Very slowly the water covers this brown leaf with a thin film until it slowly turns gray.

Next shot is outside the well, now almost covered with leaves. Heavy Japanese boots trample the leaves, and CAMERA PANS upward to take in the twelve Chinese, being given the dipper to drink. Now there is a definite gauntness and grayness on their impassive faces.

We flash to the fourth face in line, which is that of an aged Chinese woman, with a face like parchment. Obliquely, while the dipper is being passed to her right, we get a cross shot across her face, to show the dipper passing down the line, so that all we see are the mouths of the Chinese as they are drinking. Her eyes are obliquely raised toward the topmost line of the cherry tree, from which gently flutters one of the dried leaves. Apparently idly, her oblique glance registers the falling of that leaf right into the center of the well. At that moment, her hand goes up with the dipper, which has reached her, and with a slow, inscrutable smile twisting the corners of her mouth, she puts the ladle to her lips and drinks deep.

LAP DISSOLVE TO:

Uneven, lagging footsteps now treading on a heavy mass of leaves outside the well. Coping of well is covered with seared leaves. We see the bottom itself filled with leaves . . . Japanese soldiers dragging water in low-slung pails, their boots seeming weighted to show the weariness that comes from accumulative poison.

LAP DISSOLVE TO:

Dead bodies of dozens of Japanese soldiers lying about, with the twelve Chinese drinking hostages fallen where they stood.

As we see these dead bodies, CAMERA slowly moves to the cherry tree and we find the branches over and around the well completely denuded, as if by a blight . . . the rest of the tree is covered with healthy foliage.

DISSOLVE TO:

HOUSE OF JAPANESE COLONEL   CLOSEUP OF SMALL HEAP OF
BROWN DRIED LEAVES ON A TABLE

Scene expands to take in full table at which is seated the heavy-lidded, fleshy Japanese colonel. Behind him stands an orderly. Two guards at the door and a Japanese captain standing before him a short distance from the table.

    COLONEL Fools! You should have known! Why should leaves be falling in the spring?

He sweeps the leaves aside violently with both hands. They swirl upward and fill CAMERA.

DISSOLVE TO:

EXT. ROAD   NIGHT

Mama Mosquito, the cart halted, bending over Wei Lin, who is lying in the road. He is about twenty, has been cruelly beaten, appears dead. She looks quickly about, then stoops over him, turns him over. When she moves him, he cries out with pain, rouses.

MAMA MOSQUITO   What did you do, then?

WEI LIN   It is my arms. They broke them both, I think. Because I would not tell if I had seen the dynamite or not. I did not tell.

MAMA MOSQUITO   But you did see it?

WEI LIN   Yes.

MAMA MOSQUITO   Why did they not kill you, then?

WEI LIN   Then I am not dead?

MAMA MOSQUITO   (*glances anxiously and quickly about again*) Can you get into the cart? You will have to help.

His arms are broken, but with her help he gets into the cart and she covers him quickly with the vegetables and straw it contains, and goes on.

ANOTHER PART OF ROAD

A Japanese patrol stops her.

JAP SOLDIER   (*appearing suddenly out of a side path*) You— stop!

Old woman stops suddenly, stiffening as she does so. Her hands hold tightly to the shafts of the cart. She stares straight ahead. The Jap comes closer, peers at her.

JAP SOLDIER   (*contemptuously*) Ah—it is *you*, old one!

He bends over the cart, sees the ripe peaches, smacks his lips. He calls in Japanese to others behind him. Grinning, their bayonets held ready, five others run up to the cart, jabbering in Japanese. The first sentry snatches a peach . . . two of the others spear ripe peaches with the points of their bayonets, while the old woman keeps a stiff mask of indifference to her face. Only every so often her eyes flicker sideways to the center of the pile of hay, fearful of what they might find if they searched it.

The first Jap sentry, who has rested his bayonet against the cart, now picks it up, waves her on, part of the peach still in his hand.

JAP I Get on with you, old one—

Relieved, she begins to move forward—CAMERA on her and the front part of the cart. She has escaped with her burden . . . but suddenly the sound—

JAP II Wait!

And she freezes in her tracks. A Jap walks into scene, leering.

JAP II You are sure it is only fruit and vegetables you carry, old woman?

Old woman nods quickly, continues to try and pull her cart forward, but now the Japs press closely, intrigued with the promise of game.

JAP I We will see for ourselves—

Lifts his bayonet and plunges it quickly into the hay. The old woman stiffens sharply, and for an instant her eyes close as if she herself had been stabbed. The Jap laughs aloud as he draws out his bayonet, only to plunge it in again. The others follow suit, grinning and talking as they plunge their bayonets into various points of the hay . . . the fruit and vegetables are sheared and spoiled by the bayonets. The old woman's face seems to grow gray and marble-like. Little beads of sweat appear on her upper lip. But her face stays immobile.

JAP II *(motioning her to move)* Get on, now, old woman— there is nothing there—

The old woman moves slowly away from them, hearing their laughter and mockery behind her. CAMERA picks up her face, close-up, the eyes grim and bitter. Her eyes turn once to stare toward the middle of the cart. The CAMERA follows her glance. Almost imperceptibly the straw in the middle seems to settle, ever so slightly . . . CAMERA closeup of a few strands of hay—it assumes an almost translucent, dark-red, burnished quality . . .

As the CAMERA concentrates on it, a tiny, blood-red drop of liquid rolls down one strand, like a little rivulet, and drops off.

CAMERA back to closeup of old woman . . . her eyes fastened on the drop, enlarged with a look of dread . . .

DISSOLVE TO:

Old woman rolling the cart into her back yard. Looks guardedly around. Calls softly to someone in the house.

WOMAN   Lu Ping—Lu Ping—come quickly—

CLOSE GROUP   MAMA MOSQUITO AND LU PING

—as they bend over the cart while Mama Mosquito drags the vegetables and straw aside and raises her porcelain bowl. It is in fragments now, but it has saved Wei Lin's life. She flings the fragments away, then she and Lu Ping lift Wei Lin from the cart and turn with him, carrying him toward the house.

INT. HOUSE

Mama Mosquito and Lu Ping enter with Wei Lin and lay him on the bed.

MAMA MOSQUITO   Get hot water.

Lu Ping exits. Mama Mosquito looks down at Wei Lin, then turns. Her face is grim again, calm, not quite exultant.

MAMA MOSQUITO   Dynamite too.

LAP DISSOLVE TO:

CLOSE SHOT   MAMA MOSQUITO

—seated beside the lamp, her feet in another bowl of water, writing up her ledger, entering in it the number of Japs who died of the poison, and the number of machine guns taken, entering them as vegetables.

LAP DISSOLVE TO:

EXT. NIGHT   MED. CLOSE SHOT

Shadowy men carrying the machine guns and the ammunition up a wild path into the mountains.

FADE OUT.

FADE IN

Kitchen. Early morning. Mama Mosquito and Lu Ping are in the kitchen. Mama Mosquito stirs broth on the stove, fills a bowl and hands it to Lu Ping. She goes to a small door, opens it and walks carefully down the stairs into cellar room. The boy is lying on a cot against the wall. CAMERA moves closer to boy. He is lying on his back, the empty left sleeve hanging over the edge, his right arm strapped to his side. CAMERA closeup of his face. His eyes are staring straight upward, the tears welling in them and slipping down his cheeks onto the pillow. Lu Ping comes to the side of the cot, sits down on a low chair. The boy's eyes go obliquely to the empty sleeve and avert quickly, half closed.

> **LU PING** (*pityingly—low voice*) It had to be done . . . my grandmother found you on the road to Suchen and brought you home . . . she had to cut if off.

His head rolls to the right side and an oblique look takes in the strapped right arm.

> **LU PING** The right one will heal—

The boy continues to weep, shaking his head from side to side in negation.

> **BOY** I am like a dead tree in a forest—

Mama Mosquito enters.

> **MAMA MOSQUITO** A tree still lives, even though one limb is gone. Feed him, daughter.

Lu Ping rises. Mama Mosquito sits in the chair and with one arm she half lifts Wei Lin so that Lu Ping can feed him. With her other hand she begins to massage softly his remaining arm as he begins to eat.

> **MAMA MOSQUITO** Now, the dynamite.

> **WEI LIN** No! See what the knowledge of it has already—

> **MAMA MOSQUITO** (*implacable*) Yes. The dynamite. Think. (*she touches the empty sleeve*) You have not lost this arm when you can make a purchase with it.

WEI LIN   *(reacts, his face becomes firm)* Yes. The dynamite—

LAP DISSOLVE TO:

EXT. NIGHT   A WAREHOUSE   CLOSE SHOT

—as a shadowy man strangles the Jap sentry. Other shadowy men emerge from everywhere apparently, with Mama Mosquito's cart. They open the warehouse and begin to fetch out boxes of dynamite and load them swiftly into the cart.

FADE OUT.

FADE IN

INT. HOUSE

Wei Lin can sit up now. Lu Ping sits beside him, massaging his arm. Mama Mosquito sits at a table, arranging vegetables for her cart. Her feet are now in a battered bucket which is a discarded piece of Japanese military equipment. She finishes the job.

MAMA MOSQUITO   Now then, lazybones.

Lu Ping rises, dries her feet and puts her sandals beside them. Mama Mosquito rises.

MAMA MOSQUITO   Lock the door now. And put more ashes in your hair, fool.

She goes out with the vegetables. Lu Ping locks the door and returns. Scene ends on a note of tenderness between Lu Ping and Wei Lin.

AT HOUSE OF JAPANESE COLONEL

Mama Mosquito arrives with her cart of vegetables. She is again the stupid peasant, whining and cringing when necessary, a little brash and familiar with the private soldiers, who have become accustomed to her daily visits with vegetables which the colonel buys, playing her part cleverly. The cook is a Chinese, a villager whom we have seen before. He passes her a message secretly, perhaps through double talk. She departs, letting herself be kidded by the Japanese sentries, still playing her part as an old fool.

DISSOLVE TO:

EXT.   A RAILROAD BRIDGE   NIGHT

The guerrillas crouch among the bushes, waiting, as the train comes up; the bridge and train are blown up.

LAP DISSOLVE TO:

MAMA MOSQUITO

—her feet in the steel bucket, writing in her ledger.

LAP DISSOLVE TO:

ANOTHER EXPLOSION

—damaging to the Japs.

LAP DISSOLVE TO:

MAMA MOSQUITO

—writing in her ledger, Wei Lin and Lu Ping in b.g.

WEI LIN   I wish I could help.

MAMA MOSQUITO   *(does not look up)* You will in time. Wait.

LAP DISSOLVE TO:

ANOTHER EXPLOSION

DISSOLVE TO:

INT. JAP COLONEL'S OFFICE

The colonel and two captains.

COLONEL   Last week the supply train at Mukden. Two days ago, the dam at Kiangsu. And last night a train of our troops blown to bits. And you have found nothing!

1ST OFFICER   Excellency, at Kiangsu they found only a bent old grandmother walking through the woods for fagots—

COLONEL   And at the poisoned well only a bent old grandmother with a cart of vegetables!

2ND OFFICER   At Mukden they said a young woman ran into the woods—

COLONEL   Idiots! Fools. What is the reward now?

1ST OFFICER   Twelve thousand yen, Excellency.

COLONEL   Offer fifteen at once!

DISSOLVE TO:

Bridge as it explodes.

LAP DISSOLVE TO:

POSTER: TWENTY THOUSAND YEN FOR INFORMATION LEADING TO CAPTURE OF WOMAN KNOWN AS MAMA MOSQUITO!

LAP DISSOLVE TO:

A Jap column, a land mine explodes under it, the guerrillas firing into the wounded Japs.

LAP DISSOLVE TO:

HUGE POSTER: THIRTY THOUSAND YEN FOR BODY OF WOMAN KNOWN AS MAMA MOSQUITO!

DISSOLVE TO:

GARDEN OF MAMA MOSQUITO'S HOUSE

Wei Lin is kneeling on the earth. It is early dusk. Lu Ping kneels before him, making furrows. As she draws them, Wei Lin, with his weak right hand, drops seeds along. She smiles with tender encouragement as she watches. Their eyes meet now and then with a supreme, almost sublime contentment. Lu Ping is exquisite without her gray make-up.

Pausing to let his eyes rove over her face, he does not speak, but she flushes and becomes starry-eyed beneath his look. To break the silence, she speaks.

LU PING *(shyly)* Grandmother will be angry with me for leaving off the ash-dust.

WEI LIN *(simply)* The anger of all the world would melt, could it but look upon your face, Lu Ping.

She drops her eyes and continues with the furrowing. He drops the seeds, looking at her. She turns her hand upward and one of the seeds falls into her palm . . . They both stop and observe it. Her hand gently closes over the seed.

WEI LIN   In the tale of Chang Tao there was a truly remarkable man whose ears were filled constantly with celestial music, and who sought many ways to find the cause of it.

LU PING   *(breathlessly)*—And did he find it?

WEI LIN   Yes—and she was beautiful.

LU PING   *(her hand opens, turns, the seed falls into the open furrow; lip trembles)* It is easy to love where beauty is—

WEI LIN   Where love is, there is beauty.

They pause and gaze at one another for one long, tender moment, she grateful for his words. Then her eyes droop and his mood changes, quickly becomes mischievous.

WEI LIN   Look you, Lu Ping, I am a worthless son of illustrious ancestors. When I was but a boy, my honorable parent warned me I would come to no good end, because it was my habit always to go on in advance both of my feet and of my head.

LU PING   *(falling in with his mischievous mood)* I have not found it so, Wei Lin. *(a little merry look in her eyes as she swiftly glances up, then down again)* I have found yours a very steadfast nature.

WEI LIN   *(matching her)* As the mountain rises, so the river winds—

LU PING   *(merrily)* Your father taught you many things, Wei Lin—

WEI LIN   To speak with humility of one's ancestors—to love China fervently—and to kneel with reverence before her beauties. *(a merry twinkle in his eye)*

LU PING   *(delighted with him)* He taught you well, Wei Lin. What more?

CLOSE SHOT   WEI LIN AND LU PING

—kneeling, facing each other, the planting forgotten, their hands joined, their faces drawing nearer and nearer. Lu Ping has become sober, a little frightened. Wei Lin is grave too. It is as if she would withdraw her hands, but she cannot.

WEI LIN   There is another thing I know, but he did not teach it to me. It was a young man, a young white man, from far away across the East Ocean who told it to me. I have not tried yet. It is done in his country. He said it is beautiful. Do you wish to know what it is?

Now Lu Ping is trying to withdraw, but she cannot, though it is not only because hers and Wei Lin's hands are joined together.

WEI LIN   It is called kissing. It requires a man and a maid to do it, like us. Shall I show you? *(their faces draw nearer and nearer)* Lu Ping. Lu Ping. Thy name is like a little temple bell that the wind trembles . . .

Their faces touch. Wei Lin moves his face until their lips meet.

FADE OUT.

FADE IN

COLONEL'S OFFICE   COLONEL AND A CAPTAIN

COLONEL   This time there will be no blundering. At last we have a picture of this woman . . .

He extends a photograph.

INSERT: PHOTOGRAPH

It can be Mama Mosquito, or any other old woman or even a man. It wears a man's trousers and shirt, the face is half-turned as if the subject had tried to avoid the camera an instant too late. A few guerrillas can be seen in b.g.

CLOSE SHOT   COLONEL AND CAPTAIN

—as the captain takes the photograph.

COLONEL   Have every old woman in the district rounded up and compared with it.

CAPTAIN   Yes, Excellency.

COLONEL   And the men too. She is dressed as a man here; perhaps that's why you dunderheads haven't found her yet.

CAPTAIN   Yes, Excellency.

COLONEL   And increase the reward to fifty thousand yen, to anyone who will betray her.

The captain salutes, exits.

LAP DISSOLVE TO:

CLOSE SHOT   AN OLD WOMAN'S FRIGHTENED FACE

—as a rough hand jerks it around and holds the photograph beside it.

LAP DISSOLVE TO:

ANOTHER FACE   THE SAME

LAP DISSOLVE TO:

ANOTHER FACE   THE SAME

LAP DISSOLVE TO:

COLONEL'S OFFICE   COLONEL AND THE CAPTAIN

COLONEL   *(repressed, about to explode)* So you have not found her.

CAPTAIN   *(cringing almost)* We have compared the photograph with every old woman and old man in the district. We have even thought of trying the men and women in this village here . . .

COLONEL   *(explodes)* This village? *This village?* You have not sought for her here?

CAPTAIN   We thought—right here under our noses—

COLONEL   *(restrains himself)* You will have every man, woman and child in this village rounded up at once and compared with that picture. You will then report back here and prepare yourself to be relieved of duty here for transfer to the front.

CAPTAIN *(stiffly)* Yes, Excellency.

He salutes, exits.

CLOSE SHOT   AN OLD WOMAN'S FACE

—turned aside and down as the rough hand tries to raise it. It resists, the hand drags it up. It is Lu Ping, disguised. The hand holds her while she stares in terror. The man's other hand enters, rakes a smear of the ashes from her hair and face.

INT. MAMA MOSQUITO'S KITCHEN

Lu Ping and Wei Lin are preparing hurriedly to leave. Mama Mosquito is getting them started. Lu Ping is terrified. Mama Mosquito is grim, hides her alarm.

    MAMA MOSQUITO   Never mind now. It's too late. Go to the mountains.

    WEI LIN   I will protect her. I have one arm left.

    MAMA MOSQUITO   Use it. And your head too. Go.

Lu Ping and Wei Lin exit.

EXT. THE EDGE OF THE VILLAGE

As Lu Ping and Wei Lin hurry along, the Jap captain and two soldiers ambush them. They don't even do the one-armed Wei Lin the mercy of killing him. While the captain holds the girl, the two soldiers beat him with their gun butts into the ditch. He tries again with his one arm to rise. A rifle butt strikes him back down. They take Lu Ping on and leave him there.

                                    DISSOLVE TO:

INT. MAMA MOSQUITO'S HOUSE   NIGHT

Mama Mosquito, Wei Lin, and another young man. Wei Lin has recovered somewhat, is battered and bloody, but is making no effort to clean his wounds. He is grim and determined. He tells Mama Mosquito his plan. He realizes that after he does his deed, the Japs will wipe out the whole village in retribution. He has brought his friend to help Mama Mosquito save them, by sending them into the woods. Perhaps they can all be saved, but certainly Mama Mosquito must be; China needs her.

WEI LIN   As you can see, I cannot live now. But you cannot afford to die.

MAMA MOSQUITO   I gave you your life once. It now belongs to me. You cannot save her now.

WEI LIN   That I know. So how better can I use this life you gave me than by avenging her?

He turns.

MAMA MOSQUITO   Wei Lin!

WEI LIN   *(doesn't pause)* No. *(to the other young man, over his shoulder)* Warn them all. It will take me a little time yet. But guard Mother Chau as you would your own life. Farewell.

He exits. For the first time Mama Mosquito breaks down.

MAMA MOSQUITO   Aihe! Aihe! That I have seen the day to wish one of my children stillborn.

WO CHONG   Come, Mother—

Mama Mosquito recovers.

MAMA MOSQUITO   No. There are old men and women and young children here who could not travel that far. Go to the mountains. Tell Captain Chu—

WO CHONG   But you. Wei Lin said—

MAMA MOSQUITO   Have not these little men from the East Ocean been seeking Mama Mosquito for months?

WO CHONG   *(stares at her, comprehends, comes to her and stands before her in respectful humility)* You are a man, old Mother. Let the little men who love fighting cry loud when they have taken thee. Give me thy blessing as if I were thy son.

Mama Mosquito blesses him, already pushing him toward the door.

MAMA MOSQUITO   Go. To the mountains.

Wo Chong exits. Mama Mosquito takes out her ledger and ink and brush and sits with the brush poised, motionless, waiting, her face implacable and grim.

EXT. NIGHT   THE COLONEL'S HOUSE

—as Wei Lin crawls toward it with his charge of dynamite.

CLOSE SHOT   JAPANESE SENTRY   NIGHT

—as Wei Lin rises quietly behind him, flings his one arm around the sentry's neck and slowly chokes him to death and lets the body drop.

CLOSE SHOT   WEI LIN

—peering through a window, through which the colonel and the captain can be seen. He sets off his dynamite. He and house and all vanish in the explosion.

DISSOLVE TO:

DAY

The destroyed village, smoke drifting from the smoldering houses. SHOT of bodies hanging from trees. CAMERA comes down along these bodies, to show a few bodies on the ground. A small distance away, the guerrilla captain and the school teacher stand among a few guerrillas, with grim, bitter faces.

SCHOOL TEACHER   *(bitterly)* We are too late—

There are sounds of a scuffle off scene, and they turn. Four Japanese prisoners, hands tied behind them, are pushed into the circle. Three are insolent—but the fourth, looking up at the hanging bodies, shivers as if with a chill. The blacksmith moves forward, addressing one of them.

BLACKSMITH   How many were in your company?

Jap soldier, grinning insolently, murmurs something beneath his breath. From behind the Japs comes a grim, implacable voice.

MAMA MOSQUITO   You must speak louder—*(there is a quick startled flash of surprise from all as they turn to the voice)* it is difficult for them to hear— *(camera flash to hanging bodies; back to frightened faces of the Japs and the grim faces of the guerrillas surrounding them)*—and it is they who sit in judgment here.

CAMERA pans to a body lying on the ground. The head has been resting sideways. As we watch it, the head suddenly rolls downward as if passing quick judgment, and the force of the fall continues in a gentle nodding movement before settling in the last rigidity of death. Quick flash to the guerrilla captain. He jerks his head sideways, and the jaws of the Japs drop in real fear. Guerrillas grab them in implacable hatred.

DISSOLVE TO:

MED. FULL SHOT   JAPANESE MOTORCYCLE DETACHMENT

—coming up the road.

INT. MAMA MOSQUITO'S HOUSE

She has gathered a few women and children to try to protect them. They hear the approaching motorcycles in terror. Mama Mosquito sends them down to the cellar. As the sound of the motorcycles roars up, she has changed herself again into the stupid, frightened, apparently idiot old peasant woman. The motorcycles stop just outside. A pounding on the door.

Mama Mosquito opens it, shrinking timidly back as a Japanese captain and soldiers crowd into the room, with a wizened Chinese merchant shoved before them.

JAP CAPTAIN *(barking)* Well—is this the old woman?

YEN TANG *(peering)* Lift the lantern that I may see her well—

Lantern is flashed into the face of Mama Mosquito. She shrinks sideways against the wall, seeming shrunken and aged. Turns face in sudden gesture away from light as lantern flashes on her.

YEN TANG *(triumphantly)* It is she—the old devil! She goes with her cart to the hills—the only one who leaves our village.

MAMA MOSQUITO *(quavering)* I do not understand—

YEN TANG It is she who sends word to the guerrillas!

MAMA MOSQUITO *(old quavering voice)* He tells lies, honorable ones— *lies.* How could an old woman like me get up into those hills?

YEN TANG   *(shouting to stop her)* The dead man who threw the bomb was betrothed to Lu Ping! It was he who sent word to the hills!

MAMA MOSQUITO   *(cannily, peering up into the captain's face)* Aihe—and how would that one know—unless he too were there? And how could he be there and still be faithful to you?

Jap captain looks uncertainly from her to Yen Tang. Yen Tang's face is suffused with fury.

YEN TANG   *(shaking)* I told you she would lie—

JAP CAPTAIN   *(curtly)* Be still . . . *(to Mama Mosquito)* I will take you to sit awhile in a locked place, old woman—until you tell us the truth. How did you get word to the guerrillas?

MAMA MOSQUITO   *(whining)* Why should I get word to them, Excellency—and kill those who buy my vegetables? Was not the Honorable Colonel one of my best customers—and did he not always pay me well—nay, better than any other? Just as he paid this one—this traitor—to bring him news of the Chinese? *(voice rises a little)* Just as the Chinese pay Yen Tang for news of the Japanese!

YEN TANG   *(moves forward, lifting his arm to strike her; she shrinks back)* It is not true! Lies—all lies—*(the soldiers stop him)*

CAPTAIN   A traitor wears two coats—*(roughly)* But why should I believe *you,* old woman?

MAMA MOSQUITO   *(again half-whining)* Because I have no reason to lie, Excellency. I am only a poor old woman who has harmed no one and wishes only to be let alone with my garden—but this Yen Tang would kill even his children for money. It was he who took word to the guerrillas and was well paid for it.

Yen Tang breaks away from the Jap soldiers. Face contorted,

hands clawing at the old woman . . . Jap captain strikes him with his hand. He turns with a howl on the Jap captain, screaming:

YEN TANG Lies—lies—I have done nothing!

Soldier hits him on the head with the butt of his gun, Yen Tang falls . . . captain looks closely at Mama Mosquito and then points quickly to unconscious body of Yen Tang.

CAPTAIN *(curtly)* Take him—

They go. Mama Mosquito locks the door after them and leans against the doorjamb wearily. Orchestra in softly to mood.

MAMA MOSQUITO *(bitter sarcasm)* Fools! Stupid fools!

VOICE *(speaking from the other side of the room)* So it *is* true!

Orchestra hits sharp chord and holds ominous. Mama Mosquito's head comes up startled, with the first moment of terror we have seen. She stares into the darkened corner of the room from whence the voice came, and barely breathes the words. The stranger is another ragged yet hard and capable Chinese guerrilla, a new face which we have not seen before.

MAMA MOSQUITO Who are you?

STRANGER *(comes forward)* So you *are* the woman known as Mama Mosquito—

Flash to Mama Mosquito's face. Pale—resigned—lips barely moving.

MAMA MOSQUITO How did you get in?

STRANGER The others came the front way—I used the back. My orders are to bring you to Chungking! Come!

DISSOLVE TO:

CORRIDOR OF PALACE

—with soldiers on guard. Music carries theme of New China. We see the drooping tired figure of Mama Mosquito hobbling along slightly behind the stranger, bewildered.

MAMA MOSQUITO What place is this?

STRANGER *(smiles)* Come this way, please.

Door opens, showing a large hall filled with people, all standing at attention, looking toward the door through which Mama Mosquito is to pass. She looks to her guide with a startled expression. He nods and smiles . . . and now we know it is the flyer[3] . . . takes her arm and leads her gently down the aisle between the long lines of Chinese dignitaries and the military, all gathered as if at a function. They make way for her and the stranger, Mama Mosquito glancing in growing confusion to the right and left. Then slowly as she sees what is ahead of her, her little, tired, shriveled body straightens up. The guide has moved aside, leaving her standing before a raised dais before Chiang Kai-shek and his retinue.

> STRANGER Your Excellency—I have brought you Madame Chau Yutang.

> CHIANG KAI-SHEK Welcome, Madame Chau Yutang—we have been waiting for you.

Mama Mosquito kneels before him, head touching the ground, hands outspread. Chiang motions. Soldiers gently raise her.

> CHIANG KAI-SHEK We have heard much of the glorious exploits of your guerrilla fighters against the enemy, Madame Chau Yutang. *(twinkle in his eye)* How many have you slain? . . . eight hundred and sixty-three?

> MAMA MOSQUITO *(humbly)* Sixty-five, Excellency. I shot two more soldiers on the Chu Yen Bridge last week.

> VOICES IN B.G. *(muted, repressed)* Sheng Li!

> CHIANG KAI-SHEK *(smiling)* Madame Chau Yutang—

> MAMA MOSQUITO *(voice quavering a little)* Excellency— there is another name they call me in the hills. I should like you to call me by that name too—*(proudly)* Mama Mosquito.

> CHIANG KAI-SHEK *(gently)* Very well, then, Mama Mosquito. I have brought you here to offer you a commission in the mountain forces. An angel of liberty like yourself should be in my army.

3. In his revision of the "Mama Mosquito" material Faulkner eliminated the role of the flyer, but he failed to delete this reference.

MAMA MOSQUITO Excellency—you would think me a foolish and stubborn old woman—and you are right. But you see—I know the only kind of war I can fight against the Japanese.

Pause—voice deep with bitterness and repression. CAMERA goes close to her to take in each graven line of her face, as she slowly draws from the neck of her dress a small bag. She bends down and pours the contents of the bag on the edge of the dais, then sinks slowly to her knees and smoothes out the rough clumps of soil. Her hand touches it with a fierce kind of reverence. She seems absorbed to the exclusion of those around her. They move a little forward to look. Chiang Kai-shek bends closer.

MAMA MOSQUITO Here is a little of the earth of China, Excellency. *(her eyes look up with a deep glow in them)* From this earth, fed with the blood of her youth, will grow the New China—but this earth will not be planted again until the invader has been driven from our land forever. I have made that pledge—and all the thousands of guerrilla fighters with whom I fight. *(through the above line her hand clutches the earth with that same fierce gesture we saw once before, then slowly, tiredly, the hand goes limp—tiredly)*—but I am a poor, sick old woman who talks too much. I have not many days left to fight. May I go back to my people?

CHIANG KAI-SHEK You may indeed. And the blessing of all China go with you. But is there nothing you would ask of me?

Mama Mosquito pauses. She is shy, suddenly, diffident. Chiang watches her.

CHIANG Come, what is it?

MAMA MOSQUITO *(apologetically almost)* I am old. I—I have much walking to do. I have trouble with my feet. I had a bowl in which to bathe and ease them. But I have lost it. If your Excellency—*(her voice dies away as if in shame of her request)*

CHIANG You shall have it, old Mother. *(he turns)* Captain Mu.

Captain Mu turns, speaks rapidly out of scene. Two soldiers enter, carrying a magnificent brass bowl. As they hand it to Captain Mu, a VOICE speaks over the scene from the TRACK.

> VOICE Ay, a magnificent bowl, an imperial bowl, with the imperial five-toed dragon gripping it in bas relief. A bowl cast five thousand years ago for an emperor's luxury and pleasure, and now to be used that an old peasant woman may soak her tired feet in it—

Captain Mu takes the bowl, stands before Mama Mosquito, raises the bowl in one hand and speaks again in dialect to the soldiers. One of them draws his bayonet and hands it to Captain Mu. Captain Mu strikes the bowl with the bayonet. It gives forth a single sonorous bronzelike martial gonglike sound.

> CAPTAIN MU Sheng Li! *(he strikes the bowl again)* Sheng Li Chiang Shi Women Di!

He strikes the bowl again, increasing the beat gradually as he chants. Each time it gives forth the single martial ringing crash.

LAP DISSOLVE TO:

CLOSE TRUCKING SHOT   MAMA MOSQUITO

—marching proudly toward CAMERA, carrying the bowl in her arms. The sound of the GONG still punctuates the shouts from all the people in the room.

SLOW FADE OUT BEGINS.

> VOICES Sheng Li! *(the gong)* Chiang Shi! *(the gong)* Women Di! *(the gong)*

The GONG changes to the SOUND of the FREEDOM TRAIN, becomes louder and faster in—

FADE OUT.

FADE IN

(The rollicking, tinkling, merry SOUND of the DULCIMER can be heard as FADE IN begins.)

82. INT. HOUSE IN THE DESERT   GROUP SHOT   NIGHT

America on his pallet, Akers, Battson, several other soldiers gathered, squatting, kneeling, sitting and reclining about America's pallet. Akers sits in the center, playing "Porterhouse Sadie" on the dulcimer. In b.g. the Italian and German officers and the two guards. The German still wears his cold, sneering, detached air, as if he were not listening. The Italian and the two guards are listening, the Italian with obvious intentness and pleasure.

Akers finishes the piece with final theatrical twang of the strings.

> **BATTSON**   *(extends his hand)* I used to play a banjo, myself. Come on. Give it to me.

83. MED. SHOT   GROUP   FAVORING BATTSON

He takes the dulcimer from Akers, strikes a few chords, hunting the key. Then he plays "Porterhouse Sadie." He plays it competently, but with something mechanical about it: correctly, but without Akers' rollicking and careless verve and fire. While he plays, the Italian approaches, listening, his guard following. Battson finishes the piece.

> **ITALIAN**   I also could play one once. *(to Battson)* You permit, Signore Corporal?

> **BATTSON**   *(looks at the Italian a moment, then he extends the dulcimer)* Sure. Try it.

84. MED. SHOT   GROUP   FAVORING ITALIAN

The Italian takes the dulcimer, kneels among them as they make room for him. He hunts among the strings for a while, testing them, meticulously yet absorbed; he, too, has forgotten Africa, battle, defeat. The others watch him.

> **BATTSON**   The smoke here can probably beat us all. *(to America)* Can't you move your hands even?

> **AMERICA**   *(peacefully)* It hurts. *(Battson looks back to the Italian)* I'm saving it.

> **BATTSON**   You're what?

AMERICA   *(peacefully)* I'm saving moving my hands.

BATTSON   Saving it until when?

AMERICA   Until we need me to move them.

They all look at America. Battson watches him with a peculiar intensity.

BATTSON   But if you could move them, ain't there something you could play?

85. ANOTHER ANGLE   FAVORING AMERICA

—as he watches Battson, peacefully still, but with faint curiosity at Battson's curious eagerness.

AMERICA   I reckon so. What something?

BATTSON   Something the rest of us never heard.

America lies peacefully, sweating, looking at Battson as Battson leans eagerly forward, looking at America. The others watch both of them, puzzled a little.

AMERICA   I reckon not.

He turns his head to look at the Italian with the dulcimer.

86. WIDER ANGLE   TO INCLUDE THE OTHERS

AMERICA   *(to the Italian)* You ain't holding it right.

ITALIAN   Yes. How shall I hold it?

AMERICA   If you wants a banjo to talk back to you, you got to hold it strong yet easy too, like you would hold a girl.

BATTSON   *(reaches his hand)* Let me show you . . .

ITALIAN   *(quickly)* No. I know now. America has told me exactly how to hold it.

He changes the position of the dulcimer; he at least knows exactly what America meant, and shows it. He finds his key almost at once, begins to play "Porterhouse Sadie." He plays it better than Battson did, but still it is mechanical, foreign. He breaks off himself, before anyone can speak. He speaks to Akers and America; it is as if he has already divined that they are the masters, he the disciple, the acolyte; the others are merely listeners.

ITALIAN   There. You see? There is something—something . . . *(to Akers)* Perhaps if there was a lead, that I could follow, until I . . . If you could whistle it, perhaps?

87. CLOSER SHOT   AMERICA, AKERS, BATTSON

The others in b.g.

AMERICA   Inside my shirt. Easy, now.

AKERS   *(to America)* What?

AMERICA   My mouth organ. Easy, now.

Akers begins to unbutton America's shirt, easy, not to cause him to move. The others watch.

BATTSON   His what?

AKERS   *(busy with America's shirt)* His French harp.

BATTSON   His what?

AKERS   His French harp, durn it. Where you been all your life?

They all watch while Akers slips his hand inside America's shirt, carefully, not to cause him to move, while America lies motionless, his face peaceful, only a new stillness in his body to show the anticipation of the pain which he expects at any moment. Akers' hand creeps on, fumbles.

88. CLOSE   AKERS

—becomes still, his face reacts to what he has found.

AKERS   Well, well, well!

89. CLOSE TWO   AKERS AND AMERICA

AMERICA   *(quickly)* That ain't it.

AKERS   I know it ain't.

Akers' hand begins to withdraw, gently. His face is mischievous.

AMERICA   *(quickly, urgently)* No, no, Mr. Akers.

AKERS I ain't going to hurt you. Lay still.

90. THE GROUP FAVORING AMERICA

The others lean forward, interested. America's eyes roll a little as Akers' hand comes out.

91. CLOSE SHOT AKERS' HAND

—holding a razor, looped on a string around America's neck.

92. WIDER ANGLE THE GROUP

A SOLDIER What does he carry it there for?

AKERS That's what I'm going to show you. *(to America)* Ain't that all right?

AMERICA Looks like it will have to be. Ain't nothing I can do about it, anyway.

Akers supports America's head, gently as a woman, lifts the looped string from around his neck, lowers his head again. As they watch him, he drops the string over his own head and lowers the razor down his back, inside his shirt. He is talking all the while.

AKERS In mine and America's country, when America's folks don't like somebody, they don't waste no time standing up and knocking with their fists like fool white folks do. When they have trouble, they want to hurt the other fellow quick and hurt him bad and finish it. *(to America)* Ain't that right?

AMERICA *(helpless, his eyes still rolling a little)* That's done over now. All folks got better fighting than that to do now.

AKERS *(facing Battson)* So this is how they do it. Watch.

As the others watch, Akers' right hand goes quickly back over his shoulder, fumbles at his back, then flashes forward.

93. FLASH NAKED BLADE OF RAZOR

—glinting along Akers' closed fist.

94. CLOSE AKERS AND BATTSON

—as Akers strikes at Battson's throat. Battson jerks violently back.

BATTSON *(angrily)* What in the . . .

AKERS *(easily)* That's how they do it.

BATTSON *(angrily)* Give me that damn thing.

AKERS *(draws razor back)* Now, Corporal. A fellar that went to Oxford don't need no book to tell him this razor don't belong to his squad.

BATTSON Well, hang it back on America, then. Go on.

AKERS *(puts razor down beside America)* I'll put them both back at the same time. I ain't found the French harp yet.

95. MED. SHOT   THE GROUP

Akers' hand creeps underneath America's shirt, and withdraws, holding a harmonica.

BATTSON Oh. A harmonica.

AKERS Sure. That's what we both told you three times.

He taps it on his knee to knock the trash out, wipes it on his sleeve, runs a rapid scale on it. Obviously, he can play it, too.

AKERS *(to the Italian)* All right. Maybe you can get it now.

He plays "Porterhouse Sadie" on the harmonica. The Italian follows him on the dulcimer, carefully and intently at first. Then the Italian catches the American rhythm; they go through it with a good swing and verve.

96. CLOSE   AKERS   (TO INCLUDE GROUP)

—listening quietly as Akers nurses the harmonica, bent over it, rapt, swinging his body to the rhythm. He and the Italian are going full out now. Behind the group now is a pair of legs standing. Akers sees them. For just a second he stops playing. Then he picks up the tune and continues as CAMERA PANS SLOWLY UP the standing man's legs and body, REVEALING REAGAN, standing over them, grimly.

97. WIDER ANGLE   TO INCLUDE REAGAN

REAGAN All right. Break it off.

Akers and the Italian stop. All look up at Reagan.

REAGAN So this is the way you hold an outpost in the face of the enemy: with a damn banjo and a harmonica.

A SOLDIER We ain't on guard now. Riley's squad's on now.

ANOTHER SOLDIER *(confidentially, as if Reagan were not there)* It ain't that that hurts the sergeant's feelings. It's this unmilitary music.

Reagan looks toward the speaker. As he does so, a third man behind him speaks: he never does quite catch up, as usual.

THIRD SOLDIER Look in the book.

As Reagan looks toward this speaker, a fourth speaks, again behind him.

FOURTH SOLDIER We thought you had come to tell us when we are going to pull out of here and go home.

Reagan looks toward that speaker as Akers speaks.

AKERS He'll have to look in the book for that, too. Come on, Wop. *(he raises the harmonica)*

Battson stops him.

BATTSON *(to Akers)* Didn't you hear him say break off? *(to Reagan)* What's wrong with it?

REAGAN *(baffled, still grim, worried)* All right. But at least they can play something decent, that they wouldn't be ashamed to have their mothers and sisters hear. And I want four men: one man at a window on each side of the house while this vaudeville show is running.

BATTSON O.K. *(he calls out four names)*

The four men rise reluctantly, take their rifles and exit. Reagan glares grimly at the others for a moment longer, then he exits.

98. MED. SHOT   THE GROUP

A man in b.g. sighs, prolonged. The others stir, shift position to listen again.

A SOLDIER All right, Alabama.

BATTSON *(quickly)* But not that one again. I'm tired of it, too.

He looks at America. Again that curious intensity is in his manner, as if he were trying to prompt or tease America into answering a question which he—Battson—does not want to ask.

BATTSON Come on, America. If you don't want to move your arms, tell us what it is. Maybe Alabama can pick it up.

99. ANOTHER ANGLE FAVORING AMERICA

—sweating, peaceful, watching Battson again with that curious questioning, speculation.

BATTSON Something us white folks don't know, that will be different . . .

AMERICA What's this here something you keep on thinking I knows?

BATTSON *(suggestive, prodding America carefully, eager and intent)* Something from your people. Something, say, about Abraham Lincoln, about that train that brought him home to Springfield . . .

Battson and America stare at one another. The others watch in b.g., curious, puzzled, alert; Fonda in particular reacts.

AKERS *(suddenly, breaks the silence)* Here's one he knows. We can all pick this un up.

He blows a chord on the harmonica, lowers it, begins to chant, beating the rhythm on the floor with one foot.

AKERS Is you bendin' low?

AMERICA *(weakly, his face lighting a little—changing too)* Yes, Lawd! Oh yes, Lawd!

AKERS *(chants: stamping)* Is you seed de glory?

When America responds, others join, they begin to stamp the rhythm also.

VOICES Yes, Lawd! Oh yes, Lawd!

AKERS *(all stamping the rhythm now)* Is you teched de cross?

VOICES *(louder)* Yes, Lawd! Oh yes, Lawd!

AKERS *(wickedly)* Is you 'fraid to go, and 'fraid to stay?

VOICES *(very loud, stamping rhythm)* YES, LAWD! OH YES, LAWD!

BATTSON Stop it! Stop it!

They hush quickly, watching him in alarm.

BATTSON If that's the best you can do, I agree with Reagan. *(he glares about at them)*

They look aside.

FONDA That's the trouble. We ain't got any good tunes in this war. They had some tunes in the war my Grandpap and Alabama's Grandpap fought back in '65.

BATTSON *(quickly)* That wasn't a war. That was a delirium. We were sick then. We almost died. But we didn't. Forget it.

AKERS *(with dry insult)* Yeah. If I was a Yankee, I'd want to forget it, too.

FONDA *(stares at Akers)* Sure. We can afford to forget it. We won.

BATTSON Stop it, I say! Stop it! Both of you. Whether that was a war or not, you're in one now. *(to Akers)* I'm not a Yankee. I don't know what I am. I don't care. Battson's not even my name. I don't know what my name is, and I don't care about that either. I grew up in an orphanage. Reagan did too, only he looked like a grown man when he was twelve years old, so the army took him. He's been in it ever since. The trouble is, he has either gained or lost six years of his life: if he dies tomorrow, he'll be officially six years older than he has actually lived; if he don't, he will have to live to be seventy before he can retire on his pension.

100. CLOSE BATTSON

—as he continues.

BATTSON . . . But I didn't. I was adopted by a man and his wife who raised sheep in Colorado and they gave me their name and let me go to a school where I could win a Rhodes scholarship to Oxford in England. So I don't need to care. All I need to do is to try and be like people who will take a nameless tyke out of an orphanage like they did me. Come on, now. Play something decent, if you're going to play.

101. MED. SHOT   THE GROUP

FONDA There were some good tunes in the war after we got over what you call that delirium.

BATTSON All right. Play one of them.

FONDA You're right. The best war tunes are the ones about the end of it, about the coming home.

BATTSON All right, play it.

Akers with harmonica, Italian with the dulcimer, one man now has a pocket comb with a piece of toilet paper, another a small cheap tin flute. They are playing "When Johnny Comes Marching Home," shrill and high, fast and loud, the others listening raptly. The tune ends with a flourish. For a moment longer they are held by it. Then they relax, stir.

A SOLDIER Well, that's what we'll do when the fighting's over. We all know that. But what I want to know is, what are we fighting for while the fighting still goes on?

They are quiet for a moment, alert without looking at one another, even avoiding one another's eyes as they wait for someone to speak.

FONDA (*at last*) For freedom.

SOLDIER Sure. We all know that. We ought to. They been dinning it into us for going on two years now. What do you mean by freedom? Or do you know?

102. CLOSE   FONDA

His face is rapt, as if he still heard his grandfather's voice. He gropes.

FONDA Yes, I know. I . . .

103. THE GROUP

> **SOLDIER** But you can't say it. How can you know it if you can't say it?

> **FONDA** I do know it. I . . .

> **SECOND SOLDIER** Liberty.

> **BATTSON** *(turns)* All right. Your turn now. What is liberty?

> **SOLDIER** *(defensive: covering up)* Everybody knows what liberty is.

> **THIRD SOLDIER** Sure. Elbow-room to get all you can get, while you can get it.

> **BATTSON** That's not liberty. Your liberty must stop where mine begins. If it doesn't, there's no such thing as liberty.

> **SOLDIER** You mean that you or anybody else can tell me what I can and can't do?

> **BATTSON** Certainly. Somebody usually is doing it.

> **SOLDIER** *(belligerently)* Who?

> **BATTSON** *(calmly)* The police. Reagan, right now. Your conscience, if you've got one.

The soldier stares at him, baffled. The others listen gravely.

> **THIRD SOLDIER** Well, I don't know about you fellows. But my father was in France in 1918 and he come out all right. So if what he fought for was good enough for him, it's good enough for me.

The tension is eased now. They all look at the speaker.

> **BATTSON** And what was that?

> **SOLDIER** Souvenirs.

They laugh, the tension is broken.

> **ANOTHER SOLDIER** That's right. And don't forget these Arab gals that are so good-looking they have to wrap their faces up before they let them go outside . . .

ANOTHER SOLDIER   Yes. I heard about them, too. In the moving pictures. I ain't seen one though, wrapped up or not. I ain't seen nothing in Africa but wrecked tanks and sand.

They laugh again. Battson turns to Akers.

BATTSON   I suppose you left home to fight Yankees again, didn't you?

AKERS   *(stares steadily at Battson—quietly)* Sez you.

BATTSON   What's that story they told back in 1918, about the man and his son, both of them barefooted, that walked a hundred and ten miles out of the Mississippi swamp to the draft board to Vicksburg, and the man said he . . . *(assumes whining dialect)* . . . heerd the Yankees had broke out agin and so he brung his boy to help fight um back?

104. CLOSE   AKERS

—staring steadily at Battson.

105. WIDER ANGLE   TO INCLUDE THE OTHERS

They watch. There is a definite unease, discomfort; they all feel it, save Battson, who stares sardonically at Akers.

FONDA   *(to Battson)* Wasn't you the one that just finished yelling shut up on that subject?

BATTSON   *(recovers—ashamed)* Yes. *(to Akers)* I'm sorry, Alabama. Forget it, will you?

AKERS   Shore. It's all right.

FONDA   *(to Akers)* Sure enough, what are you doing here? If you ain't but eighteen, you must have enlisted.

AKERS   *(looks about at them—they watch him)* I reckon I don't know either. Maybe that's why I am here: to find out.

A SOLDIER   To find out?

AKERS   *(quietly)* Yes. Because I almost knowed it once. It was back home, one night. I was possum hunting in the woods . . .

DISSOLVE begins. THEME from "CANTATA" enters softly.

> **AKERS' VOICE**   *(over)* An old church in the woods, a nigger church . . . niggers. . . .

LAP DISSOLVE TO:

106. CLOSE   AKERS   EXT. NEGRO CHURCH

—standing beside the window of a shabby paintless Negro church, peering in. He wears overalls, a battered hat. He has a smoked lantern, an axe, a sack. Two hounds are beside him. The VOICES come from inside the church. "CANTATA" THEME continues.

> **PREACHER'S VOICE**
> You may bury me in the east,
> You may bury me in the west,
> But I'll hear that trumpet sound in the morning.

> **WOMAN'S VOICE**   *(antistrophe)*
> Yes, Lord, in the morning!

> **PREACHER'S VOICE**   *(chanting)*
> This evening, brothers and sisters,
> I come in the holiest manner,
> To tell how he died.
> He was a-laying there,
> His blood on the ground;
> And while he was laying there the sun riz,
> And it recognized him;
> Just as soon as the sun recognized him
> It clothed itself in sackcloth and went down!
> Went down in mourning!
>
> He was a-laying there,
> And the sky turned dark,
> And seven angels lepp over the battlements of glory
> And come down to get him;
> And just when they come near him, he riz,
> Yes, Lord, he riz up and walked down among us,
> Praise God,
> Walked back down among his people!

WOMAN'S VOICE
Lord, he's living now!

PREACHER'S VOICE
We got a new land!
Ain't no riding boss with a whip,
Don't have no backbiters,
Liars can't go, cheaters can't go,
Ain't no deputy to chain us,
No high sheriff to bring us back!

WOMAN'S VOICE
It's a new land!

OVER scene, gradually FADING IN, is SUPERIMPOSED: A TREMEN-
DOUS SHADOW OF ROBESON'S HEAD AND UPPER BODY, covering
Akers. He turns quickly, as if he felt the shadow touch him,
stares up BEYOND CAMERA, not frightened but surprised, alert,
not like a frightened superstitious person who has seen a ghost,
but as if at this moment he can accept anything. The shadow
grows denser as the preacher's voice concludes:

PREACHER'S VOICE
You may bury me in the east,
You may bury me in the west,
But I'll hear that trumpet sound in the morning!

The PREACHER'S VOICE CEASES. Akers still stares. ROBESON'S
SHADOW is complete now, gradually blotting out the whole
scene.

ROBESON'S VOICE   *(sings)*
Freedom's a thing that has no ending,
It needs to be cared for, it needs defending;
A great long job for many hands,
Carrying freedom through all the lands . . .

The screen is completely DARK for an instant, as we slowly—

DISSOLVE BACK TO:

107. INT. HOUSE   GROUP SHOT AS BEFORE   THE MEN ABOUT
AMERICA'S PALLET

Akers has stopped speaking. Reagan sits back, triumphant, vindicated. He has got what he wanted now. He takes out his cigarettes, takes one, puts it in his mouth, takes out his matchbox and holds the cigarette pack out without looking at it. A man takes it, takes a cigarette, passes the pack to the Italian. The Italian raises his hand to take one, stops.

ITALIAN I thank you. I have one.

108. CLOSE ITALIAN OTHERS WATCHING

—as he takes the other half of the cigarette from his pocket, takes the pin from his lapel, sticks the pin delicately into the cigarette, snaps his lighter, leaning his head aside to keep from burning off his whole face. Just as he approaches the lighter to the cigarette, Finnegan takes it quickly and deftly out of his mouth, snaps it away, offers him a whole one.

ITALIAN (*a take—then recovers, takes the cigarette*) Thank you. The other would have smoked itself.

FINNEGAN Sure. But I never did like to watch fire-eaters. They make me nervous.

109. SHOT OF GROUP AS BEFORE

BATTSON (*calm and triumphant*) At last. So that's it. I thought . . .

Levine extends his hand with the cigarette pack in it. Battson takes it, is about to put it back into his pocket, pauses, his fingers mashing the paper flat, looks into it, crumples it and throws it aside. The others watch him.

AKERS That's what?

BATTSON The rest of it. The part I couldn't find. I found . . .

FINNEGAN The rest of what?

BATTSON The freedom train, the legend. I found the rest of it. Fonda there knew some of it, from his grandfather, and I found other people that knew some of it from their grandfathers. If you were not careful, you would have thought that was all of it, enough anyway. But I knew better. Because the rest of it, the core and meaning of it, would be among America's people . . .

LEVINE   The freedom train? The legend?

BATTSON   That's what I'm going to tell you.—So I looked for the rest of it among America's people. I went through Mississippi, Louisiana . . . *(to Akers)* . . . through your state and Georgia and the Carolinas, asking them. But they wouldn't tell me, just like America here wouldn't tell me . . .

110. ANOTHER ANGLE   FAVORING AMERICA

—motionless, sweating with pain, watching Battson intently, peacefully.

BATTSON   They wouldn't tell me. So it remained for a red-necked Alabama country boy who just happened to be prowling the woods one night with two mongrel curs . . .

AKERS   *(coldly yet calmly, too)* Curs, hell. One is a Redbone and the other is half pure Trigg. You ought to hear them on a fox.

BATTSON   All right. I hope I can.—remained for Alabama here to tell me what I had been hunting for and asking questions for . . .

LEVINE   So that's what you were needling America about. All right. What is it?

111. ANOTHER ANGLE   FAVORING BATTSON

The others are listening. Battson, with that calm triumph and a calm enthusiasm which they all miss except Levine and America, is sweeping Levine along with him. America, though, lies calmly on the pallet, sweating with pain, watching Battson intently yet inscrutably.

BATTSON   *(with reserve)* I'm a musician. I . . .

AKERS   You sounded like one. Trying to play this banjo. Or maybe you don't consider a banjo as music.

BATTSON   *(to Akers)* All right. Touché. Through the guts, if it makes you feel better. *(to all)* I can't play any of it, on anything. It was the theory of music, making music for other people who

can play to play it. That's what I majored in at Oxford, and
came back home and still studied it, at Cincinnati and Boston:
to make music for other people who could play it to play. To put
America into a piece of music as Wagner[4] had put Germany
and Tchaikovsky[5] had put Russia and Palestrina[6] had put that
primitive Catholic church which was to sire Torquemada[7] . . .

112. ANOTHER ANGLE   CENTERING ON THE MEN

—staring at Battson, interested by his suppressed fire, yet
puzzled, too.

> **BATTSON**   Then I began to find it, bits of it here and there,
> until a moment ago Alabama there told me the missing
> part: the part that I knew was among America's people but
> that they wouldn't tell me just as America wouldn't tell
> me . . .

113. CLOSE   BATTSON'S FACE

> **BATTSON**   To the United States of America, the nation.
> Not born in 1776 but just conceived then: a dream, a
> shape, a splendor in human dignity dreamed by men who
> were not politicians but poets, dreamed for three thousand
> years before there was any America, by men whose nation-
> ality was only the human race: in Greece, in Italy, China,
> Russia, Poland, Germany, France; Pagan, Gentile, Jew . . .

114. ANOTHER ANGLE

> **BATTSON**   . . . until that little handful of men behind a
> locked door that day in Philadelphia, taking Christ at His
> word that man cannot live by bread alone, signed what
> might have been their death warrants by putting their

4. (Wilhelm) Richard Wagner (1813–1883), German poet, composer, and
theorist whose work had a revolutionary impact on the development of western music.
5. Peter Ilich Tchaikovsky (1840–1893), noted Russian composer of ballets,
symphonies, and other orchestral works.
6. Giovanni Pierluigi da Palestrina (c.1525–1594), Italian composer of
motets, hymns, and Masses.
7. Tomás de Torquemada (1420–1498), Spanish theologian and inquisitor
general whose name has come to symbolize the fanaticism and cruelty of the
Spanish Inquisition.

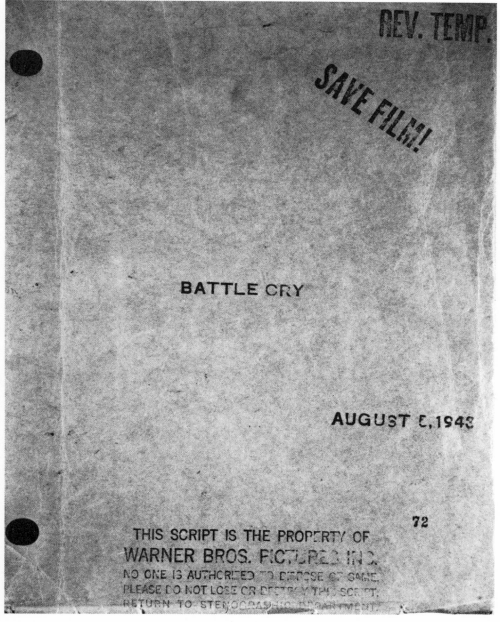

18. Revised temporary script ("Second Temporary Draft") of "Battle Cry"

names to that old poetic dream of the inviolable right of
man to his own dignity.

115. MED. SHOT   GROUP

—watching Battson in slack-jawed astonishment.

> **BATTSON**   So the United States was not born then. Because
> those men behind that locked door that day, while they
> were behind that locked door anyway, were poets and mys-
> tics, divinely touched. And, because they were prophets,
> they were not believed. So that for the next seventy-five
> years there was section against section, party against party,
> stupidity and blindness and greed and corruption while
> they still tried to interpret the first sentence in that paper
> as applying only to the rich and the ruthless and the
> shrewd whose skins were white. It was not born then, not
> until 1861–1865. 1776 was the honeymoon. 1861–1865
> was the confinement: the suffering, the agony, the blood
> and grief and travail out of which rose a nation which can
> become in reality the shape of man's eternal hope and
> which, for that reason, must not and shall not perish from
> the earth.

116. ANOTHER ANGLE   FAVORING BATTSON

> **BATTSON**   That's what I have been hunting for. And now
> I've found it—a little here, a little there, until finally Ala-
> bama told me the missing part, which belonged among
> America's people and which they wouldn't tell me, not
> even America. And, as Alabama says, I can't play it myself.
> I can only arrange it. So it must be played by people who
> can only play it but not arrange it . . .

117. MED. FULL SHOT   THE ROOM

Battson sits up, triumphant, with that suppressed enthusiasm,
while the others watch him. He lifts his hand, pointing toward
the WALL beside them. As the WALL begins to fade into LAP
DISSOLVE, Battson's voice continues OVER.

> **BATTSON'S VOICE**   . . . amateurs, who can play it without
> scores almost, who can play it because they know it and feel

it and believe it far beyond that point where anything can ever shake their believing . . .

LAP DISSOLVE TO:

118. GROUP SHOT   MUSICIANS, ALL NEGROES

Robeson standing, others seated at instruments, chorus in b.g. They are of various sorts, in work clothes, poor people, little people, country people who work hard for their bread. The instruments are crude or old, some out of tune.

The "CANTATA" THEME intact, with MONTAGES as the musicians fade out and in from time to time.[8]

FADE OUT.

RAILROAD SWITCHMAN   (*speaking slowly, heavily*) Abraham Lincoln—is dead.

A MIDDLE-AGED WOMAN   (*as if unable to believe it*) Abraham Lincoln—

AN OLDER MAN   (*heavily, shoulders drooping*) Abraham Lincoln—

A SOLDIER   (*stupefied*) Abraham—Lincoln—is dead?

RAILROAD SWITCHMAN   (*heavily, voice builds*)
Yes—John Wilkes Booth shot Lincoln dead
With a pistol bullet through his head!
Here was a man who stood for freedom!

CHORUS   (*low moaning*) Free—dom—Free—dom—

SOUND TRACK (music from "Cantata")

1st BALLAD SINGER   (*railroad switchman*)
They sent the news from Washington
That Abraham Lincoln's time had come;
John Wilkes Booth shot Lincoln dead,
With a pistol bullet through his head.

SCREEN

Now the crowd seems to realize the enormity of the tragedy. The low, moaning sound goes on like a dirge behind all the singing and the spoken words. They huddle together, as if for protection not only from the rain, but from the sorrow and suffering that they seem to feel must in-

---

8. The lengthy cantata sequence that follows is comprised of three separate sections (pages 19–24, 36–40, and 57–61) from a previous version (or versions) which have been inserted between pages 73 and 74 of this version. One segment duplicates scene 106 above.

evitably follow this news. Dejection and sadness seem to cloak them.

CAMERA PANS ALONG FACES, PICKING OUT THE FOLLOWING . . . ALL FACES GLISTENING WITH RAIN.

A Union soldier . . . puts his arm around the shoulder of his wife. She turns her face against his shoulder, weeping . . .

A Negro, unloading crates from a wagon on the outskirts of the crowd, stops and bows his head . . .

A young soldier with an empty left sleeve pinned across his tunic, looks down at it, contemplatively.

A middle-aged woman wearing (what signified lost sons in the Civil War?) smoothes it with her fingers; the tears roll down her cheeks.

An old white-haired man stares upward; his eyes drop and he shakes his head, sorrowfully . . .

The CAMERA picks up the patient, heavy faces of colored men and women, some with children in their arms . . . the faces of white men and women . . . soldiers, showing the scars of battle . . .

Voices speak from the crowd, or sing their ballads . . . these voices are all part of the chorus, which is all part of the group, not segregated from it. CAMERA picks up faces as they speak or sing.

2ND BALLAD SINGER (*a middle-aged Negro with a lined, intelligent face . . . the one who had been unloading the crates) or (a scholar, with a thin face and eyes of a zealot, clasping a book)*
The slaves are free, the war is won,
But the fight for freedom's just begun;
There are still slaves,
The hungry and poor,
Men who are not free to speak.

3rd BALLAD SINGER (*the thin-faced soldier with the empty sleeve)*
Freedom's a thing that has no ending;
It needs to be cared for, it needs
    defending;

A little boy leans over the edge of the platform, peering through the mist, up the tracks from which direction the funeral train must come. His tired-looking, patient mother draws him back, holds his hand as he struggles to get away. He becomes quiet as the third ballad singer begins.

A great long job for many hands,
Carrying freedom across the lands!

1st SPEAKER *(the stationmaster)* A job for
all the people.

2nd SPEAKER *(the old white-haired man)* A
job for Lincoln's people!

THE GRANDFATHER Sam's right. A job
for all people everywhere, to send the
word of freedom across the United States
and across all America and across the
oceans; His people are there too. They
are wherever people want to be free and
will be free: Europe—Russia—China . . .

MUSIC SOFTLY IN

1st BALLAD SINGER
A Kansas farmer, a Brooklyn sailor,
An Irish policeman, a Jewish tailor;

2nd BALLAD SINGER
An old storekeeper shaking his head,
Handing over a loaf of bread;

1st BALLAD SINGER
A buffalo hunter telling a story
Out in the Oregon territory.

2nd BALLAD SINGER
They were his people, he was their man;
You couldn't quite tell where the people
        left off
And Abraham Lincoln began.

THE MIDDLE-AGED WOMAN
There was a silence in Washington town,
When they carried Mr. Lincoln down—

Train sounds begin b.g. CAMERA moves
back to show whole group, in an attitude
of quickened listening . . . Heads slowly
turn toward the tracks. The little boy
pulls his hand from his mother's and runs
to the edge of the platform. Out of the
listening silence, the crowd sings softly as
the CAMERA MOVES OVER HEADS OF CROWD
toward the rails.

SHOT of long, endless railroad tracks.

CHORUS
A lonesome train on a lonesome track;
Seven coaches painted black.

3rd SPEAKER
Mr. Lincoln's funeral train,

As the Chorus (unseen now) and the
voices speak, DISTANT SHOT of train moving, type of 1865, seven coaches painted
black, its ghostly whistle mingling with

Traveling the long road from
     Washington to Baltimore, Baltimore
     to Philadelphia,

CHORUS
New York, Albany, Syracuse, Cleveland,
Chicago, to Springfield, Illinois.

CHORUS
A slow train, a quiet train,
Carrying Lincoln home again.

4th BALLAD SINGER
It wasn't quite mist, it was almost rain,
Falling down on the funeral train.
There was a strange and quiet crowd,
Nobody wanting to talk out loud.
Along the streets, across the square,
Lincoln's people were waiting there.

YOUNG SOLDIER You'd think they would
have warned him; even a rattlesnake
warns you.

OLD MAN This one must have been a
copperhead.

MUSIC IN SOFTLY AGAIN

CHORUS (*quietly, begins to fade very slowly*)
They carried Mr. Lincoln down,
The train started, the wheels went
     round,
You could hear the whistle for miles
     around,
Crying, Free—dom!
Crying, Free—dom!

the equally ghostly sound of the wheels.

Superimposed on the moving train, the
station signboards:
     Washington
     Baltimore
     Philadelphia
     New York
     Albany
     Syracuse
     Cleveland
     Chicago
     Springfield
The sign "Chicago" dissolves into the sign
"Springfield, Illinois" and CAMERA MOVES
DOWN to show the silent crowd waiting at
the station at Springfield, crowding at the
edge of the platform, looking up at the
track. The train for a moment is lost to
view.

As the fourth ballad singer begins, the
CAMERA MOVES BACK to show the people
crowded in a dark mass, faces glistening
in the rain, and the faint outline of the
funeral train rounding the curve.

CAMERA MOVES BACK further, showing
streets, with people massed in groups, silent, waiting, showing the square, with
horses and carriages almost as still as pictures.

There is something ghostly by now, un-
real almost, about the scene, as if it were
actually more a figment of Fonda's imagi-
nation than reality and substance. The
weird sound of the train's whistle and the
Freedom Train music combine to produce this effect.

SOUND OF FREEDOM TRAIN.
MUSIC FROM "CANTATA."

DISSOLVE BEGINS.

1st SOLO
They tell a story about that train,
They say that Lincoln wasn't on that
    train;
When that train started on its trip that
    day,
Abraham Lincoln was miles away.

SHOT of moving 1865 train.

DISSOLVE TO:

SPOKEN
Yes, sir, down in Alabama
In an old wooden church,
Didn't have no paint,
Didn't have no floor,
Didn't have no glass in the windows . . .

SHOT of small, shabby Negro church.

NEGRO WOMAN
Great God Almighty, Lord

1st SOLO
Just a pulpit and some wooden benches,
And Mr. Lincoln sitting in the back,
Listening to the sermon,
Listening to the singing.

DISSOLVE TO:

INT. OF CHURCH

Negro preacher and congregation, country men and women
and children, negroes, laborers, music from the "CANTATA."

CONGREGATION   Amen, brother, amen.

PREACHER
You may bury me in the east,
You may bury me in the west,
But I'll hear that trumpet sound in the morning.

WOMAN   Yes, Lord, in the morning!

PREACHER   *(chanting)*
This evening, brothers and sisters,
I come in the holiest manner,
To tell how he died.
He was a-laying there,
His blood on the ground;
And while he was laying there the sun riz,
And it recognized him;

Just as soon as the sun recognized him
It clothed itself in sackcloth and went down!
Went down in mourning!

He was a-laying there,
And the sky turned dark,
And seven angels lepp over the battlements of glory
And come down to get him;
And just when they come near him, he riz,
Yes, Lord, he riz up and walked down among us,
Praise God,
Walked back down among his people!

WOMAN   Lord, he's living now!

PREACHER
We got a new land!
Ain't no riding boss with a whip,
Don't have no backbiters,
Liars can't go, cheaters can't go,
Ain't no deputy to chain us,
No high sheriff to bring us back!

WOMAN   It's a new land!

PREACHER
You may bury me in the east,
You may bury me in the west,
But I'll hear that trumpet sound in the morning!

CONGREGATION   In the morning, Lord! In the morning!

SOUND TRACK	SCREEN
1st SOLO	
Down in Alabama,	DISSOLVE BEGINS.
Nothing but a pulpit and some wooden benches,	
And Mr. Lincoln sitting in the back, away in the back.	
CHORUS	
A lonesome train on a lonesome track,	MONTAGE of 1865 train running. Over it the station signs follow one another: Washington, Baltimore, Harrisburg, Philadelphia.
Seven coaches painted black,	
A slow train, a quiet train,	
Carrying Lincoln home again.	
Washington, Baltimore, Harrisburg, Philadelphia,	

Coming into New York town,
You could hear the whistle for miles
    around,
Crying, Free—dom!
        Free—dom!

SPOKEN
From Washington to New York people
    lined the tracks.

CHORUS
A strange crowd,
A quiet crowd,
Nobody wanting to talk out loud.

SPOKEN
At lonely country crossroads there were
    farmers
And their wives and kids standing for
    hours;
In Philadelphia the line of mourners ran
    three miles.

OLD WOMAN
Mr. Lincoln! Mr. Lincoln! You ain't dead,
    Mr. Lincoln! You can't be dead!

COTTON SPECULATOR   *(turns away)*
Well, boys, I'll buy the drinks.

CHORUS
For there were those who cursed the
    union,
Those who wanted the people apart;
While the sound of the freedom guns
    still echoed,
Copperheads struck at the people's
    heart.

SPOKEN
I've heard it said,
I've heard tell that when that train
    pulled into New York town,
Mr. Lincoln wasn't around.

1st SOLO
He was where there was work to be
    done,
Where there were people having fun.

SPOKEN
When that funeral train pulled into New
    York

1st SOLO
Lincoln was down in a Kansas town
Swinging his lady round and round!

Mourning and anxious crowd on station
platform.

CLOSE SHOT of an old Negro woman, decently dressed, but poor, in shawl and
widow's bonnet, at the coffin. Behind her,
a cotton speculator, a gambler type, in
frock coat, etc.

MONTAGE of stations, train.

Battle SHOT, flag.

MONTAGE: Lincoln's figure superimposed
on train, stations, etc.

DISSOLVE TO:

A country barn dance, rustic 1860–80,
two fiddlers, a triangle, a banjo, on crude

platform, dressed in Sunday clothes, a caller. The dancers are farmers, young, middle-aged, the old people sitting in chairs or on benches along the wall. Lincoln's figure is superimposed, or he is one of the dancers, maybe.

CALLER
Swing your maw, your paw,
Don't forget the girl from Arkansaw!

CHORUS *(off scene)*
When young Abe Lincoln came to dance,
Those Kansas boys didn't have a chance!

Lincoln as a young man, dancing, taking the prettiest girl. Lincoln and Fonda here.

CALLER
Grab your gal and circle four,
Make sure she ain't your mother-in-law!
Now, promenade!
Feed your chickens, milk your cows,
Have all the fun the law allows!

CHORUS *(off scene)*
They were dancing people, you could
        see,
They were folks who liked being free,
The men were tall and the girls were
        fair,
They had fought for the right to be
        dancing there!

A couple, young man in remnants of 1865 uniform, with a pretty girl. The man is Fonda.

CALLER *(points the couple out)*
Pretty little gal, around she goes,
Swing your lady for do-si-do!

The couple follow the caller's directions.

First to the right, and then to the left,
And then to the gal that you love best.

Duck for the oyster, dig for the clam,
Pass right through to the promised land!

The young man surprises his partner, kisses her before she can resist, the others react, applaud.

CHORUS *(off scene)*
These Kansas boys didn't have a chance
When young Abe Lincoln came to dance.

Lincoln dancing.
(Lincoln in this sequence is young, is Fonda)

DISSOLVE TO:

FADE IN

CHORUS FROM CANTATA
A lonesome train on a lonesome track,
Seven coaches painted black.
The train started, the wheels went
        round,
On the way to Cleveland town.

The train, 1865, moving.

Poughkeepsie, Albany, Utica,
Syracuse, Cleveland.
You could hear the whistle for miles
    around.
    Crying Free—dom!
    Crying Free—dom!

SPOKEN
In Cleveland the crowds were there;
Two hundred and fifty came from
    Meadville, Pa.,
Five hundred with two brass bands from
    Detroit,
A million people came from northern
    Ohio,
They came to mourn,
And some went home to celebrate.

1st BALLAD SINGER
When that train rolled into Cleveland
    town,
Mr. Lincoln wasn't around;
Lincoln sat in a hospital ward, far from
    the funeral train,
Lincoln sat in a hospital ward, talking to
    quiet a soldier's pain.

LINCOLN'S VOICE
Where were you wounded, son?

2nd SOLO
Lincoln said,
Standing by the soldier's bed.

SOLDIER'S VOICE
At Bull Run, sir, and Chancellorsville.
I was shot when we stormed the hill.
And I've been worried since
    Chancellorsville,
About killing, sir—it's wrong to kill.

2nd SOLO
Lincoln said,

LINCOLN'S VOICE
That's been bothering me,
How to make the war and the Word
    agree.

2nd SOLO
Lincoln said,

CHORUS
Until all men are equal, and all are free,

MONTAGE of mourning crowds at the stations, the station names superimposed as the VOICE repeats them.

The MONTAGE CONTINUES, following the NARRATIVE.

Station sign "CLEVELAND" DISSOLVES TO:

Lincoln sitting beside a wounded soldier's bed.

Lincoln beside the soldier's bed.

There will be no peace.
While there are whips and chains,
And men to use them,
There will be no peace;
After the battles,
After the blood and wounded
When the chains are smashed
And the whips are broken
And the men who held the whips are
    dead!
When men are brothers and men are
    free,
The killing will end, the war will cease.
When free men have a free men's peace.

SOLDIER'S VOICE   Lincoln beside the soldier's bed.
I'll be going home soon,

4th SOLO
The soldier said.
Lincoln turned from the side of the bed.   Lincoln turns.

LINCOLN'S VOICE
I'll see you there,

2nd SOLO
Mr. Lincoln said.   DISSOLVE TO moving train.

CHORUS
A lonesome train on a lonesome track,
Seven coaches painted black;
The train started, the wheels went
    round,
On the way to Joliet town,
You could hear that whistle for miles
    around,
Crying, Free—dom!
        Free—dom!

SPOKEN   MONTAGE to follow NARRATIVE.
Lincoln's people came;
Farmers from over in the next county,
Shopkeepers and shoemakers,
Men who'd hired him for a lawyer,
Men who'd split rails with him;
They came from Mattoon and Salem,
Fellows who'd swapped stories with Abe
    Lincoln during those long Illinois
    winter nights;
Lincoln's people were there.

CHORUS   MONTAGE: the moving train. Gunfire in
A slow rain, a warm rain,   b.g. DISSOLVE TO: the box in Ford's Thea-
Falling down on the funeral train.   ter as Booth fires, Lincoln falls, Booth

While the sound of the freedom guns
   still echoed,
Copperheads struck at the people's
   heart!

SPOKEN
When that train pulled into Joliet, you
   know where Lincoln was?
He was standing with his friends in the
   back of the crowd!
Yes, sir!

CHORUS
Standing tall, standing proud,
Wearing a shawl instead of a shroud!

SPOKEN
Abe Lincoln was with his friends, telling
   jokes!

LINCOLN'S VOICE:
I presume you all know who I am. I am
humble Abraham Lincoln. My politics
are short and sweet. Like the old
woman's dance.

(appreciative laughter from the crowd)

CHILD'S VOICE
Mr. Lincoln, how does it feel to be
President?

LINCOLN
Well now, it feels sort of like the man
they ran out of town on a rail: if it wasn't
for the honor, I'd just as soon walk.

(crowd guffaws)

WOMAN
Mr. Lincoln, isn't it right that some men
should be masters and some men should
be slaves?

LINCOLN
Ma'am, if God intended some men to do
all the work and no eating, He would
have made some men with all hands and
no mouths.

MAN'S VOICE
I say, America for Americans! What
happens on the other side of the ocean
ain't no skin off our backs!

LINCOLN
The strongest bond of human sympathy,

leaps to the stage, flourishes the pistol,
runs out. Pandemonium follows.
                              DISSOLVE TO:

"JOLIET" DISSOLVES to crowd on platform,
Lincoln tall among them.

MONTAGE follows:

Child speaks to Lincoln.

A woman speaks to Lincoln.

A man speaks generally.

Lincoln in the crowd.

outside the family relation, should be
one uniting all working people, of all
nations, tongues and kindreds. (Can't
vouch authenticity of this)

WOMAN'S VOICE
Somehow I wouldn't expect the
President of the United States to be such
a common man!

LINCOLN
I think God must have loved the
common people; He made so many of
them.
(If I remember correctly, Lincoln said,
intent humorous, "God surely must love
the poor people; He made so many of
them." Am a little inclined to think the
author stopped being a musician at this
point in order to insert a little foreign
matter.)

CHORUS   Lincoln's train leaves Joliet.
They were his people; he was their man;
You couldn't quite tell where the people
     left off and where Abe Lincoln
     began.

                                                   The train roars up the track toward CAM-
                                                   ERA.

A lonesome train on a lonesome track,
Seven coaches painted black;
Coming into Springfield town,
You could hear the whistle for miles
     around,
Crying, Freedom! Freedom!

(the TRAIN SOUND increases)   The train LAPS to a modern locomotive as
                                                   it roars past the CAMERA and the cars fol-
                                                   low.

                                                   As the train roars past, we see the win-
CHORUS   dows filled with the cheering faces of
Abe Lincoln had an Illinois face,   American troops.
And he came of a pioneer race;
He had power, he had drive,
And he liked the idea of being alive!

His heart was tough as a railroad tie,
He was made of stuff that doesn't die;
He was made of hopes, he was made of
     fears,
He was made to last a million years!

                                                   DISSOLVE TO:

FADE IN   MOONLIGHT

119. EXT. DESERT   MED. CLOSE   FONDA   NIGHT

—on sentry post, rifle on shoulder. He stops quickly, turns, brings rifle to challenge. SOUND of feet in sand, off scene.

> **FONDA**   Halt! *(sound of footsteps stops)* Who goes there?

> **RILEY'S VOICE**   *(off scene)* America.

> **FONDA**   Advance, America, and be recognized.

120. WIDER ANGLE

Battson and Riley, with three men, enter, halt before Fonda.

> **BATTSON**   New Guard, Number Two: relieve.

Wo Hong advances, stops and turns beside Fonda.

> **RILEY**   Old Guard, Number Two: dismiss.

Fonda leaves the post. Riley and Battson and the remaining two men go on toward the next post. Fonda, his rifle at trail, starts back toward the house.

121. CLOSE SHOT   LOUGHTON

—sitting on the sand in the moonlight. The house and the palm trees some distance away in b.g. He sits motionless and alone, like a man who knows he cannot escape his grief, but at least he can find solitude. He is smoking a pipe. Fonda is passing in b.g. Loughton hears him, looks toward him, then away again. Fonda sees Loughton, pauses, turns and approaches, enters.

122. MED. CLOSE   LOUGHTON AND FONDA

Loughton looks up again, then away. If Loughton does not want company, Fonda has not seen it yet.

> **FONDA**   I wondered what had become of you.

Loughton puffs his pipe, musing on the empty desert. Fonda still notices nothing. He sits down, too, lays his rifle beside him, makes himself comfortable.

> **FONDA**   Long time no see, huh?

> **LOUGHTON**   *(staring off)* That's right.

FONDA *(notices nothing—glad to see his friend again)* This is a far piece from London.

LOUGHTON *(staring off—monosyllabic)* Yes.

FONDA We had some good times there. I was wrong about you English. I had some funny ideas, I reckon. The same ideas all American troops had. Until I got to England and met some English people. *(shyly)* Met you that night in the pub when I thought the fellow was trying to cheat me because I couldn't count English money and you came up and straightened it out.

LOUGHTON *(staring off—puffing his pipe)* Yes.

FONDA *(noticing nothing)* Yes, sir. We had some times there. *(quickly, remembering)* You remember that night—what was that place? That night club forty feet underground in a bombproof, where they warned you to watch your gas mask like the signs in back-street cafes at home that say, "Watch your overcoat" . . .

Loughton stares off, apparently not listening. Fonda continues, quicker yet, turning to face Loughton.

FONDA Say, that was when you had just started to tell me about that girl. The one in Paris, the . . .

LOUGHTON *(harsh and quick, to shut Fonda up)* We were tight then.

FONDA *(missing it)* I'll say we were.—What was it?— Midyette. . . ?

LOUGHTON *(harshly)* Midinette.

FONDA Meedy Nett. That's it. All right. Go on. I want to hear it.

LOUGHTON *(restrains himself)* I was tight then. I told you.

FONDA *(still misses it)* We both was: I'll say so . . .

123. CLOSE   FONDA

He stops, gets it at last.

FONDA I'm sorry, I never meant . . . *(takes up his rifle, starts* *to get up with assumed ease)* Well, I reckon I'll get on back to the . . .

124. MED. CLOSE   THE TWO

LOUGHTON   *(staring off)* Wait.

Fonda watches him, sits slowly down again. Loughton stares off.

LOUGHTON   I knew her when I lived in Paris, working in the bank. She worked too, for one of the swank Rue de la Paix milliners. We loved one another. She had been . . . no better than she should be. Poor, you know. Had to, to have something to eat and a place to live. But that was all past and done, before we—she and I— Not anymore after that, not even for a long time before that. We were to be married. Then I was called up, back to England. Went back out to France in Gort's army. Got out with the rest of them at Dunkirk. Never saw her again.

FONDA   *(sympathetically)* Oh. And she's dead now.

LOUGHTON   *(grimly)* I hope so.

FONDA   You—what?

LOUGHTON   *(harshly)* So what, as you Yankees are always saying? Haven't you been in this war long enough to know that people die in it?

FONDA   I never meant to tromp on your toes. Excuse me.

LOUGHTON   Right. Sorry myself.

FONDA   *(mollified)* Maybe our trouble is we just ain't ready for this war. *(grins wryly)* Maybe what we need is a battle cry. My gran'pap had one in his war.

LOUGHTON   You've got one.

FONDA   What is it, then?

LOUGHTON   I don't know, if you don't.

FONDA   Have you folks got one?

LOUGHTON   *(grimly, slowly)* Well, they're dying . . .

LOW SOUND of FREEDOM TRAIN—slow fade on Loughton.

FADE OUT.

"Battle Cry"
English Sequence[9]

FADE IN

1. LONG SHOT   CONVOY AT SEA

—in fairly heavy weather. The ships are strung in lines to the horizon, and on their fringes the escort vessels move in zigzag patterns.

> **LOUGHTON'S VOICE**   The battle cry of the English is heard in many places . . . In the thunder of armies on the march . . . In the pounding engines of battleships . . . In the drone of bombers across the sky . . . Or in the quiet voice of the Englishman who fights alone. For he is England, as much as the Crown and the Sceptre . . .

LAP DISSOLVE TO:

2. MED. SHOT   A CATAPULT-ARMED MERCHANT SHIP

—a large, heavily-loaded tanker, carrying on her bow a Hurricane fighter, resting on its catapult.

LAP DISSOLVE TO:

3. MED. SHOT   BRIDGE OF FREIGHTER

Captain Ferguson and Third Officer Lowry are on watch. The former is a heavy-set, ruddy type of Scotsman who has been to sea the greater part of his 55 years. Lowry is a young man.

> **FERGUSON**   I hope the wind keeps down. I'd like to see Greenock tomorrow.

> **LOWRY**   What do you think, sir? Will we make London this trip?

> **FERGUSON**   I doubt it. They'll push us out again as fast as they can. But at least we'll be on home ground.

> **LOWRY**   It's not home to me, sir, unless it's London. I suppose it's changed. I haven't seen it since the blitz.

> **FERGUSON**   I was there, too. Pretty nasty.

9. This section of the script, prepared by John Rhodes Sturdy, is a dramatization of Sturdy's short story, "Maitland's Reply," subsequently published in *Scholastic*, 45 (November 13, 1944), 21ff.

LOWRY Yes, sir. But even with all that muck falling and the blasted guns, I felt I was home. It's only a quick hop on the train from Greenock, sir, and—

FERGUSON I'll see about it, Mister Lowry. *(looking through binoculars)* What's happening over there?

4. FULL SHOT   A CORVETTE

—wheeling off from the convoy.

5. MED. SHOT   BRIDGE   FERGUSON AND LOWRY

LOWRY It's those pesky little corvettes. They've probably picked up another contact. Oh, oh!

6. FULL SHOT   A CORVETTE

—dropping depth charges. There are explosions in the sea.

7. MED. SHOT   BRIDGE OF CAM SHIP   FERGUSON AND LOWRY

FERGUSON I hope somebody's splitting his trousers.

LOWRY I shouldn't be surprised.

8. FULL SHOT   DEPTH CHARGES

—exploding in the sea as they are fired from a corvette's throwers.

9. MED. SHOT   BRIDGE OF CAM SHIP   FERGUSON AND LOWRY

LOWRY That little fellow's making a run out. We probably won't hear from him for a time. Hope he finds the fishing good.

As he and Ferguson look through their binoculars, a sailor comes on the bridge with a signal message.

SAILOR *(to Ferguson)* Excuse me, sir.

FERGUSON *(good-naturedly)* Why are you always interrupting me, Smith?

SAILOR I'm very sorry, sir.

FERGUSON Never mind. It's intermission. What have you got there?

He takes the signal, and the sailor exits.

> **FERGUSON** *(continuing)* We may have company.

> **LOWRY** More U-boats?

> **FERGUSON** And planes. It says here we can expect them for tea. You'd better inform Maitland.

> **LOWRY** What do you think of him?

> **FERGUSON** Who? Maitland? He's a nice chap.

> **LOWRY** How can you tell? With me, he never opens his mouth. Just sits in the saloon and reads books, or writes letters that he never seems to mail . . . Or he and his mechanic . . . *(pointing)* . . . tinker with that.

10. FULL SHOT   HURRICANE ON CATAPULT

11. MED. SHOT   BRIDGE   FERGUSON AND LOWRY

> **FERGUSON** I wouldn't like his job.

> **LOWRY** Neither would I. Never knowing when you may have to go up . . . in a land plane and no land in sight. But all these Air Force chaps are a little batty. I'll take the signal to him, sir.

Lowry exits. Ferguson looks through his glasses for a moment.

> **FERGUSON** *(calling)* Smith!

The sailor Smith comes round the corner of the bridge.

> **SMITH** Yes, sir.

> **FERGUSON** My compliments to the Chief Officer. Tell him to close up his gun's crew.

> LAP DISSOLVE TO:

12. INT. SHIP'S SALOON

This is a fairly large room, and is well furnished. There is a long table in the center, surrounded by chairs. An electric grate is in one corner, and a small settee against the outboard side. A serving pantry is situated off the saloon. A steward is serving a cup of coffee to Maitland as we enter the scene. Maitland is dressed in the uniform of the Royal Air Force. The jacket is unbuttoned, and instead of shoes he is wearing heavy carpet slippers. His jacket carries the one stripe of a Flying Officer. Maitland is in his thirties. Beside him on the settee is a thick pad of paper and a pencil.

MAITLAND Thanks, steward.

Lowry enters and crosses to the settee with the signal.

LOWRY Here's some news for you, Maitland. You may not be having guests.

MAITLAND *(taking signal)* Thanks. What happened up top?

LOWRY One of the escorts dropped a few. The Heinies are still pocking at us.

Maitland is reading the signal.

LOWRY *(continuing)* Does it bore you very much?

MAITLAND Huh?

LOWRY Forget it.

Maitland hands him the signal.

MAITLAND *(to steward)* Find Sergeant MacDonald and tell him I'd like to see him here.

The steward exits as the Chief Officer, Harvey, and the Second Officer, Cunningham, enter. Harvey is dressed for the deck. He is in his late thirties. Cunningham is slightly younger, and he wears an old sweater and dirty trousers.

HARVEY What's the good word, Lowry? I just had orders to close up the gun.

CUNNINGHAM True or false?

LOWRY True, according to our friends in the navy. Ten U-boats and a swarm of bombers. For tea.

HARVEY This is it, then.

CUNNINGHAM I rather expected it before now.

HARVEY I didn't. They've just been jockeying around into position. Now, apparently, they're ready.

CUNNINGHAM *(to Maitland)* Did you get the dope, Maitland?

MAITLAND Yes.

HARVEY When do you expect the planes?

MAITLAND If they're not intercepted . . . around five o'clock.

LOWRY Tea will be served early, today.

HARVEY Anybody feel like cards?

CUNNINGHAM I do. Do you play gin rummy?

HARVEY What's that?

CUNNINGHAM An American game. Great favorite with the Hollywood stars.

LOWRY Hollywood! I found a movie magazine yesterday. Filled with pictures of gorgeous women. Enough to make a sailor go slightly mad.

CUNNINGHAM I wish we were Russians.

HARVEY I know what you're thinking. Women in the crew. Imagine making love to the Chief Engineer.

LOWRY I'd rather look at pictures.

MacDonald, a sergeant in the Royal Air Force, enters.

MACDONALD Begging your pardon . . . Is Mr. Maitland here?

MAITLAND Yes, Sergeant. Turn over the engine and check the guns.

MACDONALD Yes, sir. Is that all, sir?

MAITLAND That's all.

MacDonald exits. There is a sudden silence in the saloon. The men are lost in thought.

HARVEY How about that card game, Cunningham?

CUNNINGHAM Absolutely.

Maitland gets up and crosses the saloon.

HARVEY   Will you be in for tea?

MAITLAND   No. . . . I have to look after a few things.

HARVEY   Right. See you later.

Maitland exits.

LOWRY   *(after a moment)* That chap gets on my nerves. He's too quiet.

HARVEY   You'd probably be quiet, too, if you were going to die.

LOWRY   Who's going to die?

HARVEY   *(simply)* Maitland.

CUNNINGHAM   Oh, say, it's not as bad as all that.

HARVEY   Figure it out for yourself. If we're attacked this afternoon . . . and I mean really attacked . . . he'll be going up. We're too far out for him to make land.

CUNNINGHAM   That chap Struthers made it the last trip.

HARVEY   He did. But we were practically in the North Channel.

LOWRY   He could smile once in a while. He could at least open his mouth.

HARVEY   You're exaggerating things.

LOWRY   I'm not. He's got a rotten job, but what's the use of brooding about it? And, at least he'll get a crack at them when the time comes. All we do is wait and take it.

HARVEY   Are you unhappy?

LOWRY   Don't be silly. But we'd be a nice mess, wouldn't we, if we just sat around and stared at one another.

CUNNINGHAM   Hear, hear!

HARVEY   Well, he's not part of the family, really. He must get bored . . . I'm going up top to check the gun. Coming along, Cunningham?

CUNNINGHAM   You've forgotten the gin rummy.

HARVEY   You can teach me at tea time.

CUNNINGHAM   All right . . . See you later, Lowry.

Harvey and Maitland exit. Lowry lights a cigarette and walks back and forth across the wardroom. He stops at the settee and NOTICES THE WRITING TABLET THAT MAITLAND HAS LEFT. Curiously he picks it up, then sits on the settee with the pad on his knees. He BEGINS TO READ.

13. INSERT: WRITING PAD

In a strong hand, in pencil, we READ the following words:

"MY SHIPMATES ARE VERY DECENT FELLOWS. ALL OF THEM HAVE BEEN TORPEDOED ONCE, AND LOWRY THREE TIMES. BUT I NEVER HEAR THEM COMPLAIN. I'M STILL WAITING FOR MY CHANCE, AND I HOPE IT WILL BE SOON. I'M THINKING OF JACK AND PETER AND MICHAEL . . . AND MOTHER—"

SLOW DISSOLVE TO:

14. EXT. A STREET

—in an English coastal town that might be Dover. The buildings are old, and they are pock-marked from the explosions of German bombs. Along the street are one or two craters. The street has been badly smashed many times, but it has been neatly cleaned up. As we enter the scene, a group of people which looks like a delegation is coming upstage. The delegation is led by the mayor, who wears his chain of office.

15. CLOSE SHOT   A WINDOW

—of one of the houses on the street. JANIE'S FACE IS SEEN AT THE WINDOW. Janie is a girl of twelve. In excitement she turns.

JANIE   Mother . . . . . Mother!

16. INT. A BEDROOM

—as Janie runs across the room and out the door.

17. INT. A HALLWAY

—as Janie continues running.

JANIE   Oh, Mother!

She goes through another door.

18. INT. A SITTING ROOM

Janie enters on the run. Close to the window, on a chair, sits Mrs. Maitland, a tall, white-haired Englishwoman. She is knitting. Beside her stands Maitland, in the uniform of the R.A.F. *without wings.*

JANIE   Mother, they're coming!

MOTHER   For heaven's sakes, Janie . . . who?

JANIE   All the people . . . And the mayor . . . and he's all dressed up.

MOTHER   Coming where?

JANIE   Here, of course. And I know why. It's the Spitfire. I heard Mrs. Paige talking about it. They got the last of the money yesterday. And they're buying the Spitfire.

MOTHER   All right, Janie . . . run downtairs and wait for them.

JANIE   It's marvelous! It's . . . oh!

She exits on the run.

MOTHER   I'm glad you got a leave, Frank. I wanted you to be here.

MAITLAND   It's good to be home.

MOTHER   I don't think I could face the mayor without you.

MAITLAND   You can face anything, Mother.

MOTHER   Perhaps. How is the work getting on?

MAITLAND   It's all right. Rather busy.

MOTHER   Don't you really like it?

MAITLAND   I'd rather be in the Spitfire Janie's so excited about.

MOTHER   I had three sons who were fighter pilots. It's only right that God would save me my oldest son.

MAITLAND   I know, Mother. *(smiling)* But sometimes I wish you and Dad hadn't been so impatient to have me. Then I wouldn't be dispatching planes. How have things been here?

MOTHER   They were shelling over the weekend. There wasn't much damage. The school was strafed last week.

MAITLAND   Damn them!

MOTHER   Oh, yes. But it's not the same as it used to be. It's not just waiting any more. We're winning now. I used to stand on the roof and watch for the Germans. But now I see the sky dark with ours. It's altogether different now, Frankie.

A DOORBELL is heard.

MOTHER   *(continuing)* I'm frightened.

MAITLAND   Courage, Mrs. Maitland. They want you to remember this day.

The mother takes Maitland's arm, and they exit.

LAP DISSOLVE TO:

19. FULL SHOT   LIVING ROOM

—of the Maitland home. It is typically English lower middle-class room. The furnishings are old, but they are clean and they are neat. On the mahogany table near the bay windows are the photographs of three young men in R.A.F. uniforms—Peter, Michael and John Maitland.

The mayor and delegation are already in the room. Janie is standing by the fireplace, very excited. The mayor is nervously playing with the chain around his neck. The rest of the people are typical of a small English town.

The mother and Maitland enter.

MAYOR   Good-day, Mrs. Maitland.

MOTHER   Good-day, Your Worship.

There is a murmur of greetings from the rest of the group.

MAITLAND   I'll get you a chair, Mother.

MOTHER   No, I think I'd rather stand.   *(to the group)* I'm very honored to have you visit my home.

MAYOR   It is our honor, Mrs. Maitland. I know you understand why we're here.

MOTHER   *(smiling)* I have a very young daughter.

20. CLOSE UP   JANIE

—in sudden embarrassment, as low laughter surrounds her.

21. MED. SHOT   THE GROUP

MAYOR   Well, I'm glad Janie was my forerunner. The mayors of towns used to give speeches. But I think we've forgotten speeches and other nonessentials in our town these last four years. We haven't had much time.

He looks around him.

MAYOR   *(continuing)* We're not very rich, but we've been saving our pennies, here and there. Last night we reached our objective—enough money to buy a Spitfire. The checque is going in today, and we're very proud. We wanted to give the Spitfire a name. I think we never doubted what we should like it called. We were thinking of Peter Maitland and Jack Maitland and Michael Maitland—and Frank, here, who is carrying on. Three of your sons died in Spitfires. If you'll accept, Mrs. Maitland, we'd like to have our Spitfire called "Maitland's Reply."

MOTHER   *(after a moment)* Thank you very much, Your Worship. And thank all of you. You've done my sons a great honor. And myself.

MAYOR   I know "Maitland's Reply" will do its duty well. It's a proud name.

MOTHER   Thank you, again.

MAYOR   I hope, when the plane takes the air for its first assault, it will wing over the town here. But if not, then its brothers will. It's a . . . a. . . . I'm afraid I really am making a speech.

Chorus of "no" from the group.

MOTHER   You're saying things that all of us are hoping.

MAYOR   Well, we've had a bad time, and we're not out of it yet. But we're on our way, and we're going faster all the time. I don't think we'll ever forget the boys who saved us . . . like Peter and Michael and Jack. I . . . well, ladies and gentlemen, we've done what we came to do . . .

MOTHER   And I expect all of you to stay for tea.

A WOMAN   Oh, no, Mrs. Maitland, it's too much trouble.

MOTHER   It's no trouble. It's a pleasure . . .

Her speech is BROKEN BY THE WAIL OF THE AIR RAID SIREN. The people stop and listen for a moment.

MAYOR   I'm afraid . . . we'll have to get to our posts.

MOTHER   Good-by, Your Worship. Good-by all of you. I'll keep the tea warm.

Rapidly, but without excitement, the delegation passes in front of the mother and Maitland, and the men and women exit. As the last person leaves, Janie is running towards the window. The sirens are shrieking.

MOTHER   Janie . . . keep away from the window.

JANIE   Oh, Mother!

MAITLAND   Come on, Button. Your place is in the cellar.

JANIE   Rot!

MOTHER   Janie!

JANIE   You treat me like a child.

Nevertheless, she obeys, and exits. Mother and Maitland come close to the window, and look out and up. The SOUND OF PLANES is heard.

MOTHER   There are fewer of them these days.

MAITLAND   Some time soon there won't be any left.

MOTHER   (*turning to him*) Hold me close to you, Frank.

MAITLAND   Yes, Mother.

MOTHER   It's been a long, hard pull. But the people have stuck. Weren't you proud of them just now?

MAITLAND   The little people of Hell's Corner.

MOTHER   We belong to them. And you, Frank . . . you'll be here to help rebuild the town. It's so very important. It'll be a better town when it's all over.

MAITLAND   (*looking up*) I don't think they're coming any closer. I can't hear them now.

The mother is crying.

MAITLAND   (*continuing*) Oh, say, Mother!

MOTHER   I told you I couldn't face the mayor and people. They're too wonderful. Please give me your handkerchief, Frank.

Maitland pulls a handkerchief from his pocket. Something falls to the floor.

MAITLAND   Here.

He is about to dab her eyes, but she is staring at the floor.

22. INSERT: R.A.F. WINGS

—lying on the carpet.

23. CLOSEUP   THE MOTHER

—looking at Maitland for an instant. Then slowly she bends and picks up the cloth wings. Silently she straightens.

24. CLOSE SHOT   THE MOTHER AND MAITLAND

MOTHER   These are yours, aren't they, Frank?

MAITLAND   Yes, Mother.

MOTHER   When did you get them?

MAITLAND   The other day. I've been trying ever so long.

MOTHER   But I thought you were too old.

MAITLAND   I am, for fighter combat duty. But . . .

MOTHER   But what, Frank?

MAITLAND   They've taken me for convoy work. I can't explain much about it, Mother, but it's mostly traveling back
and forth in freighters. It's pretty dull stuff, but . . .

MOTHER   I know what it is, Frank. You're very happy,
aren't you?

MAITLAND   I just want a chance.

MOTHER   Because of the other boys?

MAITLAND   I think about them quite a bit. I know you
wanted me on the ground. I know, perhaps, it's not fair to
you. But . . .

He is interrupted by the sirens BLOWING THE ALL CLEAR.

MOTHER   (turning) That's the All Clear.

She turns back to Maitland, and looks for an instant at the
wings in her hands, then into his eyes.

MOTHER   (continuing) Take off your jacket, Frank. I'll sew
your wings on.

SLOW DISSOLVE TO:

25. INSERT: WRITING PAD

—as we read the following words.

"WE'VE JUST A REPORT THAT ENEMY PLANES ARE HEADING FOR
US. MAYBE THIS IS IT. I HOPE SO . . ."

LAP DISSOLVE TO:

26. INT. SALOON OF CAM SHIP

Lowry is staring at the writing pad on his knee. Slowly he places it beside him on the settee. Then he lights a cigarette and gets to his feet. The steward enters.

STEWARD I'm setting up tea now, sir. Will you be having any?

LOWRY Huh?

STEWARD Tea, sir?

LOWRY Oh . . . no thanks . . . I don't feel like any.

He exits. The steward begins to set places.

LAP DISSOLVE TO:

27. EXT. BRIDGE OF CAM SHIP

The captain, Ferguson, and Harvey are standing there.

FERGUSON (*looking at his watch*) Shouldn't be long now . . . if they're really coming. Take over. I'm going to get a cup of something hot inside me.

HARVEY The gun's crew is itching for action.

FERGUSON They'll probably get it. Keep a sharp lookout.

HARVEY Aye, aye.

Ferguson exits. Harvey scans the ocean with his binoculars.

28. LONG SHOT   CONVOY AT SEA

29. MED. SHOT   HURRICANE FIGHTER PLANE

—on the bow of the ship. The mechanic, MacDonald, is tinkering with the engine, as Maitland climbs out of the cockpit.

MAITLAND How's it look to you, Sergeant?

MACDONALD First rate, sir.

MAITLAND Did you check on the catapult release?

MACDONALD Perfect, sir. Ought to shoot you halfway to Berlin.

MAITLAND (*smiling*) England will be far enough, thanks.

MACDONALD Pardon me for asking, sir, but how's chances?

MAITLAND Depends on how many Heinies, and how long to knock them down.

MACDONALD I'll have my fingers crossed, sir.

MAITLAND Thanks, Sergeant. So will I. Better grab a bite to eat.

MacDonald nods and exits as Lowry enters. Lowry leans against the plane.

LOWRY Hello, Maitland.

MAITLAND Oh . . . hello, there.

LOWRY Tuning up the bus?

MAITLAND Just a last-minute check, in case.

LOWRY If you have to go up, I hope you knock those Jerries cockeyed.

MAITLAND I'll try.

LOWRY I . . . understand you're from Dover?

MAITLAND (*surprised*) Why, yes . . . how did you know?

LOWRY I forget who mentioned it. Been home lately?

MAITLAND Just before this voyage.

LOWRY I've been trying to get home for a long time. London. The Old Man's holding out a little hope for me this trip.

MAITLAND That's good. Do you know Dover?

LOWRY A bit . . . before the war. I imagine it's taken quite a beating.

MAITLAND Not really . . . just on the surface.

LOWRY Your family's there, I suppose.

MAITLAND Just my mother and young sister. The house is still standing, you know.

LOWRY My family had to move out of their place. They're down in the country.

MAITLAND I was in London quite a bit. Pretty hellish for a time.

LOWRY I imagine you've found us rather stuffy in this ship.

MAITLAND Stuffy? I don't . . .

LOWRY Well, I mean, not having much to say.

MAITLAND But you've got a job. If I had to stand four-hour watches, I wouldn't feel much like entertaining.

LOWRY We do get pretty silent. But now and again you feel like talking. You know, a real old bull session.

MAITLAND (*laughing*) Yes.

LOWRY Chaps at sea get fairly lonely. And then they just crawl up in their shells and make it worse.

MAITLAND Or maybe because . . . Well, you've got things on your mind.

LOWRY You've got a lot, haven't you, Maitland?

MAITLAND I don't . . .

LOWRY I mean, you want a crack at them, don't you?

MAITLAND (*slowly*) Yes.

LOWRY Shall we get a piece of toast, or something? We've got time.

MAITLAND Righto.

They exit.

LAP DISSOLVE TO:

30. INT. SHIP'S SALOON

Ferguson and Cunningham are at the table, eating toast with marmalade and drinking tea. The steward is waiting on them.

CUNNINGHAM Ever play gin rummy, sir?

FERGUSON Gin rummy? What is that? A cocktail?

CUNNINGHAM No, a game, sir. Fascinating thing. It goes on for years.

Lowry and Maitland enter.

FERGUSON What's it look like, up top?

LOWRY Absolutely quiet.

Maitland sees his writing tablet, and stuffs it away in a drawer, while Lowry watches him.

CUNNINGHAM Sit down and have some toast. It's a little green on the edges, but you just dig out the center.

LOWRY Cup of tea, Maitland?

MAITLAND Thanks, I will.

They sit with the others, and are served.

LOWRY Been thinking over my getting a trip to London, sir?

FERGUSON It's in the back of my mind.

CUNNINGHAM I don't care if I never see London again. There's a place on the southeast coast—

MAITLAND Dover?

CUNNINGHAM Just outside of there. Do you know Dover?

MAITLAND My home.

CUNNINGHAM It's not a bad little place.

MAITLAND I should say it's the best place in the world.

They laugh.

FERGUSON Home, sweet, home! Have any of you gentlemen ever been in Aberdeen! Now there is a . . .

He is INTERRUPTED BY AN ALARM BELL. The men look at one another for a brief moment. Then they dash for the alleyway. The bell is still ringing.

LAP DISSOLVE TO:

31. EXT. DECK OF SHIP

Men are running down the deck.

32. EXT. STERN OF SHIP

Gun's crew wheeling the gun into position.

33. EXT. BRIDGE OF SHIP

Harvey on watch, peering through binoculars, as Ferguson runs into scene.

34. LONG SHOT   CONVOY

35. FULL SHOT   ESCORT VESSELS

—dropping depth charges.

36-39. SERIES OF SHOTS   FREIGHTERS AND TANKERS STEAMING THROUGH THE SEAS

40. LONG SHOT   A TORPEDO TRACK

41. LONG SHOT   A FREIGHTER BEING HIT

42. EXT. BRIDGE OF CAM SHIP   FERGUSON AND HARVEY

    FERGUSON   This is it, Mr. Harvey.

    HARVEY   Right on the dot, sir.

43. LONG SHOT   ANOTHER SHIP BEING HIT

44. LONG SHOT   DEPTH CHARGES EXPLODING

45. LONG SHOT   SUBMARINE

—coming to the surface and exploding in smoke and flame.

46. EXT. BRIDGE OF CAM SHIP   FERGUSON AND HARVEY

    FERGUSON   Erase another iron cross.

They suddenly wheel and look upwards o.d.

    HARVEY   And here comes the boy friends, sir.

47. EXTREME LONG SHOT   GERMAN BOMBERS

—in the sky.

48. MED. SHOT HURRICANE FIGHTER

As Maitland starts to climb into the cockpit, Lowry stops him.

> **LOWRY** Good hunting, Dover.

> **MAITLAND** Thanks. Glad to have known you, Lowry. Look . . . there's a writing pad of mine down in the saloon. I wonder if you'd send it to the address on the cover.

> **LOWRY** Sure thing!

> **MACDONALD'S VOICE** All ready, sir!

> **MAITLAND** *(shaking hands)* Cheerio, Lowry!

> **LOWRY** Come back to us.

Maitland settles himself in the cockpit.

> **LOWRY** *(continuing)* Get one for me! Good luck to you . . . Maitland's Reply!

Maitland stares at Lowry for a moment. Lowry is smiling and Maitland suddenly smiles back. There is the ROAR OF THE PLANE'S ENGINE. Maitland stands back and waves his hand.

49. FULL SHOT THE HURRICANE

—being shot from its catapult.

50. CLOSE SHOT LOWRY

—waving his hand.

> **LOWRY** God . . . if I only had wings!

There is a TREMENDOUS EXPLOSION. Lowry wheels around. The ship has been hit. He starts aft, and SUDDENLY THE WHOLE SCENE IS A MASS OF FLAME THAT ENVELOPS HIM AND THE SHIP.

51. CLOSE SHOT MAITLAND

—in his plane. He looks down.

52. LONG OVERHEAD SHOT THE CAM SHIP

—burning, and enveloped in curling smoke.

53. CLOSEUP MAITLAND

His lips tighten.

We go into a series of shots of a dogfight in the sky between Maitland and three German light bombers. We intercut between Maitland and the Germans. One of the enemy goes down in flames. Maitland follows another making a low dive over the convoy and shoots it down just as it strafes one of the ships. We show the third plane wheeling from the convoy and making a run for it. Series of shots as Maitland pursues the German. Maitland's plane is pock-marked with bullets. The final shot shows the Hurricane's guns blasting into the rear of the bomber and it goes down.

54. CLOSE SHOT   MAITLAND

—looking down and out.

55. EXTREME LONG OVERHEAD SHOT   THE CONVOY

56. MAITLAND   CLOSE SHOT

—glancing at his compass.

57. FULL SHOT   THE HURRICANE

—wheeling in the sky.

58.   INSERT: THE COMPASS

—of the plane, as the needle swings to "East" and stops. Slowly the map of England is SUPERIMPOSED. The echo beat of the Freedom Train comes in.

59. INSERT: THE PETROL GAUGE

—sinking to the "Empty" mark.

60. CLOSEUP   MAITLAND

He pulls his flying cap back off his head. He is smiling as we hear a voice.

> **LOUGHTON'S VOICE**   For he is England . . . as much as the Crown and the Sceptre.

The beat of the Freedom Train coming up full.

FADE OUT.

FADE IN   MOONLIGHT

125. CLOSE SHOT   LOUGHTON AND FONDA   NIGHT

—still seated in moonlight.

>   **FONDA** *(thoughtful)* I reckon us Yankees will do some dy-
>   ing too—even if we ain't found out yet just why we are
>   here. You're lucky. Your whole country ain't much bigger
>   than a shirt-tail. Ours is big. Maybe too big. Maybe that's
>   why they ain't told us yet why we are here. But you folks
>   know. You're fighting to keep an enemy out of your back-
>   yard.

>   **LOUGHTON** We are fighting for the same thing you are.
>   For the same thing the Greeks died for without ever giving
>   up, and that some of the French and Belgians and Poles
>   and Scandinavians are still fighting for, and little hantles of
>   starving men in the Balkans; Montenegro, Serbia; Croats
>   and Slovenes. We are fighting for the right to keep on
>   living in the way we want to live. Maybe that way is wrong,
>   unjust to some, and will change later . . .

>   **FONDA** *(interrupting)* . . . but you want to change it your-
>   selves, without help. It was like a man of America's people,
>   Joe Louis, who said it about as well as I know, good
>   enough, anyway: "There's a heap wrong with this world,
>   but Hitler can't fix it."

>   **LOUGHTON** Yes, that's right. We want to change it, make it
>   better for all people. But while we are making it better for
>   all, it suits us as it is, for all its folly and waste . . .

>   **VOICE** *(calling—off scene)* Fonda!

>   **FONDA** *(rises)* Here.

126. WIDER ANGLE   TO INCLUDE MANNING

—as he enters scene. He carries an empty gas mask container.
Loughton still sits on the ground.

>   **MANNING** Reagan says to come on in. We're going to vote.

>   **FONDA** Vote? On what?

MANNING   On whether we stay on here or whether we pull out before daylight, while we can, and try to get back. He's waiting.

Manning goes on.

FONDA   *(to Loughton)* Come on.

LOUGHTON   *(doesn't move)* Vote? The leader of your party is going to let his men vote on what they want to do next?

FONDA   Why not?

LOUGHTON   What sort of chap is he? I hope he shows brighter by daylight than he has tonight, or he'll never get you out of here.

FONDA   *(quickly)* You're wrong there. He's a good man. Have you seen anything wrong with the way he has run this party since Lieutenant Whitesides died?

LOUGHTON   *(rises)* No. Vote. By George, you're right. Maybe you Americans don't know yet what you are fighting for, and maybe you haven't quite learned yet how to do the fighting, but . . . No. That's wrong. I think you not only know what you're fighting for, whether you can say it or not, but you know the best way to do the fighting, too. Go on. Vote.

FONDA   Aren't you coming? You're in this, too. That's right. I forget you don't belong with us. You can leave any time, can't you?

LOUGHTON   So can you, apparently—if Reagan's going to let you vote on it. *(he turns, walks on)* Come along. Let's cast a ballot. If it's too close, I'll vote my two prisoners. That's good democratic politics, isn't it?

Fonda follows.

127. CLOSE SHOT   HOPKINS   ON HIS SENTRY POST   NIGHT

At SOUND of FEET, off scene, he whirls, brings rifle to challenge.

HOPKINS   Halt! Who goes there?

SOUND of FEET continues to approach.

HOPKINS   Halt! That's twice now!

MANNING'S VOICE   *(off scene)* Ah, put that durn rifle up. I'm in a hurry . . .

HOPKINS   You stop right there and give the password, or I'll blow you clean out from under that helmet.

SOUND of FEET ceases.

MANNING'S VOICE   *(annoyed)* America, durn it.

HOPKINS   Advance, America, and be recognized.

128. WIDER SHOT

—as Manning enters, stops before Hopkins.

MANNING   We're voting whether to stay or pull out while we can. Here.

He takes from his pocket two cartridges: a live shell and an exploded case, hands them to Hopkins and holds out the gas mask container.

MANNING   If it's "Go," drop in the live one; if it's "Stay," drop in the hull. After I'm gone, you can throw the hull away. But if it's the live one, put it in your pocket because you'll need it.

129. MED. CLOSE SHOT   HOPKINS AND MANNING

Hopkins shuts his eyes, turns his head aside, and drops one of the shells into the container. Manning shuts the container, goes on toward the next sentry. When he has gone, Hopkins puts something into his pocket, resumes his watch.

130. INT. HOUSE   GROUP SHOT   AT AMERICA'S PALLET

Akers is banging away on the DULCIMER, rapid and merry, playing "Black Market Sadie" beside America's pallet. The Italian and others are gathered around America as he lies on his back, his face sweating with pain but his eyes peaceful and quiet as he listens with rapt pleasure to the music. Fonda, Loughton and Reagan enter.

131. MED. FULL SHOT   INT. ROOM

The strain of his responsibility is showing more and more on Reagan as the crisis approaches.

REAGAN *(to Akers)* Stop that damn noise! How many times have I got to tell you?

AKERS I don't know. I reckon until it finally gets through your skull that I ain't a member of your company and so you can't tell me to do nothing. Articles of War. Look it up. One of your corporals can tell you what page.

Reagan glares at Akers, marshalling words to speak. Battson interrupts.

BATTSON *(to Akers)* Shut your trap. Since you don't belong to this party, we'll turn you out of here and you can walk around out there in the moonlight until you find Rommel. Maybe he can tell you what page it's on. Put that damn thing down now, long enough for us to vote.

AKERS Vote on what?

REAGAN On whether we stay here, or get out while we can and try to get back to the lines.

ITALIAN OFFICER *(eagerly)* Vote? Hah.

Nobody pays any attention to him.

AKERS What do we want to go anywhere for?

BATTSON *(to Reagan)* Why not tell them all at once?

REAGAN All right.

132. THE GROUP   FAVORING REAGAN

—facing the men. The men all face him, quiet, sober, attentive. Reagan unfolds his map. Battson and Fonda help him extend it.

REAGAN We are about here . . .

FINNEGAN Sure. We all know that. We are right here. It's the American and British armies that're lost.

REAGAN Silence, there!

He glares about at them. They are quiet, watching him. He turns back to the map.

> **REAGAN** The battle yesterday was somewhere about here. As far as I could tell, we were not winning it in a hurry. So the Heinies are still somewhere in here, and you heard Lieutenant Whitesides say when those two aeroplanes came and looked at us and went away, that the Heinies want this well. And they were German aeroplanes that came and looked at us—not ours . . .

> **BATTSON** (*to Reagan*) Let me tell it while you get your breath.

133. ANOTHER ANGLE   FAVORING BATTSON

—as he addresses the men.

> **BATTSON** We were sent here to meet a battalion of the 209th and hold this well. Only, the 209th never got here, and those two Jerries yesterday afternoon know it. Lieutenant Whitesides said for us to get out of here quick. But Lieutenant Whitesides is dead. So the question is: do we get out while we can and get back to the lines, or do we hold on here until the 209th gets up?—if it's going to get up . . .

Manning enters with the gas mask container.

> **BATTSON** (*to Manning*) Have Smyth and Hopkins and Shipp and Wo Hong voted?

> **MANNING** Yes.

> **BATTSON** (*to the men*) Manning will give every man two shells: a live one and a hull . . .

134. ANOTHER ANGLE   FAVORING MANNING

> **MANNING** (*interrupting—importantly*) If it's "Go," drop in the live one; if it's "Stay," drop in the hull. You can throw the hull away after the voting, but if it's the live one you still got, keep it because you're going to need it . . .

The Italian officer moves suddenly.

135. ANOTHER ANGLE   FAVORING ITALIAN OFFICER

—eager, his face alight. All stare at him in surprise. The German stands sneering and inattentive in b.g.

> **ITALIAN OFFICER** Hah. Voting. That's American. But we too, once: The men of our Garibaldi voted themselves death and glory too in their time. But that was many years ago, and now the world thinks that my race has forgotten that once it too produced free men, heroes . . .

> **BATTSON** Sure. The bright flowers of bursting Italian bombs, shot through with flying black scraps of Ethiopian women and children, I think he called it in his book. It must have looked more like caviar than corsages, though.

The Italian pauses and listens to Battson, courteous, quizzical, attentive. He shrugs.

> **ITALIAN OFFICER** Perhaps you are right. Perhaps the world is right, and what we have left is merely that for which we bartered that old glory . . .

> **GERMAN OFFICER** *(sarcastic)* And what are you going to get? . . .

> **ITALIAN OFFICER** *(turns to look at him)* . . . is only what we deserve. Yes. But I will tell a story. It happened among the race of the Herr Kapitan there. Perhaps he recalls it. If not, I will try to speak slowly and clearly enough so that he will hear it, too.

136. NEW ANGLE   FAVORING GERMAN OFFICER

—cold, sneering and contemptuous still. BEAT of FREEDOM TRAIN can be heard.

> **ITALIAN OFFICER** *(continuing)* It was in Athens. There, too, the people had a choice. But their choice was only how to die. But still they voted . . .

As the Italian continues to speak—

SLOW DISSOLVE TO:

137. LONG SHOT   ACROPOLIS   ABOVE THE CITY OF ATHENS

—to establish location. CAMERA PANS toward Acropolis, HOLDS

on it for a second, then scene begins to LAP DISSOLVE SLOWLY.
The Italian's VOICE is heard continuing OVER scene.

> **ITALIAN'S VOICE**   *(over)* . . . because there is one quality in
> human nature, in the nature of Southerners who have
> lived always close to the sun, which is stronger than oppres-
> sion, than ruthlessness and rapacity, than starvation and
> death even . . .

LAP DISSOLVE TO:

138. EXT. STREET   ATHENS   CLOSE SHOT   AN OLD WOMAN
(MEASURED TRAMP OF GERMAN FEET IN B.G.)

—gaunt and weak with hunger, a starving child beside her,
grubbing weakly in a pile of garbage. CAMERA PULLS BACK to
SHOW other people, men, women and children, sitting and lying
propped against wall in b.g. TRAMP of FEET grows louder. A
squad of Italian soldiers, in work dress with an Italian corporal
and a German sergeant, enter and stop beside a body. The
Greek people merely look up at them, then look away. The old
woman grubs in the garbage.

> **GERMAN SERGEANT**   *(harshly in German to the Italian cor-
> poral)* Come on. Come on. Pick it up.

The Italian corporal falters, obeys, approaches the dead Greek,
kneels and is turning him over gently to see if he is dead or not.

> **GERMAN SERGEANT**   *(harshly, moves forward)* Dummkopf.
> *(he kicks the body)*

139. FLASH   BODY   LYING IN STREET

It is dead.

BACK TO SCENE:

> **GERMAN SERGEANT**   Pick it up!

Two Italians take the body by the feet, drag it out. The German
moves again, STEADY TRAMP of FEET begins, carries over. The
Greek people do not even look up.

140. MED. CLOSE TRUCKING SHOT   EXT. STREET CORNER

Two spick-and-span Italian officers PASS CAMERA, marching

stiffly. Behind them are two ragamuffin boys, about ten, ragged and starving, strutting in exact imitation of the two oblivious Italians.

141. EXT. ANOTHER STREET

Starving people sitting weakly about, on steps in the sun, against walls; in b.g. carts are carrying away dead bodies. The two Italian officers enter, strut past. Behind them, strutting step for step, clowning and mocking them, are the two ragged Greek boys, aping the Italians movement for movement. Suddenly the two boys shout together.

   BOYS Heil Hitler!

The two Italians stop, whirl about, their right arms already raised in Hitler salute, find the two ragamuffin, ragged boys facing them stiffly, their right arms also stiffly raised. The starving people stir, sit up, watch. The two Italians react, the boys break and run, the Italians start to chase them. Someone laughs. The Italians stop, look toward the laughter. Someone else laughs.

142. SHOT OF THE PEOPLE

The weak people begin to laugh, the laughter passes from mouth to mouth until the whole street is filled with it.

143. EXT. THE STREET   FULL SHOT

The baffled Italians glare about, helpless to do anything. They turn and go on, while the weak laughter sounds on all sides of them.

                                                      DISSOLVE TO:

144. INT. DINING ROOM   CLOSE SHOT
GERMAN OFFICER

The fat, porcine German officer seated alone at his table, napkin tucked in his collar, clutching his knife and fork in either hand as a soldier servant sets dishes before him. The German gloats on the dishes; can hardly wait for the servant to get his hands out of the way.

ITALIAN'S VOICE *(over)* But they were only Italians, and Italians, even by German concept, are worthy only of the bedevilment of little boys. There was the German commander himself, who held the power of life and death over that whole city which had no reason to live and yet would not die and therefore had no reason to fear or even hate him;—this fat man, this hog, who had commandeered all the food to eat himself; this sick man, slave to a disease like dipsomania, in whom the very sight of the starving people around him seemed to arouse an appetite ungovernable and constant, which all the food in Greece could not assuage, whose very stomach was not large enough to contain sufficient food to quiet its own gnawing pangs . . .

The German begins to eat, gorging himself, cramming food into his mouth, drooling, while the soldier servant stands watching him with contempt and hatred and disgust.

. . . He would even take the rations from his own troops. He was like the drunkard, who hates the very drink from which he cannot restrain himself, taking the meat and bread from his own kind as the drunkard pawns his wife's and his children's clothing to buy drink, until his own men must have hated him too, as the drunkard's wife and children come in time to hate that husband and father who in the grip of his vice is no longer a human, a man . . .

The German gobbles the last morsel from the dish, sits again waiting impatiently while the servant removes the empty dish and sets a bowl before him. Almost before the servant's hands are out of the way, the German begins to spoon into it, gobbling the dessert, drooling.

. . . Until this Demetrios, this Greek who had become an American, who had lived in that land where liberty and freedom were like the air he breathed, until thoughtless men no longer realized what they possessed, where every man had as his heritage the right to that little scrap of paper which is more powerful than any bullet; this Demetrios who was safe as long as his adopted land was safe, whom you would have thought would have stayed there, since he too had breathed freedom and liberty for so long a time that he also might have had no further reason, might well have forgotten, to break down each inhalation into its components on his palate, and say to himself, "This taste is freedom; that, liberty". . .

145. ANOTHER ANGLE

The German spooning away in the bowl, gorging and drooling.

. . . But not this Demetrios, this American who was a Greek still or who perhaps had lived in and breathed freedom and liberty until he had really come to believe that all peoples were entitled to have the sort of freedom and liberty which they chose;— came back to his country's need as the son returns to the mother's need, even though not only the Herr Kapitan's people but their lesser satellites could have told him it was already too late. But he

> would not have believed them, since, be-
> ing still a Southerner and a Greek, he not
> only still owned the gift of laughing, but
> he had brought back with him the power
> of that little scrap of paper which is strong-
> er than any bullet . . .

The German puts a spoon of the food into his mouth, stops, reacts, drops the spoon, springs up, claps his hand to his mouth, spits something violently onto the table. CAMERA PANS to it as it stops rolling. It is a black marble.

146. CLOSE SHOT   THE GERMAN

—as he glares at the marble, snatches up the bowl, dashes the remainder of the food from it, is about to hurl the bowl away, stops, peers into it. A take.

147. INSERT: THE BOWL

It is empty. Scrawled across the bottom of it, inside, is the Greek word which WIPES TO: (English) "No." DISSOLVE begins, with the Italian's VOICE CONTINUING OVER.

> **ITALIAN'S VOICE** *(over dissolve)* A black ball, you see, a vote, as in America. And the soup was made by a German sol-dier cook, and there was no one else about the kitchen but one starving Greek scullery lad, and no reason to lock this starving Greek up in jail where he would have to be fed, so he was fired and another taken on because they were easy to get; a man could get a prince or a princess to do his scullery work for the privilege of gnawing the scraps. Yet on the next day . . .

LAP DISSOLVE TO:

148. CLOSE SHOT   THE GERMAN   SEATED AT THE TABLE

—napkin in his collar, knife and fork clutched upright in either hand as the servant approaches with a casserole. The German shows a repressed fury of anxiety. He is not afraid: he just doesn't know what to expect, expects something. The servant is timid, a little terrified, too. Obviously the German has been raising hell in the kitchen, has threatened and stormed at all the servants, finding nothing though. The servant approaches timidly, puts the dish down, snatches the cover off, turns and bolts back toward the door. The German stares after him, angry, nervous, faces the dish, stares at it, raises the spoon and puts it slowly into the dish as CAMERA PANS to the dish. The spoon comes slowly up. As the gravy drains away, the black ball appears in the spoon. CAMERA HOLDS on it for a second, then PULLS BACK to show bowl and spoon vanish violently as the German hurls them away. DISSOLVE begins with Italian's VOICE OVER.

ITALIAN'S VOICE   *(over dissolve)* Until presently he would not even have to wait for the next day . . .

LAP DISSOLVE TO:

149. CLOSE SHOT   THE GERMAN   INT. HALL

—as he takes his cap from a table, starts to put it on, pauses as a black ball falls from it. CAMERA PANS with ball as it rolls across the floor.

WIPE TO:

150. CLOSE SHOT   THE GERMAN AND AN ORDERLY

The orderly holds the overcoat while the German puts it on, hands the German his cap. The German puts one hand into his pocket as he turns to walk on, stops, reacts, draws the hand slowly out. CAMERA PANS to the HAND. It holds a tiny homemade Greek flag which opens and another black ball falls. CAMERA PANS it across the floor as it stops beside the first one.

ITALIAN'S VOICE   Until at last, even on the street . . .

151. EXT.   CLOSE SHOT   A BLACK-PAINTED CANNON BALL

—wrapped in a Greek flag, poised above a door. CAMERA DRAWS BACK to a:

152. FULL SHOT   DOOR

—as it opens. The German officer starts out, the ball crashes down and barely misses him. He starts back, terrified, then in furious rage as he sees the black ball and the flag. SOUND of WEAK LAUGHTER off scene. The German glares about, impotent and furious in reaction to his fear.

153. REVERSE ANGLE   GERMAN AND ORDERLY   ON THE STOOP
(ANGLE TOWARD STREET)

Greek people, weak and starving slowly to death, lying and
sitting about the street, laughing weakly and steadily, the laughter traveling on up the street until the whole street is laughing.
The German makes a furious gesture to the orderly. The orderly marches stiffly out, approaches the nearest prone laughing man, kicks him. The laughter continues, even the man who
was kicked.

> **GERMAN**   *(furious)* Again!

The orderly stands stiffly, refusing to kick the starving skeleton.
The German strides on, stiffly, passes the orderly, who falls in
behind. They go on up the street, the weak laughter all about
them, pacing them as they walk. DISSOLVE begins with Italian's
VOICE OVER.

> **ITALIAN'S VOICE**   *(over dissolve)* And not only the laughter,
> but the flags. But that was our job . . .

DISSOLVE TO:

154. EXT. STREET   MED. LONG SHOT

The German officer and two orderlies watching and directing
as a squad of Italian soldiers do the work. The whole street is
hung with tiny homemade Greek flags from balconies and windows. The German is in a cold rage. The Italians show terror of
him as they work busily, snatching down the little flags. The
Greek people lie along the walls and curbs, watching them.

155. CLOSE SHOT   A BALCONY   FROM GERMAN OFFICER'S POINT
OF VIEW

—(which we will be able to recognize again) as the Italians
snatch a flag from it.

156. CLOSE SHOT   ANOTHER BALCONY   FROM GERMAN OFFICER'S
POINT OF VIEW

—(which we will be able to recognize again) as the Italians
snatch a flag from it.

> **A GREEK VOICE**   *(off scene)* Behind you.

The German whirls, impotent, raging, glares in furious surprise.

157. CLOSE   THE FIRST BALCONY   GERMAN IN F.G.

Another flag hangs from it.

GREEK VOICE   *(off scene)* Behind you.

The German whirls again, furious.

158. CLOSE   THE SECOND BALCONY

Another flag hangs from it. The weak laughter begins, spreads steadily. DISSOLVE BEGINS, with Italian's VOICE OVER.

ITALIAN'S VOICE   *(over dissolve)* Until at last he could no longer eat—this man who lived for eating. He wished to leave, but he had no excuse to give to his superiors, for how could he confess that he could not prevent his own servants, this conquered and starving people, from putting children's marbles into his food and his cap and his coat pocket? But at last it was the flags which saved him . . .

DISSOLVE TO:

159. INT. OFFICE   MED. SHOT

The fat German stands abjectly among his packed luggage, facing his successor: a grim, stiff officer who is looking at the fat one with complete contempt.

FAT GERMAN   *(timidly)* Am I—Am I to be sent to the front?

NEW COMMANDANT   *(contemptuously)* To the front? If you cannot keep order among a handful of starving Greeks, what could you hope to do with armed Russians or British or Americans who will fight? You will go to Italy. Perhaps our worthy allies at least will not flout you.

The fat German looks down, abject, shrinking, cringing almost.

FAT GERMAN   But my—our honor . . .

NEW COMMANDANT   Luckily for Germany, her honor in Greece at least is no longer in your hands. You are relieved and dismissed.

The fat German pulls himself together, salutes, but it is a weak effort. The new commandant returns it contemptuously. The fat German exits, the orderly follows with his luggage. The new commandant looks after him contemptuously, sits down at the desk, squares his shoulders, bangs the handbell sharply.

LAP DISSOLVE TO:

160. EXT. A WALL   A DOZEN GREEK MEN   MED. CLOSE SHOT

—standing against a wall. They are so weak from starvation that they cannot stand. Two German soldiers move among them, looping a rope among them to hold them up. They show no fear. CAMERA PULLS BACK to INCLUDE the shadows of the firing squad and the officers, lying on the ground. The two soldiers exit. The Greeks stand against the wall, held up now by the rope.

> **OFFICER'S VOICE**   *(from off scene)* Load! *(the shadows move, the rifle bolts clash)* Aim! *(the shadows move, shadows of rifles extend)* Fire! *(the rifles crash)*

Smoke obscures the entire scene. As the smoke thins away—

161. CLOSE SHOT   FIVE GREEKS

—hanging from a crossbeam between two posts. DISSOLVE begins, with Italian's VOICE OVER.

> **ITALIAN'S VOICE**   *(over dissolve)* But even that did not stop them . . .

DISSOLVE TO:

162. EXT. STREET   MOVING SHOT

—of the new commandant and his orderly tramping stiffly up the street, while the Italian squad snatches down the flags. A flag hangs from every balcony and window, made of scraps of cloth, even of paper. The starving people sit and lie along the walls, watching. The German does not look behind him. As soon as the Italians snatch down a flag, another appears. The WEAK LAUGHING begins, paces the stiffly marching German, who does not dare look behind him because he knows what he

will find. The WEAK CONSTANT LAUGHTER continues, becomes
the SOUND of the FREEDOM TRAIN, as we—

DISSOLVE TO:

163. INT. THE HOUSE IN THE DESERT   GROUP   AT AMERICA'S
PALLET

The soldiers gathered about America's pallet, listening to the
Italian.

BATTSON   Well? Is that all?

ITALIAN   It will never be all, as long as they can laugh.
How can you conquer people who can still laugh at you?

A SOLDIER   You can starve them.

ITALIAN   You can only kill them by doing that. You can kill
them much simpler. But when you do that, you have failed.
The man whom you must destroy, as the only alternative to
his obeying you, that man has beat you.

BATTSON   *(turning)* Well, you should know.

ITALIAN   *(quietly)* Yes. We should know.

BATTSON   *(to Manning)* All right, Manning. Let's finish the
voting.

The men silently scatter.

164. CLOSE SHOT   AKERS AND AMERICA

They are quiet for a moment. America shakes his head slowly
and mutters something under his breath.

AKERS   *(draws closer)* Want somethin', boy?

AMERICA   *(slowly, almost dreamily—speaks softly)* Lincoln . . .
Abraham Lincoln . . .

AKERS   *(draws out soiled handkerchief)* What made you think
o' him, America?

AMERICA   Voting.

AKERS   *(mops sweat from America's face)* Yeah—he gave it to
you.

AMERICA   —give us more'n that.

Sweat beads his face again with the effort of talking. Akers mops it again.

AKERS   Better stop talkin', boy.

AMERICA   *(peacefully)* I feel fine—fine . . .

AKERS   Scared?

AMERICA   *(face by now completely covered with sweat, but smiling)* Seems like inside me there's always been votin' 'tween bein' scared an' not bein' scared.

165. WIDER ANGLE   TO INCLUDE OTHERS

—as Manning enters with the gas mask container. It is heavy with votes now. He extends a live shell and an exploded case to Akers.

MANNING   Here. If you vote "Go," drop in the . . .

AKERS   *(does not even look at the shells)* I done voted. Me and America ain't going nowhere.

MANNING   You got to vote. Everybody has voted but you . . .

BATTSON   *(takes the container)* Let him stay here, if he wants to. He don't belong to us.

166. ANOTHER ANGLE

Battson hands the container to Reagan. Now they become quiet; it is official now, as Reagan solemnly prepares to pour out the votes and count them.

167. CLOSE GROUP SHOT

—as all gather near. Reagan pours out the votes.

168. INSERT: REAGAN'S HANDS

—emptying the sack onto the floor. They are all empty cases. Nobody has voted to go.

A SOLDIER'S VOICE   *(off scene)* Hell. Didn't anybody vote to go?

169. MED. CLOSE   GROUP

> **BATTSON** *(looks at him)* You're like everybody else. You thought everybody else would vote to go. So you would vote to stay, and just for the price of one empty 30 caliber hull you would buy a reputation for being brave.

There is a moment of dead silence. Akers breaks it.

> **AKERS** *(forced jeering laughter)* Heh, heh, heh.

He begins to play "Porterhouse Sadie" on the DULCIMER, quick and rollicking.

> **REAGAN** *(angrily)* Stop that damn . . .

> **VOICE** *(in b.g.—to Reagan)* Ah, go on outside. Take a walk yourself in the moonlight. Maybe you can find Rommel and he will tell you what page to look for.

Akers begins to play the DULCIMER.

170. CLOSE SHOT   FONDA AND LOUGHTON

The others in b.g. Akers playing the DULCIMER.

> **FONDA**   The girl . . .

> DISSOLVE TO:

The DULCIMER and the SOUND of the FREEDOM TRAIN carry OVER DISSOLVE. The FREEDOM TRAIN ceases, the DULCIMER becomes the SOUND of a CARROUSEL.

French Sequence

FADE IN   DAY

1. EXT. NIGHT   A STREET IN PARIS   WORKING PEOPLE'S QUARTER

A street fair in progress, carrousel, Punch-and-Judy and other pantomime booths, vendors, a cafe with people at the tables, other people, lower middle-class, men, women and children, strolling and enjoying themselves. The time is 1938, summer.

2. CLOSE SHOT   CLEMENTE AND ALBERT LOUGHTON

(NOTE: Will verify this game.) —at a ring-toss booth. Clemente is chic and smart, even though her clothes obviously did not cost much, among this throng. She is about 20, a true Parisienne. Albert wears neat civilian suit, English in cut. He, too, looks a little better than the men about them.

The booth is filled with cheap, gaudy prizes: dolls, bottles of scent, cheap jewelry, etc. The proprietor leans against the counter beneath the gas-flare while Clemente tosses her last rings, misses. Immediately the proprietor has three more rings ready. Albert has his hand in his pocket to pay.

CLEMENTE   No, no, no. No more.

ALBERT   Oh yes.

CLEMENTE   No, no, no, no, no.

PROPRIETOR   *(offers rings, in cajoling voice)* Not just one little sou? Not even one little sou more?

CLEMENTE   *(to proprietor)* No. Finished. *(she takes Albert's arm, turns him away)* You have spent enough. Come.

ALBERT   Two francs?

CLEMENTE   Yes. That's enough, even for a rich Englishman. It's time for apéritif now.

3. CAFE TERRASSE   CLOSE SHOT   CLEMENTE AND ALBERT

—at a table, with thin, mild French drinks.

CLEMENTE   Now we speak English some.

ALBERT   I wish I spoke French as well as you speak English.

CLEMENTE   You do.

ALBERT   Yes. French to keep a set of books in an English branch bank. To pay bills of old fat English and American women who, having lived in Paris only thirty or forty years, of course, have not learned any French at all.

CLEMENTE   What kind of French do you wish to speak?

ALBERT (*puts his untasted drink down, begins to lean toward her*) I want—I want to speak—

LAP DISSOLVE TO:

4. CLOSE   CLEMENTE AND ALBERT

—at a table in a restaurant. It is still no swank place, still a place where lower middle-class Parisians would go for a mild holiday. They have finished dinner. They are leaning toward one another among the broken meal. Albert now holds Clemente's hands among the dishes. A waiter has just entered. He stands over them, tilts the empty wine bottle, looks at Albert. Neither Albert nor Clemente looks up at him.

WAITER (*suggestively*) Monsieur?

ALBERT (*not looking up*) Yes. All right.

CLEMENTE (*looks up at waiter*) Non. Fini.

The waiter shrugs, exits. Clemente looks at Albert again.

CLEMENTE (*her air is tender, yet there is something quite alert, almost watchful about it*) Yes? Why do you want to know what my life was before we met this afternoon? What does it matter?

ALBERT (*a quick take; he gets it; it is none of his business; he had not realized he was prying*) Quite. Sorry.

He begins to draw back. He releases her hands, thinks he is going to, then finds that her hands have not released his and she has not moved, still holding his hands, watching him with that expression bright and tender yet alert, too.

CLEMENTE You have a mother and father. You lived in the little village in—where is it?

ALBERT Surrey.

CLEMENTE Then you grew up and went to London and got a job in the bank and worked hard and studied French at night and your chance came and now here you are, in Paris, nein?

ALBERT Yes.

CLEMENTE   And I, too, in a little village in the Midi. Only my mother and father were dead a long time and I lived in Catholic orphans' school. Then I grew up, too, and told the Sisters goodbye and came to Paris and got a job, worked hard, and now here am I, too, in Paris.

ALBERT   I'm sorry. I didn't mean—

Clemente holds his hands. Her hands are quite strong. She sits smiling at him until before he knows it he has relaxed and gradually he is leaning toward her across the table, shifting his hands to take her hands again.

CLEMENTE   Yes? And what kind of French would you like to speak?

ALBERT   *(fumbles for the words)* I—I—

LAP DISSOLVE TO:

5. STREET, NARROW AND QUIET   IT IS VERY LATE   CLOSE SHOT

Albert and Clemente as they pause before the door where Clemente lives. They face each other. There is a quality of gentle raillery in Clemente now.

CLEMENTE   Yes? And this French that you would speak?

ALBERT   So I can say—so that I can—

CLEMENTE   Could you say it in English?

ALBERT   *(instantaneous; controlled now)* Yes. I can say it in English.

CLEMENTE   Say it then.

ALBERT   I love you.

CLEMENTE   I love you, what?

ALBERT   I love you, Clemente.

CLEMENTE   I love you Clemente, what?

ALBERT   You haven't—

CLEMENTE   It's Desmoulins. I love you, Clemente Desmoulins, what?

A take, then Albert gets it, puts his arms around her, kisses her.

LAP DISSOLVE TO:

6. ANOTHER ANGLE

—as Albert releases her. They are standing against the door. Albert steps back. Clemente stands against the door, one hand behind her.

ALBERT   Goodnight.

CLEMENTE   Goodnight? What language does anyone need for that?

Her hidden hand turns the knob; all Albert sees is that the door has opened behind her. Still he doesn't move until she extends her other hand. Then he moves toward her as FADE OUT begins.

CLEMENTE   Not goodnight: good morning!

FADE OUT.

FADE IN

7. CLOSE SHOT   DAY   STONE FACADE ABOVE A DOOR

—with letters: BANQUE D'ANGLETERRE.

DOUBLE EXPOSURE against letters:

Albert as he leaves the bank, walking. In b.g. the constant, fretful, inconsequential beep-beep-beep of Paris taxis.

LAP DISSOLVE TO:

8. PARIS STREET SIGN   ON SIGNPOST

RUE RIVOLI

DOUBLE EXPOSURE against sign:

Albert walking, sound of cabs in b.g.

LAP DISSOLVE TO:

9. SIGN

—reading: MONDL
Couturier

10. DOUBLE EXPOSURE

—against sign: Entrance to the shop, very discrete and obviously smart and expensive; a doorman opens the door as Albert enters.

LAP DISSOLVE TO:

11. INT. SHOP

A long room, suave and elegant, with customers, men and women, mostly English and American, sitting in chairs while models parade before them. Albert has just entered, is looking about. He is out of his depth here, knows it, does not like the atmosphere, but he is not going to run away. An attendant in livery approaches him, bows slightly.

ATTENDANT   Monsieur wishes? This way, Monsieur.

ALBERT   Thanks. I'll stop here.

The attendant looks at him, shrugs, bows again, retires. Albert looks on while the models enter and parade and turn and parade again.

Clemente enters, approaches him from one side. She wears what is her livery, too: a smart simple black dress. She is not a model. Albert does not see her. She pauses, watching him, sees what his obvious reaction to the place is.

CLEMENTE   Monsieur veut?

Albert turns swiftly. His face lights.

CLEMENTE   *(rapidly)* Do you not like it in here that much?

ALBERT   Almost. Yes.

CLEMENTE   Wait for me at the side door, then. I won't be much longer. Can you still say it in English?

ALBERT   I can say it in your language now.

CLEMENTE   *(rapidly turning)* But not here. I won't be long.

12. CLOSE SHOT   ALBERT

—standing beside small side employees' door as Clemente

comes out, wearing hat and coat now. Clemente looks about, breathes deep.

> **CLEMENTE**   Paris. There is no place like it. Sometimes I wish I had never seen it.

> **ALBERT**   Why?

> **CLEMENTE**   *(takes his arm; she is covering what she could have said, though he does not know it)* So that I would still have Paris to see for the first time, stupid. Or perhaps it would have been the same.

> **ALBERT**   What would have been the same?

13. TRUCKING SHOT

—as they walk.

> **CLEMENTE**   *(recovers, draws him on)* Nothing. Perhaps I was just thinking in French. You have not learned to think in French yet. You do not need to. You can speak enough French to tell the fat old ladies what to do with their money, and you need no language to love me in, and you can tell me you love me in your language. Tell me.

> **ALBERT**   I do.

> **CLEMENTE**   And I, too, in your language and in mine.

14. CLOSE SHOT   CLEMENTE AND ALBERT

—as she, holding his arm, stops him before a cafe terrasse. She speaks rapidly. There is something at once bright and strained about her, though Albert misses it. Cab sounds again.

> **CLEMENTE**   It is a friend. She is sick. I had promised to call on her this afternoon. I had forgotten it.

She leads him toward a table as she speaks.

> **CLEMENTE**   It is not far. I will not be long.

> **ALBERT**   Couldn't I go with you?

> **CLEMENTE**   No, no, no, no, no. *(she almost pushes him down into a chair, snaps her fingers for the waiter)* I won't be long. Don't get too—how you say it?

ALBERT Tight?

CLEMENTE Tight. I won't be long.

She exits. The waiter enters, stops at the table. The cab sounds are constant, fretful, inconsequential.

WAITER Monsieur?

15. FACADE ABOVE A DOOR

Letters: POLICE—eme ARRONDISSEMENT.

LAP DISSOLVE TO:

16. CLOSE SHOT   A DOOR

Letters: DOCTOR. It opens. Clemente comes out.

LAP DISSOLVE TO:

17. INT. POLICE STATION

The room is crowded with women, obviously prostitutes, some blowsy, some merely tough-looking, all ages. Among them, Clemente looks completely out of place. The women them-selves see it, look at her doubtfully, askance, some even belliger-ently. A woman recognizes her and approaches. She is fat, good-natured, in late thirties, motherly almost.

> **WOMAN** What? You again? What a country. What a sys-tem. Get your name on their books one time, and it is there forever, no matter what your life has become since. As if anyone but a fool of a policeman could not look in your face and see that your life is virtuous now, no matter if at one time when you were young and just come to Paris and no food to eat and nowhere to sleep—*(she ceases—stares at Clemente)* What? Am I wrong? *(she stares at Clemente, who looks steadily back at her, her face grave, yet faintly smiling)* When I had thought that perhaps one of us could—had—

Clemente looks at her steadily, still gravely and faintly smiling. Suddenly the woman claps one hand lightly against her fore-head.

> **WOMAN** Fool that I am. You are in love.

> **CLEMENTE** *(quietly)* Yes.

WOMAN *(eagerly)* He will marry you?

CLEMENTE We do not need that.

WOMAN *(earnest, insistent)* But he loves you? You are sure?

CLEMENTE Yes. I am sure.

WOMAN *(takes both Clemente's hands, with quick warmth)* Bless you then. *(triumphantly)* I was right. There is one of us who has—

GENDARME *(entering)* Now then, my pigeons.

He begins to herd them into some sort of line as they move out.

18. CLOSE SHOT   GENDARME BRIGADIER

—seated behind a table, with rubber stamp, as the women file past. A woman stands at the table, the policeman stamps her license, gives it to her, she passes on. Clemente is next. The policeman takes her papers, is about to stamp them automatically, seems to read the name by chance, pauses, looks up at her. For a moment she and the policeman look steadily at one another. Then the policeman stamps the paper, hands it to her. She moves on, another woman enters, the policeman takes her paper, raises the stamp without hardly looking at it.

19. CLOSE SHOT   CLEMENTE

—walking rapidly, favoring the cafe terrasse. Albert at the table as he sees her rises quickly. She pauses as he approaches.

ALBERT Friend all right?

CLEMENTE Yes yes yes yes yes. Say it now in English.

ALBERT I love you.

CLEMENTE I love you what?

Albert gets it right away this time. He starts to put his arms around her, pauses, looks about at all the people in sight. Cab sounds are constant through this scene.

CLEMENTE This is Paris, stupid. Nobody cares. Nobody watches. Or if they do, they are only glad.

Albert kisses her.

ALBERT   Now where?

CLEMENTE   *(takes his arm, turns him on)* Home. I will cook dinner for you. You did not know that I could cook?

20. INT. CLEMENTE'S ROOM   CLOSE   ALBERT AND CLEMENTE

—seated side by side at table with remains of meal on it.

CLEMENTE   You see? I can cook for you. *(suddenly, passionately, yet still with that gay vivacity)* I will slave for you. If you refuse to let me, beware!

ALBERT   *(takes her in his arms)* All right. You can slave for me.

He tries to draw her face to his. She holds back, stares at his face. Then she kisses him passionately, clings to him, draws her face away.

CLEMENTE   Forever! Always!

She kisses him again. They cling together.

FADE OUT.

FADE IN

21. CLOSE SHOT   SHEET OF PAPER, ALBERT'S HAND WITH PEN, WRITING

The letter:

Paris.
23 October, 1938

Dear Mother:
    Yes, I am going to marry her. Or ask her, that is. This will be a shock until you know her. But it will be different then, because then you will see in her what I see. Because she has taught me—

As the hand continues, DOUBLE EXPOSURE thru letter as LETTER FADES TO:

22. CLOSE SHOT   ALBERT AND CLEMENTE

—standing at bow-rail of a Sunday excursion steamer on the Seine. Clemente's hair flies in the breeze; she holds her hat in her hand. Albert is bareheaded too; they wear sports clothes, easy old clothes for walking, etc.

> **ALBERT**   I still can't seem to get over it. I thought I knew how to save money. I realize now that to save it was all I knew. You taught me how to spend it, to spend a little of it and get the most out of it, the most pleasure. But that's not it either. That's nothing. What you have really taught me . . . *(he looks at her; they don't touch one another)* There, confound it, I've run out of English, too. Clemente. Clemente.

> **CLEMENTE**   You are doing quite well, for a man who has run out of language.

> **ALBERT**   Well, I do have one word more. Forever, Clemente.

DISSOLVE begins. The LETTER begins to appear.

> **CLEMENTE**   Forever, Albert.

> > > > > > DISSOLVE COMPLETES TO:

23. THE LETTER   CLOSE SHOT   ALBERT'S HAND

—end of the letter:

> —so I am going to marry her. Will you take my word for it and send the ring? If I don't receive it, I'll understand, and when my holiday comes next summer I'll bring her to you and then you can change your mind.
> > > > Love to Father and Mary and John.
> > > > > > Albert.

As the LETTER FADES, snow begins to fall. SOUND of Christmas bells in b.g.

> > > > > > LAP DISSOLVE TO:

24. EXT. CHURCH WITH TOWER   SNOW FALLING   BELLS RINGING CHILDREN'S VOICES

VOICES   Noel. Noel.

LAP DISSOLVE TO:

25. INT. BEDROOM

Clemente sits in a chair, still, waiting, expectant. Faint sound of bells from outside. Albert enters.

ALBERT   All right. Come on.

Clemente rises quickly, goes to the door which he is holding open, looks into the next room, squeals with pleasure and surprise, claps her hands, hurries on.

26. INT.   CLOSE SHOT   ALBERT AND CLEMENTE

—at a table on which rests a tiny Christmas tree, with candles, tinsel, etc. A small package lies beneath it.

ALBERT   This is how we do at home: not a wooden shoe sitting on the window ledge in the snow.

CLEMENTE   It's beautiful. But you have spent too much money. I know it. You always do, when I am not—

ALBERT   No. The tree and the candles cost five francs. The other cost nothing.

CLEMENTE   The other?

She sees the small package. She takes it up while Albert watches her, smiling.

CLEMENTE   For me?

ALBERT   Open it.

27. CLOSE SHOT   CLEMENTE'S HANDS

—as she opens the package. It is an old-fashioned jeweler's box. It contains a ring.

CLEMENTE   Oh, didn't I tell you you had spent—

Her voice dies away. Slowly her other hand takes the ring out as she sees what it is—an old-fashioned gold wedding ring.

28.   CLOSE SHOT   ALBERT AND CLEMENTE

Clemente holds the ring, looking at it as she comprehends. Albert is unaware of her reaction. He watches her, still smiling.

> **ALBERT** It was my mother's, and my grandmother's before that. I wrote her I wanted to marry you—

> **CLEMENTE** Marry . . . Me? Me?

As she stares at him, she begins to laugh, the laughter rising, becoming hysterical as she stares at him.

29. ANOTHER ANGLE CLEMENTE'S FACE

—beyond Albert's shoulder as she stares at him, laughing, motionless otherwise, her arms at her sides, her eyes filled with despair. Tears are now running down her face as she stares at him, laughing and crying at the same time.

> **ALBERT** *(amazed)* Clemente!

> **CLEMENTE** *(laughing and crying, her voice choked, sobbing)* Marry me. Marry me. Marry me.

The laughing and crying continue into—

DISSOLVE TO:

30. INT. HALL EVENING DIM LIGHTS BURNING (SOUND OF ALBERT'S FEET)

—as he enters mounting the stairs. The SOUND of his feet indicates his frame of mind. He is worried, baffled, does not know what he will find when he enters. He reaches the door at top of stairs, pauses, his hand on the knob, opens the door at last and enters.

31. INT. LIVING ROOM

The Christmas tree still burns on the table. The dinner table is set; Clemente, wearing an apron, is just setting a dish on the table as Albert enters. She puts the dish down and runs toward him, reaching inside the neck of her dress as she runs. She draws out the ring, looped on a string around her neck, breaks the string with a single jerk, reaches Albert and as she throws one arm around his neck she thrusts the ring into his coat pocket with the other hand.

CLEMENTE   There. You see. I did wear it for one whole day. *(she puts her other arm about his neck)* We do not need it. I will slave for you without the ring.

ALBERT   *(his arms around her)* I don't want you to slave for me. I want—

CLEMENTE   Hush. Kiss me. Then we will eat. It is Noel. Noel. *(they kiss; she still talks against his mouth)* I love you. I will not marry you. I love you. I love you.

FADE OUT.

FADE IN

32. CLOSE SHOT   SAME DOORWAY

—with letters: POLICE—eme ARRONDISSEMENT.

LAP DISSOLVE TO:

33. INT.

The same group of prostitutes come for their regular police examination, a few other faces; again Clemente looks absolutely out of place among them.

34. CLOSE SHOT   CLEMENTE AND THE SAME MOTHERLY WOMAN

WOMAN   *(tensely)* Do not tell him. Marry him. Haven't you lived a virtuous life for years now?

CLEMENTE   But he is so honest himself.

WOMAN   Bah. Let him be. Then you can count on the fact that he will continue to be—as you yourself will continue to be, who have already proved that to yourself. Marry him. Tell him nothing.

CLEMENTE   *(thoughtful; her eyes have gone vague, as if she were no longer there)* Tell him nothing . . . tell him nothing . . .

GENDARME   *(entering)* Now then, my pigeons.

LAP DISSOLVE TO:

35. CLOSE SHOT   ALBERT AND CLEMENTE

—with the ring. Clemente's hair is tied back with a ribbon.

CLEMENTE   No no no no no. Not on the finger. That for later, when we—

ALBERT   And when will that be?

CLEMENTE   *(with one hand she unties the ribbon on her hair, flips it off, runs it through the ring)* On the day before you go home for your holiday in August.

ALBERT   When *we* go home.

CLEMENTE   *(slips ring inside dress, turns her back and passes the two ribbon ends over her shoulders)* Yes. Tie it.

FADE OUT.

FADE IN

36. CLOSE SHOT   ALBERT AND CLEMENTE'S WEDDING BANNS

—posted. (Will verify all this.) The paper is dated in August 1939. Albert's hand, with wrist watch as the hands reach noon exactly. Will show the present date is August 28, three days before war broke.

37. CLOSE   ALBERT AND CLEMENTE BEFORE NOTICE

Albert is watching his watch-hands. There is something strained about Clemente now. As Albert drops his hand and looks up, Clemente quickly erases the strained look from her face.

ALBERT   There. The time is exactly up. Now for the registrar, the what-you-may-call-it. Come on.

CLEMENTE   Couldn't we—couldn't we wait until tomorrow?

ALBERT   *(surprised)* Why, we leave tomorrow. What's the matter with you?

CLEMENTE   *(turns, takes his arm; her air and voice too are reckless)* Nothing. To the registrar.

LAP DISSOLVE TO:

38. STREET   ALBERT AND CLEMENTE

Clemente has stopped again. The expression of despair has come back into her face now, as if even she can no longer control it. Albert stares at her, puzzled and now even a little annoyed. In b.g. the constant toylike beep-beep-beep of taxis.

ALBERT   What is it, Clemente?

CLEMENTE   Do you ever go to church, Albert?

ALBERT   Sometimes. At home. I suppose everybody does.

CLEMENTE   Will you go with me?

ALBERT   We've got to see the registrar, then we've got to pack—

CLEMENTE   *(rapidly)* We can extend the tickets. We can go the day after tomorrow—

ALBERT   *(amazed)* The day after tomorrow?

CLEMENTE   *(rapidly, her voice breathless almost)* I want to spend all tonight in church. *(quickly, before he can speak)* I know, I know. I haven't been to church since we have known each other, nor for a long time before that. But I want to spend tonight in a church, Albert. This last night. Will you let me?

ALBERT   Of course. But I don't—

CLEMENTE   *(before he can stop her, she has raised his hand and kissed it and dropped it)* Thank you. Thank you. I can say it in English too. I love you, Albert. Always. *(she takes his arm, draws him on)*

LAP DISSOLVE TO:

39. EVENING   CLOSE   ALBERT AND CLEMENTE INSIDE CHURCH

Clemente kneels, praying. Albert sits quietly beside her. A few other people, in the church, entering and leaving from time to time; Host, altar, candles lighted, a priest moving about the altar. The priest approaches them. He is an old man. He raises his hand automatically, then sees Albert's clothes and face, desists.

PRIEST   Monsieur is English?

ALBERT   Yes. *(quickly)* But I'm not a Roman Catholic.

PRIEST   *(about to pass on)* You are welcome.

ALBERT Thanks. *(the priest moves on; Albert says quickly:)* Is it all right for me to pray here too?

PRIEST *(pauses)* He is the same God. *(he goes on)*

40. CLOSE   CLEMENTE'S FACE

—as she looks up at the Host, still kneeling. The VOICE is low, almost a whisper, grave and quiet.

VOICE There is truth.

CLEMENTE *(her lips don't move)* But there was Mary Magdalene. You raised her Yourself and told her she would be whole again.

VOICE She confessed. There is truth.

DISSOLVE TO:

41. CLOSE SHOT   ALBERT'S HANDS HOLDING CLEMENTE'S POLICE CARD

CLEMENTE'S VOICE *(brittle, rapid, dry almost)* I was young, sixteen, seventeen, just come to Paris—

42. CLOSE SHOT   ALBERT   INT. THEIR LIVING ROOM

—holding the card. His face is dazed, as if he had been struck on the head. Clemente sits beyond him. She is smoking a cigarette, the first cigarette we have ever seen her smoke. She puffs at it rapidly as she talks, holding it like someone who is not accustomed to smoking. She does not look at Albert, who looks at the card, then wipes his hand across his face as if he could not see, or could not believe what he thinks he sees. He seems to wake, jerks his head up, looks at her.

ALBERT I'm sorry. I didn't hear—

CLEMENTE *(puffing at cigarette, still not looking at him, talking in that dry, rapid voice as if she were recounting a bridge hand)* That's all. I had just my fare here, a few clothes from the school. The sisters didn't want me to come, of course. But I came. I thought I could get a job, that anyone could get a job who wasn't afraid of work. It was cold, too. Winter, and coming from the Midi, where it is never cold except when the mistral . . . That's all. There was just one, an old man he seemed to me then. As old as my father might have been.

Then the police . . . I don't know how it happened, but one day there they were. They registered me, gave me the card. And so ever since—every six months . . . If I didn't, they would arrest me, you see.

ALBERT *(same dazed, polite tone)* I see. I—*(he rises, does not seem to know why or what he intends to do next)* Yes. I see. Yes. *(tries to pull himself together, puts the card carefully on the table)* Thanks. Think I shall get out a bit, get some air—

Clemente rises quickly, crushes out the cigarette.

CLEMENTE Yes. Better still. I've packed your bags and changed your ticket. There's a boat train tonight. You can be in London tomorrow morning.

ALBERT *(dazed)* Yes. Quite. I—

She exits while he talks.

43. CLOSE ALBERT

—at the door, his bags at his feet. Clemente hands him his hat and coat. As she hands the coat to him, we see the ribbon from which the ring hung dangling from the coat pocket. She sees it, stuffs it quickly in.

ALBERT I—*(takes coat and hat)* Thanks. I can write to you—wire you when I—

CLEMENTE *(opens the door, holds it)* Yes.

After a moment Albert sees the open door, wakes again with that jerk, picks up the bags.

ALBERT Yes. I can write you. Wire you. Goodbye.

CLEMENTE Goodbye.

Albert exits. Clemente shuts the door, stands looking up as when she had knelt in the church, looking up at the Host. Her face is despairing, but peaceful now.

CLEMENTE There is truth. I did as You said for me to do.

DISSOLVE TO:

44. INT. TRAIN COMPARTMENT   TRAIN SOUND AND MOTION

45. CLOSE SHOT   HIS HAND   RIBBON DANGLING

46. FULL SHOT   COMPARTMENT

Three other passengers, dozing or asleep. Albert sits, his
clenched hand on his knee, the ribbon dangling, his head back
and his eyes closed. The train begins to slow. He opens his eyes.
At first he merely opens them as a sick man might at a change
of light in his room. The train slows more; it is going to stop.
Albert jerks his head up. His eyes wake now. He glances about
the compartment, gets up quickly, thrusting the ring into his
pocket as he jerks the door open and exits, hatless and coatless,
leaving his baggage too.

47. EXT. STATION PLATFORM

—as Albert leaps from the train. A guard is nearby.

GUARD   No descension here, Monsieur!

Albert rushes past him. Guard looks after him.

GUARD   You, Monsieur!

48. CLOSE   ALBERT

—rushes into station just as porter comes out, carrying bags.
Albert jostles the porter, who drops the bags.

PORTER   (angrily) Now, then!

Albert pauses, jerks coins from his pocket, flings them back
without counting them, runs on.

49. CLOSE SHOT   ALBERT'S HAND

—writing a telegram:

Mlle. Clemente Desmoulins,
4 bis Rue du Chat qui Peche,
Paris

IT'S ALL RIGHT   IT DOESN'T MATTER   I JUST HAD TO GET
USED TO IT   IT DOESN'T MATTER AT ALL   RETURNING FIRST
TRAIN   I LOVE YOU

Albert

LAP DISSOLVE TO:

50. INT. MORNING CLOSE SHOT

—the unopened telegram in an oldish woman's hand.

51. CLOSE ALBERT AND LANDLADY IN HALL

The landlady holds the telegram.

LANDLADY She left too. We thought—

ALBERT You don't know where she went?

LANDLADY No, Monsieur Loughton. She took her bags too. The rent is paid up. We thought . . .

SLOW DISSOLVE BEGINS.

ALBERT'S VOICE (talking to Fonda) So I tried everywhere: the shop, the places we used to go, the priest; one day I met Henri Ballin on the street, but even he—Then—

MONTAGE of September 1, Germans enter Poland, the war begins, battle sound, etc., Albert's voice in b.g.

ALBERT So I went back home, to be called up, and so it was the spring of 1940 before I got back to France and I wangled 24 hours' leave and went to Paris to look again, only I didn't even have time to do that—

Gunfire, battle sound increases, drowns his voice in—

DISSOLVE TO:

52. BEACH AT DUNKIRK GUNFIRE, AEROPLANE SOUNDS

53. GROUP SHOT ALBERT AND OTHER BRITISH TROOPS

—standing waist-deep in water off the beach, waiting for the boats to take them off. German fighters are strafing them, coming down on them one after another, ripping the water with their machine guns, zzzooming on as the next follows. Now and then a man is hit. The men show a grim and frantic impotent defiance. As each aeroplane comes in, the men face it, shooting at it with their rifles as long as they can, then ducking down under the water to try to escape the machine gun bullets as the aeroplane flashes past.

One is coming in quite low. They shoot at it, then duck. Albert does not duck. He has drawn a hand grenade. He pulls the pin, stands up in the water, times his throw, flings the grenade at the aeroplane which is shooting at him, ducks under the water as the aeroplane explodes.

SLOW DISSOLVE BEGINS.

ALBERT'S VOICE *(to Fonda)* So I went back to England—as everybody else in Europe that could was doing. And I would ask them if they knew where she was—the ones coming to England looking for a man named De Gaulle. But they did not know either, until one day—

DISSOLVE TO:

54. AN ARMY POST   ENGLAND   CLOSE   ALBERT AND HENRI BALLIN

Ballin is a Frenchman, about 30, a refugee soldier who has come to join De Gaulle.

BALLIN   Yes. I saw her. I bring you the message. She said to tell you goodbye. That she will love you always, and goodbye.

ALBERT   Goodbye. Goodbye. Then you don't—

BALLIN   *(quickly)* I do not know. *(he looks at Albert with commiseration; he puts his hand gently on Albert's shoulder)* Do not ask, my friend. *(suddenly he claps Albert hard on the shoulder; his face becomes sardonic, Gallic)* My sister was in Paris also. So we do not ask. We do not wish to know, eh?

ALBERT   Yes. We do not wish to know.

DISSOLVE TO:

55. CLOSE   ALBERT AND FONDA

—in the house in the desert, other soldiers grouped around America's pallet in b.g. where Akers plays "Porterhouse Sadie" on the dulcimer, rollicking and merry.

FONDA   So that's why you hope she's dead.

ALBERT Yes. Because I saw Ballin one time more, on his next return to England.

FADE OUT.

FADE IN

56. CLOSE   SWASTIKA FLAG FLYING FROM THE EIFFEL TOWER

TRAMP of German soldiers' feet begins in—

LAP DISSOLVE TO:

57. INT. LARGE HALL IN A PARIS PUBLIC BUILDING   A FILE OF GERMAN SOLDIERS

—march past CAMERA, CLOSE, obscuring what is beyond them, their heavy boots clashing in unison on the stone floor. The last one passes. Against the far wall is a huddle of young French girls. They are not quite terrified, just uncertain, alarmed because they have been taken from their homes and even off the streets and brought here, no reason given them yet. As the TRAMP of the soldiers' feet begins to grow fainter, CAMERA APPROACHES AND PANS THE FACES of the girls, showing that same expression, alarmed, puzzled. CAMERA reaches Clemente. She is standing beside a very young girl who is terrified. This is Henri Ballin's sister, Eugenie. Clemente's face is not terrified; merely watchful. Eugenie clings to Clemente's hand. TRAMP of SOLDIERS' FEET dies away, ceases.

EUGENIE *(whispers)* I'm afraid. What is it?

CLEMENTE *(staring watchful out scene)* Hush. It'll be all right.

58. CLOSE   GERMAN GESTAPO OFFICER

—behind desk. The girls are ranged before it. Among the girls now are a few German women agents, in uniform of sorts, grim and efficient-looking. An orderly has placed papers on the desk, steps back. The officer rises, looks about at the girls. His air is pleasant, easy; he is obviously trying to put the girls at ease.

OFFICER Don't be alarmed, young ladies. The French armies have been conquered, but that is merely a war lost, and what is one more war between Germany and France? In fact, it is because France and Germany are and will always be neighbors, that we fight one another. And what better way to put an end forever to this useless strife between us, than to mix our blood. What better destiny for the young women of France, than to bear children to the young soldiers of victorious Germany, to raise up in France a new race of men and women who will have the culture of France and the valor and strength of Germany—

59. ANOTHER ANGLE

Clemente faces the desk. She has brought Eugenie with her, holds Eugenie's hand. One of the German policewomen has followed, is about to put her hand on Clemente's shoulder.

> **OFFICER** *(to woman)* Bitte. *(the woman retires; the other girls watch in b.g.)*

> **CLEMENTE**   This girl is a—

> **OFFICER**   Ah. You speak German, Mademoiselle?

> **CLEMENTE**   Yes. Even German.—This girl is a child, as you can see. Look at her—

> **OFFICER**   She is related to you?

> **CLEMENTE**   No. Look at her. You can't—

The officer speaks out of scene without turning his head, a short order obviously in German; Eugenie and the other girls do not understand it. They still watch, wide-eyed, puzzled and terrified. TRAMP of FEET begins, two soldiers enter. The officer speaks another short command in German. Clemente understands it, releases Eugenie, turns as the two soldiers grasp her, carry her struggling out. The policewoman enters, leads Eugenie back to the other girls as the officer continues, smooth-tongued again.

> **OFFICER**   I am sorry that happened. But you are still not to be alarmed. What is the action of one foolish girl—

VOICE shouts an order in German off scene. TRAMP of SOLDIERS' FEET begins and approaches, growing louder.

OFFICER *(continuing above tramping feet)*—to this plan be-tween us which will give to the French race—

Soldiers enter, their feet drown his VOICE, they pass tramping, their boots ringing. They obscure the huddled girls.

60. A DRESSING ROOM   SOUND OF FEET FAINT YET STEADY B.G.

The girls are huddled. The German policewomen pass among them, distributing garments: negligee, boudoir, etc. Another follows, gives each girl a big placard bearing a number. The girls accept them, dazed.

LAP DISSOLVE TO:

61. SAME

The girls are now dressed in the sheer, more or less diaphanous garments, each with a number placard on her back. They hud-dle, cringe. TRAMP of FEET grows louder and louder.

62. CLOSE SHOT

A German sergeant with a notebook stands beside a sort of barred peephole in a wall. The steady TRAMP of FEET continues through the scene.

SERGEANT Heinrichs!

A young German soldier enters, stiff and military, turns, ap-proaches the peephole, looks through it awhile.

SOLDIER Twenty-nine.

SERGEANT *(writes in book)* Twenty-nine.

Heinrichs about-faces, marches stiffly out.

SERGEANT Wittel!

Another young soldier enters, emulates Heinrichs exactly.

SOLDIER Two.

SERGEANT Two.

Wittel exits as Heinrichs did.

SERGEANT Koebler!

Another young soldier enters, exactly as the others had done.

TRAMP of FEET DIES AWAY in—

DISSOLVE TO:

63. INT. OFFICE   DESK AND A COUCH

Clemente is standing. SOUND of DOOR as it opens and closes. Clemente looks quickly toward it, becomes alert yet still shows no fear as SOUND of FEET approaches and the officer enters. He has in his hand Clemente's police card.

> OFFICER   This is yours? Camille Desmoulins, registered with the Paris police?

> CLEMENTE   *(watchful)* Yes.

> OFFICER   Then it is well that you spoke when you did. Naturally, with this record, we could have no one of the men we have chosen for this . . . However, you will still need a friend in Paris—if you wish to continue to eat. For, permit me to say it with no intention whatever merely to flatter you, Mademoiselle: your old profession can and must do without you—for a time at least. *(he indicates the couch with one hand; he almost bows)* If you please.

> CLEMENTE   No.

> OFFICER   Once more. *(indicates the couch)* Be advised. If you please.

> CLEMENTE   No.

The officer raises his voice, gives a sharp order out of scene. The door opens and closes again, TRAMP of FEET, four soldiers enter, stop in unison at attention. The officer gives another short harsh command. Clemente turns as the soldiers grasp her. The officer watches calmly. Clemente struggles furiously as the soldiers overpower her. She does not cry out: there is only the sound of her panting as they drag her to the couch, which is now out of scene. From out of scene still comes the sound of her panting breath as she still struggles apparently. The officer turns and walks toward the sound of her panting, out of CAMERA.

FADE OUT.

FADE IN

64. A DUTCH CITY   AUGUST, 1940   CLOSE   A DOORWAY

—with temporary sign of German police attached to it. Steady, measured sound of tramping German soldiers in b.g.

LAP DISSOLVE TO:

65. INT.   STEADY TRAMP OF GERMAN SOLDIERS' FEET IN B.G.

The scene resembles that one in the police station in Paris before the war, but with differences which show the oppression under which these people exist. The TRAMP of the FEET continues over the scene as an oppression motif.

A group of prostitutes, Clemente among them. She has changed completely. She is not only poorly dressed, but sloven, even dirty, almost hopeless, though the character and courage which enabled her to resist the Germans in Paris to the last is still there. She is not afraid of them; she has just given up. She is simply an animal now, wanting food and shelter in order to live.

The other women resemble her, ill-clad, with the expression in their faces which the constant dread of hunger, starvation, even though it has not quite come yet, gives. They are of all ages, from girls in 'teens to women of middle age. Some are grim, some are merely hopeless, have given up. Some have even gone beyond that, the young ones especially. They have a recklessness, a quality of mirth, ready laughter, gaiety even of people who know they are lost and no longer even care.

As the scene opens, a young girl is laughing, loud and continuously, as at a good joke. The others pay no attention to the laughter. One or two look apathetically toward the sound, then look away. A German soldier (police) enters.

    GERMAN   *(to the girl)* You, there. Hush that!

    GIRL   *(pertly)* I passed the doctor. My license is still good. Can't I laugh on it, too?

    GERMAN   *(to all of them; roughly)* In line, there! Come on.

He passes down the group, shoving them into line, forcing the flavor of militarism, regimentation, even on these drabs from the alleys and gutters. The German backs off, still facing them, stiff and military.

> **GERMAN** All with military permits—Forward! (*Clemente and the other younger ones come forward*) Turn—March!

Clemente and her group turn and go out. The TRAMP of soldiers in b.g. seems to become the sound of their shuffling feet.

66. CLOSE SHOT   GESTAPO SERGEANT

—seated behind a table as the women file past, almost exactly like the scene with the Gendarme Brigadier in Paris. He checks each license, stamps it, takes a food card from the pile on the desk, hands it and the license to the woman, who goes on as the next comes up. The third one is Clemente. The German stamps her license, hands her it and her food card. She does not move on. She looks at the food card. Her face, expression, is that of an animal which is interested only in food.

> **CLEMENTE** Is that all?

> **SERGEANT** (*reaching for the next card, pauses, looks at her*) It's like the others.

> **CLEMENTE** (*shows the first of any kind of life, animation*) I'm licensed for troops. I—

> **SERGEANT** Then work harder. Earn more. (*examines her a moment*) Borrow a cake of soap. Wash that dress and your face and comb your hair, and maybe you can earn more. Next!

> **CLEMENTE** But I—

German orderly enters, shoves her on.

> **ORDERLY** Get along, there!

Clemente turns, walks toward CAMERA, her face hopeless.

> DISSOLVE TO:

67. STREET   CLOSE   CLEMENTE

—standing, hopeless. In b.g. a constant stream of people: abject

Dutch men and women, now and then German soldiers, arrogant. Clemente is looking out of scene. Suddenly she starts, her face wakes; she has recognized someone she did not expect to see here. She moves out, beginning to walk fast, her face now alight with a sort of unbelieving hope.

68. TRUCKING SHOT   HENRI BALLIN

—walking toward CAMERA. He has a beard now, wears rough workingman's clothes, is disguised. Clemente in b.g. hurrying to overtake him, her face wearing that expression of incredulous hope. She reaches him, is just behind him.

   CLEMENTE   *(not loud)* Henri.

He hears her. Only his eyes shift a little. He pretends not to, strolling on, not increasing his gait, doing nothing to indicate to any passing German that his name is Henri or that he believes Clemente is addressing him. He turns easily, still strolling, toward a show window while Clemente, anxious, a little puzzled, follows.

69. CLOSE   HENRI AND CLEMENTE

—facing the shop window. Henri has done this to see Clemente's reflection in the glass, see who it is that knows his name. He recognizes her by the reflection. He is thinking quickly. He does not want to be recognized. But she has done so. Even if he could bluff his way out of this, she might pass him again on the street someday, and call his name, this time with a German policeman in hearing. He turns, pretends to recognize her for the first time.

   HENRI   Why, Clemente.

There is still that hope in Clemente's face, even though she does not know it. She has not even rationalized the matter. She knew Henri went to England, got off safe. Yet here he is in Holland. She has not thought herself of escaping; it has not seemed possible. But already, subconsciously, she has thought of the possibility for the first time on recognizing this man who did find the way to escape.

   CLEMENTE   What are you doing here?

HENRI *(shrugs)* What are you? I'm working in the shell factory at Douellens.

He glances quickly, a little furtively, about.

HENRI My name's not Henri Ballin now, too. I have a Dutch name now.

CLEMENTE *(hope dies)* Working, for them? *(Henri shrugs; she stares at him)* I thought you had gone to England. I thought . . .

Her voice dies away as she stares at him, as the vague irrational hope she had had for a moment dies in her. To her he seems to have the same hopeless fatalism which she has been living in. She had not believed it, but apparently it is so.

HENRI *(rapidly)* What for? England will be next. Then they will have all Europe, for our time at least. Better to dig in now and be safe with a job and enough to eat. Let the others fight on, if they want to.

CLEMENTE *(quiet, hopeless again)* Yes.

She looks away. He is impatient to be gone. She feels it.

CLEMENTE I suppose you know I saw Eugenie—

HENRI *(roughly, quickly)* No. Don't tell me. I don't want to know.

CLEMENTE I tried—

HENRI I know that, too. Thank you. But I don't want to know. Well—

CLEMENTE *(turns to him quickly)* Henri—

HENRI Hush. Not that name. I'm a Dutchman now.

CLEMENTE Yes. *(then humbly, in a kind of fumbling rush)* Let me come live with you. I won't bother you. I can sleep on the floor. I have a food card. If I didn't have rent to pay, I could . . . I wouldn't have to . . . Maybe you could even get me a job in the factory—

He looks at her with pity, but he cannot do this, as we will see later.

HENRI   No. I'm sorry. *(rapidly)* You did what you could for Eugenie. Do this for Eugenie, too. Forget that you saw me. Or forget that I was ever a Frenchman. Will you promise that?

CLEMENTE   *(dully)* Yes. I promise.

HENRI   Then goodbye.

He is about to turn away, stops, takes a small handful of money from his pocket without counting it and offers it to her.

HENRI   Here.

CLEMENTE   *(rouses)* You are poor, too. I don't need it. I can earn enough.

HENRI   Take it. *(he puts the money into her hand and turns)* Goodbye.

Clemente holds the money. She has not even looked at it. Henri goes out. She looks out of scene after him, dull and hopeless again.

CLEMENTE   Goodbye.

DISSOLVE TO:

70. CLOSE SHOT   A PHOTOGRAPH OF HENRI

—without the beard, in French uniform, as he appeared before the fall of France. It lies on a desk.

71. INT. GESTAPO OFFICE

The officer who raped Clemente in Paris sits behind the desk as the door opens and two policemen enter with Clemente between them. An orderly stands behind the GPO officer. The policemen march Clemente to the desk, halt.

OFFICER   All right. Dismiss.

The two policemen exit. The officer examines Clemente—her slovenliness, dirtiness, shabbiness, etc. Clemente stares back at him.

OFFICER   You do not seem to have done as well as you should. Perhaps it is that same—shall we call it modesty?—

which you showed me once. You should try to break yourself of it. Come here.

Clemente approaches the desk. He turns the photograph
around to face her, still holding it, watching her face.

OFFICER   Do you know this man?

CLEMENTE   *(gives picture a brief glance, looks up)* No.

OFFICER   *(still watching her face)* Come. When you assaulted
two of my men that day in Paris, to defend his sister?

CLEMENTE   *(meets his stare)* No.

OFFICER   Give me your license and food card. *(Clemente
stares at him)* Or shall I call in four men to hold you, as I was
forced to do that day in Paris?

Clemente, still staring at him, produces the two cards. He takes
them and hands her the picture.

OFFICER   So. We exchange. *(Clemente stares at him)* Since
you do not know this man, you will need the photograph.
He is now in Holland, without doubt under a false name
and disguised. From now on, you will spend your time
looking for him. Meanwhile, I will hold these two cards.

CLEMENTE   But how will I eat?

OFFICER   Fritz here will see to that. Each day at noon you
will return here, and Fritz will give you food—until you can
come to me and report that you have found this man. I
would advise you to begin at once to seek him.

Clemente stares at him. He stares back at her. She turns and
exits. The officer looks at the door which has closed behind her.
His tone is musing.

OFFICER   She was beautiful once. She could be now, if
she—*(catches himself, sits back)* Ah, bah. These French. What
a race. How they have lasted this long even—*(to the orderly,
taking up other papers to resume work)* Give her three days. Let
her get good and hungry. Then—

ORDERLY   Yes, sir. Then I will know what to do.

DISSOLVE TO:

72. CLOSE SHOT   A BOWL OF FOOD

—in Clemente's hand. It is not quite full.

73. CLOSE   CLEMENTE AND THE ORDERLY

> CLEMENTE   *(looking at bowl, her face dull, hopeless)* Is this all?
>
> ORDERLY   You must look harder for him.

LAP DISSOLVE TO:

74. CLOSE SHOT   THE BOWL OF FOOD

—in Clemente's hands. It is about half full.

> ORDERLY'S VOICE   You must look harder for him.

LAP DISSOLVE TO:

75. CLOSE SHOT   THE BOWL OF FOOD

—in Clemente's hands. It is almost empty.

LAP DISSOLVE TO:

76. INT. GARRET ROOM

A broken-down cheap bed. The bedclothes tumbled. Clemente sits on the bed, her clothes disarranged, her hair straggling. She has a plate of food on her lap, is crouched over it like an animal, wolfing it ravenously, like a starved dog. The orderly stands beside the bed, fastening his coat, belt, etc., while she eats the last morsel from the plate, leaving it clean. The orderly takes it. She watches the plate hungrily as he moves it and sets it aside.

> ORDERLY   You are not looking hard enough for this man.
>
> CLEMENTE   *(rouses, begins to straighten her clothes; dully)* Why do you want him?
>
> ORDERLY   Never mind why. But you can see what will happen to you if you don't find him.

Clemente gets up from the bed, still straightening her clothes. The orderly is fastening his belt, almost dressed now.

> CLEMENTE   Maybe if I knew why you wanted him, I would know where to look.

ORDERLY *(pauses, his belt in the buckle but not hooked yet; he stares at Clemente)* Aber Gott, that's sensible. I wonder why the Chief—*(he pauses, watches her as she fastens her blouse, looking at what she is doing)* That will help you, you think?

CLEMENTE *(looking down)* It may.

ORDERLY He is a De Gaullist spy. He is here from England by the underground.

Clemente has stopped dead, her hands motionless on the buttons, her face still lowered. The orderly doesn't notice. He fastens his belt, steps to her, puts his arms around her. She recovers.

ORDERLY Ja, a De Gaulle agent. You catch him and eat again, ja?

He tries to kiss her. Clemente holds back.

CLEMENTE Haven't I already paid for that plateful?

ORDERLY *(draws her to him)* You may need another—if you don't catch him pretty quick.

He draws her to him. Clemente submits to his kiss.

DISSOLVE TO:

77. CLOSE SHOT   THE BOWL OF FOOD

It sits untouched on a wooden plank table.

LAP DISSOLVE TO:

78. CLOSE SHOT   CLEMENTE

—as she searches for Henri. Her face is dirty, gaunt with hunger; she looks dazed, but there is now in her face hope again, as she moves along, while people, the abject Dutch and now and then an arrogant German soldier, pass her. She is weak from hunger. She walks like a sleepwalker, blundering into people, going on.

LAP DISSOLVE TO:

79. CLOSE SHOT   THE BOWL OF FOOD

—still untouched on the wooden table.

LAP DISSOLVE TO:

80. STREET NIGHT POOR QUARTER CLEMENTE

—moving along, her face lifted, the hope in it as she seeks Henri. She is weaker now as she walks slowly and unsteadily on, looking at the furtive Dutch faces. A bearded man passes in the dim light.

    CLEMENTE *(stops; weakly)* Henri.

The man looks at her, hurries on. She turns, moves on, stumbles, falls to her knees, catches a post, pulls herself painfully up again, stops dead, listening. Faint steady TRAMP of SOLDIERS' FEET in distance. She shows alarm, then terror, tries to run, exits running unsteadily.

81. CLOSE CLEMENTE

—crouched in a dark doorway in a deserted street, panting, listening. The TRAMP of FEET continues, nearer now. She hurries on, panting, running unsteadily.

82. A NARROW ALLEY

Clemente hurries toward CAMERA, staggering. TRAMP of FEET is nearer. She staggers into a doorway, stops, panting, looking back. Two men appear suddenly from the dark doorway behind her, one claps his hand over her mouth, the two of them snatch her backward out of sight. TRAMP of FEET is louder and nearer: a steady Whack. Whack. Whack. Whack.

83. INT. A BASEMENT CELLAR

—crude table, chairs. An old fat Dutchman in a shabby mariner's jacket and cap, a younger one, a young Belgian and Henri have just turned from the table as two other men enter, half carrying Clemente between them. They have to hold her up. She blinks in the light, at the faces. Henri rises. She sees him.

    CLEMENTE *(weakly)* Henri.

She sways, collapses. Henri springs forward; he and the other two catch her. Henri holds her.

DUTCH CAPTAIN *(in Dutch; removes his heavy curved pipe)* What's wrong there?

HENRI Nothing's wrong with her, any more than is wrong with the rest of Europe. She's just starving.

FADE OUT.

FADE IN

84. CLOSE CLEMENTE AND HENRI MORNING

Clemente sits up on a bed: a mattress on the floor, with rough quilts. She has a bowl of soup, is wolfing it down. Her face is dirty, her hair uncombed, her clothes soiled and ragged.

HENRI You were getting too close to us, you see. We were watching you too. We knew they had set men to follow you, and you were getting too near. We had to do something.

She is scarcely listening. She empties the bowl. Henri takes it. She follows it with her eyes like a hungry dog.

CLEMENTE More. Please.

HENRI *(rises)* No. You'll be sick. You can have more after a while. You'd better rest again now. *(he turns to leave; Clemente watches him; she has waked, roused)*

CLEMENTE *(quickly)* Henri—*(he pauses, turns back; she continues, rapid, breathless)* They said you came here from England. Then you can go back, are going back. Take me with you.

HENRI You rest now. Try to sleep again. I'll bring you more soup after a while.

He goes out. Clemente looks after him.

DISSOLVE TO:

85. CLOSE CLEMENTE

—cooking a meal on a stove. She dishes up the food, turns. Her face is quiet, dull, apathetic, but at least she is no longer worried and hungry.

86. INT. LARGER ROOM   THE TABLE, CHAIRS, ETC.

Henri, the young Dutchman, two young Belgians, another young Frenchman, all with a seagoing air, clothing, etc., are seated about the table. Clemente has just entered with a dish in each hand. The men are quiet, as if they had stopped talking when she entered. As she approaches the table, the young Dutchman rises quickly, diffidently, respectfully. The others, without rising, make room for her to reach the table and put the dishes down. She looks at none of them, sets the dishes down, goes on and sits on a low stool before the hearth, becomes motionless, chin propped on her hand, brooding. The young Dutchman, Willem, sits down again. Henri draws his chair back to the table.

FIRST BELGIAN   We will not wait for Captain Maas?

HENRI   No. He may be late.

The others draw up to the table, are about to begin, pause as the door opens. Captain Maas enters. Willem, the two Belgians and the young Frenchman rise quickly, stand stiffly as Captain Maas comes to the table. Henri stops too, watches Maas intently.

HENRI   So?

MAAS   Ja.

He removes his cap, hangs it carefully up, takes the chair at the head of the table, lays his pipe beside it. When he is seated, the young men sit down. But they sit stiffly, waiting until Maas has served himself first, showing the discipline which is observed on Maas's tugboat as if it were a liner or a man-of-war even. Henri still watches Maas intently.

HENRI   Well?

Maas pauses, turns his head slowly. The others all turn their heads to look at Clemente as she sits on the stool, staring into the dead ashes on the hearth.

HENRI   *(impatiently)* You see? Besides, what does it matter, anyway?

87. CLOSE   CLEMENTE

—on the stool, motionless, brooding, dirty, disheveled, apparently a thousand miles away.

    MAAS'S VOICE   Ja. Soon now. The wind is west today. It rains in England now.

Clemente starts slightly, raises her head, her eyes wake. Her head comes slowly up.

88. GROUP AT TABLE

The others leaning forward, all intent and grave, listening as Maas talks.

    MAAS   Tomorrow the wind will haul south and the fog will come. The tide will be right at daylight the day after tomorrow morning.

    HENRI   It will be then, you think?

    MAAS   It will be then, I think—

They pause, look up. Clemente stands over the table. She is awake now, tense, passionate.

    CLEMENTE   *(to Maas)* You're going to England. Let me go! *(they look at her, Maas frowns; Willem again has sprung respectfully to his feet)* Don't leave me here! *(she looks imploringly from face to face as the young men watch her, gravely, pityingly; she looks at Henri)* Henri! I did what I could for Eugenie—

    HENRI   *(rises quickly, takes her arm)* Come.

    CLEMENTE   You won't leave me here? You'll take me away with you?

    HENRI   *(gently)* Come along, now.

He leads her out.

89. KITCHEN   CLOSE   CLEMENTE AND HENRI

Henri stands. Clemente sits in a chair, clinging to his hand. She is trembling.

    HENRI   *(gently)* It's for Captain Maas to say. He's in command of the boat. We'll have to talk about it. You wait here, now.

CLEMENTE *(clings to his hand)* Don't leave me here, Henri. Promise me you won't leave me here.

She stares at him, imploring, shaking, fumbling at his hand. He looks down at her.

HENRI *(suddenly)* Yes. I promise.

She releases his hand. He exits. She looks after him. There is hope in her face and peace too, eagerness. She is panting, trembling still, clenching her hands together to stop the shaking.

CLEMENTE *(whispers)* England. England.

90. GROUP AT TABLE

Henri has returned. Maas is smoking his big pipe.

MAAS It will be dangerous, a risk.

HENRI She can go as a crew member—cut off her hair, in men's clothes.

MAAS Ja. And papers for her.

They had not thought of that. The young men remain quiet. Maas puffs steadily at his pipe.

WILLEM *(suddenly)* She can go on my papers. I will remain here.

The young men do not move. Slowly Maas takes the pipe from his mouth, turns his head deliberately and stares at his son. He puts the pipe back in his mouth and puffs steadily again, staring at Willem. Then he turns his head, belches, pushes his chair slightly back to give his belly room.

MAAS Bah. What are a few papers? I am a friend of Germans.

LAP DISSOLVE TO:

91. SAME

All leaning forward as Henri talks. Clemente sits on the stool as before, apparently not listening. But her face is quiet now, peaceful.

HENRI   We will use the official broadcast. *(to Maas)* As soon as they notify you of the hour you will sail, Rynje will give me a copy of the broadcast and I will insert the code message for the destroyers—

FRENCHMAN   And they at the radio will find this strange sentence in the broadcast and they will return to Rittner to see what it means, if it belongs there—

HENRI   That is the chance we must take. Unless we could keep Rittner incommunicado for an hour, until the time arrives when the broadcast must be made—

FIRST BELGIAN   That will be easy. Rynje and I will leave him quiet and uninterested in radio or anything else forever.

HENRI   *(quickly)* No. That will be too risky. The messenger who comes to see if the broadcast is correct will find him dead, if nobody before him does. We will see when the time comes. The principal thing is the broadcast and the sailing—

MAAS   *(puffing at pipe)* And the fog.

HENRI   Yes. The fog.

DISSOLVE TO:

92. STREET   FOG COMING IN

—gradually blotting out the houses, etc.

LAP DISSOLVE TO:

93. INT. THE ROOM

Clemente is seated as before on her stool in the corner. The others, except Henri, have just risen as Maas enters. They all watch him, the intensity has increased, as he hangs his cap deliberately and carefully on its peg and takes the head of the table, sits down and lays the pipe beside his plate. The young men sit down. They all stare at Maas, as he begins calmly to serve himself with food.

MAAS   Ja. Tomorrow.

HENRI *(rises quickly)* Then it will be the broadcast tonight. I will—

FRENCHMAN And Rittner, when the messenger comes to him.

The two Belgians rise quickly.

FIRST BELGIAN You see? There is but one way. Rynje and I—

SECOND BELGIAN And I. Then the girl will have two sets of seamen's papers to use.

HENRI No, I tell you. Captain Maas will need you. I will attend to Rittner; all you need to do is get the barges there—

He stops, all pause.

94. ANOTHER ANGLE

Clemente stands beside the table while they look at her. Her face is awake now, quite calm. Her voice is a little reckless as she throws away forever her last and only chance to get away. She is dirty, disheveled, ragged: a tramp.

CLEMENTE Can you get me a clean dress?

HENRI *(puzzled)* A dress?

CLEMENTE A silk negligee. And some soap and a bottle of scent. I'll take care of Rittner.

All stare at her, Maas puffing steadily at his pipe.

HENRI *(quietly; reminding her)* You will not go to England, then.

She says nothing. She is looking above their heads now, her face quiet, composed. A take.

HENRI *(quietly)* Yes. I will get them for you.

He takes her dirty hand, kisses it. It seems dead as he lowers it gently to the table, releases it, turns and exits. Clemente remains motionless, looking beyond them, above their heads. Willem moves forward, diffidently, takes her hand.

WILLEM *(timidly)* Mademoiselle?

She doesn't move. Willem lifts her hand, kisses it, lowers it. As he does so, his father heaves himself deliberately from his chair, approaches, removes his pipe, takes Clemente's lax hand, raises it, pauses, turns his face aside, spits, wipes his mouth on his sleeve, kisses the hand, releases it, puts his pipe in his mouth and returns toward his chair. Clemente does not move. The Frenchman moves forward.

FRENCHMAN And I also, Mademoiselle?

As the DISSOLVE begins, the FREEDOM TRAIN SOUND and MOTIF enter briefly, become TRAMP of GERMAN FEET over—

DISSOLVE TO:

95. A CORRIDOR   A SENTRY

The sentry is tramping back and forth before a closed door. A German soldier-clerk enters hurriedly, with a paper in his hand, approaches the door.

SENTRY Hold on there. Not that one.

CLERK *(hurriedly, alarmed)* I've got to see the Chief. It's about the broadcast. It's got to go out in thirty minutes.

SENTRY The Chief ain't interested in radio for the next few hours. If I was in there where he is now, I wouldn't never be interested in nothing else again.

CLERK You mean—?

SENTRY Exactly. And if you had seen what I saw—

CLERK But the broadcast.

SENTRY Broadcast it. The Chief left specific orders he ain't to be disturbed until morning.

The clerk exits with the paper. The sentry begins to pace again. The TRAMP, TRAMP of FEET continues into—

DISSOLVE TO:

96. AT SEA   FOG   A BIG TUGBOAT

—towing a long line of invasion barges loaded with German troops.

97. INT. PILOT HOUSE OF TUG

Willem is steering. One of the Belgians and Captain Maas are bending over a clumsy homemade wireless with a key for sending Morse. Maas is working the key.

LAP DISSOLVE TO:

98. A SMALL GROUP OF BRITISH DESTROYERS AT SEA   FOG

99. INT. BRIDGE, WIRELESS ROOM OF A DESTROYER

Operator at the key, an officer leaning over him.

OPERATOR   Here it comes, sir.

100. CLOSE   OPERATOR'S HAND

—as it writes on a pad:

"POSITION 22 MILES, BEARING (DEGREES) FROM (POINT ON LAND)"

OPERATOR'S VOICE   He's repeating it, sir. He says he can receive by voice, but he can't send that way.

OFFICER'S VOICE   Put me onto him. Give me the mike.

The operator's hand takes mike from hook, passes it out of scene, throws a switch.

OFFICER'S VOICE   We have you. And thanks. We've not much time, you know; they are picking us up. Cast your barges loose and get yourself clear. We'll give you two minutes. Set your course 280 degrees. Jump to it.

OPERATOR'S VOICE   Here he comes, sir.

His hand writes slowly on the pad as the message comes through:

YOU—WILL—LOSE—THEM—ON—THIS—TIDE—IN—THAT—TIME—WE—ARE—CLEAR—COMMENCE—FIRING

The clicks become a steady buzzing.

OPERATOR'S VOICE He's holding his key down, sir. Giving us a beam to range on.

OFFICER'S VOICE Hello! Hello! Are you there?

The steady buzz breaks into clicks. The operator's hand writes:

YES—RANGE—ON—ME—AND—COMMENCE—FIRING

OFFICER'S VOICE Right. And thanks again. And good luck.

The steady buzz continues. As DISSOLVE begins:

VOICES Range blank, 2000. Commence firing. *(fainter as dissolve increases)* Range blank, 2000. Commence firing. *(very faint)* Range blank, 2000. Commence firing.

Firing begins, carries through—

DISSOLVE TO:

101. THE TUG AND THE BARGES

—as shells begin to fall among them, destroying them.

102. DESTROYER'S WIRELESS ROOM AND BRIDGE

The firing is continuous. The steady buzz continues, then is cut short off. The firing becomes the SOUND of FREEDOM TRAIN in—

FADE OUT.

FADE IN

(SOUND of the men SNORING in various keys as FADE IN begins.)

171. INT. HOUSE IN DESERT   FULL SHOT   DAY

It is just before sunrise. The men, including the two prisoners, are sleeping, some lying on the floor, some sitting against the walls. A sentry lies on the ledge beneath the window where we first saw Akers, asleep too, his rifle lying across the window sill, pointing out. Even America is asleep now, Akers propped against the wall beside him, snoring. The rifles are stacked in one corner, the pistol belts and the grenades hung on the stacked rifles and piled about the butts of them. The sun rises, the first ray fills the window beside the sleeping sentry and enters the room. The Italian machine gun is in the same corner with rifles.

172. EXT. HOUSE   CLOSE   LEVINE   AT ONE OF THE OUTPOSTS

He is half-crouched, holding his rifle between his knees while he drags frantically at his binoculars case, staring off into the desert. He jerks out the glass, claps it to his eyes. The sun has risen; his shadow lies long beside him.

173. INSERT: SHOT THROUGH BINOCULARS

A cloud of moving dust in the early sun, with movement in the dust. The dust thins, a tank emerges from it. The tank bears a swastika cross.

174. CLOSE SHOT   THE SENTRY

—as he fires his rifle, pumps the bolt to fire again.

175. INT. HOUSE   MED. FULL SHOT

The men have waked, been waked suddenly by the sentry's first shot. They are still half asleep, sitting up, dazed in the instant before they can gather themselves. Another FAINT SHOT sounds from outside.

Battson springs to his feet, first as usual, though Levine, Finnegan and Gomez are close behind him.

    BATTSON   Up with you! Everybody!

He runs toward the door as the third SHOT SOUNDS. Reagan is up now; but before he can move all the others have leaped up and go piling toward the door after Battson. Reagan leaps between them and the door, flings out his arms, stops them. Battson exits.

    REAGAN   Back! Back! What the . . .

    GERMAN'S VOICE   *(off scene)* Achtung!

The men turn, stop dead, staring.

176. SHOT AT DOOR   ANGLE TOWARD ITALIAN MACHINE GUN

The unarmed men huddled about the door. Facing them across the room, the German officer squats easily behind the Italian machine gun, holding it trained on them. The Italian stands a short distance away. The two guards have snatched up their rifles. They stand tense at one side; the German has moved too fast for them. Now they dare not make any move. The men at the door stare at the German in helpless amazement. He seems to read their thoughts.

GERMAN   That is true. One or perhaps even two of you might possibly reach the rifles and the grenades. Perhaps one of them might even be able to fire. But . . . *(he swivels the gun, to show how it will traverse)* . . . the rest of you will be dead, particularly if I should put a bullet into that pile of grenades. *(they stare at him)* In fact, two of you hold rifles just beside me here. Why do they not shoot?

REAGAN   *(to the guards)* You, Grady and Two Horses. Don't move.

GERMAN   What? A few lives are not worth the destruction of a single enemy? Well, perhaps you are wise. To an American, a bad trade is worse than no trade, eh? *(to the Italian—his voice is no longer sarcastic, but sharp, businesslike: the fun is over now)* Disarm these two guards.

ITALIAN   *(mildly)* I?

GERMAN   Yes, Garibaldi. You.

177.   WIDER ANGLE   TO INCLUDE AMERICA

—lying quiet on his pallet, his face calm, his eyes calm and wide as he watches. Akers had run to the door also, stands now with the others.

The Italian approaches the two guards.

ITALIAN   *(courteously)* You permit, signores?

He takes their rifles courteously.

ITALIAN   *(to guards)* Thank you.

The German still watches the men at the door. He speaks over his shoulder to the guards.

GERMAN   You may join your friends now.

For a moment the two guards do not move.

GERMAN *(sharply)* Go, fools! Have you not discovered yet that you are in a war?

The two guards join the group at the door. The German speaks to the Italian over his shoulder, still without turning his eyes from the men at the door.

GERMAN Lay them behind me.

The Italian lays the two rifles on the floor behind the German.

GERMAN Now the other rifles. The pistols, too. Then gather up the grenades.

The Italian goes and gets the stacked rifles and the pistol holsters and returns to lay them down. His air is still quizzical, Latin. The German watches the men who face him. The Italian puts all the rifles down. Then he moves rapidly. He puts the pistols down, draws one from its holster, pulls back the slide to see there is a live shell in the chamber, all in one rapid movement. He is now slightly behind the German.

178. CLOSER SHOT   THE ITALIAN AND THE GERMAN

ITALIAN Herr Kapitan.

The German turns his head. As he does so, the Italian continues rapidly:

ITALIAN I too would have you looking at me, even though the bullet does go into your back.

He fires as he speaks.

179. CLOSE SHOT   THE GERMAN

—as he slumps forward, dead.

180. CLOSE SHOT   THE GROUP   AT DOOR

There is a take for a second.

181. MED. SHOT

Then the Americans rush toward the Italian. Before they can reach him, he snaps the safety on, spins the pistol on his finger and tosses it toward the Americans. Riley catches it, not because he intended to or had time to, but because the Italian threw it right into his hands.

RILEY You murdered him!

ITALIAN So what? Between us we have murdered all Europe. What is one more little stain of blood on the hands of either of us—especially our own.

FONDA On your soul, then.

ITALIAN *(in mock amazement)* What? Is there a man any-where who still believes we have souls?

Reagan enters between them, a little slow as usual, but catching up at last and efficient enough when he does catch up.

REAGAN All right. That'll do. Get your rifles.

182. ANOTHER ANGLE   FAVORING REAGAN

Akers and America in f.g.; men recovering rifles in b.g. Battson runs in to Reagan:

REAGAN *(to Battson)* Well?

BATTSON Yes. It's them. About two miles yet.

REAGAN You sure?

BATTSON I saw the crosses.

REAGAN *(still calm)* All right. Take four men. Reinforce each outpost. If they're going to rush us from all four directions at the same time, I want to know it. As soon as you are certain where they are coming from, and how many near as you can tell, fall your outposts back on the house. Don't wait too long.

BATTSON Right. *(he turns, calls out four names)*

The four men, armed now, follow Battson out. Reagan faces the men.

REAGAN All right, boys. *(as he talks, Manning enters, hands him his pistol belt; he buckles it on)* It's coming now. A man at each window, another man behind him to load for him. *(to*

Manning) Manning, pile the grenades at the door there. You and me'll handle them. *(he turns, sees Akers beside America's pallet, pauses again)* What're you going to do? Use that banjo, I guess?

AKERS Don't you worry about me. What I want to know is, what about America here? I ain't going to leave him . . .

AMERICA Don't leave me here, Sergeant. I can . . .

REAGAN All right. All right. I'll tend to you in a minute. *(he turns)*

183. CLOSE REAGAN

—standing over the Italian machine gun, examining it.

184. WIDER ANGLE TO INCLUDE THE OTHERS IN ROOM

Akers is beside America's pallet. The men are manning the windows. Manning is piling grenades beside the door. The Italian stands quietly to one side.

REAGAN Anybody know how to work this gun?

The men pause, look back at him. Nobody answers.

ITALIAN I.

They all look at the Italian.

AKERS *(harshly; he is slightly hysterical)* How do we know who's the next one you'll decide to shoot in the back? Your Kraut buddy couldn't trust you. Why should we?

They all watch the Italian, wait for his answer. He looks quietly about at them, Latin, sardonic, mild and courteous.

ITALIAN You can't. I am now twice apostate, even for an Italian. In fact, if you were to trust my simple word, I would doubt not only you, but my own five senses. An Italian of this day and time believes in nothing else, but he does believe in his five senses. When once he doubts them . . . *(he shrugs)* So I do not waste your—our—time protesting to you my good faith. I only say that I can operate this gun . . . *(he slaps the breech of the gun, looks about at them)* Well?

They watch him, then they watch Reagan. Reagan stares at the Italian as though he were trying to stare through the Italian's skull and read what is there. The Italian has looked at Reagan for only a moment, but he has read Reagan.

ITALIAN   I would suggest in the door there, where there will be room to traverse it. To cover your outside party when they fall back, if necessary.

REAGAN   *(quietly—turns)* All right. Give us a hand here, Franklin.

Franklin, Reagan and the Italian approach. They wheel the machine gun to the door. The Italian takes charge of it, prepares it for action. Reagan and Franklin turn back, Franklin to his former post. Akers is still beside America.

185. MED. SHOT   INT. ROOM   ANGLE TOWARD AMERICA'S PALLET

AMERICA   *(to Reagan)* Don't leave me here. I can . . .

AKERS   *(hysterically)* You durn right we ain't. *(to Reagan)* At least we can lay him close to the wall, where a stray bullet won't . . .

AMERICA   No, no. Up there at a window, where I can see out. I can shoot the pistols.

AKERS   You durn right you can! *(he turns to the others)* Come on, you guys . . .

REAGAN   *(to Akers)* Will you shut up a while? *(to America)* Can you move your arms all right?

AMERICA   Yes. *(he moves his arms and hands and turns his head to prove it—the sweat of the pain beading his face again)* I can shoot.

REAGAN   All right. *(he turns)* Four men here.

Four men join them.

186. CLOSE SHOT   AT AMERICA'S PALLET

The six prepare to pick America up.

AMERICA   *(sweating)* Easy now. Pick me up easy, please.

AKERS Durn it, you better be easy with him!

The six men raise America, as gently as they can. But the pouring of sweat on his face shows the agony of movement, though his calm face and his eyes do not change; only the increased sweat.

AKERS *(panting)* You durn clumsy sons, can't you be easy?

AMERICA *(sweating)* They're easy. I'm all right. I feel fine.

CAMERA PANS with them to the ledge where we first saw Akers. They lay him on a ledge, where he can look out the window.

REAGAN *(to Manning)* Bring all the pistols here. Akers can shoot from this window, too, and load for him.

Manning gathers up the pistols and returns. Akers bends anxiously over America. He is almost crying.

AKERS You durn black son, what did you want to get shot for? Are you all right now?

187. CLOSE AMERICA

—peacefully, a pistol in his hand. He draws back the slide to see the live shell.

AMERICA I'm all right. I feel fine.

A volley of FIRING SOUNDS from outside.

188. FULL SHOT INT. ROOM

The men become alert. Through the open door, where the Italian crouches behind the machine gun, Battson and his men can be seen retreating, stooping, running. The FIRING CONTINUES. Battson and his men enter. The FIRING outside INCREASES.

BATTSON *(to Reagan)* Here they come.

REAGAN How many?

BATTSON *(laconic)* Plenty.

A SOLDIER *(turns from his window)* You mean *enough*, don't you?

```
FORM 68 5M                    WARNER BROS. PICTURES, INC.        BADGE
                                 OFF PAYROLL NOTICE              NO.

NAME        FAULKNER, WILLIAM                              NO

DATE  August 13, 1943      HOUR FINISHED          RATE  $400.

OCCUPATION        Writer.

DEPARTMENT

REMARKS      Contract suspended for approximately
             4 months.


ALL COMPANY PROPERTY HAS BEEN CHECKED IN AND PAYMENT TO EMPLOYEE
                    IS HEREBY AUTHORIZED

STOREKEEPER                          APPROVED  R. J. OBRINGER
```

19. Off Payroll Notice for Faulkner

BATTSON Naw. I just said plenty.

REAGAN All right. Place your men.

Battson places his men at windows. The FIRING outside IN-
CREASES.

LEVINE Manning? Where's Manning?

MANNING Here. Whataya want?

LEVINE Ain't it about time to make another vote whether
to leave or not? We'll get a good majority this time.

FRANKLIN (*fires through his window—ejects the empty case*)
Yeah. The same majority. There won't be nothing for Man-
ning . . . (*he fires again, ejects the empty; others begin to fire*) . . .
to pick up to vote with but hulls.

Now they are all firing, America too, as Akers fires, puts his
rifle quickly down, loads another clip for America's pistol, picks

up his rifle and fires again. The FIRING outside INCREASES. The Italian's machine gun begins.

189. EXT. DESERT   FULL SHOT

German tanks in f.g., as they approach, firing. SOUND of BATTLE INCREASES, very loud and steady. As DISSOLVE begins, the SOUND of the TANKS and the FIRING becomes the SOUND of the FREEDOM TRAIN.

The FREEDOM TRAIN FADES IN—SUPERIMPOSED on the TANKS. The TANKS begin to FADE OUT, leaving the moving train, HEAD-ON SHOT, the locomotive of 1865 rushing toward CAMERA.

> **ROBESON'S VOICE**   (over)
> Freedom's a thing that has no ending,
> It needs to be cared for, it needs defending;
> A great long job for many hands,
> Carrying freedom through all the lands,
> Crying, Free—dom!
>   Free—dom!

From train of 1865—

LAP DISSOLVE TO:

190. TRAIN OF 1943

Locomotive rushes into CAMERA, filling the scene. The SOUND INCREASES, roars over and drowns the "CANTATA" and ROBESON'S VOICE as CAMERA PANS with the train as it rushes past. CAMERA HOLDS the last car with its row of cheering young faces of American troops in the windows. On the car is scrawled in huge letters:

BERLIN   TOKYO   OR   BUST

FADE OUT.

THE END

KNOW ALL MEN BY THESE PRESENTS:

I, _____ William Faulkner _____,hereby
certify that I wrote, created and composed and/or collaborated
in the writing, creation and composition of the screen play

entitled "BATTLE CRY"

~~xxxxxxxxxxxxxxxxxxxxxxxxxxxxxxxxxxxxxxxxxxxxxxxxxxx~~

~~xxxxxxxxxxxxxxxxxxxxxxxxxxxxxxxxxxxxxxxxxxxxxxxxxxx~~

based on material owned by Warner Bros. Pictures, Inc.

and the original dialogue used therein, as an employee of
Warner Bros. Pictures, Inc., pursuant to an agreement of
employment dated   July 27, 1942,
in performance of my duties thereunder and in the regular
course of my employment; and that said Warner Bros. Pictures,
Inc.is the author and entitled to the copyright and all
other rights (including the moral rights of authors) therein
and thereto, and with the right to make such changes therein
and such uses thereof as it may determine as such author.

     IN WITNESS WHEREOF, I have hereunto set my hand
this 16th day of   August   , 1943 .

                              William Faulkner

Subscribed and sworn to
before me this 16th day of
August , 1943 .

_____
Notary Public
NOTARY PUBLIC
In and for the County of Los Angeles, State of California
My Commission Expires July 20, 1947.

20. Contract between Faulkner and Warner Bros.

TEXTUAL COLLATION

Page.Line	Volume	Manuscript
198.25	becomes	become
206.24	knows	knew
230.1	jounces	jounced
235.3	he	we
248.1	takes	take
249.28	begins	begin
265.30	foot touches	feet touched
274.17–275.31	Wei Lin	Li Wen
305.22	a man	man
346.30	begins, carries	begin, carry
368.20–21	indicates	indicate
375.7	Loughton	Lofton
382.20	of any	on any

These are the
substitute pages
for the original
which Mr. Howler
already has.

... les, just
right at the
we kin shove
off ...

The VOICE CEASES. F
rouses, remembers wh
is well, turns.

CLOSE TRUCKING SH

walking again.
Fonda's face is
to the beat of
grows definite

Fonda lowers

da
o

TWO HORSES
Riley and
turns aw

FONDA